The Mage's Ghost

Book Four in the Mages of Martir

by Timothy L. Cerepaka

An Annulus Publishing Book

Annulus Publishing, Cherokee, Texas, 2015

Published by Annulus Publishing

Copyright © Timothy L. Cerepaka 2015. All rights reserved.

Author: Timothy L. Cerepaka

Layout by Timothy L. Cerepaka

Contact: timothy@timothylcerepaka.com

Cover design by Elaina Lee of For the Muse Design
(http://www.forthemusedesign.com/)

ISBN-13: 978-0692481011

ISBN-10: 069248101X

Acknowledgments

I would like to thank my uncle, James Wilhite, for helping me get this manuscript into publishable shape. I'd also like to thank the rest of my family for supporting me while I wrote this novel. You guys rock.

Chapter One

The harsh wind of the Great Berg bit at Darek Takren's ears and fingers. He normally wouldn't have noticed this much, due to his specializing in ice magic; but now that he no longer could use magic, it was impossible to ignore. He slid his hands into the sleeves of his white robes to keep them out of the wind.

Auratus, on the other hand, didn't seem cold at all, despite being an aquarian. She wore the usual green-and-silver uniform that all Institute students did, but she was quite literally radiating a warm temperature—no doubt due to the heat spell she had cast on herself prior to their teleporting from North Academy a few minutes ago—a heat spell that, despite extending to Darek, still didn't make him feel as warm as he should have. Yet even Auratus shivered slightly when a particularly gelid gust of wind tore through, cutting through them both like the tusks of a baba raga.

Darek looked around at their surroundings, as he always did whenever they teleported somewhere new, because in recent days it was more necessary than ever to do that in order to avoid getting killed. The grounds of the Xocionian Monastery—a monastery designed for monks dedicated to serving Xocion, the God of Ice—was completely empty of all monks.

The reason for that was no mystery. Wherever Darek looked, he saw chunks of rock piercing through the icy ground. A nearby storage building had collapsed on itself, and a statue of Xocion himself lying on the ground in pieces, likely knocked over by the shock waves that had shaken Martir after the death of Skimif. The finely carved stone pathway leading from the steps of the Temple to the gates on the other end of the Monastery was cracked and broken in several places, while the gates themselves barely appeared to be standing, holding on only because they had fallen in such a way as to support each other.

The Temple of Xocion itself was still in one piece. It was made entirely out of ice, having been designed ages ago by the first Xocionian Monks who traveled from the Northern Isles to the Great Berg. It looked almost like a castle, with turrets and towers, but much smaller, with a main building with a tall spire in the center that resembled an oversized icicle.

Above the main doorway—which was shut, though not locked—was the Monks' motto, carved in ice: *TO SERVE XOCION WITH ALL OF OUR HEART, SOUL, STRENGTH, AND MIND.*

If that was the only thing we had to do, then life would be so much easier, Darek thought as Auratus and he walked up the steps toward the large ice doors.

Though the doors to the Temple were large and thick, Darek knew he wouldn't have any trouble opening them. As he had done many times before, Darek waved his wand at the doors, expecting them to push open thanks to his mastery over pagomancy.

But nothing happened. The doors stood as closed as ever, making Darek confused for a moment before he heard Auratus's voice in his mind say, *No magic, remember?*

Darek blushed in embarrassment. "Oh ... right." He had forgotten that he could no longer use magic anymore, not after losing his magical power to Uron a couple of months back. The sight of the ice doors must have triggered an old habit of his, though that didn't lessen the embarrassment of what he had just tried to do.

Thankfully, Auratus did not push the point. She waved her own hand toward the doors and they opened inwards, albeit slowly, allowing Darek and her to enter without trouble. Though as they entered, Darek noticed how unused the doors appeared, as if they had not been opened regularly.

Of course they haven't, Darek thought. *The Monks have been holed up in here ever since Skimif's death, too afraid to leave or go anywhere else.*

Thinking about the God of Martir's death caused a heavy depression and even panic to settle on his heart before Darek forced the thought away. No time to be afraid or scared. In desperate times like this, you had to be stronger and braver than you normally were, even if you didn't feel like it. *Especially* if you didn't feel like it.

The interior of the Temple of Xocion looked essentially the same as Darek remembered it: High arches, ice sculptures of Xocion in the nooks in the walls, closed doors leading to different rooms (such as the Prayer Room and the Sculpting Room), and a staircase to the left of the doors that led to the second floor. None of that concerned him at the moment, because he knew, from experience, that the Monks were currently gathered in the room at the very end of the Temple lobby, the room known as the Mourning Room.

So he and Auratus strode toward the doors at the end of the Temple's lobby, doors that were smaller than the front doors, small enough that Darek could easily open them with his hands. The interior of the Temple was eerily quiet; at least, until Darek heard the sounds of mourning from the Monks, muffled by the doors of the Mourning Room, coming from the other end of the Temple.

He looked at Auratus. He had gotten better at reading aquarian facial features and body language over the last two months, ever since he and Auratus had started working more closely together. Though she walked as naturally as an aquarian used to swimming underwater could walk on dry land, he could tell by the way her shoulders slumped that she did not believe their current mission was going to be anymore fruitful or successful than their last few attempts had been.

What should we do, then? Darek had asked Auratus once, about a week ago, after their last attempt to convince the Xocionian Monks to join them had failed. *Leave them here, where Uron will eventually get to them? They are my brothers in ice, so I don't have the luxury of abandoning them, even if they are stubborn as icebergs sometimes.*

Auratus had agreed that they needed all the help they

4

could get, but she clearly didn't think that this mission was a good investment in their time. He understood her desire to return to North Academy, but he didn't want to, mostly because he was getting tired of the endless debating over how to deal with Uron among the people there.

We need as many people on our side as possible, Darek thought. *Even if we aren't strong enough to kill Uron, this is better than standing around doing nothing.*

Upon reaching the doors, the mourning of the Monks was louder than ever. They sounded very similar to the howling wind outside, except Darek could distinguish actual words among the Monks' mourning. It was a prayer, a prayer he had memorized over the past month or so after so many visits to the Monastery. As he listened, he could tell they were about halfway through it:

"*O great Powers/Please save us/Your gods are scattered and weak/Your world is at its edge/The Fire grows ever closer/It burns away at every island and every god/There is no hope to be found/None, not even in the Wisdom of Xocion/Help us, O great Powers/Help us.*"

Darek bit his lips. The 'Fire,' in Xocionian mythology, was the term for the force that was said to end the world in its final days. The Xocionian Monks had taken to identifying Uron with the Fire, no doubt due to Uron's attempts to destroy Martir. It was a depressing prayer, written by the very first Xocionian Monk, that was supposed to be prayed only in times of great despair.

There were only a couple of times that the prayer had ever been prayed, to Darek's knowledge. Once, around thirty years ago, when the Powers had come to destroy Martir (but had decided not to after being convinced to spare the world by King Malock of Carnag and Skimif, who at the time had been a mortal and not a god); and second, recently, after Skimif's death.

Just hearing that prayer made Darek depressed; however, he shoved the doors open anyway, determined not to let this prayer of sadness continue to sap the confidence and energy from the other Monks.

The scene laid out before him and Auratus was almost exactly like the scene they had seen several times before: Two dozen Xocionian monks, each wearing the same white-and-blue robes that all Xocionian monks wore, lay prostrate on the floor around a massive statue of the God of Ice, a statue said to have been carved by the founder of the Monastery. There used to be more, many more, Monks than the two dozen around here, but when Skimif's death rocked the world, Darek had learned that many had died in the chaos, while many more had simply fled to parts unknown, even though there was nowhere in the known world to flee to.

The Monks did not seem to notice Darek and Auratus's entrance, because they continued to pray just as if the two had not entered:

"*Great Xocion/Ruler of Winter and King of Cold/Intercede on behalf of your followers/Implore the Powers to send a savior to our world/Your followers plead with you to fulfill your promises/Prove our faith in you/And we will serve you forevermore.*"

One of the Monks, a large burly man named Vian, was actually crying as he prayed. His tears fell down his large cheeks and landed on the ice floor, where they immediately froze. Another Monk, a short elderly woman named Fajan, had both of her hands on the toes of the Xocion statue, without any gloves to keep her hands warm. He could already see the tips of her fingers turning blue from the cold.

It pained Darek to see them like this. Darek had only been a Xocionian Monk himself for about a month before Skimif's death; even so, he had grown close to his brothers and sisters in ice and thought of them as his family, in a way. To see them all in such despair was saddening; to know that they had refused, repeatedly, to listen to his pleas of forming an alliance with them, was depressing.

Nonetheless, Darek walked over to the nearest Monk, a man with a full gray head of hair and a long gray beard named Abbot Carcello, and patted him on the back.

"Abbot?" said Darek, raising his voice to be heard above the Mourning Prayer of the Monks. "It's Darek Takren again. I am here to—"

Without warning, Carcello stood up, causing Darek to step back in surprise. Carcello whirled around to face Darek, his ice blue eyes cold with anger, his fists shaking at his side.

"Get out of here," Carcello said, pointing over Darek's shoulder at the doors behind them, the grief in his voice vanishing like a rock tossed into the ocean. "You and your aquarian friend. Out."

Darek had expected Carcello to react a little less than happily at his arrival; nonetheless, Darek didn't back down, despite being completely powerless himself and standing in front of the most powerful pagomancer in all of Martir.

"Can't we at least talk?" said Darek. He gestured over his shoulder toward the open doors. "In the lobby, where we won't interrupt the other Monks?"

Not that they were in any danger of doing that. Despite Carcello's sharp tone and sudden movements, not a single one of the other Monks had so much as glanced up to see them. They were all too absorbed by the air of despair that seemed to hang over Martir like a heavy fog.

To Darek's relief, Carcello's shoulders slumped and he sighed. "All right. We can talk, but only briefly. I do not have time to listen to any half-cooked, harebrained schemes to save our world from a god-killer like Uron, so we shall make it quick."

Darek nodded and walked out of the Mourning Room with Carcello. Auratus joined them, pulling the doors closed behind them as they left. The prayer of the Monks became muffled once again, although it sounded a little louder now, as if the Monks had raised their voices in an attempt to be better heard by Xocion and the Powers.

Carcello put his hands together in his white sleeves and looked Darek straight in the eye, as he always did whenever he talked to anyone, and asked, "What is your mother's offer now?"

Darek cringed at Carcello's tone. Darek's mother, Jenur Takren, was technically the Magical Superior at the moment, albeit only a temporary one. Carcello knew that, but ever since Skimif's death, he had taken to calling her 'your mother' whenever he spoke to Darek, like he did not really accept her authority as genuine, even though the previous Magical Superior had passed the title on to her prior to his death.

Carcello hadn't always been this way. When Darek had first come to the Xocionian Monastery, he had accepted Mom's position as the Superior, as he had known Mom already and understood that the position was temporary until Skimif chose someone more suited for the position. He had even sent her a letter of congratulations, which Darek remembered because Carcello had asked him to deliver it to her personally.

But ever since Skimif's death, Carcello had been rather hostile toward Mom. Though Darek didn't know for sure, Carcello seemed to think that Mom's authority as Magical Superior was no longer legitimate and, thus had, for all intents and purposes, cut ties with North Academy, despite the Monastery being located very close to that school. It was primarily the Abbot's hostility toward Mom that had made it difficult for Darek and Auratus to convince the Xocionian Monks to work with them.

Still, Darek didn't back down or apologize for Mom's authority, which was as legitimate as ever, even without Skimif to affirm it.

He simply said, "The same as always, Abbot. If you would just stop praying to Xocion—who is in no position to intercede on your behalf more than any of the other gods are—we might be able to figure out how to defeat Uron. Your wisdom and guidance could be of immense help to us, you know."

Carcello lifted his nose up at Darek's words and scoffed. "Oh? So I am supposed to believe that your mother, the teacher, has a better idea of how to defeat Uron than Skimif himself? What a silly notion, though I have always held that Jenur Takren was a silly woman."

Darek grit his teeth. "It's not just the Magical Superior, as you very well know. Archmage Yorak, the head of the Undersea Institute, is also working with us, as are Ranama, the God of Language, and the Ghostly God, the God of Ghosts and Mist. All of us are working together to figure out how to defeat Uron before he destroys us all."

Carcello laughed. "Don't take me for a fool, Darek. The gods are practically powerless against Uron, especially with Skimif dead. Having two gods—especially two as obscure as Ranama and the Ghostly God—on your side means *nothing*. And as for Yorak, I have never believed her to be particularly wise, so dropping her name does not impress me."

Auratus stepped forward, an angry look on her goldfish-like features, but Darek held out an arm in front of her and gave her a brief, but very clear, glare. He understood that Auratus respected Yorak more than any other mage in the world, but there was no point in her arguing with Carcello right now, who already had a low opinion of aquarian mages anyway.

"Our only hope lies in praying to Xocion and hoping he

brings our prayers to the Powers, as the Apocalypse Prayer says," said Carcello. Then his eyes narrowed. "You, as a Xocionian mage, should know that better than anyone, Darek. I wonder if you lost your memories of our teachings along with your magic."

That was another thing that had made bargaining with Carcello so different. If Carcello's opinion of aquarian mages was low, he held non-magical humans in even lower contempt, despite his great wisdom. He seemed to think that any human who did not wholeheartedly pursue the study and practice of magic was inferior to those who did in every way; morally, spiritually, even physically.

That Darek had lost his own magical power—a fact that he couldn't hide from Carcello even if he tried—had put Darek even lower than humans who had simply chosen never to study magic at all in Carcello's eyes. This in spite of the fact that Darek still honored Xocion and tried to worship the God of Ice as best as he could without his magic.

"I know that praying to Xocion feels good," said Darek. "And trust me, I've prayed to him plenty of times over the last couple of months, but the fact is, Xocion is as scared and weakened as the rest of the gods. This is not the time for us mages to be scattered and afraid; we have to be united and strong, even if the gods aren't."

"How can we be strong when the God of Martir himself is dead?" said Carcello. His voice almost broke when he said that. "I do not believe in instilling false hope in my brothers and sisters in ice. The only hope we have is the same hope we've always had: Relying on Xocion to do what our forefathers and ancestors promised he would do in our blackest times of need."

"If you guys continue to stay here, praying to a god who can't do anything about Uron, then you *will* die once Uron reaches the Great Berg," Darek said. "But if you come with us, you might live, maybe even live long enough to see Uron fall for good."

"You cannot guarantee that," said Carcello. "I will not let you tempt me with your high-sounding 'ifs' and 'maybes.' I was not made the Abbot of the Xocionian Monastery because I listened to magic-less mages who try to instill false hopes in my Monks."

"It's not a false hope," said Darek. "It's a hope that is far more reliable than praying to Xocion to do something he cannot. No one, not even the gods, know where the Powers are; how, then, can you expect Xocion to find them and ask them to save us?"

"It is what we were always taught and is what I believe," said Carcello. "Now, I am done arguing with non-believing youth. I must return to my *true* brothers and sisters in ice, the ones who continue to believe and who do not doubt, unlike you."

That was the last straw. Darek grabbed Carcello's beard and forced Carcello to look him in the eyes again. He didn't care that Carcello appeared shocked and angry at Darek's impropriety, nor did he pay any attention to Auratus grabbing his arm and trying to get him to let go of Carcello.

"Listen here you old fool," said Darek, in the sharpest,

lowest tone he could speak in and still be understood. "Martir is currently on the very edge of apocalypse. It is even closer to apocalypse than the day when the Powers returned and tried to destroy everything. As much as I hate to admit, this time, we can't rely on a Carnagian prince or a leader of a social movement to intervene, nor can we rely on the gods to intercede, either. But if you want to lie on the floor and whine like a baby, fine. Just don't come whining to us when Uron knocks down the doors of the Monastery and kills you all."

Though Darek was pulling on Carcello's beard hard enough to cause some pain, the Abbot showed none of it. He simply glared into Darek's eyes, a strong glare that reflected his own authority and conviction, and said, "And who, I wonder, is to blame for that? The blizzard whispers that it was the result of a silly young mage freeing Uron by sacrificing his own magical power. Tell me, might you know who that is?"

"It was an accident," Darek growled. "I didn't know any better. If you had been there—"

"I would have berated you for being the idiot that you are," Carcello snapped. "Now, either let go of my beard or I will turn you into another ice statue. Would you like that?"

Darek was about to respond, but then a resounding *boom* echoed through the lobby, causing all three of them to freeze. Even the praying of the Monks went silent, as if they, too, had heard that crack.

Still clutching Carcello's beard, Darek looked back down the lobby the way he and Auratus had came. The front doors of the Temple were cracked, like something large had hit them hard. The cracks were thick and ugly, too, reminding Darek of how the ground outside had looked.

"What ... was that?" said Carcello, the anger in his voice replaced by fear. "What's out there?"

"I don't know," said Darek. "But whatever it is, it can't be —"

Another *boom* and the doors went crashing inward. They landed on the floor hard enough to shatter into chunks of ice, which scattered all over the icy floor like dropped coins. Darek gulped and let go of Carcello's beard when he saw who stood behind the door, though Carcello didn't even try to run away.

The being that had knocked down the door was large and bearlike in appearance, with thick red hair and massive ape-like fists that looked more than capable of crushing human skulls. She looked like a monster, but Darek knew who and what she really was, even though it had been quite some time since he had last seen her.

"Who in the name of Xocion is that?" said Carcello with a gulp. "No, *what* is that?"

"Not a *what*," said the new arrival, her tone harsh and cruel, "though I will tell you I am a katabans. It is *who*, though I don't think I need to tell you that, as Darek and Auratus already know who I am."

"Yeah, we do," said Darek. He glared at her. "She's Durima the Demon, a servant of Uron."

"Indeed I am," said Durima calmly. She gestured at the shattered doors at her feet. "Like these doors, Martir, too,

14

will be shattered into a million pieces by Uron. It is only a matter of time before he hunts down and kills every last god in the world; after that, it will be even less time before Martir itself is no more."

"A servant of Uron, eh?" said Carcello. He drew his own wand out, which was made out of ice, and pointed it at her. "I don't know how powerful you are, but I have the power of Xocion flowing through me, and he is no weak god. If I were you, I would run back to Uron now."

Durima smiled an ursine smile. "Why would I ever do that? Old, fat mortals wielding icicles don't scare me."

"This 'old, fat mortal' is the Abbot of the Xocionian Monastery," said Carcello. "But what does that matter to you? Whether or not you understand the significance of my position, I will kill you where you stand."

Durima rolled her eyes. "Right. Well, why don't we test that theory? It's not like I have anything better to do, after all."

"Why are you here?" said Darek. "Did Uron send you?"

"Yes," said Durima. "He hasn't made his way to the Great Berg yet, but he wanted me to take out any possibly obstacles on his way to destroy North Academy once and for all. He's already had me destroy more than a handful of other magical schools. They died screaming."

"How monstrous," said Carcello, shaking his head. "If you are truly a servant of the gods, why would you choose to serve him?"

Durima crouched low to the ground, like she was going to jump at them. "My reasons for why I do what I do are my

15

own. Anyway, talk is a waste of time. I came here to tear this Monastery to the ground, and to do that, I must first kill you."

Carcello marched forward, his wand glowing icy blue. Darek reached for his arm to get him to stop, but Carcello was already out of his reach.

"Stay back, you two," Carcello said, glancing over his shoulder at Darek and Auratus. "I will take care of this traitor in less time than it takes for a cup of water to freeze in the Great Berg."

"Quite confident," said Durima. "Too bad you won't be able to back up that confidence with anything even remotely resembling talent."

"I need not talent to do away with the likes of you," said Carcello. "For I have the guidance of Xocion, the God of Ice, the Frozen Lord, to—"

Durima vanished and reappeared in front of Carcello so fast that Darek didn't even realize it until her massive hands grabbed the Abbot's head and neck and twisted.

A terrible *crack* shot through the air like a bullet. Carcello immediately collapsed onto the ground, dropping his ice wand, which Durima crushed with one of her big fists before it even stopped bouncing on the ground, shattering it like the doors she had knocked down.

The next moment, the doors to the Mourning Room opened and the other Monks peeked out. Many of them looked confused until they spotted Carcello's corpse lying on the floor underneath Durima, at which half of them yelled in fear and the other half just stared in horror.

Seeing an opportunity, Darek yelled, "Run, you idiots! Or you'll end up like Carcello!"

He didn't need to say that twice. The Monks shut the doors to the Mourning Room, but he could hear them hurrying out of the secret exit at the back of the Mourning Room. He had no idea where they would run to. He hoped that they would go to North Academy, as they would be safe there, but considering how fearful everyone was, he wondered if it would even occur to them to do that.

Darek thought for sure that Durima would get angry at him, maybe even attack him right away. After all, he had just saved the lives of two dozen people she was supposed to kill. That had to make her angry.

Instead, however, Durima cocked her head to the side, confusion spreading over her beastly features.

"Let me get this straight," said Durima. She pointed at Carcello's corpse. "After I kill one of your allies, you tell a dozen well-trained Monks—who specialize in ice magic and live in a temple made of ice in the coldest place on Martir— to run away from me. Thus leaving you two, a mage who can't use any magic and an aquarian who clearly doesn't like the cold. I don't think you thought this through very well."

Darek opened his mouth to say that he had, but then it struck him that Durima had made a very good point. He stepped back in fear, because he knew that he couldn't take on Durima in a straight fight, though Auratus stood her ground, like she wasn't afraid of Durima at all.

"Based on your silence, I'm going to say that you have realized just how dumb your 'heroic' efforts were," said

Durima. Her wicked smile revealed row upon row of sharp, ursine teeth. "Not that it matters. I will kill you two and smash the foundations of this useless Temple, which I think should be more than enough to clear the path for Uron's eventual arrival in the Great Berg."

Not unless stop you, said Auratus, her voice in Darek's head, though Durima must have heard it, too, because she simply shook her head.

"Stop me?" the katabans laughed. "Little fish, I am three centuries old and have killed mages far more powerful than you during that time. If you had not been stupid enough to tell your allies to run, you might have stood a chance; as it is, this will be a brief, yet bloody, slaughter."

Faster than someone of her size should have been able to move, Durima slammed her fist onto the floor, cracking it. A moment later, Darek heard something burrowing through the ground underneath, like a massive drill spinning, but before he could do anything about it, a massive spire of rock burst through the floor like the fist of a giant.

The spire's breaking through the floor sent both Darek and Auratus flying. Darek screamed, but was cut off when he crashed onto the floor again, sliding across the icy, slippery surface until he bumped into the wall. One of the Xocion statues in the nooks in the wall crashed beside him, spraying him with ice, the statue's ice sword sliding away across the floor from him.

Shaking his head, Darek smelled wet animal fur and instinctively rolled to the right. Just in time, too, because Durima's fists suddenly came down on the spot where he had been lying not a moment before, smashing it and sending ice shards flying into the air.

Rising to his feet, Darek walked backwards away from Durima, who lifted her ice-covered fists and shook the frozen chips off them as she glared at Darek.

"You will be the first to die," said Durima as she began to advance on him. "I've always believed in picking off the weakest first ... and you, Darek Takren, are the weakest of them all, being that you lack magic."

Darek didn't dare take his eyes off Durima, even though he wanted to look around to see if Auratus was still conscious or not. For that matter, he also needed a weapon of some sort.

Then he almost tripped over something, causing him to glance down. It was the ice sword from the Xocion statue that had fallen over next to him earlier. It was large and likely heavy, but he bent over and lifted it up with both hands anyway.

His hands burned under the cold hilt of the sword, making him almost scream from the painful gelid blade. Not only that, but it was indeed heavy; perhaps not as heavy as an actual sword (though Darek didn't know for sure, as he had never wielded a real sword before), but heavy enough that he was unsure he could wield it effectively.

Durima must have thought the same thing, because she just smiled even more widely at him. "Do you honestly believe that a fake 'sword' like that will hurt me even slightly? It's not even designed right. Just look at that edge; whoever sculpted that piece of crap has clearly never seen an actual sword in person before."

Whether or not Durima's criticism of the sword's blade was accurate, Darek didn't know or even really care. He just held it before him, looking for an opportunity to strike, even though he doubted he would be able to attack her before she took him down.

Then Durima swiped at him with one of her claws. He just barely managed to bring up the ice sword in time to block it. It was useless, however, because Durima's claw smashed through the sculpted sword like a toy, leaving nothing but a freezing hilt in Darek's hands.

It was enough for Darek, however. He threw the hilt at Durima, but she knocked it out of the air like it was nothing more than an annoying bee.

"Now you're really unarmed," said Durima. "Time to die."

Just before she leaped at him, a fountain of water came out of nowhere and struck her in the back. Durima roared in shock from the water blast, while Darek looked in the direction the water was coming from and saw Auratus shooting it from her hands, her magic stone glowing bright blue around her ankle.

But then a portal to the ethereal opened in front of Durima and she rolled into it. The portal closed with a *pop*, while Auratus ceased shooting water from her hands and lowered them. Her eyes darted around the now-ruined lobby in search of Durima, but the katabans was nowhere to be seen.

She gone, said Auratus. *Maybe forever?*

Darek shook his head. "I doubt it. Durima doesn't strike me as the kind to give up, even after being sprayed with water in an ice cold room. She'll probably—"

He heard the *pop* of an ethereal portal opening behind him. Instinctively, Darek dove forward, just as he felt the air from Durima's claw pass him by. He hit the floor, rolled to his feet, and looked over his shoulder in time to see Durima's arm disappear back into the ethereal.

"What did I say?" said Darek, looking up at Auratus. "We have to keep our guard up at all times. Durima's a veteran of the Katabans War, so she knows how to fight even better than we do."

Auratus nodded, turning her head this way and that in an attempt to find Durima. Darek stood up and walked over closer to her and looked around as well, even though there wasn't much he could do against Durima if the katabans showed up again.

The Temple of Xocion was once again quiet, aside from Darek and Auratus's breathing. The rock spire that Durima had summoned earlier still stood where it had burst through the floor, while Carcello's corpse lay near its base. Darek tried not to look at Carcello; he could not afford to let his emotions get the best of him.

Darek picked up a nearby chunk of ice to use as a weapon. It was by no means threatening or intimidating, and it probably wouldn't be very effective at all, but Darek didn't like being weapon-less in this situation. His hands tingled against the cold ice chunk, but he gripped it anyway.

Leave, Auratus suggested. *While Durima gone, we*

leave.

Darek frowned. "Not a bad suggestion. Can you teleport through solid objects yet?"

Auratus's silence told him that she had not yet mastered that particular skill, which did not make him very confident about the likelihood of their survival in this particular situation.

"Our only way out would be if we walked out the front doors and immediately teleported," Darek said, nodding at the open doorway and the shattered remains of the front doors. "But there's a clear gap between here and the doorway. If we run, we might make it ... or just give Durima an opportunity to burst out of the ethereal and kill us."

Understood, Auratus thought. *Keep fighting?*

"Until we can get a safe opening, yes," said Darek.

So the two ceased speaking, Darek straining his ears to listen for the usual *pop* of an ethereal portal opening. That would likely be the only signal they would get before Durima attacked; therefore, it was imperative that they listen for it.

What's she waiting for? Darek thought. *Maybe trying to dry off her fur so she doesn't instantly freeze when she returns? Looking for the perfect opening?*

That was when Darek heard that familiar *pop*, causing him to look wildly around for its source. Auratus looked as well, but no matter where Darek looked, he didn't see Durima anywhere, which made him wonder if his ears were playing tricks on him.

"Auratus, did you hear that?" said Darek. "That pop?

You heard it, right?"

Auratus nodded without looking at Darek. *Yes. Where is?*

"No idea," said Darek. "Thought you might—"

He was interrupted by the floor rumbling beneath his feet, almost throwing him off-balance. He looked down just in time to see another rock spire tunneling through the clear ice floor under him.

Without thinking, Darek shoved Auratus to the side, sending her out of the way of the incoming second spire. He then tried to move himself out of the way, but he was too slow. The spire broke through the floor, sending shards and chunks of ice flying everywhere. The spire only glanced him in the side, but it was a powerful glance that sent him staggering like a man shot by a gun.

He heard Durima's growl and looked up in time to see her jumping at him from the other spire. Her claws were flashing, forcing him to duck to avoid getting his head taken clear off his shoulders.

Durima soared over his head and landed on the floor hard. Nonetheless, she turned around and slashed at him with the fierceness of an enraged baba raga. Darek dodged as best as he could, but he was so tired and could feel the cold starting to seep into his bones, which made it harder to move as smoothly as he normally did.

Then his foot slipped on the ice and he stumbled. A second later, Durima's right claw flew at him and tore through his chest.

Durima's claws were as sharp as knives. Darek cried out

in pain, falling down onto the cracked ice floor underneath him. His bloody chest stung against the cold air of the Temple and he found it hard to breathe, though he could scream just fine.

He saw Durima's claw—with his blood—coming at him again before another burst of water flew over Darek's head, dropping tiny droplets on his face, and struck Durima head on. Durima once again roared in anger before disappearing through another ethereal portal.

Then Darek felt Auratus's hands, colder than ever, grab his shoulders. Their whole world went black for a brief moment and then they were outside of the Temple in the snow, having teleported through the open doorway that Durima had created earlier.

Yet the icy weather out here was even worse to Darek's bloody chest than the interior of the Temple of Xocion had been. It was like a cat was clawing at him, a cat that had dunked its paws in freezing ice water, and there was nothing he could do about it.

Hold on, Auratus said, her grip on him tightening. *Going back to North Academy now.*

Just as their world went dark, Darek thought he saw another ethereal portal open and saw Durima's head staring out it in rage. But it was only briefly that he thought he saw that; the next moment, he was too distracted by the darkness of teleportation and the pain in his chest to think much about what he had seen.

Chapter Two

When Durima saw Darek and Auratus teleport, she jumped out of the ethereal portal after them.

Of course, even before she landed on the icy path under her feet, she knew she was too late. They vanished just as quickly as mist in the light of the sun. No doubt by now, they were already back at North Academy, getting Darek the medical attention he clearly needed.

She considered following them. Traveling from the Temple of Xocion, which was located on a tiny ice island on the edge of the Great Berg, to North Academy, which was located a few hundred miles to the north, would take no time at all in the ethereal.

Then Durima remembered that the Academy was protected by a spell that prevented anyone from entering via the ethereal.

If I went after them now, I would have to climb those damn Walls to get in there, Durima thought. She smiled, though it was a bitter smile. *Just like when Gujak and I first visited that stupid school a little over a year ago.*

Durima shook her head. Doing that would be suicide. She wasn't afraid of Jenur Takren or Archmage Yorak or even the Ghostly God or Ranama. However, she recognized that she was no match for any of them by herself. If she tried to break into North Academy now, she'd probably be dead within minutes, or at best, captured and tossed back into those awful catacombs beneath the school.

I'm not an idiot, Durima thought. *Once Uron decides to go there himself, then I'll join as back-up. Until then, let those stupid mortals and gods plan and argue and debate about how to kill the un-killable. It's not like they'll come up with a way to defeat Uron, after all.*

Durima shivered when a particularly cold gust of wind blew through. Her fur was not quite as wet as it had been even just a few minutes ago, but it was still damp and if she didn't dry off quick, she'd end up with what those mortals called a 'cold.' She had rarely experienced those things (as katabans were immune to most mortal diseases) but once, when she had been one-hundred and fifty, she had come down with one that had knocked her out for a week.

I should finish up here, Durima thought, turning around to face the Temple of Xocion, which looked like little more than a fancy, over-sized ice sculpture to her, *and then go back to Uron and report back the success of my mission.*

Balling her fists, Durima was about to bring them down on the ground to cause an earthquake that would have completely demolished the remaining buildings on the Monastery grounds when she felt a familiar slimy, cold, snake-like hand rest on her shoulder.

Pausing, Durima looked over her shoulder and saw a tall, muscular being with purplish-black skin staring down at her. His face was serpentine and he smelled faintly like a corpse, though she would of course never say that aloud.

Lowering her fists, Durima said, "Lord Uron. What are you doing here? I thought you were on Ikadori Island killing the Loner God."

Uron smiled that same unsettling smile he always made whenever he wanted to creep Durima out. "Call me 'Uron,' please. The 'Lord' part is too formal. I am not looking to rule any world. I wish only to save my own."

Durima nodded. "Yes, sir. You still didn't answer my question."

Uron took his hand off her shoulder. "The Loner God ran away. I rampaged through his jungle, but he didn't stay and fight. My hunt for the gods has mostly been this way: Go to their domain, try to fight them, learn they have run away to parts unknown."

Durima frowned. "So what, are you going to play hide-and-seek with them for the next few centuries or however long it takes for you to kill them all?"

"Of course not," Uron snapped. "Don't take me for such a fool. I have a better plan for destroying the whole lot of them. I have yet to use it because it's not yet the right time to do it."

Durima's eyes darted to the metallic, ancient gauntlet on Uron's right hand. "Does the God-killer have anything to do with it?"

Uron held up the God-killer. "Yes, it does. But I don't want to talk about it aloud. The ice has ears."

He said that while pointing at the Temple before them. Durima understood that he was referring to the fact that

Xocion, the God of Ice, was likely listening to them, or at least had the ability to do so if he wanted. It still sounded a bit silly to Durima, however, as she had a hard time imagining what ice with ears would even look like.

"Anyway, I came to check on your progress," said Uron. He put his hands behind his back. "Did you kill all of the Xocionian Monks?"

Durima turned to face him. "I killed their Abbot. A fat, old mortal, very arrogant. But I ran into some trouble."

"Trouble?"

"Darek Takren and Auratus," said Durima. "They were here before me. They convinced the rest of the Xocionian Monks to escape to North Academy. I tried to kill those two, but then they teleported away."

Durima expected Uron to be angry at her failure. After all, Durima was actually rather angry at herself for doing it. Thinking back, she realized that she had had several opportunities in which to kill Darek or Auratus or both together, opportunities that she had missed.

Much to her surprise, however, Uron didn't hit her or threaten her with some kind of punishment. He just tapped his chin as if Durima had just told him an interesting story. He didn't even look mad.

"No matter," said Uron, shaking his head. "I'm sure you did your best. What matters is that they are scared and in one place now, which will make it so much easier to kill them later."

Durima could not believe her ears. In all of her years of serving the gods, she had never, ever been told 'I'm sure you did your best.' Uron wasn't a god, of course, but her relationship to him was similar to her servant relationship with the gods.

She was too stunned to say even one word. She tried to, but she found she couldn't, no matter how hard she tried.

"I don't know if you understand, Durima, but Darek and Auratus and those Monks are not much of a threat to me," said Uron. "I only sent you here, not because I knew you could kill them all, but because I wanted you to scare them. I wanted you to be a statement from me that my hand reaches everywhere and that I can and will strike wherever and whenever I please."

Uron walked around her toward the Temple. Still incapable of talking, Durima followed, not shivering even when another gust of cold wind nipped at her wet face.

"No doubt the Monks are even more despondent than they were before," Uron continued as they approached the Temple. "They probably have lost all faith in their god, Xocion, now. And believe me, once a mortal loses faith in their god, they might as well be dead."

Durima finally found her tongue. She asked, "So you just wanted to destroy their spirit?"

"Exactly," said Uron as they climbed the steps of the Temple. "The fools at North Academy are already desperate and depressed, their alliance fractured by stress and their own interpersonal conflicts with each other. I may not even have to kill them all myself. They might just end up killing each other, leaving me to sweep up the ashes."

That did not surprise Durima. Uron did not usually go in

for the direct kill. He always manipulated his enemies to get what he wanted. He only stepped in directly when his plans weren't going the way he wanted them to or when he absolutely had to, which is why he killed Skimif personally.

"But sooner or later, I *will* have to go to North Academy," Uron continued, stopping at the open doorway to the Temple's interior. He placed a hand on its icy frame. "I cannot have that place taking up precious space that belongs to Harnum."

Durima nodded. "May I ask how you plan to bring back Harnum in the first place?"

"You will find out soon enough," said Uron. He patted her on the head again. "After all, you are my faithful servant, who will join me in the new Harnum by my side."

Durima didn't like being petted like some kind of pet, but she tolerated it anyway, partly because she trusted Uron, partly because she didn't think he would take kindly to her biting his fingers off.

"Which brings me to my next question," said Uron. "How are the katabans currently doing? I have not kept track of them since I killed Skimif."

That sounded an awful lot like a lie to Durima. Uron may not have known everything that was happening on Martir, but she was always under the impression that he always knew more than he let on. He had to know about the current state of katabans society, probably even better than she, which made her wonder why he was asking her that question.

Still, Durima knew she had no choice but to answer it, so

she said, "Scattered. Katabans society is organized almost entirely around worship and service to the gods. With the gods as frightened and disorganized as they are now, you can imagine how we katabans are, especially because World's End was still under reconstruction after your half-god army's failed attempt to destroy it."

Uron nodded. "I expected as much. What about those old fools, the Katabans Council, I believe they were called? Where are they?"

"No idea," said Durima with a shrug. "Last I heard, they had fled World's End after Skimif's death. I haven't been keeping as good a track of them as I normally would. I imagine they're probably scared and hiding, most likely not doing much law-passing or criminal-punishing."

Uron stroked his chin. "That is exactly what I wanted to hear. Do you know why I asked you that?"

"Do you want me to track them down and kill them?" Durima asked.

"Of course not," said Uron, shaking his head. "At least not right away. The Council is not much of a threat to my plans; instead, I have a much better job for you to do."

"What might that be?" said Durima.

Uron looked down at her and said, "If what you say about your people being disorganized is true, then I want you to find as many katabans as you can and organize them under your leadership."

Durima blinked. "Why?"

"Because I promised to spare the katabans people, don't you remember?" said Uron. "I want you to tell the katabans

31

that if they would only listen to me, if they would follow my orders, then they will be allowed to live in the new world I am going to build. How does that sound?"

"Amazingly generous," said Durima. But then her shoulders slumped. "I don't think anyone else will actually listen to me, though. The katabans may be scared, confused, and disorganized, but they are still servants of the gods first and foremost. And everyone already knows I am working for you, so they will probably try to kill me as soon as they see me."

"Perhaps," said Uron. "But if there is one thing all living beings have in common, it's this: If their very lives are threatened, but you offer them even the slightest chance of survival, they will take it, even if it means abandoning their principles or serving someone they hate."

"Maybe," said Durima. "The urge to serve the gods is a powerful one in us katabans. There is a reason there has been no widespread rebellion of katabans against the gods in history; it's because most katabans can't even imagine betraying the gods."

"But you did," said Uron. "And you appear to be a katabans just like everyone else."

Durima looked down at the ice steps under her feet. "That's because I'm different. I've always been more an independent-minded katabans, so switching my loyalties wasn't as difficult for me as it could have been."

"I suppose every species has its black sheep that go against the stereotype," Uron mused. "Or maybe it is more accurate to say that every species has its leaders and revolutionaries, who see a grander future for their kind that the rest are too scared and frightened to see."

Durima looked up at Uron again. He was looking down at her, his face partially shadowed by the sun shining behind him, though his yellow eyes glowed well enough.

"What do you mean?" said Durima. "Do you mean ... I'm a leader?"

"What else do you call an individual who takes the first step toward a new era for her people?" said Uron. He patted her on the head again. "Because that is what you are. You saw that I would crush the gods, and I will. You saw that your people would be freer, better off without the gods abusing and ruling them. Only a true leader, a revolutionary, has that kind of insight and clarity of vision."

Durima had never really thought of herself as a leader before. Sure, when Gujak had been alive, she had always sort of bossed him around, and yes, during the Katabans War, she had been in charge of her own unit every now and then, but bossing around a partner or leading a military unit was not the same thing as being a revolutionary who would lead her people to a grander future.

As a matter of fact, Durima had always hated those kinds of people. She remembered Jakuuth Grinfborn, who had held that kind of visionary leadership status among some of the katabans before he was defeated at the end of the Katabans War. Those people always turned out to have some kind of sneaky ulterior motive that was often never as noble as their vision for their people.

On the other hand, even if Uron was wrong about her,

would it really hurt her to obey him? As much as she might have loathed the gods, Durima still felt some loyalty to her species. If she really could convince even some of them to join her and Uron, then the katabans species could continue, maybe even prosper, in the new Harnum. It was almost impossible for her to imagine what katabans society would be like without the gods; however, that did not mean it was not the next step that they as a species needed to take.

"But you know, even the most radical revolutionary is rarely unique," said Uron. "There are probably more, many more, katabans who share similar views to you. If you could seek them out and give them my message, well, wouldn't that be a good thing?"

"It would," Durima agreed. "Yes, it would be. One of the reasons I decided to join you is because I was tired of how the gods treated my people. I just don't know what to tell them to join us."

"Tell them they can live in a world without gods or not live at all," said Uron. "Because ultimately, those are the only two choices they have, if you haven't already realized that."

"I know," said Durima. "I'm just afraid that many of them would rather die serving gods who do not appreciate their talents or their lives than live independent of them, free to live as they wish."

Uron began walking into the Temple, kicking aside the chunks of ice that had once been the double doors as he did so. Durima followed, wondering why Uron was going into the Temple in the first place, as she didn't think there was anything in here that would interest Uron much.

"Many beings are afraid of freedom," said Uron, "like how children are afraid of bad-tasting medicine they need to take; therefore, if you are to convince the katabans to join us, you should appeal to their animalistic drive to live no matter what."

"I suppose so," said Durima. "I just don't know where to look for them. The katabans are scattered everywhere."

"Then find a way to unite them," said Uron as he turned to the left, toward one of the closed doors along the walls. "Call a Convocation of the Katabans on some island somewhere, perhaps on Bleak Rock, as good location as any, if a bit cramped."

How Uron knew about the Convocation of the Katabans —a special type of meeting held only in grave emergencies that was usually only called by the Katabans Council but which could technically be called by any katabans, no matter how important or unimportant they were—Durima didn't know. Then again, she supposed it wasn't exactly a secret, since it was at the last Convocation that the Katabans War had been officially declared.

"Once the people are gathered there, make your case and give them an ultimatum," said Uron. He opened the door, but did not enter the room. Instead, he looked at Durima. "Either join us, and live, or stand with the gods, and die. Simple enough for even the dimmest katabans to understand."

"I guess you're right," said Durima. "It's not like there's

anything else I can do right now. But what do I do if I succeed?"

"I will give you further instructions afterward," said Uron. "You don't need to worry about that right now."

As curious as Durima was to know what these 'further instructions' might be, she simply nodded and said, "I better leave right away, then."

"Of course," said Uron. "Don't worry about me. I will be doing what I have always been doing: Hunting gods, killing any too stupid to escape me, and having a good time all the while."

"Yes, sir," said Durima. "But before I leave, can I ask you something?"

"What?" said Uron.

She gestured at the open door, though she could not see beyond it, as Uron stood in her way. "Why are you going into this room?"

Uron's smile returned, though it was much more mysterious this time. "You will find out soon enough, Durima. I am looking for something that I think might have been put here, but I don't know for sure. I can find it on my own, which is why I am telling you to leave."

Though Uron's tone wasn't very threatening—in fact, it was kind of nice—Durima sensed that if she pressed the issue further, Uron would quickly become threatening. Especially when she noticed his hand wrapped around the ice door handle; he was gripping it so tightly that the handle was cracked.

"Very well," said Durima. "I wish you luck in whatever

you are looking for. I'll go and call a Convocation, and if I have any success, I will let you know right away."

"I am expecting it," said Uron.

Durima turned and ran out the open doorway of the Temple. As she did so, she glanced over her shoulder to see Uron enter the side chamber, closing the door behind him as he did so. She thought she caught a glimpse of books in there, but why Uron would be interested in a bunch of books written by Xocionian Monks, she didn't know.

Not really any of my business, Durima thought as an ethereal portal opened in front of her. *I'm sure that whatever Uron is looking for, he has no malicious intent. Well, maybe malicious intent for the gods and Martir, but certainly not for me or any of the katabans who might join me.*

Still, Durima did hesitate a moment before plunging into the ethereal, like a tiny voice in her head was telling her to stop before she did something she would regret for the rest of her life.

But then Durima ignored the voice and entered the ethereal. She was already thinking of a good location to call the Convocation and wondering just how many katabans, if any at all, would come to the Convocation once they learned who had called it.

Chapter Three

Darek lay in one of the beds in the medical wing of the Arcanium, too exhausted from the cold and Durima's assault to even sleep. His chest was better—it had been healed by Archmage Yorak—but he found the actual recovery process hard. He suspected it had to do with the fact that he couldn't use magic anymore; without his ability to use magic, he was as weak as any normal mortal and would take about as long as a normal mortal to recover from a wound like that, even now that it was magically healed.

When he and Auratus had reappeared on North Academy's grounds, he had been immediately taken to the school's medical wing, where Yorak had healed him. He had then been given a decent meal of lime fish soup (his favorite dish, actually) and water and told to rest, which was the usual treatment for wounds like his.

No one had asked him about what happened at the Temple of Xocion, which was fine by him, as he was too tired to answer any questions. He had, however, seen Auratus going with Yorak to fill her in on the details of Durima's attack, though he wondered what else there was to say.

After all, he had learned the Xocionian Monks had

indeed fled to North Academy, so they had probably already explained most of the situation to everyone else. Darek had caught a glimpse of the Monks when he had been taken inside the Arcanium. They had been gathered in the Arcanium's courtyard, talking to Mom, who had appeared to be listening to them very intently.

She must still be talking with them, Darek thought. *Or maybe talking to Auratus, because she hasn't shown up to see if I am all right yet.*

That did not surprise Darek very much. Mom was the Magical Superior now, after all, and would probably remain that way for the foreseeable future. Mom was supposed to have made a list of potential candidates for the position of Magical Superior and given it to Skimif for him to make the final decision, but with Skimif dead, Darek wondered whether it was even possible to pick a new Magical Superior now.

Of course, we first have to worry about stopping Uron, which is the more pressing issue, Darek thought, sinking a little deeper into his soft pillow and sheets. If *we can stop him at all, that is.*

As much as he hated to admit it, the late Carcello had been more than a little accurate when he accused Darek and his friends and allies of arguing endlessly about how to stop Uron with no real progress. Mom, Yorak, Ranama, and the Ghostly God argued every day about how to deal with him; that wasn't even counting their discussions about the Void, which, though not seen since Skimif's death, was still very much a real threat to Martir, albeit not as urgent a one as

Uron.

Every discussion on the matter that Darek had participated in seemed to go exactly the same. Mom would ask if anyone had any ideas about how to stop Uron. Yorak would state that they needed to seek the guidance of the Powers, which would then be countered by Ranama, who would argue that going to the Powers was completely outside of their ability to do because no one knew where the Powers were or how to contact them. The Ghostly God would then chime in, usually to make some snide remark about the uselessness of their discussion and the stupidity of mortals, and then everyone would argue even more loudly than before.

Because the simple fact was, Skimif had been their best bet against Uron. He had been the only god who could go toe-to-toe with Uron due to their identical power levels. Indeed, the only reason Skimif had ever had trouble with Uron was due to Uron's possession of the God-killer, an object, sadly enough, to which Skimif was not immune.

Darek didn't want to think about any of this. He just wanted to close his eyes and sleep, which was what he should have been doing in the first place. Thinking about their terrible situation succeeded only in depressing him. Maybe things would look better after he woke up later.

Just as Darek closed his eyes, a familiar deep voice to his right said, "Hello, Darek."

His eyes snapped open, causing Darek to look up and grimace openly at the being hovering beside his bed.

He was a large, pale-armored being, with dark blue skin

and a nose-less face. Where he should have had legs, he had a wispy, ghost-like tail instead; and his fingers resembled chain links, though they acted just like normal fingers nonetheless.

"What do you want, Ghostly God?" said Darek.

The Ghostly God held up a finger. "Ah, ah. Remember, your agreement with me still has another nine and a half years left on it. So you have to call me *Master*. I thought we already went over this."

Darek sighed. "I remember, I remember, uh, Master."

"Better," said the Ghostly God, crossing his arms over his chest. "But I expect you to say it with more enthusiasm next time."

"I'm tired and still healing from Durima's attack," Darek said, gesturing at his chest, which was covered by his blankets. "So forgive me if I don't remember every last formality, Master."

Though Darek was usually respectful towards all gods, even those he didn't like much, he found it hard to keep a respectable, level-headed tone toward the Ghostly God. It was probably because he still remembered how it was technically the Ghostly God's fault Uron even had a body in the first place, though he did not say that aloud.

The Ghostly God, thankfully enough, did not seem inclined to push the point. "Well, I suppose I can forgive a few mistakes here and there. There are far bigger things happening in the world today than a mortal man who cannot remember to be respectful of his inherent superiors all the while."

"I still want to know why you're here," said Darek. "I'm not in any position to help you with anything, you know."

"True," said the Ghostly God, "which is why I am not going to ask you to do anything for me right now. Instead, I want to talk about Aorja Kitano."

Darek scowled and looked toward the window on the opposite side of the room, though he could only see the sky outside, rather than what he actually wanted to see. "What about her?"

"I thought she used to be your best friend," said the Ghostly God. "She and you were once very close, weren't you?"

"At one point, yes," said Darek, "before she revealed she was a psycho by trying to kill me and Jiku. On your orders."

The Ghostly God didn't even look slightly sheepish. "I don't remember ordering her to kill you or your other friend. When Aorja worked for me, I only gave her orders to distract you and the other mages so Durima and Gujak, my former servants, could sneak in and get their job done without error. Her trying to kill you was entirely her own choice."

It was hard to tell if the Ghostly God was telling the truth or not. That his tone was more matter-of-fact and less apologetic might have meant that he was telling the truth, or simply was so apathetic about it that he didn't see the need to apologize. Either way, it did not improve Darek's opinion of the Ghostly God.

"Besides, she's no longer under my employ," the Ghostly God continued. "She hates me as much as she hates you,

you know. She seems to think that I abandoned her on Rock Isle. What she forgot is that she was only ever a tool to me and nothing more."

"I don't care," said Darek. "Why are we even talking about her? I'd rather talk about someone else."

The Ghostly God either didn't hear him, or didn't care about what Darek just said, because he continued, "I do find it amusing, however, that your mother has allowed Aorja to stay on North Academy's grounds, along with that freakish half-god pet of hers, because, if I am not mistaken, it was your mother who helped put Aorja behind bars in the first place."

Darek bit his lower lip. He hadn't forgotten about Aorja being in North Academy, although she was not allowed to stay in any of the dorms or the Arcanium. Instead, Aorja had built a tiny stone hut out on the far edge of the sports field, near the Walls, where everyone could keep an eye on her but where no one would ever run into her accidentally.

It may have seemed strange to allow Aorja, a known hater of North Academy and everyone who lived or worked or learned within it, to live there, but Aorja had said she hated Uron and the Void even more than North Academy and had agreed to work with them to help save Martir.

It was probably the most controversial decision that Mom, in her short tenure as the Magical Superior, had ever made. Even Darek didn't agree with it. Though Aorja mostly kept to herself, only occasionally coming up to the Arcanium to listen to the meetings about how to defeat Uron, no one trusted her at all. Darek would have been happy to let her and her half-god pet nicknamed Zeeree fend for themselves outside of the school, but Mom had insisted that they needed all the help they could get, which was why Aorja still had her wand and wasn't locked away in the deepest, darkest corners of the catacombs, rotting away like the walking corpse that she was.

"I suppose your mother is desperate," said the Ghostly God. "And indeed, these are desperate times, the most desperate I can think of, at least since the time the Powers almost destroyed Martir. Of course, back then we had Skimif and that Carnagian prince to save us."

"Isn't King Malock still alive?" said Darek. "Why don't we ask him for help?"

"He's a weak, pathetic mortal, that's why," said the Ghostly God dismissively. "Carnag is on fire at the moment, thanks to Grinf running away, so I imagine that that is keeping his attention occupied. Anyway, we're getting off topic. I wanted to talk about Aorja."

"What's there to talk about?" said Darek. "She's a psychopathic musician who has only agreed to work with us because she thinks Uron and the Void are bigger threats. She'll probably turn on us the minute those two are no longer a problem."

"Speaking of her being a musician, have you heard her playing her guitar at night?" said the Ghostly God. "I have. And she's quite good, though shaky."

Darek rolled his eyes openly at that. "I don't care if she's the best musician in the world. She's a disgrace as a human being and as a student of North Academy."

"Right," said the Ghostly God. "Well, I wanted to talk with her about you because I wanted to know if you were interested in working alongside her on a mission."

Darek looked at the Ghostly God again in disbelief. "A mission? What kind of mission? And why would I want to work with her?"

"Just gauging your interest," said the Ghostly God, "though you will have no choice but to do it anyway once I tell you to do it. Remember your agreement with me."

"I remember, I remember," said Darek. "Have you asked Aorja if she wants to do it?"

"She doesn't listen to me anymore," said the Ghostly God, "though I imagine she might once I tell her what I have in mind for her."

"Does this mission involve stopping Uron somehow?" Darek asked.

"In an indirect, roundabout sort of way, yes," said the Ghostly God, nodding. "But it is supremely dangerous. I would not suggest it to even my worst enemies; however, these are desperate times and I believe we have no choice if we are going to have any hope of defeating Uron once and for all."

Darek folded his arms across his chest. "Why haven't you mentioned this in the dozens and dozens of meetings we've had over the past couple of months?"

"You have ears," said the Ghostly God, tapping the side of his head where his ears should have been but weren't (which made Darek wonder how the Ghostly God could even hear him). "Listen. I said it was dangerous ... and in truth, I don't even know if it will work."

"That's why you didn't bring it up around Mom and the others?" said Darek.

"I plan to do it at our next meeting," said the Ghostly God. He glanced at a clock hanging on the wall opposite Darek. "Coincidentally, our next meeting is only an hour away. Will you be there?"

Darek gestured at his blankets. "Considering how tired and exhausted I am, I doubt it."

"No," the Ghostly God said, shaking his head. "You *have* to be there. I want everyone to hear about my plan, especially you. Let me take away your exhaustion."

The Ghostly God wrapped one of his cold, metal hands around Darek's upper arm and squeezed.

A surge of power shot through Darek's whole body, similar to how Darek had felt back when the Ghostly God had healed him so many months ago. It was almost too much at first, but then the surge faded and Darek felt normal again.

Removing his hand from Darek's upper arm, the Ghostly God said, "There. Now you have no excuse for not being there. It will be in Jenur's study, as usual, so make sure to be there within the next hour."

Darek nodded. He would have thanked the Ghostly God, but then his stomach growled and he said, "I'm hungry."

"Do I look like your mother?" said the Ghostly God. "Go feed yourself. Anyway, I must see Aorja now and invite her to the meeting. See you in an hour."

With that, the Ghostly God vanished, leaving behind a

misty outline of himself that quickly evaporated.

Darek sat up his bed. He really did feel a lot better; however, thinking about the Ghostly God's plan—even though he didn't know the specifics—and how the Ghostly God's last plan had turned out, he wasn't sure whether to be excited or afraid.

Both, he decided.

But then he felt his stomach grumble, so he decided to think more about the Ghostly God's plan later. He would go to the Arcanium's kitchen, get something to eat, and then go up to Mom's study and find out just what the Ghostly God's plan was. At this point, he was willing to try anything if it would give them even the slightest chance of defeating Uron for good.

Chapter Four

Durima walked across the barren sand dunes of King's Desert, pacing back and forth across the same stretch of sand. She had been doing so for about an hour now, ever since she had called a Convocation of the Katabans. She had chosen King's Desert—a tiny, desert island located fifty miles to the east of a human island called Destan—as the meeting place for the Convocation because it was uninhabited by mortals due to its hostile climate, but roomy enough to allow for hundreds if not thousands of katabans to gather and listen to her pleas.

Not that she expected many to show. Though all katabans were technically required to attend a Convocation, that was only in normal times. No doubt many of her fellow katabans were hiding from Uron and the Void. And even if they had heard it, there was little chance any would answer it; after all, Durima had been the one to call it, and she was pretty sure that every other katabans in the world hated her now.

They probably think it's a trap, Durima thought as she continued to pace.

This particular area of King's Desert was intimately familiar to her. During the Katabans War, one of the battles had taken place on this island, as it had been where Jakuuth Grinfborn, under the guise of Grinf, had intended to begin his initial invasion of the Northern Isles. Jakuuth's forces had set up camp here discreetly, though their camp had soon been discovered, and Durima's side was sent to take them out.

That had been over three decades ago. There was no sign of the tents set up by the enemy soldiers, aside from a few poles sticking out of the sand here and there. Durima had found an abandoned knife, though it had looked more human in design than katabans, so it had probably been abandoned by some human long ago. Durima had also found a few scraps of cloth and pieces of armor, although they were so sandy and old that it was impossible to tell which side or species they had belonged to.

Indeed, as Durima surveyed the tan sand around her, she found it odd how natural the place looked now. It was like Kano, the Goddess of the Sea, Sand, and Art, had reclaimed King's Desert, devouring the bodies and other signs of battle that had taken place here.

But Durima remembered. She remembered how hot she had been in her armor under the boiling sun; remembered the screams of agony that her dying enemies had screamed as they went down under her; and remembered how she had been stabbed in the shoulder by a particularly large enemy soldier, a wound that had eventually healed but which sometimes still hurt anyway.

Yet Durima did not allow any of it to affect her right now. The Katabans War had ended twenty-five years ago;

she had had plenty of time to get over her trauma. Still, her fighting senses were on high alert nonetheless, as if her body expected an enemy soldier to pop out of the sand and attack her at any moment.

Old war instincts, Durima thought. *I guess they never really go away.*

Just then, Durima heard a small *pop,* the sound of an ethereal portal opening. Surprised, she stopped pacing and looked around until she spotted a single katabans standing about a dozen yards away from her.

This was not a katabans that Durima had seen before. He looked like a katabans from World's End, if his human-like features were any indication, though he was completely bald. He didn't wear much clothing; just a simple black toga, with sandals on his feet.

The newcomer looked terrified to Durima, though whether he was terrified of her or terrified of everything that had happened over the last couple of months, she couldn't tell.

"A-Are you Durima?" said the young katabans. His voice pegged him as being less than fifty-years-old. "The Demon?"

His shaking, uncertain voice reminded Durima of Gujak. It was a painful memory, however, so she pushed it away in order to keep her focus on the present.

"Yes, that's me," said Durima, nodding. "And you are?"

"Garvan," said the katabans. Then he added needlessly, "I used to own a ship salvaging company on World's End before Skimif's death. I had to abandon the building it was based in when Uron got out of the ethereal and I don't know if he destroyed it or not."

Uron hadn't done much to World's End since escaping the ethereal, to Durima's knowledge. She suspected that Garvan's company building was probably fine, though she didn't know for sure.

"Am I the first one here?" said Garvan, looking around the wide, sweeping desert.

"Yep," said Durima. "I didn't think anyone would show. What made you come?"

Garvan gulped and wiped the sweat off his brow. "Oh, uh, well, I, er, wanted to hear what you had to say. I mean, I know everyone says you're a traitor and everything, but ... oh, everything is just so scary and crazy nowadays, I mean, what else am I supposed to do?"

He sounded lost and confused and frightened. That described roughly ninety-nine percent of Martir's inhabitants at the moment, although something about Garvan's way of expressing it reminded her of Gujak.

"And, well, I just want to survive," said Garvan. He threw his hands up hopelessly. "I mean, I want to serve the gods and I want to help, but Skimif's dead and the gods are scattered and afraid like everyone, so I thought, what do I have to lose by seeing what you have to say? I mean, I'm going to die anyway, probably, so what do I have to lose, you know?"

He even rambles just like Gujak, Durima thought. *Almost like Gujak reincarnated.*

"So is anyone else going to show up?" Garvan asked,

rubbing his hands together worriedly.

"No idea," said Durima with a shrug. "It might just be you and—"

She was interrupted by dozens and dozens of popping sounds as ethereal portals opened all around her and Garvan. The sudden popping noises caused Garvan to jump, but Durima simply looked around at the dozens of katabans stepping out of the portals onto the hot sand all around her.

There was quite a variety of katabans here today. Some looked as animalistic as her, such as the katabans who resembled a giraffe, though with a more humanoid body; others were closer in appearance to humans, such as one female who looked almost exactly like Aorja Kitano, save for her nose, which was larger. There was even a Soldier of the Gods, identifiable thanks to his crystalline armor, the reflection of the sun's rays causing Durima to look away to save her vision.

More and more katabans kept coming, until soon the desert appeared as full of katabans as it was of sand. Friends reunited with friends, business associates talked with their partners, and couples embraced, though everyone kept a wide berth around Durima, like she was infected with some kind of virus that could be caught through close contact.

There were too many katabans for Durima to count; however, she estimated there to be anywhere from five hundred to one thousand katabans present. That wasn't the entire species, but it was a pretty good number, considering Durima was a hated traitor with no real authority over the rest of her kind to speak of.

Maybe there are more katabans like me than I thought, Durima thought as she watched the gathered katabans talk and chat among each other. *Or maybe they just want to listen to what I have to say so they know exactly why they will be killing me today.*

She did not see any members of the Katabans Council, though that hardly surprised her. She had never gotten along very well with the Council, especially after they unjustly banished her and Gujak to the Void a few months back. They probably didn't want to see her face ever again, which was fine by Durima, as she was not very fond of their faces, either.

Besides, without their influence, she thought it would be easier to convince the few katabans who had arrived to join with her. If they had already chosen to come of their own free will, then they were probably not entirely hostile to the idea of serving Uron.

Then again, as she noted earlier, most of the katabans did seem to avoid her. Even Garvan kept his distance, though he looked uncomfortable in the crowd, like he didn't like being so close to so many other katabans at once like this.

Durima waited a little while longer to see if any other katabans would show up. When she no longer heard or saw any other ethereal portals opening, she decided to start the actual Convocation.

The problem was that she could not see everyone and she doubted everyone could see her, so Durima placed her fists against the sand and used her geomancy to search for any rock below. It took her a moment, but soon she detected some rock deep underneath the sand.

It took her only a brief moment to make the rock rise. It rose up underneath her, forming a platform wide enough for her to stand and walk on, and raised her above all of the other katabans in the area. Sand poured off the platform as it rose, while most of the katabans who had been gathered around Durima moved back, surprised by the sudden appearance of the platform she had summoned.

Once she was at least five feet above everyone else, Durima forced the platform to stop rising. She then looked down on them all and was pleased to see every head in the desert looking up at her. Each face had a similar questioning expression on their face, like they were wondering what Durima was going to say to them.

Durima was not much of a public speaker; it had simply never been something she was terribly interested in. Still, she knew how to speak to an audience without stuttering and wasn't very nervous at all. In fact, she could tell that the katabans looking at her were far more nervous about her than she was about them.

They no doubt see me as the servant of Uron, Durima thought. *Maybe they even think I will kill them all, although of course I won't.*

Still, that thought made her feel more powerful than she had in a while. She was hardly a power-hungry maniac (a term that much better described the Katabans Council), but she liked the feeling nonetheless.

So Durima said, "I am glad to see that you all made it. I didn't expect quite so many of you to show; I originally estimated that only about a dozen, if even that much, of you would appear. That so many of you decided to come is an encouraging sign to me."

"Are you going to kill us?" one of the katabans, a tall, lanky fellow with purple hair, asked. "Is that why you called this Convocation?"

The crowd moved collectively away from Durima's platform, even though she hadn't even responded to his question yet. She found it amusing, however, that she had been right that at least one of the katabans thought she had gathered them here to kill her, though she tried not to appear that way, otherwise she might make the people get the wrong idea.

"No," said Durima, shaking her head as a warm breeze blew through her fur. "Of course not. And all of you know it, too, otherwise you wouldn't have dared to risk coming here."

"But you work for Uron!" another katabans cried out. "And everyone knows that Uron wants to destroy all of Martir! He killed Skimif himself, for the gods' sake!"

Quite a few people in the crowd were nodding in agreement with the second katabans; in fact, Durima noticed a handful of the more frightened ones on the edge of the crowd slip away into ethereal portals. Many more looked like they were thinking of leaving as well, which forced Durima to act quickly.

"You're correct that I work for Uron and that Uron wants

to destroy Martir," Durima said as quickly and clearly as she could. "Being an honest katabans, I always tell the truth, no matter the circumstance. But Uron does not want to destroy literally everything on Martir; in fact, he has offered to spare the entire katabans species if we will only serve him."

At that, the katabans in the crowd began muttering among themselves, like this was a surprising new development that none of them knew how to deal with. The general tone was skeptical, which meant Durima still had some work to do to convince them that she was telling the truth, but on the positive side, none of them looked like they were about to leave, at least.

With no one objecting, Durima went on, "What I just said was also the truth. Though Uron wants to destroy Martir, he doesn't want to destroy everything. Any katabans who swear allegiance to him will be allowed to live in the new world he will build on the ruins of Martir. It doesn't matter who you are now or what you do; you will live and be able to live your life as you see fit if you would just work for him."

Thousands of questions burst from the crowd at once, the collective sound of so many katabans speaking together in unison making Durima cringe. She wished she was a better audimancer because then she might have been able to silence them or at least lower the volume of their collective questions to a more reasonable level.

She held up her hands and shouted as loudly as she could, "Hold on, hold on, one question at a time! I can't answer a million questions at once."

Though Durima barely heard her own voice over the countless questions coming at her, she noticed the crowd's questions began to die down. Perhaps the katabans nearest her had heard her words and sent word back to everyone else to settle down, or maybe it was the general katabans instinct to listen to their superiors, but eventually the crowd went quiet, though they continued to look at her like she had heard every single question and was going to give each one a thorough and detailed answer.

In truth, Durima had heard a whole lot of shouting, much of it angry and confused, but nothing else. So she pointed at Garvan, who was closest to her platform, and said, "You. What's your question?"

Garvan shrank back as the katabans standing around him turned to look at him, but he did manage to stutter, "I-If we agree to serve Uron, will Uron spare the gods?"

"The youngling has a good question," said an elderly standing next to Garvan, slapping him on the shoulder as he did so. "We know that Uron wants to kill all of the gods; in fact, he has already killed several. You didn't say if Uron would spare the gods or not."

"He won't," said Durima. "He has extended this offer only to katabans who are willing to serve him. The gods—both northern and southern—will die."

She probably could have used a little more tact when saying that, but Durima saw no reason to sugarcoat or hide the truth. It wasn't like they would believe her if she lied anyway; if Uron had really intended to spare the gods, after all, then the gods would not currently be in hiding, trying to avoid being killed by him.

"Then why should we serve Uron?" the elderly katabans demanded. His voice sounded louder than it should have; a result of his audimancy, no doubt. "When the Powers first created us katabans eons ago, our job—our whole purpose for existing—was to serve the gods wholeheartedly. While the gods maintained the world, we did the little tasks and jobs they had no time or interest for. Even during the Godly War, we served them, because it was as the Ancient Words say: 'Thy purpose is to serve the gods of Martir forever and ever, until the Day ends.'"

Durima—and every other katabans in the desert—knew exactly what this old coot was talking about. The Ancient Words were the oldest written words in Martir, said to have been given to the katabans people by the Powers shortly after Martir was finished. Whether or not the Ancient Words actually had been written by the Powers, no one knew for sure, but the writings had influenced katabans thought for untold centuries, even though most katabans had never even read the Words and few ever consciously thought about them.

Durima was one of those most who had never read the Ancient Words, but she remembered Gujak, who actually had read some of the Ancient Words prior to his death, explaining to her once that the 'Day' was a poetic term thought to refer to Martir.

It's why that passage was always thought to describe the end of Martir, Gujak had said. Some scholars think that it means that the katabans are supposed to serve the gods until the last day of Martir, though there is some disagreement because it seems to contradict a passage in the Later Words which says...

That was where her memory of Gujak's explanation ended, as Durima had stopped listening to him prattle. She immediately felt guilty, however, because her memories were all she had about Gujak, so not being able to remember every last detail made her feel like a terrible friend.

But she pushed aside that feeling for now. She was losing the crowd. Some were wiping the sweat off their foreheads, looking thirsty and ready to leave; quite a few others, more than she wanted to see, were nodding in agreement with the elderly katabans, like he had just made a point that was impossible to argue with.

Durima wasn't going to back down that easily, though. She did not want to let her people die, not when there was a chance to save even just a small portion of them.

Thus, Durima stood up straighter and said, "But does anyone here deny that the Day is about to end? Look at the world. Skimif is dead, Uron is running rampant, the Void draws ever closer to the Northern Isles, and the gods are scared, confused, and scattered like sand in the wind. There is no way for anyone to defeat Uron or the Void; not even the gods can stop them. Does this not seem like the end of the Day to everyone?"

She must have struck a chord, because many of the people who were once nodding solemnly in agreement with the elder had stopped and now looked a bit more doubtful about their earlier certainty. That was good.

"But the Katabans Council hasn't told us that it's the end of the Day!" another katabans shouted. "They—"

"The Katabans Council are hiding," said Durima, in the harshest voice she could muster, "like the cowards they are. I thought they were supposed to lead the katabans; if so, where are they? What are they doing now? Why do you bring them up, like their opinions are relevant to anything anymore?"

The katabans who had been dumb enough to bring up the Council hung his head in shame. No one came to his defense, probably because most of the other katabans present did not appear to be big fans of the Council.

"Listen here," Durima continued, though she lessened the harshness of her voice. "Deep down inside, all of us know we have only two choices now: Either stand with the gods, and be slaughtered, or stand with Uron, and live."

"What good has Uron ever done for us?" asked the elder from before. "He led an army of half-gods and overpowered mortals to destroy World's End, the only island that any of us katabans could call home. He has made traveling the ethereal, our true home, dangerous, because one never knows whether he will show up on it or not."

"Uron has only made our lives more dangerous," cried out another katabans. "Not less!"

"And have the gods been much better?" Durima asked. She tapped the side of her head. "Think about it. The gods only see us as tools. They never appreciate anything we do, even if we follow their orders correctly. Tell me, how many of you have ever felt appreciated by any god?"

The silence that followed her question was deafening. The only sound to be heard was a handful of them shifting their feet uncomfortably, scuffing the sand upon which they stood.

Durima nodded slowly. She began walking in a circle on her platform in order to get a fuller look at everyone. She saw uncomfortable faces, averted eyes, and more than a few defiant expressions, although even the most defiant of them had some doubt in their eyes, as if they were unsure if they had any good reason for their defiance.

"Your silence is answer enough," said Durima, keeping her tone calmer now, though she put some tension into it in order to keep the crowd on edge. "It is true that the gods have spared us, but it is only the kind of mercy that a soldier shows to his sword. If the soldier no longer needs the sword, do you think he will continue to use it? Of course not. He will discard it and find a different weapon, just like how the gods discard us whenever we complete whatever job they've given us."

Again, no answer, likely because Durima was absolutely correct. It was not a popular topic to talk about in polite katabans society; however, considering the situation, she did not hesitate to continue to speak about it, as she doubted no one would even think about interrupting her.

"I have served many gods myself over the years," Durima continued. "Nimiko, Hollech, the Loner God, the Ghostly God, and many others. Some were fairer than others—such as Nimiko—but trust me when I say that none of them thanked me for anything I did. Why? Because the farmer doesn't thank his shovel for a job well done, that's why."

Even the elder did not look like he was going to argue that point.

"We katabans have known since time immemorial that we have always received rotten and unfair treatment from the gods," Durima said. She gestured at them all. "But our instincts have always compelled us to listen to and obey the gods no matter what. Most of the time, we've let those instincts guide us under the mistaken belief that, because they are natural, they are right. Well, I'm here to tell you that they are wrong."

Worried muttering broke out among certain members of the crowd, a trio of brothers from the look of it, but no one joined them in muttering. Nor did Durima stop and listen; she was on a roll and she wasn't going to sacrifice her roll just yet.

"Look at the humans," said Durima. "And the aquarians, too. Both species are not compelled to worship or serve the gods. Does anyone remember the infamous Brotherhood of Heathens, that group of mortals that Skimif founded prior to his ascension to godhood? Why are mortals allowed to rebel against the gods, but not we katabans?"

Much to her surprise, the elder spoke again, though this time, he didn't sound quite as confident as before. "Because the mortals are different. When the Powers created the peoples of Martir, they gave the mortals the ability to become gods themselves, if necessary. The mortals were never supposed to be loyal servants of the gods, at least not all of them, because if they did, then they would not make very good gods themselves."

"But why must we katabans serve the gods?" said Durima. "Why did the Powers design us to tolerate slavery and abuse from the gods? Once you think about it, we katabans have always been the butt of Martir's intelligent species. Always scrambling to please gods that can't be pleased, always lacking the freedom to enjoy the many things humans and aquarians take for granted; even on World's End, many of you only settled there to be near the gods, leaving you little time to enjoy life's pleasures or live your lives the way you see fit."

She could tell that her words were starting to sway some. Some were even nodding in agreement with her. None of them looked like they wanted to leave now.

"But if we serve Uron, we will be the only, or at least the dominant, species on his world," Durima said. "The humans won't be there. Neither will the aquarians. And of course, the gods will not even be a faint memory. We katabans will be free to live how we want ... and no one will be able to tell us otherwise."

Durima stopped and then looked around at all of the people below. Out of the thousand or so faces looking up at her, only a handful continued to look skeptical or doubtful, but she saw fear mixed in with that skepticism and doubt, the kind of fear one feels when one is the only person to disagree with the crowd.

"We are back to my original offer," said Durima. She held up one hand. "Agree to serve Uron, and you will live and be part of the new katabans that will be their own masters. Oppose him, and die."

She said 'die' with little emphasis, but it was enough. Even before the katabans began raising their hands, one by one, to show their agreement, Durima could tell that she had finally convinced them for good.

Soon, every katabans standing in the desert was holding up their hands. The hot sun burned the rock beneath Durima's feet, but she ignored it. She merely raised her own hands higher, smiling down on all of her people as she did so.

And, no matter where Durima looked, she did not see anyone who was going to leave now. Those few skeptical faces she had spotted before had vanished, drowned by the sea of believing, assenting faces looking up at her like she was some kind of goddess.

Of course, I am no goddess, Durima thought, her toothy smile growing ever larger the longer she looked at the people, *and this is only a small portion of the katabans as a whole. Still, I now understand why the gods like to be worshiped so much.*

"Good," said Durima aloud. "Once I let Uron know about this, he will spare every one of you, just as he promised. Today, you have all made the right choice."

There was no answer from the people, but there was no need. Not when the only question now was what to do next.

Then a voice that Durima had never heard before said: "Today, I think you have all made the wrong choice."

Chapter Five

His stomach full from a good lunch of rice, beans, and cheese, Darek Takren sat on a small wooden stool next to Auratus, who sat next to Archmage Yorak around the round oak table in the center of Mom's study. Auratus had nodded at Darek when he entered the study and had asked him, via telepathy, how he felt, but that was all she had asked him, because they were waiting for the meeting to begin.

Across from Darek sat Ranama, the God of Language. He still looked like an aquarian, despite being on land among humans. He had said he preferred this form, which no one had argued with him about because he was a god and you generally did not argue with gods. His glasses, at least, weren't cracked anymore, having been repaired a while ago by Ranama himself, allowing his intelligent blue eyes to be seen whole.

The god was looking at an ancient—something of an understatement, really, as it had apparently existed before Martir—stone tablet, its writing so faded that Darek wasn't sure how anyone could possibly read it. That tablet had taken up much of Ranama's time over the last couple of months; indeed, every time he wasn't in a meeting with everyone else, he was deep in the catacombs, trying to translate whatever was written on that tablet.

Unfortunately, he had not had much luck, from what Darek knew. The tablet was believed to have been written by someone from Uron's old world, which meant it was written in a non-Martirian language, which was the main reason he had not yet succeeded in translating it.

The whole reason Ranama was trying to translate it was because he believed it might hold the secret to defeating Uron. No one knew for sure, however, but no one had discouraged him from ding so, as they didn't have any other real ideas for dealing with Uron. It was somewhat rude, though, how Ranama would keep trying to translate it even during these meetings, but considering how little Ranama contributed to the usual discussions, it wasn't as big a loss as it could have been.

Aorja sat on Ranama's right. This was not because she liked Ranama; she simply did not want to sit next to Darek. She avoided looking at Darek by looking at the table in front of her, even though there wasn't anything on it to look at. Her normally blemish-less skin still had faint round sores on it, left over from an attack by a pseudo-net a couple of months back, though most of it was hidden thanks to the red-and-black student robes she had been given to wear when she first returned to the school a while ago.

And the Ghostly God sat—floated, really, as he didn't have a bottom to sit on—on Ranama's left. He had only just recently arrived, having been the last one to arrive as always, even though the whole reason they were gathered was to discuss his possible plan to stop Uron.

Then Darek looked over at his mother, a middle-aged woman named Jenur Takren, who as the current Magical Superior got to sit at the head of the table. She sat on a somewhat nicer chair than what everyone else sat on; however, she looked far more tired than everyone else. Her hair was normally a dark black, but ever since Skimif's death, it seemed like she had been aging faster than normal to Darek. Her hair had many gray hairs now, and seemed to be getting more every day; not to mention that her skin looked far more wrinkled than it usually did.

Then again, she's had to lead the entire school all by herself since the Magical Superior sacrificed himself, Darek thought. *Add Jakuuth's earlier attack on the school—which killed quite a few students and teachers—and then Skimif's death not long after that and I am amazed she hasn't completely fallen apart under the pressure.*

But then, Mom was always a tough woman. More than once, she had shown no hesitation in arguing with the gods, even the southern gods, and that was before she became the Magical Superior. He had always thought it would take a lot to break her, and he was pleased to see that he was correct.

"All right," said Mom. Her voice was still strong; however, Darek caught a tinge of weakness in it that he had never noticed before, or, more likely, hadn't been there in the first place. "This is, I believe, the twenty-fifth meeting we have held since Skimif's death, though I doubt anyone here except for me has been keeping track."

"Let's skip the pointless preliminaries," said Yorak. She pointed at the Ghostly God. "Ghostly God, I have been told you have a plan to defeat Uron."

The Ghostly God actually scratched the back of his neck, like he was embarrassed. "Yes, I do."

"And you didn't mention this to any of us right away because—?" Mom said, propping her chin on her hand as she looked at him.

"Because it is theoretical," said the Ghostly God. "Theoretical ... and dangerous."

"You said that already," said Aorja. Darek noticed how she kept her eyes firmly on the Ghostly God, not even looking at Darek. "We know how much you hate being clear and specific, but you know, it might actually help us kill that bastard if you were."

The Ghostly God glared at Aorja. "How dare you speak to me that way. Then again, I guess I shouldn't be shocked, as you mortals never respected us southern gods very much in the first place."

"Yeah, it's really unfair how we mortals don't respect the gods that killed a lot of their siblings in a massive war because they wanted to eat us for dinner every night," Aorja commented. "Very strange, isn't it?"

"Enough," said Mom. She pointed her wand at Aorja. "We don't have time for petty, senseless arguments or insults. This is exactly what Uron wants, and there's no way in hell I am giving that monster anything."

Aorja closed her mouth, but didn't say anything in response. She just looked down at the table once more, again pointedly ignoring Darek. Darek felt somewhat annoyed by that, even though he no longer liked her as much as he used to.

"Very well," said the Ghostly God. "I hate these meetings, so I might as well get straight to the point."

The Ghostly God slid one hand into the breastplate of his armor and withdrew an old-looking notebook with a blank cover. Carefully, he laid the notebook on the table before him. All eyes were drawn to the notebook, which looked mostly innocuous, though something about it made Darek feel wary, like it was some kind of wild animal that would jump up and bite your fingers off if you weren't careful.

"This is my notebook," said the Ghostly God, gesturing at the old book. "It was a notebook made by my brother, Yoreth, who you mortals know as the God of Reading and Writing. This was before the Godly War that divided us."

Even Ranama had torn his attention away from the tablet before him to look at the notebook. A look of recognition dawned on Ranama's features. "I remember that. Yoreth gave everyone those notebooks because he wanted to encourage us gods to write down everything we did for our personal development."

"Where is yours?" the Ghostly God asked.

Ranama adjusted his glasses sheepishly. "Well, uh, you see, I seemed to have misplaced it after the War. Haven't seen it in centuries."

"And here I thought you had kept yours in order to write about your translation efforts," the Ghostly God remarked. "Then again, I suppose you don't need to rely on pen and paper to help you translate anything, now do you, brother?"

"Don't tell Yoreth I lost mine," Ranama pleaded. "He will

be very angry with me if he finds out. Very angry."

"I won't," said the Ghostly God. "Though I do wonder where Yoreth is nowadays. Haven't felt his death, so I assume that Uron hasn't gotten him yet."

"Lord Ranama, Lord Ghostly God, can we please get back on topic?" said Mom, looking at the two gods in annoyance. "Yoreth is probably still alive, since we can all still read and write. Though I don't know how much longer that will last if we keep getting off-topic like this."

"For once, I agree with you," said the Ghostly God. "Anyway, I kept the notebook because it is unique among notebooks: It can never be filled. You can write and write in it to your heart's content, but there will always be at least a few more blank pages for you to fill."

"How does that work?" Darek asked.

"I don't know and have never cared to ask Yoreth how he did it," said the Ghostly God with a shrug. "I've just found it extremely useful, as this notebook is also incapable of breaking down. It only looks as old as it does because it has gotten exposed to the weather a few times and I am not the God of Cleanliness."

"Why do you keep a notebook, Ghostly God?" Yorak said. She covered her mouth. "To keep a record of the mortals you eat?"

"I write about that sometimes," said the Ghostly God, "though it has been a while since I last ate a mortal. Most of the time, I write about the secrets that lay beyond the domain of my brother, Diog; which is to say, what lies beyond the grave."

"But you're the God of Ghosts," said Aorja. She nodded at the notebook. "Doesn't that mean you already know everything there is to know about what exists in the afterlife?"

"My understanding of it is naturally deeper than that of other beings," said the Ghostly God as he rested one hand on the notebook. "But it is not perfect. The Powers gave me power over ghosts and spirits, such as katabans, but my power is largely limited over spirits in this world, not over spirits in whatever world might lie beyond this one."

Darek looked over his shoulder. He felt like someone was watching him, though he saw nothing except the tall bookshelves that went all the way up to the ceiling. "You mean ghosts actually exist?"

"Of course they do," said the Ghostly God, gesturing at himself. "Why would the Powers have give me power over them if they did not? I will admit, however, that they are extremely rare. Most mortals, when they die, go on to the afterlife and never return. Only a few ever return as ghosts, and they are easily dealt with."

"Let me guess," said Mom, "the ghosts who return are usually the ones who did not get a proper burial when they died, right?"

"Sometimes," said the Ghostly God. "Generally, however, it doesn't matter whether the ghost's body was 'properly' buried or not. Quite a few ghosts came back because they were not 'allowed' to go further."

"Allowed?" said Yorak. She leaned forward, causing Auratus to move as if to catch her in case she fell. "Allowed by who?"

"Your guess is as good as mine, mortal," the Ghostly God replied. "Every time I ask who does not allow them to go to the afterlife, the ghosts only ever reply, 'I don't know. I am simply not allowed to enter.'"

"So ..." Darek hesitated to speak up, but the Ghostly God's words had gotten his mind turning. "Does that mean that the Heavenly Paradise doesn't exist?"

"Again, I don't know," said the Ghostly God. He patted his notebook. "The afterlife might be the Heavenly Paradise, or the Beautiful Blue, or something else entirely. My research into the subject has been inconclusive, if only because every ghost I've spoken to always uses the least descriptive words to describe it."

"How spooky," said Aorja, though she rolled her eyes as she said that. "Maybe all of the ghosts you've dealt with are just bad at describing things."

"Perhaps," said the Ghostly God. "In any case, I always end up sending them back the way they came, and they never return, so I have always believed that they must be allowed inside for some reason."

"This is all very interesting," said Mom, "but I don't really see the point of it. How will knowing all of this help us defeat Uron?"

"It won't," said the Ghostly God. "I am simply explaining to you all of this so you understand the context of my plan better. I have spent several centuries learning the secrets of ghosts and the afterlife and I have recorded everything I know in this notebook."

"I think everyone here understands the context now, Ghostly God," said Mom. "We're ready to hear your suggestion for getting rid of Uron once and for all."

The Ghostly God leaned back, even though he wasn't even sitting down, and said, "To put it simply, I suggest that we send Darek and Aorja to this afterlife in order to convince whoever the gatekeeper of the afterlife is to take back Uron's soul."

That was not what Darek had been expecting to hear, and based on the puzzled expressions of the other people in the meeting, no one else had expected to hear that, either. In fact, he was certain that he had heard it entirely wrong. The Ghostly God couldn't have suggested that he and Aorja go to the afterlife, could he?

But of course, he did, because it was Aorja who recovered from the initial shock first and said, "Wait a minute. How is that even possible? How are we supposed to communicate with some gatekeeper of the afterlife? What do you mean by, 'take back Uron's soul'? And why does it have to be me and *Darek*?"

She said Darek's name like an insult, and she didn't even look at him when she said it, either. Again, Darek found it annoying, as he wasn't above looking at her when he talked about her. He was sitting across from her, for the gods' sake. It just reminded him about how petty Aorja could be.

"You finally have the sense to ask the right questions," said the Ghostly God. He put the tips of his fingers together. "I have a theory about Uron's true nature that I think explains his survival of the end of his world better than any other, as well as gives us a possible method to defeat him."

"Before we get onto that, why not just send Darek and Aorja to find Skimif's ghost?" asked Mom. "If we could get back Skimif, and maybe the other gods Uron has already killed—"

"We would be in the exact same situation we were in before," the Ghostly God finished, glaring at her in annoyance. "Besides, I don't think the ghosts of gods can return from the dead. In all of my years, I have never met any divine ghosts; merely confused, lost, and sometimes angry mortal ones. Not even after the Godly War, in which many gods died, and certainly not with any of the recent deaths caused by Uron. A god, once dead, can never return to our world, it seems."

Mom and Yorak both looked disappointed by that, as did Auratus and Ranama. Aorja, on the other hand, folded her arms across her chest and snapped, "Then get on with your theory about Uron. We're listening."

Darek held up a hand before the Ghostly God could speak. "Forgive me for interrupting, but I don't understand why we need a theory about Uron's nature. Uron already explained his origin to us last year, when he got his body. He was a 'scientist,' whatever that is, on his world, who put his soul in the center of his world right before it ended. His soul then survived the destruction of his world and lay dormant for years until it was awakened by the Powers's creating Martir. Then he came up with a plan to get a new body and, well, I think everyone here knows the rest."

"I am no expert on how the physics of a pre-Martir world

might have worked," the Ghostly God admitted. "Maybe it was indeed possible for a being to house his soul in an exterior object, but I doubt it, as souls and bodies are so intimately linked as to make hiding them inside external objects a complete impossibility. No, I think Uron is either lying or mistaken about how he, and he alone, survived the end of his world."

"Let's hear your theory, then," said Mom.

"My theory is this," said the Ghostly God. He gestured at the ceiling. "When Uron's world ended, he died with it. There was not a single survivor from the destruction of his world; it was a total apocalypse, like the kind Uron is trying to inflict on Martir."

"If Uron didn't survive, then is this some imposter we're dealing with?" said Aorja. "Because either way, I am going to kill that bastard with both of my hands."

"This is the real Uron, the only Uron that exists, in fact," said the Ghostly God. "What I believe occurred is that Uron, upon dying, attempted to go to the afterlife with the rest of his people, but for some reason, he was turned away. He returned to the ruins of his world, but without a physical body, he was unable to rebuild his home. With nothing to do, he most likely decided to rest under what remained of his world, perhaps promising to himself to rebuild his world once he awoke."

"That would explain how he was able to house his ghost inside the remains of his world," Ranama said. His eyes had returned to the tablet, but he clearly must have been listening if he said that. "Since he no longer had a body to return to, he could only go asleep in his world's ruins."

"Precisely, brother," said the Ghostly God, nodding. "But his spirit was still free, which is how he was able to possess that teleporter snake in his original form. I still don't understand how he was able to take the skeleton of Braim Kotogs and fuse it with the snake to create a new body for him, however. It is yet another secret of the beyond that I have yet to learn."

Then the Ghostly God pointed at Darek and then at Aorja. "I believe that you two need to go to the afterlife and convince its gatekeeper that it is time for Uron to go to his final resting place."

"Us?" said Darek, pointing at himself (he didn't point at Aorja because he didn't want to somehow piss her off). "Why us? You have experience sending ghosts back to where they're supposed to go. Why don't you do it?"

The Ghostly God's smile revealed his green teeth. "Because Uron is not a mere ghost anymore. I can no more tell him what to do than I can order my linguistic brother here around like a stupid katabans."

"But you're the Ghostly God," said Darek. "Can't you just go into the afterlife yourself?"

"No," said the Ghostly God. He gestured at the study all around them. "I am still a living being, just like everyone else. I would have to die in order to do this myself, but I think we can all agree that we do not need another dead god with Uron still active."

"I think I get what you're saying," said Yorak, rubbing the rainbow-colored stone on her arm. "You believe that the gatekeeper of the afterlife might be able to recall ghosts that it originally sent away."

"Bingo," said the Ghostly God. "I know nothing about this gatekeeper's powers or identity; however, it is the only way of permanently dealing with Uron that is available to us."

"But why Darek and Aorja?" Yorak asked. She glanced at Darek and then glared at Aorja. "While Darek is a noble human, he completely lacks the ability to use magic; as for Aorja, she is nothing more than a vile, sociopathic, selfish girl who threatens people for the pettiest reasons."

"Petty?" said Aorja, slamming her fist on the table. "You want to come here and say that to my face, bottle nose?"

"See?" said Yorak, gesturing at Aorja. "I am not normally one to question the wisdom or dictates of a god; however, I cannot help but wonder if there are individuals more qualified to go to the afterlife than they."

"I picked Darek because he still owes me nine and a half years of service," said the Ghostly God, gesturing at Darek. "So I knew he would have no choice but to serve me. Besides, ghosts cannot use magic; therefore, it doesn't matter if Darek can use magic or not because he won't need to use it."

"Then why me?" said Aorja. "It's not exactly a secret how much Darek and I hate each other."

"Because you have a tendency to keep going after something that wronged you even if you can't kill it," said the Ghostly God. "I can only assume that the afterlife is a dangerous, confusing place. Therefore, you are the perfect candidate to keep going even if everyone and everything there tries to stop you."

"Why can't we send Auratus with them?" said Yorak, putting one hand on her pupil's shoulders. "Auratus is as strong and brave as Aorja, minus the insanity. She would at least work with Darek much better than Aorja, that's for certain."

Auratus was nodding as Yorak said that, like she agreed with everything her headmistress was saying. She didn't even seem frightened by the prospect of going to the afterlife, which made her braver than Darek, as he wasn't so sure he wanted to do that.

The Ghostly God, however, shook his head as if it was the dumbest idea he had ever heard. "While Auratus may be saner than Aorja, that doesn't mean she is more capable of handling what lies beyond the grave. Besides, I want nothing to do with a mortal cursed by my sister; Amare can be quite vindictive when she wants to be."

"We can do it on our own," said Aorja, looking at Auratus with a smirk. "Actually, *I* can do it on my own, probably. I'm not afraid of the afterlife or ghosts."

"If I trusted you, I might have considered sending you by yourself," said the Ghostly God. "But I don't. I don't trust any mortals, to be honest, but Darek is far more stable than you are. He will make certain that you stay on track and do not get distracted from your purpose."

Aorja sighed heavily. "Fine. Maybe I can use Darek as a distraction if there are any enemies in the afterlife or whatever."

"That's the spirit," said the Ghostly God, sounding like he meant it. "Teamwork is a human virtue, is it not?"

"That kind of 'teamwork' isn't," Mom said. "If you can even call it that."

"Nonetheless, I hope everyone here understands my reasoning behind choosing Darek and Aorja," said the Ghostly God, once again gesturing at the two. "If they work together, then we might stand a chance of defeating Uron and saving Martir, just like the heroes we are."

"I like the idea," said Ranama, looking up from the tablet in front of him, "but how can we send a couple of mortals beyond the grave? Are you suggesting we kill Darek and Aorja?"

Aorja jumped out of her chair at the suggestion and pointed her wand at the Ghostly God. Strands of hair curtained her eyes as she stepped away from him.

"Hold on," said Aorja, "I am *not* going to die. No way. Not even to save Martir. I'm not that kind of a person."

"Killing you two might not even work," said the Ghostly God. "The gatekeeper will probably treat you two like regular ghosts and the whole plan will fall apart. Instead, we'll use a method I devised to send you two to the afterlife while remaining alive."

"What is it?" Aorja asked, although she still kept her distance from the Ghostly God like she thought he was going to kill her anyway.

"I will show it to you only if you agree to allow me to test it on you," said the Ghostly God. "It is a theoretical method of traveling to the afterlife; in fact, I've never even used it on anyone before, mortal or otherwise. It might not even work."

"If you can't guarantee it will work, then why are we even talking about it?" said Mom, throwing up her hands in exasperation. "I'm not going to let you experiment on my one and only son, even if he is bound to serve you for nine years. Especially if even you don't know exactly what exists in the afterlife."

"So you have a better idea, then?" said the Ghostly God. "You know of some other, more effective way for us to defeat Uron once and for all? I am very much interested in hearing it, if that's the case."

Mom looked flustered. She said, "I, well, I—" She went silent when the Ghostly God held up a finger.

"Of course you don't," said the Ghostly God. "But if you would, notice how long it took for me to bring this up. I took as long as I did because I know how dangerous it is to mess with things like spirits and ghosts. I would not suggest sending Darek and Aorja if I thought we had any other reasonable options of stopping Uron left."

"My brother is right," said Ranama. He then paused and adjusted his glasses. "We don't have much choice. I am no advocate of putting the lives of mortals in unnecessary danger; however, we have literally no other option on the table. It seems to me that we either choose to go along with the Ghostly God's plan, or we argue until Uron extinguishes the sun and the Void envelops us all in its darkness."

"I agree with Lord Salor," said Yorak, using Ranama's aquarian name. She still had a hand on Auratus's shoulder, though she didn't look very happy. "This may be our only hope, and it would be foolish of us to ignore it just because it might not work."

"Would you be saying the same thing if this plan put your own son at risk, Yorak?" said Mom. "I know you don't have any children, but you know what I mean, don't you?"

"If I had a son, I would be proud to let the Ghostly God send him to the afterlife if it was the only way we could save the world," said Yorak. She nodded at Darek. "And knowing how brave and strong Darek Takren is, I have no doubt in my mind that he will do a good job, even if he must keep an eye on Aorja while he does it."

"I have to, Mom," said Darek, before Mom could argue with Yorak. He gestured at the Ghostly God. "I said I would do whatever the Ghostly God asked me to do when I agreed to work for him. So I don't have any choice."

"Your son is correct," said the Ghostly God. "He can only stay if I order him to, but I obviously am not going to order him to do that, now am I?"

Darek didn't like disagreeing with Mom too often, even though he knew she wasn't always right about everything. Still, in this case, he was willing to handle the way she looked at him in disappointment.

This was, after all, a way to be useful, which was something he hadn't felt since losing his ability to use magic two months ago. He may have been the one to bring Uron back into this world, but if the Ghostly God's plan worked, he would also be the one to take him out of it, and that was worth all of the danger and uncertainty that this plan presented.

Mom was now looking at everyone, like she was trying to find any allies who would join her in objecting to this plan. Unfortunately for her, however, everyone had voiced their support for the plan already, except for Auratus, although she didn't look like she was going to object anytime soon.

Finally, Mom rubbed her forehead and said, "All right. I guess I'm out-voted this time. I want to keep Darek safe; but if putting him in danger will save Martir, then I guess I'm for it."

She sounded very reluctant and still seemed to be waiting for someone else besides her to object. No one did; in fact, Ranama actually smiled, like he was happy she was for it. Darek did feel a little bad about his mother's reluctance, but he knew it was for the best.

The Ghostly God picked up his notebook and flipped it open to somewhere in the middle. "Then what are we waiting for? We don't have time to lose, so we might as well get started right away."

Chapter Six

The voice that had spoken rang out clear through the hot desert air, as mighty and unquestionable as that of a god. It sounded almost human-like underneath the divine tone that was impossible to deny or ignore.

The various katabans below looked around the desert in alarm, searching for the owner of that voice. Durima, too, looked around as hard as she could, wondering who would dare say something like that. She hoped at first that it might have been a katabans until she spotted a figure standing on the dunes not far from them, a figure she was sure hadn't been standing there even just five seconds ago.

He was no katabans; that much was obvious. He wore a long, gray traveling cloak that had probably seen better days, considering how worn and torn it looked. He had a straw hat on his head, but underneath it, she saw a small nose, piercing golden eyes, and tanned skin almost as dark as volcanic rock.

The traveler, because that is what he looked like, leaned on a simple traveling staff, which, like the cloak, looked worn. He leaned on it like it was the only thing he trusted, and considering how his golden eyes looked over them all with displeasure, that was probably truer than even Durima believed.

He looked like a human, but there was something about him that was clearly not. It might have been the way he looked at the crowd of nearly a thousand katabans—many of whom were strong enough to kill a regular human even without magic—as if they were a bunch of rowdy children that needed discipline, or it might have been the sheer magical aura radiating from his form, much stronger than any mortal mage who wasn't a Limitless could possibly be.

"Who are you?" Durima demanded, pointing at the traveler. "A mortal lost in the desert? Do you even know what we are?"

"A better question is, do you even know who *I* am?" asked the traveler. "Or has your anger towards the gods so blinded you that you can no longer even tell when you are talking to one?"

The crowd backed away immediately when the traveler said that. They hid behind Durima's platform, or hid as well as a large crowd of noisy katabans could, anyway. Durima herself almost stepped back, but caught herself before she did so, as she did not want to show a sign of weakness to this god, whoever he was.

"Which god are you?" said Durima. "Forgive me for not knowing, but there are many gods and goddesses in the world and I am not familiar with each one."

"What a poor excuse for a katabans you are, having to ask me my identity," said the traveler, putting his hand on his hat to keep it from fluttering away in a sudden breeze that stirred up. "I guess that's why you are working for Uron. No *true* katabans would ever work for that killer of the gods. Nonetheless, I will introduce myself: I am the Human God, the God of Humans."

"The Human God?" said Durima. "I didn't know the humans had a god of their own, and a southern god at that."

"My relationship with humans is ... murky, at best," the Human God admitted. "I was on the side of the southern gods in the Godly War, but unlike my brothers and sisters in the south, I have since realized the error of my ways, though that doesn't mean I deny how tasty humans can be, when cooked right."

He licked his lips, like just thinking about a properly cooked human was a delight. Durima was quite thankful she was not a human; if she was, she would be running the other way, even though they were beyond the Dividing Line, which meant the Human God could no more eat a human than Durima could sprout wings and fly.

"But that is irrelevant," said the Human God, shaking his head. He pointed at Durima. "I've been hiding here in the north ever since Uron killed Skimif. I didn't want to come out of hiding, but when I saw so many katabans heading to this island, I had to come and see for myself what you were doing."

"We're gaining our freedom from the tyranny of your brothers and sisters," said Durima. Her instincts demanded that she bow to him, but she fought them down. "Uron has promised us that freedom and it is a promise we intend to hold him to."

"Yes, I heard every word of your stupid speech to the crowd," said the Human God, nodding. "But that doesn't mean I accept one word of it. You katabans are naïve if you believe Uron actually cares about you, or has any intention of letting any of you live in freedom in his new world."

Durima sensed the katabans below and behind her starting to shift uneasily. While the Human God may not have been known to most of the katabans present until just now, he was still very much a god, which meant that most of the katabans had to listen to him even if they didn't want to. Even Durima found it hard to stand strong in the face of his disapproval and the hot sun overhead did not make it any easier.

The Human God pointed his staff at them like the gavel of a judge. "Look at you all. You're pathetic, nothing more than a bunch of scared and confused minor spirits who think that allying with the monster that wants to destroy their world will give them freedom. How stupid do you have to be to believe that?"

"Not stupid at all," Durima said, shaking her head. "Just practical."

"Practical? Don't make me laugh," said the Human God. "I smell fear in the air, and it ain't mine. Every last one of you katabans is afraid, like a bunch of sheep being chased by a big bad wolf. As one of the gods of Martir, I order you not to help Uron."

Durima looked over her at the crowd. Many of the katabans held their heads in shame; a few had even fallen on their hands and knees like they were asking for forgiveness for their unpardonable sins.

She then looked at the Human God again, who was still

leaning on his staff. He looked quite pleased at how submissive the katabans behaved toward him, which angered Durima more than anything else.

She pointed at him and demanded, "You talk tough for a god who was hiding from Uron. Why should we work for you if you are afraid of Uron? You cannot protect us any better than we can protect ourselves."

The Human God shrugged. "I share many qualities with the humans, one of which is my inability to give up even in the face of insurmountable odds. My siblings and I may not stand a chance against Uron, but that doesn't mean I am just going to lie down and let him walk all over me like a carpet. Nor will I let any of you cowardly katabans do the same. You will stand and fight him, just like you're supposed to."

He said those last words with such authority that Durima felt her knees buckling beneath her. Every instinct in her body was telling her to join the rest of her katabans and slobber at his feet. She wanted to apologize to the Human God for daring to stand against him, tell him that she would never even think of doing anything like this again, and then ask him what she wanted him to do next.

She bent her knees, but then straightened up. No. She was not going to fall down and worship him, worship a god who clearly did not care for her or any of the other katabans assembled here. She was no mere dog, to be ordered about and bossed around like she was too stupid to know what to do for herself.

Fighting against her instincts, Durima stood up and said

to the Human God, "No. I will not fight Uron. Nor will anyone else here."

She heard some gasps of horror behind her, but she did not turn around to look and reassure everyone that she was fine. She continued to stare at the Human God, who was now looking at her in disbelief.

"Did you just openly defy my orders?" said the Human God. He stopped leaning on his staff, which Durima did not take to be a good sign. "Like you have any choice?"

Durima did not know for sure how often katabans defied the gods; however, she knew it wasn't common. The Human God looked so taken aback by her refusal to obey him that she thought that that alone might have been enough to convince him to leave and look for easier katabans to boss around.

But of course, it wasn't that easy. He glared at Durima with the kind of divine hatred that only a god could muster. It was a look Durima was familiar with, as the Ghostly God had fixed her with that look every time she failed him, and it was a look she had a hard time standing against.

"Well, we gods have ways of dealing with uncooperative katabans," said the Human God, tugging at his cloak. "Ways that are often cruel and unusual and more than a little violent."

Durima knew exactly how cruel the gods could be. She had no idea what kind of punishments the Human God preferred, having never served him before; however, she was in no mood to find out.

"If you harm me," said Durima, gesturing at herself,

"then Uron will find out, hunt you down, and kill you."

"Is that supposed to scare me?" said the Human God. "Uron will come after me even if I treated you like royalty. I will make an example out of you, which should be more than enough to convince the rest of you cowardly traitors to get back in line."

He raised a hand—probably to use some kind of magic—causing Durima to say quickly, "Is that it, then? You're going to prove me right by violently putting down our rebellion without even asking us if we still want to serve you?"

The Human God paused. The sweat on his hand glistened, which made Durima feel even hotter than she already did; nonetheless, she could tell she had hit a weak point.

"What do you mean?" said the Human God.

Relieved to have an opportunity to speak, Durima raised her voice to make sure her fellow katabans heard every word she said. "Well, Human God, you said you heard my whole argument, didn't you? I argued that the gods, which includes you, by the way, have always denied us katabans the freedom we deserve. By punishing me and forcing us to obey you, you are proving that we really would be better off without you."

The Human God's golden eyes were hard to read from a distance, though it seemed like he was thinking about what she just said. Of course, there was no reason for the Human God to listen to her; he could just as easily choose to ignore her point and go ahead with whatever punishment he intended to deal to her.

But then the Human God lowered his hand and pushed up the brim of his straw hat with his thumb. She could see his face much more clearly now, and it was smiling.

"You're absolutely correct, Durima the Demon," said the Human God in a cheerful voice. "It would have been very stupid of me to prove your silly argument right, even though the end result would have been the same, with you dead and this little rebellion squashed. You're too smart for a katabans; you should have been a goddess instead."

Durima could hardly believe that that had worked, especially on a southern god, who were not known for their ability to reason or their love of logic.

"So will you leave us alone?" said Durima. "Because I can summon Uron right now to kill you."

"By the time he gets here, you will be dead and I will be long gone," said the Human God with a chuckle. "Besides, brother Xocion tells me Uron is a little busy in the Great Berg right now. Not sure what he's doing, but I doubt he could go from the Great Berg to here very quickly even if he teleported."

"Then what are you going to do?" said Durima.

"Make you an offer," said the Human God. He gestured at the desert. "Just look at this big, old wide desert. Perfect place for a fight, with plenty of room for a thousand or so spectators to stand and watch, wouldn't you say?"

Durima looked around the area. It was indeed wide-open, which was why she had picked this place as the location of the Convocation in the first place. She did not understand what that had to do with anything, however.

"In case you were wondering, my offer is pretty simple," said the Human God. He pointed at Durima. "You and I fight. If I win, this dumb little rebellion ends before it even starts and you katabans have to swear allegiance to me. If you win, then I leave you guys alone and go back into hiding from Uron. How does that sound?"

Durima gulped. All of her courage drained from her body, making it almost impossible for her to stand. She knew she was no match for any god. While katabans were generally stronger than humans, they were no match for gods. Even just one god could, on his own, take down an entire army of katabans if he wanted.

And there was no ignoring the sheer power radiating from the Human God right now like heat from the sun. She sensed that if he wanted to, the Human God could slaughter the entire crowd of katabans behind her just as easily as a fire burned through a dry forest. Even if Durima unleashed the Demon within, she doubted it would give her enough strength to defeat the Human God.

On the other hand, if she refused the offer, that would do more to destroy the trust she had built up in her fellow katabans than anything else. The Human God must have known that; why else would he make that offer unless he was sure that she would accept it and that he would win?

"Of course," said the Human God, lowering the brim of his hat again, "if you want to give up and skip this battle entirely, that would be fine by me. With Uron running around killing gods left and right, I really don't have any time to waste fighting rebellious katabans."

Still unsure what to say, Durima looked back at the katabans behind her. Though they were all now on their hands and knees, a few were now looking up at her, trying to figure out if she was going to accept the Human God's offer or not. One of them was Garvan, who shook in his spot like he was bowing in the middle of the Great Berg rather than in the middle of the King's Desert.

What would Gujak do? Durima asked herself suddenly.

The answer came to her immediately: He would get down on his hands and knees and plead for forgiveness from the Human God. That wasn't an option for Durima right now. Therefore, she had only one choice.

So she said to the Human God, "All right. I accept your offer. When do you want to begin the fight?"

The Human God stroked his chin and looked up at the sun. "I'd like to get it out of the way immediately; however, I think we can put it off for half an hour, and no more. I would like to give you a chance to prepare against me, even though I know for a fact that you can't beat me. It's only fair."

"Very well," said Durima, though only with great reluctance, because she was pretty sure that she was going to lose this fight no matter how much time she was given in which to prepare. She just hoped that Uron would still honor his promise to her to spare the katabans even if she died, as unlikely as that seemed.

Chapter Seven

Darek and Aorja sat cross-legged next to each other in the Chamber beneath Mom's study. The green lights running along the ceiling helped to illuminate it a little, though they also made the Ghostly God —who floated before them with his notebook opened in one hand—look even ghastlier than normal, his pale armor sickening under the green light.

The little podium that had usually stood in the center of the Chamber had been moved next to the doorway. Mom stood by it, leaning on the podium with a worried expression on her face, while Ranama, Yorak, and Auratus stood next to her. They all kept their distance because the Ghostly God had said he didn't need them all standing around getting in the way, though he had said they could watch if they wanted to.

Darek looked down at the floor underneath him. He and Aorja sat together inside a thin salt circle, laid out by the Ghostly God himself, who had said that it was crucial he do it in order to get the width of the circle just right. As a result, the Chamber smelled a little saltier than usual, although it wasn't as noticeable as it could have been.

"Are we ready to do it yet?" Aorja asked, brushing a few stray strands of hair out of her eyes in annoyance. "Because we've been sitting here for at least half an hour and this stone floor isn't exactly comfortable, you know."

"I am going over my notes again to make sure I did not skip any important steps," said the Ghostly God, without looking up at Aorja. "Though I must say, I have never met any mortal as eager to go beyond the grave before as you are."

"That's because I'm not afraid of ghosts," Aorja replied. Then she added, "Can Zeeree come with us? He could be really helpful."

The Ghostly God scowled. "Of course not. I have no idea if this even works for mortals; half-gods are another thing entirely. Besides, I doubt your little pet could even fit down here, at least not without crowding out the rest of us, anyway."

"Well, take good care of him while I'm away, okay?" said Aorja. "He can be violent and angry sometimes, but he's really a very sweet half-god. You just have to watch out for the poison he sometimes secretes."

Seeing Aorja act so concerned about Zeeree reminded Darek about how Aorja had acted before she betrayed them. He used to think of her as an exceedingly kind and sweet person herself. He had thought that that kind and sweet person had died when she first tried to kill him, but maybe, deep down inside, the old Aorja was still alive somewhere, albeit weak and ineffectual.

"I will make sure he does not cause too much trouble while you are away," said the Ghostly God, turning the page of his notebook as carefully as he could with his big fingers, though he didn't sound like he meant it.

Darek, for one, was quite thankful that Zeeree was not coming with them. The big, lumbering half-god lived with Aorja out on the sports field, but had already caused a lot of trouble for the mages at North Academy, such as the time he got into a fight with Guardian, the automaton protector of the school, which had ended with the Ghostly God and Ranama working together to end the fight before it got too serious.

Then again, he supposed that Zeeree wasn't entirely useless. It had been Zeeree, after all, who had delivered the final blows to the Void back in the Old Ruins, thus saving them all from a terrible fate. And sure, Zeeree could be thoughtful, though he only acted that way around Aorja, who he seemed to think of as his mother, strangely enough.

Shaking his head, Darek said, "Well, we'll try to be quick. Ghostly God, do you know how long it will take us to find this gatekeeper you told us about?"

"No," said the Ghostly God, shaking his head, his eyes still fixated on the worn pages of his notebook before him. "I am not sure this gatekeeper even exists. It might instead be some sort of natural force that allows or prevents ghosts from entering the afterlife. You might not even be able to reason with it, in the same way you cannot reason with a tornado or an erupting volcano."

That thought made Darek shiver a little where he sat, but then a new thought occurred to him that he had never considered before. It caused his fear to melt away, because if there was any truth to it, then it might make the journey beyond the grave worth it even if they could not find this gatekeeper.

"Right," said Darek. He leaned forward, ignoring the pressure on his legs caused by this movement. "Ghostly God, if this works and Aorja and I go to the afterlife, do you think we'll run into the ghosts of people we know? Like Kuroshio, the Magical Superior, Eyurna, and maybe others."

The Ghostly God still did not look up from his notebook. "It is possible, though unlikely. All of the beings you mentioned have gone on to the afterlife. Their spirits are at rest. I doubt you'll even find Skimif's ghost; as I said, a god, once dead, can never return. That is what all of the evidence suggests."

"But it is possible to bring back mortals," said Darek. "Could we then—"

The Ghostly God's notebook snapped shut and he looked up at Darek, his eyes blazing with anger. "Don't even suggest it. Bringing back any ghosts from the dead, for any reason, is one of the most foolish things I have ever heard any mortal suggest in my lifetime ... and I have heard many foolish things from many mortals."

"Why?" said Aorja. "I mean, not that I would do it anyway—don't really have anyone I'd want to bring back—but I don't see what the problem is."

The Ghostly God sighed, just like how some of Darek's old teachers would sigh whenever he failed to grasp what they considered a simple magical concept. "When someone dies, they are supposed to stay dead. Look what happened when someone who was supposed to stay dead came back; you know, Uron, also known as the whole reason we are even attempting to do this."

"But Uron is different," said Darek. "He's not a Martirian, and anyway he's evil and crazy, which is probably why he came back that way."

"It is unnatural," said the Ghostly God. "There is a very good reason why the Powers did not grant any of us gods—even Skimif—the ability to resurrect the dead. It is too much power for any one god to wield, even for a good god. Besides, why bring back your departed friends when they are now at rest? Don't you think that would be cruel?"

Darek frowned. He found it a bit humorous that the Ghostly God, easily one of the cruelest gods he knew, was appealing to their own hatred of cruelty in order to get them to do what he wanted. He found it especially funny that the God of Ghosts and Mist apparently believed that it would work at all on Aorja.

Nonetheless, Darek nodded and said, "I guess you're right, Master. We don't need to distract ourselves trying to save people who are already dead."

"Excellent," said the Ghostly God with a relieved sigh. "Very good. Yes, it's very important that we keep our focus on finding the gatekeeper and convincing him to recall Uron's soul. As long as you two keep your focus on that, you should be fine."

"Can we just get on with it already?" said Aorja, patting her knees in annoyance. "Is there anything else you need to do before we can leave?"

The Ghostly God shook his head as he slipped his notebook back into his breastplate. "No. I believe we have completed all the steps: Picked out two willing mortals, put them in a circle of salt out of the sun light, in a place where some have died. All I need to do now is activate the spell and you should be well on your way to saving the world."

"What will happen, exactly?" Darek asked. His bottom was starting to get numb from sitting for so long, so he shifted his weight a little to get the feeling returned to it.

"If all goes according to my research, your souls should be severed from your bodies and you should be sent directly to the place between Martir and the afterlife," said the Ghostly God. "You should then, theoretically, be able to find the gatekeeper to the afterlife and inform him of Uron's recent revival. From there, I can only assume that the gatekeeper will recall Uron back and Martir will be saved."

"But Skimif will still be dead," Mom spoke up. The green lights made her face look older than it normally did, even made her look a little sickly. "And those other gods Uron has already killed, too."

"True," said the Ghostly God. "But we will deal with that after we have gotten rid of Uron. First things first, as I always say."

Then the Ghostly God held out one hand toward Darek and Aorja. A whitish mist, sparkling like ice in the sun, began to form at the tip of his index finger.

"I have no idea if this spell will hurt or not, so don't even think about asking," said the Ghostly God. "And again, it might not even work."

"What if it backfires?" said Aorja. She sounded more than a little worried now, perhaps because a god was pointing a glowing finger at them. "Maybe it will actually kill us, instead of temporarily separating our souls from our bodies."

"Possibly," said the Ghostly God. "Though it's too late to back out of this now. And if it does end up killing you, then no matter; you will become ghosts who can then go on and complete the mission just the same, the only difference being that you would not be able to return to this world."

The Ghostly God didn't sound disturbed by that fact, even though Darek found himself wondering if the Ghostly God might actually just go ahead and kill them instead. Of course, he doubted the Ghostly God could kill them, as they were still on the northern side of the Dividing Line, not to mention that Ranama was here and he was unlikely to sit back and let the Ghostly God kill any mortal, even if they weren't his followers.

I still wish he would at least pretend to be bothered by that idea, Darek thought with a gulp. *Then again, the Ghostly God never has cared much about whether anyone thinks he's cruel or kind.*

Then an important question occurred to him that he had almost forgotten to ask. He looked at the Ghostly God and asked, "How will Aorja and I return, assuming we succeed in our mission? You didn't say."

"My studies have not helped me figure that out," the Ghostly God said. "It may not even be possible for you to come back, but I am certain you two will find a way home,

99

though I don't know how long it will take."

"How wonderful," said Aorja in a sardonic voice. "So there's a good possibility that this spell will make it impossible for us to come back; in other words, it might actually kill us."

"Do you have any better ideas, then?" asked the Ghostly God, tapping his ear that had appeared out of nowhere. "Because I'm all ears, you know."

Neither Darek nor Aorja answered that, mostly because they did not have any better ideas. Still, Darek wished the Ghostly God could at least have guaranteed them a safe return home, if nothing else.

"Now, before I cast the spell, do any of you have any last words to impart to us?" said the Ghostly God. "You may not return for some time, so I thought I would give you two this opportunity to say good bye to your friends."

"Tell Zeeree I will be back very soon," said Aorja, in a tone similar to the kind Mom always used whenever she tried to calm Darek as a child. "And that he shouldn't worry or be afraid of the man in the fox mask."

The Ghostly God looked confused by that last line, though Darek didn't. Zeeree had, for some reason, been afraid of Junaz Esperon, the metomancy teacher of North Academy who wore a fox mask under the belief that it would make him as clever as a fox. Granted, Junaz was a bit strange, but hardly terrifying, in Darek's opinion, though considering how simple-minded Zeeree was, he doubted it had occurred to the half-god that he was much stronger than Junaz.

But Darek pushed that thought out of his mind for now. He looked over at Mom, Ranama, Yorak, and Auratus, and said, "Mom, you don't have to worry about me. We'll go there and back so fast it will be like we never left at all."

"Just be careful, all right?" said Mom.

"I will," said Darek, nodding.

"And keep Aorja in check," Yorak added. "If she does anything, don't be afraid to knock her around a bit."

"As if I would ever let Darek so much as touch me," said Aorja, throwing a dangerous smile in Darek's direction. "Especially since you can't so much as light a candle with your thoughts nowadays."

Darek glared at her, while Ranama, who looked up from the stone tablet, said, "I wish there was some way I could help you, but alas, I cannot. I will do my best to decode this diary while you are away. Perhaps it will also hold some information we could use to defeat Uron."

Then Darek heard Auratus's voice in his mind, saying simply, *Good luck.*

"Are we all done talking now?" said the Ghostly God. "Because I am tired of standing here with my arm up like this."

"Fire away," said Aorja, resting her hands on her knees as she looked directly into the white light on the tip of the Ghostly God's finger. "We're ready when you are."

Darek also looked at the white light, but he did not get to say anything. The white mist leaped out of the Ghostly God's finger like a snake from the ground and entered Darek's mouth, eyes, and ears. It tasted like mist and ice, an odd taste that made Darek feel sick to his stomach.

Though he had little time to dwell on that feeling, because in the next moment, Darek's whole world went black and he fell into unconsciousness.

When Darek woke up, he felt like he had taken a good, long nap. He yawned, stretching his arms and legs, ready to get out of bed for another day at North Academy when he looked at his hands and realized that they were so faded that he could see straight through them.

Panicking, Darek sat up and tried to pinch himself, thinking this was only some kind of terrible nightmare that would go away if he felt some pain. Unfortunately, pinching his arm only hurt, but did not wake him up.

Then Darek realized that his whole body was transparent. Even worse, he was completely naked; he did not see his Xocionian Monk robes on his body, nor were his feet shod. Oddly, he could not see his genitals; they seemed to be hidden by a strange white glow that covered his body, which made him feel a little less shameful, even though he was still acutely aware of his nudity. What was even stranger was how he couldn't feel them at all, as if they had actually vanished (as disturbing a thought as any, for sure).

"Good morning," said Aorja's musical and mocking voice somewhere above him. "I thought you were just going to sleep there forever. Did you have a bad nightmare or something?"

Darek looked up and would have blushed when he saw Aorja, although for some reason he couldn't or at least didn't feel his face grow hot when he saw her naked body.

All right, Aorja was technically similar to him in appearance. While she was most definitely not wearing any clothes at all—not even the skimpy clothing he had seen her in back in the Old Ruins—her genitals, like his, were hidden by some mysterious white glow. He still found himself staring at her chest, however, although it was more out of confusion about where her breasts had gone than out of lust.

"There's not much to see of my amazing body," Aorja said, causing Darek to look up at her face, which was as clear as ever. "For some reason, ghosts don't have genitals. I guess it must be because ghosts can't have sex or something. I can't even feel turned on, and trust me, I've been thinking of some fine male specimens to help me there."

Darek blinked and looked down at his own body again. "Wait, we're ghosts?"

"Of course we are," said Aorja in annoyance. "I know you're an idiot, Darek, but I thought you would at least remember how we got here."

Darek rubbed the back of his head. "That's right. I remember now. The Ghostly God's spell must have been a success."

"Got that right," said Aorja. She looked around, a frown on her face. "Only question now is, where the hell are we?"

For the first time since he woke up, Darek noticed his surroundings.

He and Aorja were in the middle of what appeared to be

a long dirt road; at least, he assumed it was long, though he did not know for sure, as a thick, heavy mist obscured the path ahead of him. He could not see what lay beyond the mist. They might have been sitting on the edge of a tall cliff or were just outside a town. All he saw was what appeared to be a thick stone archway standing only a few feet away from them, though the mist was so thick that he still couldn't make out much of its actual appearance.

The area was quiet as well. He didn't hear any people or animals, no wind or rain or any other weather phenomena. It reminded him of the Void, though at least the Void had felt like there might be something living within. Here, he saw no sign of life at all, though that made sense, seeing as this was the afterlife, after all.

"How long have you been awake?" Darek asked as he rose to his feet unsteadily.

"Ten minutes longer than you," Aorja replied. "I would have left you behind to complete the mission, but I decided I wanted to have you on hand in case I needed a distraction. You know, that teamwork thing the Ghostly God mentioned?"

Darek grimaced. "I'm finally starting to understand why the Ghostly God originally hired you in the first place."

Aorja shoved him. "Shut up."

Regaining his balance, Darek looked around again. "Well, what direction do you think we should go in? Under that arch?"

He pointed at the stone arch barely visible in the mist. It was wide enough that the two of them could walk side by side underneath it if they wanted to, though with the mist as thick as it was, it was impossible to see what lay beyond it.

"Don't have any other better ideas, I suppose," said Aorja with a shrug. "Even if it's dangerous, I doubt it will hurt us that badly, considering we're already ghosts."

"Try not to say anything like that," said Darek, looking around worriedly.

"Why not?" said Aorja.

"Because you might jinx us," said Darek.

"Don't be stupid," said Aorja, now walking toward the arch. "Jinxing people doesn't actually work. You're just paranoid."

Darek walked after her, keeping his eyes wide open as he looked around the area. "I just think we should be very careful about this place. Not even the gods know what this place is like. There could be literally anything here. Maybe there are even monsters that eat ghosts."

"That's a stupid thought," said Aorja, rolling her eyes. "Just what I would expect from someone as dumb as you. Monsters that eat ghosts ... that sounds like something a kid would make up to scare his friends."

"Dismiss my fears all you like, but that doesn't mean they are unfounded," Darek said. "We need to exercise extreme caution here until we know just how dangerous this place is."

"Yap, yap, yap," said Aorja, miming him talking by opening and closing her right hand. "Right now, there's just mist and this weird arch, neither of which look very dangerous to me. As long as we keep walking, we'll be just fine."

Darek didn't know if he believed that, but he didn't want to argue with Aorja anymore, either, seeing as he couldn't get her to believe him.

So he looked at the arch as they approached it. It was twice as tall as he and looked quite old, though clearly in good condition, which either meant that the weather around here was usually temperate or someone took good care of it.

Then he started to notice that the arch's surface was not as smooth as he initially believed. Carved into the arch's legs, running all the way up to the top, were carvings of beings he did not recognize. They were humanoid, but only up to the waist; below the waist, they had wispy ghost-like tails that reminded Darek of the Ghostly God's.

He stopped to look at the carvings more closely, causing Aorja to snap, "What are you doing? We don't have time to stand around and stare at dumb arches all day."

Darek glanced at her. "I am trying to get information so that we're not walking in blind. Maybe this arch will give us an idea about what lies beyond it."

Aorja sighed and folded her arms across her chest. "Fine, fine, whatever. Though if you take too much time, I won't hesitate to drag you the rest of the way myself."

Darek ignored her threat. He stroked his chin in thought, trying to understand what he was looking at.

His initial thought was that the carvings were random, with no real order or plan to them. But the longer he stared, the more he began to make out some kind of story or at least an orderly progression of events featured on the carvings.

At the bottom of the arch's right leg, he saw a carving of what appeared to be a hand sticking out of a pool. The next carving showed one of the ghost-like beings he had noticed in the first place, followed by another carving of multiple ghost-like beings dancing around what appeared to be a fire. The carving of the fire even seemed to glow, though it might have been Darek's mind playing tricks on him.

Above that was a carving of some kind of woman. He assumed it was a woman, anyway; it had what appeared to be breasts, but its face was absolutely hideous, scarred and pitted with frazzled hair that looked like the hair of a corpse. The carving showed the woman rising from a pit, grasping the ghostly tail of one of the beings from earlier. The look of terror on the ghostly being's face was so real that Darek almost forgot he was looking at a stone carving, not the real thing.

Closer to the top of the arch was another carving of a dozen or so ghostly beings fleeing in terror from the woman. It didn't actually show the woman, but he recognized the claw-like hand that was reaching toward them just the same.

The next few carvings, running down the arch's left leg, showed the ghostly beings fleeing beyond some kind of door. The mad woman was following, her carved teeth resembling sharpened knives, but in the next carving the door was closed and the woman was pounding on it in anger.

That was where the carvings ended. Darek looked at Aorja and asked, "Any idea about what it means?"

"No," said Aorja, shaking her head. "Old hag looks kind of like my mother, though. It's probably just some art made by someone just to scare anyone who passes through here."

"I'm not so sure about that," said Darek. He spread his arms to indicate the whole arch. "It's too detailed and meticulous to just be some scary story thought up by a bored storyteller. It's even more detailed than the work of the Divine Carvers. It most definitely has some kind of purpose."

"Unless this purpose will help us find that gatekeeper guy, I don't see any reason to worry about it," said Aorja. She began walking under the arch. "Now if you will excuse me, I am not going to let a bunch of silly carvings on a dumb arch scare—"

She was cut off abruptly by a wild howling sound that tore through the mist like a knife. It was unnaturally loud, like a scream amplified by audimancy, and it actually made Darek cover his ears to protect his hearing (though he was unsure if he could even lose his hearing as a ghost).

It was a wild, whooping scream, and it sounded like it came from everywhere at once. Darek looked around, trying to spot its source, but it was impossible because of the thick and heavy mist that covered everything around them. All he heard was that awful scream, more like a screech, really, that sent shivers down his spine (again, he was unsure if he had a literal spine as a ghost).

Then he saw it. Dragging itself along the ground, black

smoke rising from its nostrils, was what looked like the decapitated corpse of a woman; different from the carving of the woman monster on the arch, but similar enough that he staggered back away from it anyway.

"What in the name of the gods is that?" said Aorja. She reached for her wand, but then cursed. "Damn it. I forgot we couldn't take our wands with us."

Darek gulped. "And we can't use any magic, either. Do you know what that means?"

Aorja nodded. "Run?"

"Run," said Darek.

They turned and ran through the archway, neither looking back over their shoulder at the screaming, shrieking woman crawling after them. Not that passing under the archway would do anything by itself; after all, the archway had no gate or anything to prevent the corpse from following. Still, the other direction would take them straight into the arms of the monster corpse, so it was worth risking whatever lay beyond the arch if it meant escaping the beast.

Or they *would* have passed under the arch, if they hadn't ran straight into an invisible barrier. It felt as hard as the stone archway itself, yet Darek could still see through it as plainly as air, still see the stone path stretching out into the mist to parts unknown.

Aorja slammed her fists against the barrier, but it didn't budge even one inch under her attack. "Damn it. Who put an invisible wall here, of all—"

Another ugly shriek caused Darek's head to whip around. The corpse was still dragging itself toward them. Its head was upside down and its eyeballs hung out of its sockets, eyeballs as black as ink and as slimy as a snake. A strange black wetness trailed behind the corpse, a wetness that smoked and burned wherever it touched the ground.

"Let's go around the arch," Darek suggested, gesturing at both sides of the arch. "I mean, it's not part of a wall or building or anything, so we should be able to go around, right?"

"Five hundred coins says that this invisible wall extends beyond this arch," said Aorja, tapping the barrier with a scowl on her face. Her violet eyes darted over to the corpse dragging itself toward them. "Let's kill it."

"How?" said Darek. "In case you forgot, not only are we incapable of using magic anymore, but we're also weaponless. Unless, of course, you happen to be a professional martial artist and never told anyone?"

"I was hoping *you* would know something, seeing as you always manage to get out of the stickiest situations somehow," Aorja replied. "But I should have guessed that you'd be just as useless as ever."

"Forgive me for not being an instant expert on fighting ghost corpses," Darek snapped. "I don't even know if we *can* kill it."

Aorja smiled that crazy smile of hers that Darek had learned to hate. "Then let's find out, shall we?"

Without warning, she grabbed Darek and shoved him toward the corpse. Taken by surprise, Darek staggered forward and fell on his hands and knees onto the ground. It did not hurt—as a ghost, he seemed incapable of feeling pain—but the sudden movement did shock him for a moment, even though he should have seen that coming from a million miles away.

He then looked up in time to see the corpse almost right up in his face. He looked into its eyes, which were completely black, and quaked with fear. He was so paralyzed that he could only watch as the corpse drew closer and closer to him, smoke trailing behind it. Its claws were like the talons of a falcon, but sickish yellow and cracked in many places, though he had no doubt they could tear right through him if given the chance.

Then Darek heard Aorja shout, "Who the heck are *you*?" but before he got a chance to look over his shoulder and see who it was (not that he could, because he was too paralyzed with fear by the sight of the corpse), he felt someone grab his neck and pull him back. The person shoved him onto his behind so fast that Darek almost didn't even comprehend what had happened until it did.

Shaking his head, Darek looked up to see someone standing in between him and the corpse. It was another ghost, that much he could tell, because the being was humanoid and whitish and transparent just like him and Aorja, and naked, too, though of course he saw nothing that should be clothed.

Beyond that, however, Darek couldn't see anything else about this person, because the newcomer's back was to him. He did, however, appear to be carrying some kind of short blade that resembled an overgrown knife.

Through the gap between the newcomer's legs, Darek

saw the corpse had not slowed down its dragging at all. He wasn't even sure that it had registered the appearance of the new ghost, though he supposed it didn't matter either way because that corpse could probably kill all three of them if it wanted (or do whatever it would do to ghosts, because they probably couldn't die again).

The new ghost raised his short blade and slashed at the corpse. Some kind of greenish light lanced from the blade's tip and struck the corpse, which shrieked again, though this time it shrieked in pain instead.

"Take that, you dumb beast," said the new ghost, in a voice that was familiar to Darek, though where he had heard it before, he didn't know. "Get out of here. No one wants to see your ugly mug anymore."

Much to Darek's surprise, the corpse actually retreated. Still howling and shrieking, it retreated back into the mist, crawling away even faster than it had been moving before. In fact, it crawled so fast that when Darek blinked again, it was gone, the only clue of its existence being the trail of black wetness that followed it wherever it went.

Then the being lowered his short blade and said, "Well, that was easier than expected. A shame such a pretty woman had to end up looking like that. Can't even imagine what it must feel like."

Darek shook his head again as Aorja ran up next to him. She didn't even bother to ask Darek how he felt. She just hauled him up to his feet like he was a disobedient little child and then growled at the newcomer, "Who are you? What do you want?"

The new ghost turned around. His body was just like Darek's—vague and covered in a whitish glow—but his face was completely different. He had outgoing eyes, a smile that had clearly spoken many jokes and quips, and had a full head of hair that resembled the kind of hair that the Nikon people back on Martir had, which might have been red back in his old life. There was something incredibly familiar in the ghost's face, again like Darek had seen it somewhere before, but again, he was not sure why.

"Is that really the kind of tone you use to address the guy who just saved you, beautiful?" said the newcomer. "Because I didn't technically have to do it, you know. I only stepped in because beautiful women in danger are my only weakness."

"Don't be such a pig," Aorja snapped. "Just tell us who you are."

The newcomer held up his hands in a pacifying sort of way. "Okay, fine. You remind me of a girl I used to know, though I don't remember her name, sadly. Straight to the point, she was. Didn't much like it when I called her 'beautiful,' even though she clearly was."

"Tell us your name or I will break your neck," Aorja said. And based on how tightly she grasped Darek's shoulder, he was fairly certain she would break his neck as well, given the chance.

"The woman I remember never threatened to break my neck before," said the newcomer. "But anyway, I'm rambling. My name is ... oh, that's a tough one. Ever since I came here, my memory has been sort of fuzzy. I barely even remember what I did an hour ago, but I'll try my best."

The newcomer looked down at his blade and seemed to be focusing very hard on it. He then looked up again abruptly and smiled.

"That's right." He held out a hand. "Name's Braim Kotogs. I've lived here for as long as I can remember. What are your names?"

Chapter Eight

Durima stood on the hot sand, trying not to look weak as the Human God stood before her with his poncho discarded, lying underneath a rock he had put on it to keep the wind from blowing it away. He had thrown it off in order to help him move more freely, he had said, but Durima didn't think he needed to do that. He was a god, after all. He could just as easily blink and end Durima's life in an instant if he wanted to, rather than 'fight' her (though she had a feeling it was going to be the type of fight where a human stepped on an ant).

Surrounding the scene of the battle were all of the katabans who had originally come to the Convocation. Durima was glad to see that none of them had left or even tried to leave yet. She took that as a sign that maybe there were more katabans on her side than she originally thought, though in all likelihood they were staying here because they had nowhere else to go.

If I lose this, then they will certainly have somewhere to go, Durima thought, watching the Human God crack his knuckles. *To wherever the Human God tells them to go.*

Without his poncho, the Human God wore a simple white shirt that showed his muscular body quite well. He had taken off his boots, too, again to grant him greater mobility, he said. He didn't seem bothered by the heat in the sand under his feet, though considering he was a god, she was not surprised.

This has to be the stupidest thing I've ever done, Durima thought. *Why did I ever agree to fight a god? I am going to die and Uron will be extremely angry. In fact, he'll be so angry that he will probably find some way to get my soul from beyond death just to punish me for it.*

She shook her head. She was starting to think of Uron like how she used to think of the Ghostly God, her last master. Of course Uron was different from the Ghostly God; unlike the Ghostly God, Uron had actually complimented Durima on a job well-done.

As for Durima herself, she was doing some push-ups. She technically didn't need to do them; she was already in great shape. However, she didn't want the Human God to think she was nervous and the best way to hide one's nerves was through a good workout. That was what she had learned over the years and it was knowledge she always tried to put into practice whenever she was in a situation where she needed to hide her nerves.

Then Durima heard someone walking toward her and she looked over her shoulder in time to see Garvan approaching. He kept his eyes firmly averted from the Human God, like he was afraid of making eye contact with or perhaps angering the god. Durima understood; southern gods like the Human God could be very unpredictable, as Garvan no doubt knew already.

Still doing her push-ups, Durima said, "Hi, Garvan.

What do you want?"

Garvan stopped. The sun was reflecting off his bald head almost like a mirror. Sweat ran down the side of his face, which he wiped away with a handkerchief he had pulled out of the folds of his toga.

"I just wanted to say ..." Garvan glanced at the Human God and then looked at Durima again. "I just wanted to say good luck. I think you're really brave for fighting a god, even if you can't beat him."

Durima almost stopped doing her push-ups she was so surprised by Garvan's support, though she caught herself and kept up her workout as if she had not been surprised at all. "Thanks. Though you do realize, of course, that the Human God is listening?"

Garvan nodded, still keeping his eyes on Durima. "Yes. And I don't care. I listened to your speech earlier and I believed every word of it."

Another surprise, though again, Durima tried not to show it. She only had a few more minutes, if even that much, before her fight with the Human God would start, so she could not let him see any weakness on her part just yet.

"You did," said Durima, her tone slightly breathless as she did her push-ups. "That's good to hear."

"Yeah," said Garvan. "I wasn't so sure what to believe before, but now I believe that we would be better off following Uron and gaining our freedom, rather than die serving the gods who don't even care about us that much."

As Garvan spoke, Durima noticed the Human God still cracking his knuckles, his head bowed as if he was listening to Garvan, like the young katabans was talking to him instead. His hat blocked his face, though Durima doubted the Human God was pleased with what he heard.

Then Durima stopped doing her push-ups. Standing up, she looked at Garvan and said, "There's a good chance I will die here. What will you do then?"

"I don't know," Garvan admitted. "But I'll think of something. For sure."

"Well?" the Human God barked, causing Durima to start and look in his direction. He was now looking up, his golden eyes glowing under his hat. "Are we going to get this fight started or what?"

"May Dranyx's luck be with—" Garvan said, before catching himself and frowning. "Wait, why am I wishing Dranyx's luck on you? She would never give you luck against one of her siblings, at least in this situation."

"It doesn't matter," said Durima, gesturing for Garvan to return to the watching crowd. "I'll just have to do my best. Now go back to everyone else; I don't need you or anyone else in my way while I'm fighting this god."

Garvan nodded and ran off back to the crowd. Durima watched him go, just to make sure he actually was going (she had the sneaking suspicion that he wanted to try and help her). Once she saw him take his place next to the elder from earlier, Durima turned to face the Human God once again.

He had taken off his hat now. It hang off the back of his neck via a thin string. That did not seem like a very good place to put one's hat in a fight, but again, it didn't matter because the Human God could have fought with his eyes closed and all of his limbs broken and Durima still wouldn't stand a chance against him.

His hair was dark and wild, despite having been under that hat for a while. The Human God wasn't even sweating in the sun overhead, which made Durima envious, as the heat was starting to get to her.

Sweeping his staff before him, the Human God said, "It has been a good, long while since I last fought anyone. Thinking of taking my time with this one. Maybe I'll play around with you for a bit before I crush you totally."

Durima stepped forward, her hands balled into fists. "Maybe you should think twice about underestimating your opponents. Just because I'm a katabans doesn't mean I don't pack a punch."

"Sure, bear," said the Human God. "Keep talking and I might actually believe that you pose a legitimate threat to me. But why are we still talking? Talk is cheaper than dirt. If you're truly as strong as you believe, then show me your moves."

Durima slammed her fists into the ground, activating her geomancy as she did so. The impact of her fists sending geomancy waves through the ground sent a massive wave of hot sand hurtling toward the Human God, the wave so thick that Durima could not even see the Human God on the other side, even though she knew that he was there.

"Throwing sand at me?" the Human God's voice roared from behind the incoming wave. "Ha! How childish."

The Human God burst through the sand wave, the dust

getting in his hair, and landed with a roll on the ground. The wave kept going, however, and smashed back into the rest of the desert, sending up a large dust cloud as tall as a two story building.

Not that Durima had any time to focus on that, because the Human God then dashed at her with shocking speed. His golden eyes glinted with glee as he drew closer to Durima, who was now pretty sure that she was going to die.

Nonetheless, she rolled out of the way just as the Human God's staff came flying at her. Rolling to her feet, she tried to punch the Human God, but he dodged it easily. Not even a second later, his staff came flying out of nowhere at her face.

The staff—which had appeared to be made out of wood—struck her as hard as a crowbar. In fact, it struck her so hard that she went flying through the air, unable to control her trajectory or register her surroundings, until she slammed straight into the sand and rolled and tumbled across its hot, dry surface.

She eventually stopped tumbling, though with the way her head spun and ached from the blow, she still felt like she was flying. Her head felt like it was cracked open, even though she couldn't feel any bleeding, and all she wanted to do was lie there and hope her pain went away on its own.

But Durima had experienced worse pain during the Katabans War, so she shook her still-aching head, sat up, and looked up in time to see the Human God walking toward her. His staff on his shoulder, the Human God smirked as if she was more of an amusing distraction than a real threat.

"Throwing sand at me," the Human God repeated, shaking his head as he did so. "What a pathetic first attack. And here I was expecting to see the Demon come out, but I guess that's just the way the dice rolls, eh?"

Durima also wanted the Demon to come out, but she had no way of accessing that more violent version of herself at the moment. Right now, she had to rely on her good old military and combat experience, a feat made slightly difficult by her aching head and body, though she had experience in ignoring pain in order to survive.

Stepping back, Durima tried to analyze the Human God, and fast, because though he was taking a more leisurely pace at the moment, she knew how fast he could move when he wanted to. She was not going to give him an opening in which to take her down.

She knew very little about him, except that he was the God of Humans. That was certainly an odd domain to control, but that was not worth thinking about at the moment.

If he's the God of Humans, does that mean he shares common human weaknesses? Durima thought, eying his body and muscles. *But gods don't get tired or hungry or thirsty or sick. They can keep fighting forever.*

She walked backwards as fast as she could, putting some distance between herself and the Human God, though this was a temporary measure at best.

"If you want to give up now, I won't fault you for it," said the Human God. "One of the traits of intelligence is knowing when to fold 'em, after all."

Durima said nothing to that. She was analyzing his every movement to look for that one weakness she could take advantage of. She analyzed his feet, his clothes, his arms, his staff ... but she saw nothing she could take advantage of, nothing that would give her the edge over him that she needed in order to win.

Think! Durima told herself. *What kind of weaknesses do humans have that the Human God might share with them? As powerful as he may be, he must still have some sort of exploitable weakness.*

"Based on the way you haven't fallen to your knees and begged for my forgiveness, I'm gonna assume you aren't going to give up," said the Human God with a sigh. "Oh, well. I guess you really *have* gone over to the dark side. A shame, but what can you do?"

He was gone just as quickly as Durima could blink. She at first didn't know where he could have gone, but then it hit her like lightning and she jumped to the left just as the Human God's staff came falling down where her head had been.

The blow actually shook the ground, causing Durima to almost lose her footing, though she managed to regain it just as the Human God stood up to his full height and laid his staff on his shoulder again.

"Saw that one coming, didn't you?" said the Human God. "Of course you did. It was obvious."

Durima didn't understand why the Human God was explaining to her how obvious his attack had been. She understood even less why he didn't seem angry about her dodging and predicting his move, though something told her that she should have been very afraid about that.

"But will you see this attack coming?" said the Human God, stroking his chin as he said that.

"See *what* attack—" Durima was cut off by a loud buzzing sound that made her look around wildly, but she could not see what was making that sound.

Then she felt a sharp sting on her shoulder, causing her to swat at it with her fist. She crushed something and removed her fist and saw that the sticky, blue remains of some kind of insect she didn't recognize were on her shoulder. She flicked them off with one finger, feeling disgusted as she watched the insectoid remains fall to the sand below.

"What was that?" said Durima, looking up at the Human God sharply.

The Human God smiled. "That was my favorite bug, a paralyzing stinger. They're known for their sting, which can paralyze practically anything, no matter how big it is. I always carry one around; this one I released when you dodged my last attack, which is how you did not notice it."

Durima was about to say that she didn't think that the paralyzing stinger had actually worked on her when she could no longer move her right arm. It felt as stiff as a board and just as useful in her current situation.

"Wish you hadn't smashed it, though," said the Human God with a sigh. "He was my only companion on my long journeys across the world. I guess I'll just have to go back to

Inice if we survive all this and see if she can give me another one."

The panic rising in Durima's chest was as palpable as the heat of the sun. She staggered backward, all of her confidence draining from her body in an instant. The paralysis seemed confined to her right arm, but that did not make her feel very confident because it still gave her an unnecessary handicap in this fight, a handicap she was certain would spell her doom.

"No answer?" said the Human God. "Eh, didn't expect one, anyway. I can smell your fear, though. It reeks like the stink of a corpse left out in the sun all day."

Durima could not smell her own fear, but she didn't doubt that the Human God was telling the truth when he said he could smell it. Fear was not an easy thing to hide, even for a veteran like her, especially the unique katabans fear that rose within her, the one every katabans felt whenever they thought they had displeased the gods.

The Human God was not Durima's master; nonetheless, he was a god, which was probably the prime reason she was having such a hard time analyzing him. Her every instinct was telling her to fall to her knees and worship, to apologize for her actions and to ask for the forgiveness that she knew she would not get.

But she fought her instincts. She used her geomancy again, this time focusing on the rock deep beneath the surface of the desert. She knew it would do little against the Human God; however, she had to try it, even though she did not think she could beat him.

A gigantic stone hand burst out of the sand, sending sand clouds flying, and grabbed the Human God from behind. The Human God looked genuinely shocked by this development at first, especially when the stone hand squeezed hard around his body, trying to crush him between its fingers.

But then the Human God's expression changed to one of annoyance and he shrugged. It was a subtle gesture; but it was enough, because the stone hand exploded, causing chunks of rock to go flying everywhere. Durima ducked to avoid a particularly large chunk that came flying toward her head and then stepped back as the Human God fell to the sand.

"Giant stone hand," said the Human God, dusting off his shoulders as he returned to his full height. "Gotta admit, I did not see that coming; however, it still left me unimpressed. If that's the best you got, then maybe I should just end this right here and now before Uron actually shows up."

Again he was gone. Durima jumped to the side again, thinking he was going to repeat his previous sneak attack, but then he reappeared in the direction she was jumping and he kicked her in the chest.

The blow sent her falling flat on her back, and awkwardly at that, thanks to her paralyzed right arm. Before she could get up or do anything else, the Human God pinned her to the ground with his right foot. The pressure he applied to her was intense, much more than a being of his statue and weight should have been able to apply, though considering how appearances could be very deceiving for gods, that was no surprise to her.

The Human God raised his staff above his head as he said, "This fight was boring, and you know what, I probably shouldn't have even done it in the first place. All I did was waste time, and time is one of the few resources you don't want to waste, trust me."

Durima hit his right foot with her left hand, but the blow glanced off his tough-as-iron skin like it was nothing. He just smiled down at her like her weak attempts at resistance were a minor amusement.

Then he looked over his shoulder at the other katabans and shouted, "Let Durima's fate, which shall be bloody and very messy, be a lesson to the rest of you traitors. Anyone who tries to sell out the gods to Uron is less than a worm larva in our eyes. Don't even bother to cry for her demise; she deserved it for her crimes against the gods."

The Human God then returned his attention to Durima. He held up the staff even higher over his head. "When I said your death was going to be bloody and very messy, I meant it."

Durima kept her eyes firmly open, even though she wanted to close them to avoid seeing her death come to her. Death did not really scare her as much as it scared other katabans, mostly because she had been a soldier who had seen death many times before. Her own death wasn't anything to be afraid of; it was her instinctual fear of death that made her want to close her eyes and not see it.

But then, without warning, the Human God froze. He

almost looked like a statue now, he was so still. The crowd of watching katabans gasped in horror, though Durima didn't need to hear their reactions to know that she was looking at the death of yet another god.

Then his chest faded into a dusty, ugly brown, browner than the sand upon which they fought. He gave a horrible, shuddering gasp as the disintegrating effect of the God-killer spread from his chest all over his body. His arms detached from his shoulders and fell to the ground; his legs rapidly turned into nothing, while his horrified expression soon vanished in the dust pile that he was becoming.

As the Human God's form collapsed into dust, becoming virtually indistinguishable from the dust clouds that had risen during Durima's fight with him, Uron lowered the God-killer to his side. He dusted it off with his other hand, as if he had merely gotten it dirty and had not just killed another god in cold blood.

"There," said Uron, smiling satisfactorily. "It worked out just as I planned."

Durima blinked. Some of the Human God's dust had landed on her chest, though it fell off when she sat up and rubbed the back of her head, which still ached. Unfortunately, she had to use her left hand to rub her head; her right arm was as paralyzed as ever.

"Uron," said Durima, looking up at him in surprise. "What are you doing here? I thought you were back in the Great Berg, searching for something in the Temple of Xocion."

The fingers of the God-killer rolled into a fist as Uron

said, "It wasn't there. I thought it was—it *should* have been —but it wasn't."

He sighed in frustration. Then he glanced at Durima's right arm. "What happened to your arm?"

"Paralyzing stinger," said Durima. "I don't know if you know what they do, but—"

"Irrelevant," said Uron, shaking his head. "Will it heal quickly?"

"Paralyzing stingers usually wear off after a few days," said Durima. "Though you can make them go away quicker by having another paralyzing stinger sting you in the same spot. Their venom can cure itself."

Uron looked at her with a puzzled expression. "I didn't know you were an expert on Martirian insect life, Durima."

"I'm not," Durima admitted. "Gujak told me that once, a long time ago. Surprised I remembered it."

"Surprising indeed," said Uron. He then held out his other hand, the one that didn't have the God-killer covering it. "Now, take my hand. You look like you need some help standing up."

Durima, however, did not take Uron's hand immediately. She just stared at the pile of dust lying between them that had once been the Human God, practically indistinguishable from the sand of the desert now.

"You said it all worked as planned," said Durima. She looked up at Uron again, though with the sun behind his head, his face was hard to see. "What did you mean by that?"

Uron smiled, and when he spoke, it was in a low whisper. "I knew that having you gather a small army of katabans in one place was bound to attract the attention of at least one god or goddess. That it was the Human God made it even better, as I have no doubt this will cause terrible damage to humanity—though I would have been happy no matter which god had come to teach you a lesson in respect."

"That was the whole reason you had me do this?" said Durima. "Just to draw a god or two out of the woodwork?"

"Partly," said Uron. He coughed. "But also because I will need new people to inhabit Harnum. The katabans who have chosen to follow you will be part of that new people, though they will not be the only ones, of course."

Durima tilted her head to the side. "Are you going to spare more Martirians who pledge to serve you?"

Uron chuckled, which sounded like a snake hissing. "Good joke, Durima; but no. I despise most of you. When I say I want to bring back Harnum, I want to bring back *all* of it. Do you understand?"

Durima did not, so she shook her head in response.

Uron sighed. "Never mind. I do not need you to understand, but I do need you to help me; because I promise that if you do, I will make you free from the gods."

He said that with such sincerity that even Durima, as hardened and cynical as she was, had a hard time disbelieving him. She just took his hand and allowed him to help her up onto her feet.

Then Uron turned around and faced the crowd of

129

watching katabans, not one of whom had said a thing since Uron had killed the Human God. Although Uron was clearly not going to harm them, many of them shrunk back anyway, as if they were afraid that he was.

Uron held up the God-killer, which reflected the rays of the sun brilliantly. "Did you see what I just did? You saw me kill the Human God, kill him as easily as if he was an actual human. If there are still doubters among you, then leave now or join the Human God, the Avian Goddess, Skimif, and, very soon, the rest of the gods in the beyond."

Not a single katabans left at Uron's words. Durima, on the other hand, was getting déjà vu, as this scene was playing out similarly to the time Durima had seen Uron rallying the half-gods in the Void. Back then, Durima had been frightened by what she saw and heard, but now, she felt emboldened, because she knew that Uron was on her side.

"But I know that not every katabans servant of the gods is present here," said Uron, spreading his arms wide as if to embrace the whole crowd. "Many of your friends and families continue to serve and follow the gods, as if they believe that the gods can somehow defeat me. I will not spare any of them; they have made their choice, just as you have, and there is no going back on any of our choices, not at this point."

He then stepped forward. Durima followed, even though he had not asked her to, as she wanted to show solidarity with him.

"I know that the question on all of your minds now is,

what next?" said Uron. "And that is indeed a very good question. What should you katabans do next, now that you have sworn your allegiance to me and will fight against the gods? Does anyone care to guess aloud?"

None of them answered. Even Garvan looked like his mouth had been sewn shut. The entire crowd seemed equally mesmerized by and afraid of Uron, which Durima understood, as Uron was both an impressive and frightening figure.

"No one?" said Uron, turning his head side to side to look at everyone. "Fine. I will spare you the trouble of guessing and get straight to the point."

He pointed at Durima, causing her to look up at him in surprise. He did not return the look, however, because his yellow eyes were locked on the crowd before him.

"Most of you do not know or understand the finer points of war," said Uron. "Katabans in general are not good fighters; however, very soon, I will lead you katabans as a united force, an army capable of defeating any Martirian foe who tries to stand against us. And to become that army, I will have Durima the Demon, a veteran of the Katabans War, train you in the way you should go."

Durima, still surprised, looked back at the gathered crowd. All eyes were on her now; frightened eyes, though whether they were afraid of her or of Uron, she did not know.

Then Garvan held up a hand. "Uh, Lord Uron, sir?"

"Do not call me 'Lord,' like I am one of those silly gods," said Uron in a sharp tone. "But anyway, what is your question, young katabans?"

Garvan looked like he didn't want to talk to Uron at all, but he nonetheless said, "But what about the gods? Won't they try to stop Durima from training us?"

"And risk inviting my wrath upon them?" said Uron, shaking his head. "Of course not. The gods know that if they attack Durima, then they will give me yet another reason to destroy them utterly. I cannot grant you the kind of protection that the gods can offer their servants; in practice, however, the gods' fear of me will work as well as their protection, I can assure you."

Though the katabans were hardly cheering for Uron, they no longer looked quite as scared as they once did. Then Garvan suddenly started clapping, the sound of his wide hands hitting against each other echoing loudly in the quiet desert.

At first, the other katabans just stared at Garvan, as if they thought he had lost his mind. Then the elder next to him started clapping, followed by the katabans to his right, and like toppling dominoes the entire crowd soon burst into applause—rapturous, thunderous applause, the first time Durima could remember a katabans crowd of this size ever applauding a being who was not a god.

Uron raised one arm, smiling that same grin he always smiled, while putting his God-killer hand on Durima's shoulder. Durima did not flinch or look up at him; she was too shocked by the applause of the other katabans to think about her surroundings.

"And this, Durima," said Uron, his voice as low as the

warm desert breeze that blew in at that moment, "is what will spell the true end of the gods. All because of you."

Uron said that in a happy voice. Durima knew she should be happy, but deep down, in a part of herself she rarely thought about, she wasn't so sure she should be, especially when she glanced over her shoulder at the pile of dust behind her that had once been a mighty and powerful god.

Chapter Nine

Neither Darek nor Aorja even moved when Braim said his name. Still, Braim continued to hold out his hand, smiling as happily as always, though there was a playfulness in his grin that told Darek that this ghost was cleverer than he appeared.

"What?" said Braim. "You two look like you've seen a ghost." He paused, his grin replaced by a frown. "Well, I suppose technically, you *have* seen a ghost, so that sort of ruins the joke."

"You said your name is Braim Kotogs," said Darek. "Right?"

"The one and only," said Braim. He lowered his hand. "It's one of the few memories I have that I remember with any certainty. It's not the greatest name, maybe, but it's my name, and that's what matters."

"Not the greatest name?" said Aorja. She pointed at him. "Back where we come from, you're famous."

Braim tilted his head. "Me, famous? Beautiful, you might be an eye-catcher, but that doesn't mean you have the greatest sense of humor to go along with it."

"You literally don't remember who you are?" said Darek. "Not even a little?"

"Yep," said Braim, nodding. "Sometimes I have visions

of things I might have experienced—a guy made out of smoke, another guy in auburn robes—but I'm never sure if any of that is true or real or anything."

Darek bit his lower lip. Out of all of the people he had expected to run into in the afterlife (if that's what this place was, though Darek was starting to have doubts about that now), Braim Kotogs, the deceased pupil of the Magical Superior of North Academy, was the person he had least expected to see.

Thirty years ago, Braim Kotogs had been murdered by the villainous Nijok Wirm, the brother of the Magical Superior. His tragic death had caused the Magical Superior to refuse to take on a new pupil up until the Superior's own death a few months back. And of course, it had been a mere three decades after Braim's death that Uron had taken Braim's skeletal corpse and used it to create his new body that he was currently using to terrorize Martir.

In addition, it had been Braim who had brought Darek and his mother to North Academy all those years ago, after the death of Darek's actual blood mother at the hands of the aforementioned Nijok Wirm. Darek had been five-years-old at the time, so he remembered very little about those early years. Nonetheless, he remembered enough of Braim's appearance to be absolutely certain that the ghost standing before them was indeed the same Braim he had met years ago. There was no doubt about it.

Yet it made no sense to Darek at all. Braim should have already gone onto the afterlife. After all, he had been dead thirty years. That seemed like plenty of time for Braim's

135

soul to move on. So why hadn't he?

"Anyway," said Braim, glancing over his shoulder, "we should probably leave here. I can take you to a safer place where—"

"Do you remember me?" said Darek, abruptly and without really thinking about it.

Braim paused and looked at Darek with surprise. "What?"

"It doesn't matter," said Aorja. "Darek's a little stupid sometimes. Actually, make that *really* stupid sometimes."

"Ignore Aorja," said Darek. He put a hand on his chest. "Do you remember me, Braim? Does my face look familiar to you at all?"

Braim looked a little more closely, his eyes darting over every inch of Darek's face before he pulled back and shook his head. "Nope. You're a complete stranger to me. I don't even know your name."

"Darek Takren," said Darek. "Does that name ring a bell to you?"

Braim scratched the back of his head and furrowed his brow. "Takren ... Takren ... you know, I think I've heard that name before. It rings a bell."

"You knew my mother," said Darek. "Jenur Takren. You have to remember that name."

Braim furrowed his brow even more, as if he was thinking hard about what Darek was saying. "Jenur Takren ... you're right, that name *is* familiar. Very familiar. And beautiful, too."

"You helped my mother and I," said Darek, gesturing at

136

himself. "It was years ago, before you died. You're the reason we weren't killed by Nijok Wirm."

Braim's cheerful demeanor gave way to an angry scowl. He held up his short blade, which now glowed with greenish energy. Darek and Aorja stepped back, even though they had their backs to the invisible barrier and therefore had nowhere to run to in case Braim attacked them.

"I don't remember who Nijok Wirm is, either," said Braim, his words full of barely contained rage, "but god do I hate that name. Makes me want to crack some skulls."

"You don't need to do that," said Darek, holding up his hands defensively. "At all."

Braim looked like he was going to give them both the beating of a lifetime anyway, but then he lowered his blade and sighed. "Sorry. Sometimes that happens to me. I hear a word or a phrase or a name and it triggers something in me. First time I've heard the name 'Nijok Wirm,' though I feel like I have quite the history with it."

"You do," said Darek. "But we don't have to talk about it if you don't want to. If it's gonna trigger you like that, we can talk about other matters."

Braim rubbed his forehead. "Yeah. Like how you two know who the heck I am and you haven't even introduced yourselves to me yet."

"I already told you my name," said Darek. He gestured at Aorja. "This is Aorja Kitano. If we weren't ghosts, I would warn you about letting your guard down around her, because she will kill you if you're not careful."

"This little girl?" said Braim, looking at Aorja like she

was a joke. "Really? You gotta be kidding me."

Aorja balled her hands into fists. "Little girl? I'm almost as old as Darek, but twice as dangerous."

"Twice as dangerous," said Braim, nodding. "Sure. Anyway, nice to meet you, Darek, Aorja. How did you two die?"

"What?" said Darek. "That seems like a strange question to ask."

"It's what I ask every new ghost who I meet," said Braim with a shrug. "It was the first question that the Arbiter asked me and I think it's a pretty appropriate question to ask, since, y'know, we're all dead here and everything."

Darek and Aorja glanced at each other. As much as the two had drifted apart over the years, he still found it easy to read the expression on her face: *Should we tell him the truth?*

Darek saw no reason not to. Braim was a good, trustworthy guy. Besides, he clearly seemed to know and understand the afterlife better than they did. He might even have been able to help them find that gatekeeper that the Ghostly God theorized existed.

Though when Darek thought about it further, he became a little less certain. Braim seemed as friendly as Mom had described him, but his amnesia unsettled Darek. There might have been more to Braim than met the eye, though Darek couldn't imagine what Braim might be hiding from them, if anything.

He decided that it made sense to explain everything to Braim. It was a risk, perhaps, but not as big a risk as allowing the Ghostly God to test an untested spell on them that could easily have killed them for real.

So he nodded at Aorja and then explained to Braim as much of their situation as he could. Braim folded his arms across his chest as he listened to Darek's tale. Darek hoped that Braim might say 'I remember that' or 'Hey, that guy is still around?' but Braim's amnesia must have been totally complete, because he didn't react to any of the names that Darek mentioned. He did show some interest when Darek mentioned Mom, though he still didn't actually say anything.

When Darek finished their story, Braim scratched his chin. The ghost looked at Darek and Aorja with a look that quite clearly told Darek that Braim did not believe even a quarter of their story.

"Let me get this straight," said Braim. "There is this crazy snake guy running around Martir—using *my* skeleton, of all the skeletons in the world—and he's killing gods left and right because he wants to bring back *his* world. Another god, who is a jerk, sent you two to the afterlife so you can find this 'gatekeeper' you mentioned so you can convince him to take the crazy snake guy's soul back."

"Exactly," said Darek, nodding. "So I hope you understand the seriousness of our situation."

"It's the craziest thing I've ever heard," said Braim. Then he smiled again. "But I *love* crazy! It's way better than normal, that's for sure. Crazy is awesome."

"Okay," said Aorja, tapping her foot on the ground impatiently. "Your turn. Tell us everything you know about this damn place right now or—"

Braim held up one finger. "Cool it, beautiful. I'll tell you on our way to safety. I don't like being out here like this, not when there are things like that ugly dragger around."

"Dragger?" said Darek. "You mean that weird female corpse thing has an actual name?"

"Sure," said Braim. He shuddered. "Hideous things. Good thing this one was alone; if there had been a dozen, like there usually are, we wouldn't even be standing here talking about this."

Braim walked past them both toward the arch. Darek and Aorja turned, watching as Braim walked up to the invisible barrier that had nearly gotten them killed before. As soon as he reached it, Braim knocked on its surface once.

Almost immediately, a tiny, barely visible ripple appeared in the barrier. The ripple spread out, like a rock tossed into the middle of a pond, over the whole barrier, distorting the misty clouds on the other side.

Then the barrier melted away, like a sheet of ice melting under hot water, and the misty clouds beyond it looked as normal as ever. As soon as the barrier was gone, Braim gestured for Darek and Aorja to follow.

"Come on, you two," said Braim. "No telling if more draggers are on their way ... or worse, the Dark Lady."

"The Dark Lady?" said Darek. "Who's that?"

"Like I said, I will explain it to you on our way back to safety," said Braim. "Now are you going to come or not?"

Darek and Aorja didn't hesitate to follow Braim under the arch. Nonetheless, Darek found himself looking over his shoulder at the remaining black wetness left by the dragger, though that was rapidly dissipating in the mist and becoming blurry in the reforming barrier even as he watched.

It was not long before the massive arch vanished into the mist behind them, making Darek feel like he, Aorja, and Braim were now miles away from civilization, because he could not see any other structures nearby. The only hint of other people being here was the long stone road they walked upon, though even it appeared to be a natural thing, like it had grown from the earth like a tree.

"Where are you taking us?" Aorja asked as she walked faster so she was walking by Braim's side.

Braim gestured ahead. "To the Spirit Lands, of course. It's where all ghosts go before they move on beyond the Gates. We'll be safe from the draggers and the Dark Lady there."

"Spirit Lands?" said Darek. "What are they like?"

"Usually pretty empty," said Braim, scratching his chin. "Most ghosts only stay a little while before moving on beyond the Gates. They're lucky; while these Spirit Lands may be safe, they're also boring as hell."

"What are the Gates?" said Darek, picking up speed until he was on Braim's other side. His eyes flickered onto Braim's blade for a moment. "And where did you get that sword?"

"The Gates are the last entryway to the next life, what you might call the afterlife," said Braim. He gestured around the misty area. "Right now, we're in a kind of limbo place, sort of between the physical world and the afterlife. Every ghost comes down this road at some point ... unless they become a dragger, that is. As for this sword, it was given to me by the Arbiter, of course."

"Who is the Arbiter?" said Aorja. "Never heard of him."

Braim scratched the back of his head. "Hmm ... well, best way I can describe him is that he decides who gets to go through the Gates and who doesn't. He's that gatekeeper guy you guys were talking about finding."

"So he does exist," said Aorja, She scowled. "Damn it, the Ghostly God was right."

"But that's great," said Darek, pumping his fist. "That means that you, Braim, just need to take us to the Arbiter, and we'll do the rest. So glad we found you; who knows how long it would have taken for us to find the Arbiter all on our own?"

Braim chuckled, almost laughed. "Good luck with that. The Arbiter ... he's indisposed at the moment."

"Indisposed?" said Darek. "What does that mean?"

"He's not even conscious," said Braim. "See, a while back, the Arbiter got sick. Not sick like the way living beings can get sick, but it's the best way I can describe what happened to him. Then he fell unconscious and, well, he's been out cold for a while and I haven't had any success in waking the old dude up yet."

"How did he get sick?" said Aorja. She didn't sound concerned for the Arbiter's health at all, though she did sound frustrated, like she was angry about this apparent obstacle in their quest.

"Not sure," said Braim. "This is the first time this has ever happened to him, and trust me, the Arbiter guy is older than the stars. I think the Dark Lady did it. Don't know how, but I bet she did."

"You mentioned her before," said Darek, glancing over his shoulder just to be sure that there weren't any draggers following them. "But you haven't actually explained who the Dark Lady *is*."

Braim jerked his thumb over his shoulder. "Did you see those carvings back on the Arch back there? Including the ones with the crazy-looking woman on them?"

Darek shuddered when he remembered those carvings. "Yes. What about them?"

"That wasn't just something some artist drew to scare new ghosts," said Braim, shaking his head. "That was carved by the Arbiter himself so long ago even he doesn't remember when he carved it. It's a history of the Spirit Lands and the origin of the Dark Lady."

"I thought it was just bad art," said Aorja. "I could probably carve something better if I wanted to."

"Sure you could, beautiful," said Braim. "Anyway, the carvings were pretty self-explanatory, so I don't think there's any need for me to elaborate on them."

"Uh, actually, they really aren't all that obvious," said Darek. "At least to us. Could you possibly explain them a bit?"

"All right," said Braim, though with the way he frowned, he obviously didn't want to. "So what those carvings showed was the Spirit Lands before the Dark Lady came. Everything was all peaceful and nice. Ghosts would go beyond the Gates and no one ever had any trouble. Then the Dark Lady appeared."

"Where did she come from?" said Darek. "Was she a creation of the Powers?"

Braim shrugged as he kicked a stray rock out of their path. "I don't know. The Arbiter told me that the Dark Lady used to be a normal spirit of a human woman, but when she came here, she was very petty and vengeful. She wanted to rule the ghosts, but the Arbiter told her no. She was pretty persistent, though, and eventually the Arbiter had to banish her beyond the Spirit Lands and into the Unknown."

"What is the Unknown?" said Aorja.

Again, Braim jerked a thumb over his shoulder. "Another land beyond the Arch. Don't ask me about it; I've never been. Only a few ghosts have ever been there, and every last one of them was banished there by the Arbiter for their wickedness. Most ghosts banished there are gone forever, but for some reason the Dark Lady survived and became even stronger than before."

"This Dark Lady person sounds interesting," said Aorja.

"Interesting? She's evil," said Braim, shaking his head in disgust. "What she does is use her awful powers to corrupt innocent ghosts into draggers. That's why that invisible barrier exists back there; the Arbiter made it so that the Dark Lady couldn't leave the Unknown and come back here."

"How powerful is she?" said Darek. "Is she as strong as a

god?"

"I don't know," said Braim. "All I know is that she is a force to be reckoned with. Even the Arbiter was afraid to challenge her. So far, that barrier has kept her back, but with the Arbiter currently out for the count, I'm worried she might choose this opportunity to attack again."

Darek didn't like the sound of that at all. He had hoped that the Spirit Lands would be devoid of any dangerous conflict or problems that existed in the physical world. Yet if Braim was telling the truth, the Spirit Lands had their own problems to deal with, problems that seemed worse to Darek than their own; after all, a demonic female spirit who could corrupt souls was clearly a worse threat than Uron by far.

"How did the Dark Lady even get those powers in the first place, if she's just a normal human spirit?" asked Aorja. She rubbed her hands together eagerly. "And is there any chance that I might be able to get powers like that, too?"

"I have no idea," said Braim. He shuddered. "Maybe she found some power in the Unknown or maybe there's something even worse in there that gave her that power." He looked at Aorja in bewilderment. "Why do you even want her powers? Do you want to corrupt other spirits, too?"

"No," said Aorja quickly, shaking her head. "I just thought that maybe we could use her own power against her. That's all."

She was clearly lying, though Darek saw no need to point that out, as Braim probably saw through her unconvincing lies as well. Darek knew that if Aorja had that kind of power, then she would be an almost worse threat to Martir than Uron. He was quite glad, then, that there was probably no way for her to do it.

"What is your job here?" said Aorja. "You died thirty years ago. Shouldn't your spirit have gone beyond the Gates by now, if that's where all ghosts are supposed to go after they die?"

Braim shrugged. "I was supposed to, yeah, but when I first got here, the Dark Lady was corrupting souls left and right. The Arbiter really couldn't go after her without leaving his post, so he picked me to serve as a protector of new ghosts so they don't get corrupted as soon as they get here. It's my job to search for new ghosts and save them from the draggers that go after them. Like how I met you two."

"How long are you supposed to do that?" said Aorja.

"For as long as the Arbiter needs my help," said Braim. "Since the Dark Lady is nowhere near close to being defeated, I imagine I'll be doing this for the rest of my ghostly life, which is to say, forever."

"So you'll never get an opportunity to rest in peace," said Darek. "I'm sorry to hear that."

Braim waved off his concern. "Nah. It's not a huge issue. Resting is boring. Fighting off corrupted ghosts is a lot more interesting. I'd rather do this than sleep for eternity, or whatever it is that ghosts do when they go beyond the Gates. The Arbiter never told me."

"If you say so," said Darek. "So have you ever actually

killed a dragger before?"

"Nope," said Braim. He raised his blade. "You can't actually kill draggers, seeing as they are technically already dead. The best you can do is scare them off or turn them into dark gas clouds that usually reform at some point. It's a never-ending battle."

"Well, it doesn't really matter, now does it?" said Aorja. "After all, the barrier is keeping those draggers out. So I doubt we'll see any more today, but if we do, we can rip them apart and ship them back to the Dark Lady piece by piece."

"That's some violent mental imagery right there," said Braim, "but I understand the feeling—though I don't know how right you are, what with the barrier getting weaker ever since the Arbiter went down."

"The barrier is getting weaker?" said Darek. "What do you mean?"

"It's not as strong as it once was," said Braim. He gestured over his shoulder again, even though the barrier was impossible to see through the mist. "Just recently, a dragger managed to cut a hole in the barrier; not a big hole, but a problem nonetheless. I had to fix it myself, but if the barrier is that weak, then I think it's only a matter of time before the Dark Lady and her draggers cut a hole big enough for more of them to crawl through."

"And if the Dark Lady succeeds?" said Darek.

"You don't want to know what will happen if she does," said Braim. "Anyway, we're almost to the Gates. Should be coming up any minute now. I'll take you guys straight to the

Arbiter so you can see him for yourself. Doubt it will do you any good, though, since he's probably still out."

Darek looked in the direction they were walking. The mist was as thick and impenetrable as ever. If the Gates really were nearby, Darek certainly couldn't see them, which made him more than a little nervous, as he didn't like walking into the unknown like this, even with a guide like Braim at his side.

"Are there any other ghosts here or are we the only ones?" Darek asked.

"There's only one guy," said Braim, nodding. "Only reason he hasn't gone beyond the Gates yet is because the Arbiter is out of commission at the moment."

"Anyone we might know?" said Darek.

"I don't know," said Braim with a shrug. "You'll have to meet him for yourself in order to get your answer to that question."

"But shouldn't there be more?" said Aorja. "People die all the time, especially now with Uron on the run. Shouldn't the Spirit Lands be absolutely full of ghosts?"

Braim stroked his chin, looking troubled. "There *was* another guy for a while there, someone named Helpful, who served the Arbiter along with me, but then he vanished after the Arbiter got sick and I don't know where he is. Coward."

He said 'coward' as if it was the worst insult he could come up with. Darek wanted to ask more about this 'Helpful' person, but considering how Braim's hand balled into a fist and his eyes flashed with anger, he decided against it.

148

"But anyway, you do have a point," said Braim, the anger in his voice replaced by worry. "The Spirit Lands should be full of new ghosts coming in all the time, but they aren't. I don't know why or what is going on, but I think the Dark Lady is behind it. Somehow she's getting to most of the new ghosts before I can."

"How can we stop her?" said Darek. "Is there any to defeat her?"

"The Arbiter has been trying to figure that out for eons, and he's still no closer to doing it than he was when he first started," said Braim. He sighed in frustration. "But anyway, we should be seeing the Gates any minute ... now ..."

As Braim said that, the mist before them parted, seemingly of its own accord, to reveal a sight Darek would never forget.

Their path went down a tall hill, zigzagging to a flat, white land below that seemed to stretch forever to the east and the west. There were no buildings of any sort, not even any temporary residences; just a single road, the road they walked upon, that went all the way to the north.

The road ended at the foot of a massive silver-white wall, a wall much, much larger than the Walls of North Academy. It must have been ten thousand feet tall, though its length was a mystery, as it stretched on well to the east and the west well beyond Darek's line of sight.

The wall was so huge that Darek wondered how something like that could even be constructed. Though there was no sun in the Spirit Lands, the wall nonetheless glowed as brightly as if there had been a sun built into it. He didn't know what the wall was made of; maybe metal, maybe rock, maybe crystal, or maybe all three. It was much closer to the descriptions Darek had heard of the ethereal, which described a vast, white road that stretched on forever, making him wonder if the wall and the ethereal were in some way connected.

Standing in the center of the wall was a gigantic set of Gates. Towering like massive oak trees, the Gates shone a golden sheen so bright that Darek could not look directly at them. Whereas the wall was plain, the Gates had been designed intricately, with what appeared to be a replica of the road they stood upon carved into it. Additionally, there seemed to be writing on the Gates, though it was impossible to read from their current distance, and it might not have been writing at all, though Darek did not know for sure.

"There they are," said Braim, pointing at the Gates. "The Gates to the afterlife. Once you go beyond those, you are gone for good."

"Amazing," said Darek, unable to tear his eyes from them. "Who made them? How long have they stood there? Where did they come from? What are they made of?"

"How should I know?" said Braim with a shrug. "The Arbiter always told me that the Gates have always stood. I always thought that was bull, but he's always given me the same answer every time I ask, so—"

"Big whoop," said Aorja, rolling her eyes. "So it's some big fancy Gates. Who cares? Where is the Arbiter?"

"At the Gates, obviously," said Braim. "He's the only one who can open or close them, so he has a little watchtower set up near there. He was still there when I left, so finding him shouldn't be much of a problem. Follow me."

Braim walked down the hill toward the flat plains below. Darek and Aorja followed, Darek looking around for the other ghost that Braim had mentioned was around here. He was looking for a very specific person: Chen Wirm, also known as the Magical Superior of North Academy.

The Magical Superior had died a few months back, giving his own life to stop Jakuuth Grinfborn from destroying North Academy. Just thinking about the Superior's death made strong emotions well up in Darek, though they weren't as bad as they had been shortly after the Magical Superior's death. He had had his time to mourn, after all, and had moved on since then.

But if all ghosts passed through here, then maybe the Magical Superior's ghost had also come through here at some point. Maybe he was even still here, unable to pass through the Gates thanks to the Arbiter's current unconsciousness.

Would the Magical Superior even recognize me if I saw him, though? Darek thought. *He hasn't been dead very long, so maybe most of his memories are still intact. What could I possibly say to him, though? Maybe I could just thank him for saving us.*

Darek's thoughts were interrupted when Braim stopped without warning. The deceased mage held up his blade, like he was ready for battle.

"What?" said Aorja, stopping with Darek in order to avoid walking into Braim. "What did you see?"

"It's not what I *see* that worries me," said Braim, shaking his head. "It's what I *feel*. Do you sense that?"

Darek did not know what Braim was talking about at first until he heard something soaring above them. Looking up, Darek saw nothing except for the thick mist that swirled like storm clouds, reminding him far too much of that night back in the graveyard on North Academy, when the Ghostly God had shrouded the cemetery with mist of his own creation. That had not been a good night.

"I still don't see or feel anything out of the ordinary," said Aorja, putting her hands on her hips. "I think you're just overreacting. All of these years as a ghost have just made you overly jumpy and paranoid."

"Paranoid? I'm the farthest thing from paranoid," Braim snapped. "Fact is, you two haven't been ghosts very long, and maybe aren't even ghosts at all, if your story about how you got here is true, but—"

It was at that moment that Darek saw a dark silhouette dart through the mist above. He would have dismissed the movement as his imagination going out of control when, without warning, a large, dragon-like beast tore through the misty clouds above, its silver scales shining as it flew down at them faster than something of its size should have been able to.

And worse, it was not alone; another dozen creatures, similar in design and build to the first, followed, each one roaring as they came toward them. Individually, each dragon looked strong enough to tear the three of them into shreds. That thought alone made Darek step back in fear, even though he had nowhere to run to.

"What the hell are those?" Aorja said, her voice higher than normal as she stepped back with Darek. "Braim, how do we beat them?

Braim looked at Darek and Aorja with a grim smile on his face. The next words he said were not the words that Darek wanted to hear in this situation:

"I don't know."

Chapter Ten

It was only recently that World's End, the island on the edge of the world, had been a glorious city, larger and grander than any other city in the entire world. Its buildings had been made of crystals, rubies, sapphires, emeralds, and many other precious stones and metals. The Temple of the Gods, located in the center of the city, had been the grandest of them all, radiating the powers of the gods themselves like the heat of the sun.

Nowadays, though ... well, Durima didn't know how World's End looked nowadays. She stood on the deck of the *Divine Arrow*, a warship that had once belonged to the Soldiers of the Gods before being abandoned shortly after Uron's return from the ethereal, looking at the massive wall of darkness that had consumed World's End.

The black wall appeared completely stationary; however, Durima's sharp eyes told her that it was moving, if only subtly. The sea and sky ended at the darkness, but it wasn't a clean break; it was ragged, like the wall had taken huge bites out of the skies and ocean. The clouds that drew close to the darkness were sucked into the wall when they got too close, though Durima could not feel any sucking force from within.

A warm breeze blew through Durima's fur, though she

still shivered at the sight of the wall—also known as the Void—nonetheless.

Uron stood by her side, his arms crossed over his chest. He seemed perfectly at ease now, a content smile on his face as their ship drew closer and closer to the blackness gradually consuming the world before them. The God-killer reflected the sun's rays from above, especially whenever Uron scratched his chin with it.

Durima looked about the ship restlessly. Large cannons stuck out of both sides of the ship, while three huge masts rose from the center of the ship, the symbol of the Soldiers of the Gods sewn into the sails. The steering wheel, which was closer to the center of the ship than the back, moved all by itself thanks to a spell cast by Uron. Indeed, Durima and Uron were the only two beings on the *Divine Arrow* at all.

There was a reason for that, though whether it was a good reason, Durima was not sure. Uron had told Durima that they needed to go deal with the Void, who he considered to be a threat not just to Martir, but to his own plans to bring back Harnum. Durima had assumed that Uron would bring the rest of the katabans with them, but he had said he only needed Durima for what he was going to do. The others, he said, could stay in King's Desert, where they would be safe until Durima returned to give them the proper training they needed.

Exactly what Uron was going to do, Durima did not know, as he had been mum about his plan the entire time. He had given her no clue as to how he planned to get rid of the Void. Indeed, until he announced that they were going to go confront it, Durima had assumed that Uron was simply going to leave the Void alone until he had killed all of the gods first.

Even curiouser, Uron had insisted that they take a boat to the Void. They had not literally sailed from King's Desert, which was in the Northern Isles, down to World's End. Such a voyage would take at least three months on a normal-sized sailing ship, and that was assuming the southern gods did not try to kill or eat you on your way there.

Instead, Uron had teleported the entire ship—which was as big as a schooner, but heavier due to the twenty or so guns it had—from King's Desert down here. That Uron had managed to do that, and didn't even seem worn out by it, was just another reminder of the kind of power he possessed.

The *Divine Arrow* was the only part of this entire scheme that Uron had bothered to explain so far: "I want the Void to underestimate us, to think we're idiots for not teleporting directly into her darkness, where we could cause her more damage. It is a psychological tactic."

Whether that would work as Uron intended, Durima didn't know. She did know, however, that she was experiencing a severe case of déjà vu. It had been this very ship that had taken her to the Void when she and her friend Gujak had been banished by the Katabans Council for their accidental murder of the Spider Goddess last year. She could even still feel the metal chains around her arms and legs, despite having abandoned those long ago.

Remembering that time forced her to remember Gujak.

He had been so pathetic back then, so scared; even so, her memories of him wrenched her heart. Before his untimely death, Gujak had been just as much against Uron as anyone else, despite also being the biggest coward Durima had ever known in her life.

What would Gujak think now, if he found out you were working for Uron? Durima thought.

She didn't want to answer that question, because she already knew what he would think.

So she looked up at Uron and asked, "What do we do if the Void tries to sink us?"

"She won't," said Uron, without looking at her. "She's powerful, true, but quite instinctual and animalistic. She remembers what we did to her back in the tunnel to the Old Ruins a couple of months back."

Durima nodded. She also remembered that. It had been the first time she and Uron had truly united. At the time, Durima had felt incredibly powerful, unafraid of anything; now, however, since she and Uron hadn't combined at all since that time, she sometimes felt a pang of regret at allowing Uron to control her like that, even though it had saved not just her life, but Aorja's and Zeeree's as well.

Uron patted Durima on the head again. "That is why I brought you along. The Void remembers you. If she sees both of us together, she will hesitate to destroy us immediately."

"But she will anyway," said Durima, her eyes flicking back to the wall of impenetrable darkness before them. "You do realize that, right?"

"Of course I do," said Uron. "I'm not childish enough to believe that she will allow her fear of us to prevent her from killing us. I'm banking on her fear freezing her long enough for us to do our job."

"And what is that job?" said Durima, tilting her head to the side.

"Returning the Void to her original boundaries, naturally," said Uron, without missing a beat. "Even I cannot destroy her completely; however, I understand how the Powers originally separated her from Martir. And the Void knows that as well."

Durima nodded again. "Will it be difficult to do?"

"Likely," said Uron. "The Void will not simply lie down and take it like an obedient dog. She will fight, though do not worry, because she doesn't stand a chance against us."

Uron sounded as confident as Durima had ever heard anyone before; indeed, he sounded as confident as the gods.

Still, the Void made Durima uneasy. She had too many bad memories associated with that place by now for her to have the same kind of confidence that Uron appeared to possess. She especially remembered the half-gods and the Glass Blizzard. She could still hear the Glass Blizzard cutting against the exterior of Castle Hollech, a memory that still made her wince even now, many months later.

"Remembering the bad old days?" said Uron, snapping Durima out of her reminiscing.

Durima again looked up at Uron. He had taken his eyes off the Void, his yellow orbs focused on her. He was still smiling.

"Yes," said Durima, because she saw no reason to lie or hold back any information from him. "I am remembering when Gujak and I were banished in there."

"Understandable," said Uron. "The Void is not the kind of place you ever truly forget, not for as long as you live. It is always there, always on the peripheral, ready to consume you the minute you let your guard down."

"Yes," said Durima. She hesitated, then asked, "Uron, do you remember Castle Hollech? That tiny little stone building that Hollech had made into his personal fortress before you killed him?"

Much to her surprise, Uron blinked. "He had a castle? What did it look like?"

Durima suspected Uron's surprise had to be false; after all, he had to have known that Hollech once had a 'castle,' if you could call it that. It wasn't like Hollech had tried to hide it or anything. Uron's half-gods had made regular raids on Castle Hollech and knew of its location. How could Uron not know about it?

Nonetheless, Durima described it, saying, "It was very, very old. You had to pass through an old stone gate and some old stone pillars to reach it. It looked like a tiny stone building, with only a single turret standing out of the center of the main building. Hardly much of a castle, if you ask me."

Uron stroked his chin. He seemed to be thinking very hard, as if Durima had just informed him of a surprising fact that forced him to rethink his plans. Again, Durima could not tell if he actually was surprised or if he was simply putting on an act to fool her for reasons known only to him.

"Was there anything ... was there anything *in* the castle?" Uron asked. He sounded a little hesitant, like he was afraid of Durima's answer.

"Just some Void metal armor and weapons," said Durima. "And piles of dirt that Hollech called his servants."

Uron blinked. "What?"

"Hollech was insane," said Durima in a flat voice. "Anyway, I can see you don't know anything about it. Oh well."

She watched his reaction carefully. Uron returned his attention back to the Void, but his eyes revealed that he was still thinking about Castle Hollech.

There's something important about it, Durima thought. *Something Uron doesn't even want to tell me about. I wonder if it has anything to do with that thing he was trying to find back in the Temple of Xocion or if it's something else entirely.*

She had no more time to speculate about the significance of Castle Hollech to Uron, or his own reasons for being so interested in it, because at that moment, something emerged from the Void.

Its massive head came first, resembling a sharp-toothed tiger's face, its eyes a deep purple that was almost black. Long, spidery legs followed, attached to a body that was fat and round. Wings like the wings of an eagle extended from its back, though they looked as sharp as blades.

Durima's breathing become constricted. She took a step back, thinking of opening an ethereal portal in order to escape, but Uron rested a hand on her shoulder.

"Show no fear," said Uron, without looking down at her. "The Void is far more scared of us than we are of her. Take advantage of that."

That may have been true (though it could just as easily have been false, knowing how overconfident Uron could be at times), but right now, Durima felt much weaker than the Void. The giant monster stepped toward them, though it hadn't stepped out of the Void entirely; its behind was still partially covered by the Void, like a woman standing partway under a veil.

Uron, came the Void's voice from the monster's mouth. **I see you decided to confront me directly. No matter; I will squash you just as easily as if I had come to you.**

"And therein lies the problem that has continually sabotaged your efforts to consume Martir, Void," said Uron. He gestured at Durima. "You have underestimated the strength of beings like Durima, thinking them weaker than they actually are. If we were still allies, I would suggest you learn some humility and learn how to address your enemies as they are, rather than as you think they are."

The Void doesn't need your condescending 'help,' said the Void. Drops of darkness fell from her legs into the clear ocean water below. **I have existed well before the foundations of *your* world were laid, Uron, and will continue to exist eons after Martir meets its own end. The Void is the true nature and essence of the universe itself. Any world**

established in my domain is nothing more than an aberration that must be consumed and lost forever.

"The high-and-mighty talk is starting to bore me," said Uron. He held up the God-killer. "You have done what I needed you to do; namely, keep the gods busy while I returned to Martir. Your presence is no longer needed here."

You talk to me as if I am some mindless servant who will do whatever you tell me to do, like the katabans at your side, the Void sneered. **I will not heed any orders you give me. No one rules the Void. No one.**

At that moment, gigantic tendrils of shadows burst from the water on all sides. They rose high, almost taller than the skyscrapers of World's End, and water flew everywhere as they emerged from the ocean. The water fell on Durima, causing her to hold her arms over her head instinctively, though she still got wet, as did Uron, though he didn't seem bothered by it.

The *Divine Arrow* was now surrounded on all sides by the dozen tendrils that had emerged from the ocean. They twisted and whirled through the air, but none of them yet came close to their ship; still, even just one of those tendrils was big enough to sink the *Divine Arrow* with a single blow, and Durima knew it.

Enough talk, said the Void. **I will make your deaths quick and painless so I no longer have to worry about you two getting in the way of my desires.**

Uron had not moved a muscle since the Void's tendrils

had emerged from the ocean. He simply looked to the left and to the right, as if to ascertain their current situation, and then looked back at the Void.

"I see we cannot solve this dispute peacefully, like rational beings," said Uron. "Very well."

He held out the God-killer before him, pointing it directly at the Void. Much to Durima's surprise, the Void actually seemed to hesitate, as if it was afraid of the God-killer. That didn't make any sense, seeing as the Void wasn't a god or goddess, but Durima liked seeing the Void afraid anyway.

Then the Void shook its head and roared, **Be lost forever in the darkness!**

All twelve of the massive tendrils from before became as straight as arrows. Then, as one, they crashed down toward the *Divine Arrow,* like buildings knocked over by an earthquake.

And still Uron stood there, appearing hardly fazed by the dozen giant tendrils coming down toward them or the monstrous spider/tiger creature before them. In fact, he had even closed his eyes, like he was going to take a nap.

"Uron?" said Durima, tugging at his arm. "Uh, Uron? We're going to die if you don't do something, you know."

Uron nodded, though still without opening his eyes. "I know."

The sun became blocked out overhead, because now the tendrils were directly above her and Uron. They were so close, still coming closer, that Durima could even see the ridges running along their surfaces.

Then Uron raised the God-killer above his head, in the exact spot where all the Void's tendrils were falling. Durima wanted to ask him what the hell he thought he was doing, but before she could utter even one word, the tendrils—all twelve of them—crashed onto the God-killer.

Durima expected to hear the splinter of wood as the tendrils smashed through the deck of the *Divine Arrow*. She expected to drown beneath the waves of the clear sea or maybe get swallowed up by the darkness of the Void or, in the likeliest scenario, both.

Instead, when the tendrils fell on the God-killer, they stopped. Uron didn't even grunt, even though the tendrils must have weighed a ton each. Nor did the God-killer crack or show any other signs of stress; it was like it had absorbed the combined force of so many thick, heavy tendrils falling on it at once.

The Void's tiger-like snarl turned into a hesitant, even frightened, scowl. She even stepped back a little into the mass of shadows behind her, like she was going to run away. **Impossible. How are you doing this?**

Uron did not answer.

Instead, a bright light shone from the God-killer, forcing Durima to hold her hands over her eyes to avoid damaging them. She did, however, see the light melting through the tendrils, like lava poured onto stone.

No way, said the Void. **What is this power you wield? How have I never sensed it before?**

Uron chuckled. "Unlike you, Void, I never show my whole hand. The God-killer does more than just kill gods; it can banish you back to where you belong."

Soon, the light had evaporated all twelve of the tendrils, but it didn't stop there. It rose from Uron's hand, like a rising pillar of stone, and then lanced toward the Void like a lightning bolt.

The Void let loose a roar like an angry baba raga, but that was the last sound she made, because the light struck her dead on and her dark body vanished into nothingness.

The dark wall of the Void remained, however, still an impressive, terrifying sight that looked far too big for Durima or Uron to take care of. It continued to slowly eat away at the sky and sea, advancing toward them just as if they weren't there at all.

Uron, however, didn't seem concerned about it. He lowered the God-killer, aiming it directly at the Void as he said, "I see you must have forgotten, Void, that it was I who weakened the boundaries that kept you from advancing on Martir in the first place. Why don't I remind you of that?"

He then punched the God-killer forward. The air in front of them grew distorted and bubbly for a moment, but only for a moment; in fact, it was so quick that Durima wondered if her eyes had only been playing tricks on her.

Then the Void shouted, **No! You will not return me to my original boundaries! I will—**

The Void never got to finish her sentence, however, because the dark wall before them suddenly retracted. It was like someone had punched the Void, because it just went flying back the way it had come, like an ocean wave in reverse. It was the oddest sight Durima had ever seen in her life. She watched as the darkness that was the Void kept retreating back further and further until, very soon, it was out of sight completely.

Uron lowered the God-killer to his side, a look of smug satisfaction on his face. "I really am lazy. I could have done that much sooner, but it was the kind of unpleasant task you want to put off until the very last moment."

Durima blinked. "So the Void is really gone? She can't send any of her minions into Martir or swallow up anymore islands or anything?"

Uron shook his head. "She is exactly the same way as she was before: An ominous shadow on the edge of Martir, frightening only if you forget that she has no power here."

Durima looked at the God-killer. Its fingers hung open, the writing on the knuckles as faint as ever, while the sun's rays reflected off its surface like the sea.

"Was that the God-killer's doing?" said Durima, looking up at Uron again.

"Partly," said Uron as he rubbed the God-killer. "The God-killer has a unique variety of powers that even I didn't know about before getting it. The wearer becomes godlike in his own right; and one of the perks of godhood is the ability to determine Martir's boundaries, an ability previously only allowed to Skimif, but which I now wield."

"The God-killer truly is an amazing creation," said Durima. She shuddered. "I'm just surprised that the Powers allowed it to stay inside Bleak Rock unguarded for so long; I mean, aside from the Mysterious One's protection, of course."

"Like that meant much," said Uron, holding up the God-killer to admire it. "Considering you and Gujak were able to get it fairly easily, I can only conclude that the Powers made it easy to find in case mortals needed to get it quickly."

"It wasn't *that* easy," said Durima. "The Spider Goddess almost killed us when we tried to get it."

"True," said Uron. "But she failed, didn't she? All thanks to this."

Durima didn't like thinking about the time she and Gujak stole the God-killer. At the time, neither of them really knew what they were doing. Just thinking about how they accidentally killed the Spider Goddess made her katabans instincts trouble her, which was why she didn't want to think about it.

Deciding to change the subject, Durima asked, "So what do we do now? Do we return to the King's Desert, round up the other katabans, and destroy North Academy?"

"As tempting as that it is, we will have to put it off for just a little while longer," said Uron. He gestured in the direction that the Void had retreated in. "I have something very important to do. It may or may not lead to anything; however, it is a lead worth checking out, because if it is what I think it is, then we will be that much closer to restoring Harnum to its original glory."

Durima frowned. "What is it, Uron? Is there something back on World's End that you want to look at?"

Uron just patted her on the head again. "It is a secret, one everyone will know soon enough. But I must do it alone, which means you can't come with me."

"What am I supposed to do, then?" said Durima. She glanced at the barnacle-covered deck of the *Divine Arrow* and grimaced at the disgusting stink of seaweed rising from the floorboards underneath her feet. "Wait here until you return?"

"Go back to the King's Desert and begin training the katabans army," Uron said. "In the meantime, I am going to investigate Castle Hollech. There may yet be something there I could use."

Durima was interested to know what Uron thought he could find in Castle Hollech; however, she knew better than to ask him directly. It may have been her katabans servant instincts at work, or maybe it was her years of experience serving under gods and goddesses who did not permit even the slightest bit of questioning of their orders from their servants—probably both.

So Durima nodded and said, "All right. I'll leave, but if you need me, just call me and I will be at your side without delay."

"Very well," said Uron. "See you soon; very soon, I hope."

When Durima blinked, Uron was gone. He must have teleported, because she certainly hadn't heard him open an ethereal portal. She looked out to the horizon, but all she saw was the endless sea; she couldn't even see World's End on the horizon, though if the darker color of the sky in that direction meant anything, she thought she could still vaguely see the Void.

Time to get going, Durima thought. *Not much else for*

me to do here now. I'll just leave the ship; we don't really need it anyway.

She was just about to open an ethereal portal when she heard the sound of something light landing on the wooden deck of the *Divine Arrow* behind her. She whirled around to see who it was, but something thick, heavy, and metal slammed into her face with enough force to knock her out even before her body fell to the deck under her feet.

Chapter Eleven

The next word Braim said wasn't one Darek wanted to hear in this situation, either: "Run!"

Darek didn't hesitate to follow Braim's advice. He dashed down the misty hillside of the Spirit Lands, Aorja at his side, as the dragons overhead roared and soared. Braim was ahead of them, holding his shining green blade over his head, as if that tiny thing was enough by itself to deter the dozen or so silvery dragons that appeared to be as big as the Third Dorm, if not larger.

One of the dragons—the first one—bellowed, unleashing a silver stream of energy directly at them. Darek ducked his head, narrowly avoiding the beam as it flew by. The beam struck the road behind him, causing it to explode and send strange, crumbly white rocks flying through the air and raining down on them.

Then another one of the dragons swooped down and landed in the path before them. It forced Darek, Aorja, and Braim to stop before they crashed into it, though they were running so fast that it was hard to do so.

The dragon in their path stood up and stretched its wings, which were long enough to completely block out the path. The dragon's eyes glowed an eerie ghostly green, while it clawed at the road they stood on, wisps of some kind of white smoke rising from its nostrils as it glared at them.

"Do something, Braim," said Aorja, pointing at the dragon. "Can't that blade of yours scare it off, like with that dragger from before?"

"Beautiful, I already said I don't know the first thing about these dragons," Braim snapped, though his blade was already glowing with suppressed energy. "But I'll try anyway. Never know what will work until you try."

He fired a bolt of some kind of fiery energy at the dragon. The bolt struck the dragon directly in the center of its flat head, but rather than wound or scare the dragon, all it did was make it angrier. The wisps of smoke rising from its nostrils grew thicker and thicker, until it looked like the dragon was cooking something in its mouth and was releasing the smoke made by it.

"I just pissed it off more," said Braim, looking over his shoulder at Aorja and Darek. "Either of you two have any good ideas?"

"How the hell are we supposed to know how to defeat a spirit dragon?" said Aorja in exasperation. "We haven't even been here for a day. You're the expert on this spirit stuff, aren't you?"

"Well, we experts don't know everything," Braim admitted. Then he smiled. "Wait, maybe we can go around it. We just need to distract it with—"

He was interrupted by the abrupt arrival of the other eleven dragons. They landed around the party of three, spreading their wings as they did so, effectively cutting off every possible avenue of escape for Darek and his friends.

The only realistic escape route Darek could see was the sky above, which remained open and unblocked; however, none of them could fly, and he doubted any of the dragons would be willing to give them a lift.

Therefore, Darek, Aorja, and Braim gathered closer together in the center, while the dragons moved in even tighter. What bothered Darek most about their current situation was the complete lack of smell he picked up from the dragons; for some reason, he found it disquieting, as if their lack of a scent was the worst part of the monsters.

"What are we so afraid of, anyway?" said Aorja, though despite her words, Darek sensed a very real undercurrent of fear in her voice. "I mean, we're already ghosts, right? It's not like these stupid ugly dragons can kill us again."

"Eh, it's not that simple, beautiful," said Braim, still holding his blade in front of him, even though it had already proven ineffective against the dragons. "Yeah, we can't die twice, but ghosts can be corrupted, just like those draggers back there. How much do you want to bet that these dragons could do something similar to us if we let them touch us?"

Aorja did not answer that, like she was thinking about how it would feel to be turned into a dragger. Based on her horrified expression, it was pretty obvious how she felt about it.

"Then what do we do?" said Darek. He held up his hands, even though he had zero experience fighting with his fists.

"Come up with a great idea," said Braim. "Or pray to the

gods and hope maybe they will hear us even from here."

The dragons snarled and snapped their teeth. They were so close now that Darek started to feel claustrophobic. None of them were close enough to snap up Darek, Aorja, or Braim; that meant nothing, however, because it would not be long before the dragons' teeth clamped shut around their bodies and did only the gods knew what to them.

What they needed more than anything was to find the dragons' weakness. Darek knew the three of them were no match for the combined strength of these dragons; still, that didn't mean they couldn't outsmart them in some way.

Darek's eyes darted about. He noted the dragons' claws, which were long, sharp, and silver as swords, and then looked at their wings, though those were well out of his reach. The dragons' eyes were unprotected; however, Darek had no way to attack them, so he was forced to look for something else.

Don't have much time, Darek thought, watching as that strange white energy from before began forming in the mouth of one of the dragons. *They look hungry and angry. Not exactly a winning combination.*

That was when he noticed that each dragon had a strange, string-like thing running from their mouths to the back of their necks. They almost looked like the reins of a horse, though unlike a horse's reins, these were clearly an organic part of the dragons' natural biology.

It seemed like a pointless observation to him, however, until a crazy idea came to mind when he saw it. He wasn't at all sure it would work, but the only other alternative was to stand here and let the dragons do whatever they were going to do to him, Aorja, and Braim. He decided that it was worth the risk.

"All right," said Darek, looking at Aorja and Braim. "I have an idea. Braim, I'll need your help for this."

"What is it?" said Aorja.

"No time to explain," said Darek. He pointed at the nearest dragon. "Braim, could you please distract that dragon? Right now would be nice."

Braim nodded and raised his blade. "Sure thing."

Darek nodded and then ran toward the nearest dragon, the one which had blocked their path. His sudden movement seemed to surprise the dragons, because they stopped advancing and merely watched him, as if unable to understand why this puny, unarmed ghost was running directly at them.

One of the dragons, however, must have gotten over its shock quickly, because it was already aiming its mouth at Darek. Whitish energy emerged between its teeth, but then one of Braim's green energy blasts hit it in the side of the face, causing the dragon to turn its attention away from Darek.

Have to be quick, Darek thought, glancing briefly at the dragon that was no longer looking at him, *otherwise this could all end very badly for all of us.*

The dragon he was running toward also seemed to have snapped out of its shock. It was growling and snarling, fearsome noises to be sure, but Darek didn't allow his fear to get the best of him. He just launched himself toward the dragon, reaching for the organic pseudo-reins, which he wouldn't even have had a chance of getting if another blast from Braim had not flown over his head and struck the dragon in the neck.

The blast from Braim's blade was enough to cause the dragon to look away, which happened to bring its reins closer to Darek's outstretched hand. He wrapped his fingers around the reins and held on tightly, using the momentum of his jump to swing around up onto the back of the dragon's neck.

The dragon's neck was rough and hard under his behind and the fall was somewhat jarring, but Darek got over it quickly. He grabbed the reins and pulled back, causing the dragon to roar in anger, though he didn't hold back even then.

The other dragons must have noticed what Darek was doing, because they were turning away from Aorja and Braim to look at him. That was good because it meant Aorja and Braim were safe. That was bad because now Darek was up against eleven giant dragons by himself, in addition to having to learn how to tame the one he sat on.

That was hardly an easy task. The dragon he sat on shook its head and neck violently, trying to toss him, but he tightened his grip on the reins and clamped his thighs down on the dragon's neck harder than ever. The dragon tried to turn to look at him, but he pulled on the reins and the dragon roared again as it returned its face to look at its fellow dragons.

Not that the other dragons seemed likely to help their

friend. Based on the way they watched Darek, it seemed like they were trying to figure out what was going on, as if this was the first time any of them had seen a ghost try to tame one of them before.

Doubt they'll be this shocked forever, Darek thought. *Must take advantage of their surprise and act now.*

His dragon was now charging more of that strange white energy from before. He had no idea how the dragon planned to hit him with that beam; after all, he sat on the back of its neck and it had already proven unable to turn around and bite him.

But Darek saw an opportunity and he went for it. He jerked the dragon's reins to the right as hard as he could. The dragon opened its mouth, probably to roar in anger, but instead it accidentally unleashed a beam of white energy at its brothers.

The dragons scattered when they saw the beam coming, save for one, which must have been slower than its brothers because it didn't even try to take off into the sky until the beam was almost upon it. It tried to fly, but the beam struck it directly in the heart and the dragon exploded into a whitish gray gas, an effect Darek had not expected the beam to have on a dragon, but one for which he was thankful anyway.

Aorja and Braim, meanwhile, had ducked to avoid the blast. Braim was looking at the gas cloud that had once been a dragon, while Aorja was now eying the other dragons like she was thinking of stealing one for herself.

"Come on, you two!" Darek cried out, drawing Braim

and Aorja's attention to himself. "Climb on up! We can use this dragon to fly to the Gates."

"You know how to fly that thing?" said Aorja in a highly skeptical voice.

"I can learn," Darek replied. "Now come on, before the other dragons get over their fear and attack again."

This time, Aorja said nothing as she and Braim hurried over to the dragon. They even managed to climb onto it without much difficulty, though that was less due to the dragon's gentle nature and more due to the fact that the dragon seemed shocked that it had killed one of its own brothers.

Aorja sat directly behind Darek, wrapping her arms around his waist to keep from falling off. Braim sat behind her, holding onto Aorja with one hand. His other hand, in which he held his blade, he kept at his side.

Both of them seemed secure now, so Darek redoubled his grip on the dragon's reins and pulled down.

The dragon growled in anger, even tried to throw him off again, but Darek kept his grip as steady as he could. He had never tamed an animal of any sort before, much less a ghostly animal, but he understood he had to show his dominance if he was going to make this dragon do what he wanted it to do.

Thankfully, this dragon must not have been as assertive as some, because it eventually stopped fighting against his grip. It seemed resigned to its fate, so Darek pulled down on the reins again, hoping it would understand what he was trying to get it to do.

The dragon must have been smarter than he thought, because it flapped its wings a couple of times before setting off into the misty air above. He did, however, have to direct it toward the Gates, but once he did that, it flew straight on in that direction without another peep of rebellion.

There was no wind in the mist to blow through Darek's hair, like what he expected to feel as they soared through the sky of the Spirit Lands. Indeed, it didn't even feel much like flying, even with the flapping of the dragon's wings. It was closer to floating through the water, like the air up here was thicker than the air below (though he wondered whether this could even be called air, because ghosts didn't need air to breathe, after all).

His thoughts were interrupted when one of the other dragons swooped in from the mist toward them. It came almost out of nowhere; he hadn't even heard its wings flapping in the mist.

The second dragon's claws were coming for Darek and his friends, forcing Darek to pull the reins of their dragon to make it go down. The second dragon flew by overhead, the tips of its claws just barely missing their scalps, and soon the attacker was lost in the mist again, though Darek had no doubt that it would be back soon enough.

Then a beam of white energy lanced out of the mist, aimed for Darek's head. He ducked to avoid it, allowing the energy beam to pass by his head, though it was so close that he felt the heat radiating off it. He looked in the direction the energy beam had come from, but the mist was too thick for him to see if the dragon that had shot it was still there.

A roar from above caused him to look up. Yet another dragon was almost literally falling toward them, its wings stuck to its body like the ears of a cat. Darek yanked on his dragon's reins, causing it to bank sharply to the right, allowing the falling dragon to fall past them so fast Darek only saw it as a white blur more than anything.

"Watch out!" Aorja shouted.

Darek looked around and saw three of the dragons flying straight toward them, whitish smoke flowing from their nostrils. Each one was charging an energy beam that looked even stronger than the last few, if the fact that the energy was literally overflowing from their mouths was a sign of the sheer power of their abilities.

Darek didn't even want to see what those dragons were going to do. He yanked on his dragon's reins again, causing it to fly upwards at the same moment that its three brothers unleashed their beams of energy in unison. The energy beams cut through the mist, but thankfully did not hit Darek's dragon.

Instead, Darek and his friends soared over the three dragons, quickly leaving them behind in the mist. Darek heard them turning around and coming after him and his friends, however, so he urged their dragon to fly faster, even though it appeared to be flying at full speed now.

Soon, Darek saw the golden glow of the Gates through the mist. It didn't look very far now to him, but then it occurred to him that he had no idea how or where to land the dragon.

Thankfully, he did not have to think about it very hard

because Braim behind him shouted, "Land over there!"

Darek glanced over his shoulder and saw Braim pointing at the base of the Gates. From their position in the sky, it was impossible for Darek to see exactly what was down there, but he trusted Braim, so he yanked on the dragon's reins, urging it to fly lower toward the Gates' base.

But the dragon seemed to be getting some of its old spirit back, because it jerked its head up and let out a terrifying rumble of a growl that did not sound good to Darek at all. No doubt it was getting tired of these annoying ghosts clinging to its back, forcing it to evade its brothers, and treating it like a steed.

Gritting his teeth, Darek yanked its reins down again, thinking he only had to apply a little bit more pressure to make it obey him again. After all, while he was no expert on spirit dragons (or whatever this thing was), that had seemed to work so far. No reason why it couldn't continue to work.

That was why Darek was shocked when the dragon flipped upside down. It was only for a moment—perhaps it was impossible for a spirit dragon to fly upside down for a long period of time even here—but the move was so sudden and unexpected that Darek let go of the dragon's reins and fell, along with Aorja and Braim, who hadn't had anything to keep them seated on the back of the dragon's neck, after all.

Now they were falling, falling toward the ground below, and Darek wasn't sure whether to be afraid or not because even if they hit the ground, they wouldn't die. After all, they were already ghosts, so what did he have to be afraid of?

Still, he screamed anyway as they fell through the misty sky toward the ground below. Maybe they wouldn't die, but he had no doubt the inevitable impact would hurt very badly. It didn't help that the mist around him made it impossible for him to see the ground below.

Braim and Aorja were screaming as well, which was how Darek knew that they were screwed. Yet there was nothing he could do to stop or even slow their fall and it seemed unlikely that any of the dragons would save them before they hit the ground.

Then, through a break in the mist, Darek saw the ground. It was so close now that there was no chance of anyone or anything saving them. They would hit the ground, and once they did, they would be fresh pickings for the dragons.

And then they finally crashed into the ground. Darek fully expected to feel horrible pain, maybe even enough to paralyze him. At the very least, he expected it to take him a while to recover, and by the time he did, the dragons would return and there would be no escaping them.

But when Darek, Aorja, and Braim crashed into the road, it didn't hurt at all. The impact, though sudden and shocking, did not actually hurt Darek. He lay on his stomach on the road, no longer screaming and not in any sort of pain, but hardly feeling as if he could just jump up and run around, either.

He looked to his right. Aorja also lay stunned on the ground, while Braim was already getting to his feet, saying as he did so, "Get up, you two! We're at the Gates. If we can get inside the Arbiter's station, we'll be able to escape those damn dragons."

Darek looked up. Braim was correct: The massive golden Gates now towered over them like giants, glowing so brightly and powerfully that they were almost too bright to look at. He was so mesmerized by the sheer beauty of the Gates that he almost did not hear someone—their voice high, as if they were afraid—calling, "Hey, you guys! Get in here, quick!"

Darek looked in the direction of the voice. Near the base of the Gates was what looked like a large—though not too large—watchtower, made of a spotless white brick. It looked closer to a lighthouse than a watchtower, though, because a light shone at the top, rotating in a circle just like a lighthouse.

At the base of the watchtower was a silver door that stood open. A hunched-over, astral being stood in the doorway, probably the person who had called them over, waving at them to come over.

Not knowing who that was, Darek got up to his feet anyway, while Braim helped up Aorja, who seemed too shocked by the sudden fall to stand up herself. Still, she had enough sense in her head to run with Braim and him toward the watchtower, where the astral being had stopped waving, his eyes now scanning the skies above like he was on the lookout for the dragons.

Darek also looked up as they ran, but he didn't see any of the dragons. He almost believed that the dragons might have given up and decided to go back to wherever they had come from when, without warning, one of the dragons swooped down from the sky toward them.

This dragon flew faster than the other dragons had; in fact, it was like every time Darek blinked, it covered another ten or twenty feet. Even worse, it was coming straight for them, energy building in its mouth, energy that overflowed like a waterfall.

And then the dragon unleashed its energy beam at them. Darek tried to warn Braim and Aorja, but the beam moved faster than he could talk.

Yet before the beam actually struck, Braim noticed it and shot a green energy blast in the beam's path. The blast and beam met in midair and exploded in a cascade of green and white flames that fell to the ground, leaving strange burning fires that didn't look natural even in the Spirit Lands.

As for the dragon, it had already veered out of their way after it shot the blast, perhaps originally intending to return after its beam killed Darek and the others. But now that they had survived, the dragon was roaring in anger and already turning back to go after them and probably take them out with its claws.

Not that it would get a chance to do that, because that brief period of time was enough to allow Darek, Aorja, and Braim to run into the watchtower. As soon as all three of them had passed through the doorway, the astral being who held it open for them closed and bolted it shut with a thick golden bar.

And just in the nick of time, too, because as soon as the astral being bolted the door, the sound of multiple energy beams striking the door at once echoed through the watchtower. The door even became dented with the beams, though it did not puncture any holes in its silvery surface.

The barrage of energy beams made Darek and Aorja cringe, though the door itself managed to hold against the assault. And then the explosions of energy ended, replaced by the frustrated roars of the dragons, which gradually grew fainter as the dragons no doubt flew away, probably to regroup and come up with a different strategy to get them.

Though Darek was a ghost, he still put his hands on his knees and panted. It was probably out of habit, as ghosts couldn't get tired, but he didn't bother to do anything about it, as it made him feel better.

"Wh-What were those things?" asked the astral being, addressing Braim. "Creations of the Dark Lady?"

"Probably," said Braim, "though I don't really know because I was too busy running away and trying not to get corrupted—or worse—to ask them where they came from."

The astral being groaned. "Oh, great. Just great. The Arbiter's out like a light and now these dragons are going around attacking ghosts. We might as well give up and let the Dark Lady have her way."

"Don't be such a downer," said Braim, waving off the astral being's concerns. "Everything will be all right. We just need to figure out what those things are and how they got here, that's all."

"If you say so," the astral being said with a sigh.

Darek, no longer panting, stood up and looked at the astral being more closely. He immediately knew that this being was not a human; his proportions were off, with larger feet, thicker arms, and a hunch that was no human hunch. He rubbed his hands together worriedly and was looking at the door like he thought it was going to fall down any minute.

"Oh, that's right," said Braim. He slapped the astral being on the shoulder. "Why don't you introduce yourself to Darek and Aorja? Don't worry; they're cool, though beautiful here can be a little psychotic sometimes."

Aorja glared at Braim when he said that, while the astral being looked away from the door at Darek and Aorja. He did not react when he looked at Aorja, but when he looked at Darek, he peered a little more closely.

"You look familiar," said the astral being. He frowned. "Where have I seen your face before?"

Darek shrugged. "I don't know. I don't think we've ever met."

"You're probably right," the astral being said, again sighing. "My memory isn't as good as it used to be, at least since I entered the Spirit Lands. Like most ghosts, the only thing I remember with certainty is my name."

"And what is that?" Aorja asked, sounding irritated. "Go on. We're listening."

The astral being, still rubbing his hands together in worry, said, "My name is Gujak. I haven't been dead for very long, but I already wish I wasn't."

Chapter Twelve

Wake up, traitor," said a harsh voice above her. "Nap time's over."

Durima slowly opened her eyes, even though she didn't want to. She didn't feel like it. Her face hurt, like something heavy had slammed into it; in fact, now that she thought about it, something heavy *had* slammed into it. She had been knocked out by something, but by what and why, she did not know.

Only one way to find out, Durima thought.

When her eyes were fully open, Durima found herself staring into the snarling face of a wolf. She tried to jump back in surprise, but her arms and legs were tied together, so she only succeeded in wriggling awkwardly along the floor.

A harsh, biting laugh to her right caused her to look in that direction. A young human, clearly in his teenage years, leaned against the wall, a wicked grin on his face as he looked down on Durima with clear contempt. He held a thick metal pipe in his right hand, though what he might have used it for, she didn't know.

"So the Demon awakes," said the teenaged human, although his voice was far from adolescent. He pointed at Durima with his pipe. "I think you spooked her, Valumor.

Which is funny as all hell, because you sure didn't seem easily spooked when we tried you for your crimes against the gods a few months back, Durima."

Durima blinked. *Valumor?*

She looked back at the wolf face she had woken up to. An older-looking katabans, wearing red judge robes with ragged edges, knelt over her, his wolfish teeth bared in a snarl. His hair was messy and unkempt, as if he had not bathed in a while.

Yet despite those changes in his appearance, there was no mistaking Valumor, head of the Katabans Council and a veteran of the Katabans War like herself, standing before her. There was especially no mistaking the sheer hatred with which he regarded her, a hatred he had shown back in the Hall of Judgment on World's End in what seemed like a lifetime ago.

Some movement to her left made Durima look in that direction. A katabans with an eel-like face sat on a wooden stool, a thick book in her lap, and she was now looking at Durima with an annoyed expression on her face, as if Durima had interrupted her reading time. It was Namusa, another member of the Council.

That made Durima realize that the teenage human boy she had seen was no teenaged human boy at all, but Huju, the third member of the Council. Kaxu didn't seem to be around, but that hardly comforted Durima, as these three Council members were bad enough all by themselves.

Durima tried to figure out where she was. The floor beneath her was wooden and hard; the ceiling, too, was made of the same kind of wood, although with the gaps between the boards, it didn't seem like a very good one.

She realized that she was in some kind of cabin, though where it was located was still a mystery to her. A quick glance at the chains around her arms and legs told her that she was chained up tight and unlikely to escape, at least very easily.

Huju's grinning young face appeared over her, revealing his teeth that were too white for Durima's tastes. He poked her in the cheek, causing Durima to snap at his finger, though he pulled back just before she could take his finger off.

Then he slapped her. It was a sudden blow, and didn't really hurt, but it did take her by surprise. She was grateful he didn't slam her with his pipe; that probably *would* have hurt.

"Don't bite me, Demon," said Huju. He wagged a finger at her like she was a naughty animal. "We can't have any of that, no we can't. I mean, sure, you could bite my finger off, but that would just give us another reason to kill you. Or at least beat you to a pulp with this."

Huju shook his metal pipe in her face. "I already hit you with this once. Do you really want me to hit you again?"

"Considering we already have dozens of reasons to kill you, Demon, it would not be wise for you to give us another," said Valumor. He frowned. "Though I suppose no one ever said you were very wise, now did they?"

Durima growled and tugged at her chains, though they were as tight as they came. "Where am I? How long have I been out?"

"Valumor, should we tell her where she is?" said Huju. "I don't trust her with that information."

"It won't hurt," said Valumor, waving off Huju's concern. "What good will it do her? I doubt she's heard of this island. We made sure to keep it hidden from everyone else, after all."

"Fine," said Huju. He looked down at Durima again. "You're on our secret private island, which we've always called Hideaway Isle. It's located in the southern seas, unknown to anyone who isn't a member of the Katabans Council."

"You're right," said Durima. "I haven't heard of that island before. I didn't even know it existed."

"It's a well-kept secret of the Council," said Valumor. He gestured at the cabin. "In the event of an emergency, all Council members are supposed to retreat here, where we are safe from whatever the problem is. Even the Soldiers of the Gods don't know where it is, save for a select few who were trusted with this knowledge because it was believed they would not abuse it."

"Don't bother to ask who they are," Valumor added, before Durima could respond. "They're dead. They died when trying to fight Uron after he killed Skimif."

"I suppose you're not going to tell me Hideaway Isle's exact location in relation to the other southern islands?" said Durima. "Like, say, where it is in relation to World's End?"

"That's information you don't need to know," said Huju.

"Just know that we are far, far away from anywhere else. We are not in any danger of being found by anyone; even the gods would have a hard time locating this place."

Durima scowled. "You still haven't told me how long I have been unconscious."

"Perhaps a day, at most," said Valumor. He stroked his long, lupine nose. "Though it has been harder than usual to determine how much time has passed recently thanks to the stress of the current situation."

"You mean Uron," said Durima, "who is going to show up any day now and kill all of you bastards for kidnapping me."

She expected the Council members to run or at least stand there and look horrified at the thought that Uron would come by to kill them personally.

Instead, Huju chuckled and said, "That's exactly what we're waiting for, Durima. Why else do you think we kidnapped you?"

"We've been paying careful attention to you ever since Uron killed Skimif," said Namusa as she closed her book and placed it on the rickety desk next to her seat. "We know how much Uron values your help and companionship. You are his most trusted servant; therefore, it is only logical that he would come and save you at some point if your life was in danger."

"So your big master plan is to lure Uron here so he can kill you three easily?" said Durima. "Not that I'm complaining about it or anything, as I think Martir would be better off without you three, but you guys have clearly not

190

thought this plan through completely."

"On the contrary, Durima, we have thought it through perfectly," said Huju, tapping the side of his head. "You just don't know the full details of it."

"Would you mind telling me what they are?" said Durima. She gestured with her bound hands at the ceiling. "Because all I see is three old katabans hiding in an even older shack. Speaking of you three, where is Kaxu?"

"She died," said Huju. His voice became tighter. "Killed by a freak storm that happened after Skimif's death. We never found the body."

"But her death shall soon be avenged," said Valumor. He brought his left hand to his chest. "And it will be we, her fellow Council members, who will avenge it."

"Our plan is simple," said Namusa. "When Uron arrives, we will offer him a deal: In exchange for your life, he will give us the God-killer, which will then allow the gods to defeat Uron once and for all."

"What makes you think that Uron will give up the God-killer for me?" said Durima. "It's the most important object he owns, the one thing that guarantees him the power to destroy Martir."

"We have to believe it," said Huju. He looked up at the ceiling, like he thought Uron was listening from it. "It's the best chance we have at saving Martir, though I doubt you would care, since you're nothing more than a traitor to your people."

"Traitor?" said Durima. "I'm not a traitor to the katabans. In case you haven't noticed, I have close to one thousand katabans working with me now. They've chosen to serve Uron because they're smart enough to know that there's no way for anyone, god or not, to defeat him."

Huju laughed that same harsh laugh again. "Do you honestly believe that *all* of those traitors are loyal to Uron? I mean, how else do you think we've kept an eye on you if we didn't have a spy among your so-called 'friends'?"

Durima furrowed her brow. "You mean one of those katabans working for Uron is actually a spy planted by you guys?"

"Yep," said Huju, nodding. "He's actually been trailing you and Uron for much longer than you think, as he's also an excellent tracker. A true hero, he is, because he has been working from within to help us defeat Uron once and for all."

"Who is he?" said Durima.

Huju opened his mouth, most likely to gloat, but then Valumor held up a hand and said, "Don't tell her."

Huju frowned. "What's the harm in letting her know? It's not like she can do anything about it."

"That may be so, but knowledge is power, and if she knows who the spy is, she might somehow be able to use that to her advantage," said Valumor. "Those who are careless with words tend to eat them later."

Huju crossed his arms over his chest. "Fine. I just really wanted to see the look on her face when she found out just who had betrayed her. Love seeing traitors get betrayed; it's the epitome of poetic justice."

Durima also wanted to know who the spy was, though

less because she cared about 'poetic justice' and more because she wanted to kill the bastard who had spied on her. She made a mental note to tell this to Uron once he got here. Until then, she was on her own, which meant addressing the pressing issue of being held captive by some of her worst enemies.

"Are there any gods here?" said Durima.

"No," said Valumor, shaking his head. "Despite the location's secrecy, none of the gods have tried to hide out here. The gods are constantly on the move, you know, which is the only way they can keep safe from Uron."

"It's working so far," said Namusa. "Though it cannot go like this forever, because sooner or later, Uron will kill them all."

"Unless we can get the God-killer from him, that is," said Huju with a smirk. He looked out the window. "Damn bastard is still not here. But I'm sure he'll turn up any minute now. We just have to be patient."

Valumor stood up and dusted off his knees. "Indeed. And once he does get here and gives us the God-killer in exchange for this traitor, then we will be remembered as the true heroes of Martir forever."

Valumor said that with relish, as if he could not think of a better reward for their actions than to be remembered as heroes. His happiness made Durima a little sick to her stomach, though also a little amused, too, because she didn't think this plan would work at all.

So Durima said, "Right. The Council that banished two innocent katabans beyond the Void and was reprimanded by Skimif himself for doing that will be remembered as the heroes of Martir forever. I can most definitely see that happening."

Huju kicked Durima in the side. The blow was sharp, though not terribly painful. "You're still upset about that? You and Gujak survived, didn't you? Though it would have been better, perhaps, if you two had died instead."

"If we'd died, Uron would have killed Skimif much earlier than he did," said Durima. "Either way, things would not have worked out for you guys."

"Shut up," Valumor snapped. "We don't care to hear your opinions. You are our captive, and captives never talk."

That was totally wrong, but Durima didn't care enough to correct him. Instead, she began to think about how she could escape this cabin and return to Uron. She did not know if Uron was still at Castle Hollech or not, but whether he was or wasn't, at least Durima would not be in the hands of the Council anymore.

I should try to open an ethereal portal and get out of here, Durima thought. *Idiots didn't even think to keep me from doing that. Time to go.*

She focused hard on opening an ethereal portal nearby, one she could roll into easily. She wished she could have broken free of her chains and killed these morons instead, but right now it was more important that she escape their clutches than get her revenge for the wrongs they committed against her.

But no matter how hard she focused, the ethereal portal did not open up. It should have, but it didn't.

Damn it, Durima thought, though she kept her expression neutral so the Council members wouldn't know what she just tried to do. *They must have cast a spell to make it impossible to open the ethereal here, just like what North Academy has. They must have realized I'd try to escape, so they decided to keep me from doing that.*

This frustrated her because she was so used to using the ethereal to get out of these kinds of situations; nonetheless, she was a creative katabans and so knew better than to give up right away. There had to be some other way of escape that she had not yet thought of.

So she took the time to observe her surroundings a bit more closely. The floor was old and rotten beneath her body, like it had been abandoned for years. It seemed strange to her that the Council's top secret cabin on their top secret island looked like junk; she wondered if there was a reason for that or if the Council was simply terrible at housekeeping.

In any case, the cabin's walls looked wobbly and weak. A strong gust of wind might have been capable of knocking the whole cabin down. Unfortunately, Durima did not hear any wind blowing outside, not even a slight breeze. That was probably for the best; knocking down the cabin would trap her underneath the heavy wood roof and walls. Therefore, she had to find another way to escape.

She glanced at the shackles on her arms and legs. Thick, heavy, and made of some kind of old metal, they greatly limited her movement, not to mention made her uncomfortable. If the three Council members had not been standing around her, she would have tried to put all of her strength into tearing them apart; but she didn't want the Council to kill her if they noticed her trying to escape.

Could I use metomancy to weaken the shackles enough that I could break them quickly? Durima thought. *I don't know much metomancy, though, which is the problem. I guess I could always try, but what might happen if I fail?*

Then again, a better question might be what would happen if she *didn't* try. She would be stuck here, at the mercy of the Council, until Uron decided to show up (if he decided to show up at all). Assuming the Council's plan worked the way they thought it would—which seemed about as likely as chocolate raining down from the sky—then she and Uron would be vulnerable to the gods, who would, beyond a shadow of a doubt, attempt to utterly destroy them.

Better try, Durima decided. *And if it doesn't work, then I can at least say I tried. Besides, the Council probably won't kill me if they find out what I am doing; I am their only bargaining chip, after all. Without me, they don't stand even the slightest chance of stopping Uron.*

So Durima focused intently on the shackles around her arms and legs, though she tried to do it discreetly. The Council would undoubtedly try to stop her if they noticed what she was doing, so she had to make sure none of them did.

Metomancy was always trickier for Durima than geomancy. Geomancy was a wilder magic than metomancy, because earth and rock could be found practically anywhere, while metal was often only found artificially. One of the reasons Durima had become so good at geomancy was because it was one of the easier magical fields to master due to the sheer abundance of rock and earth everywhere you went.

The two magical fields were related—after all, metal had to be mined from the earth first—but different enough that they were considered two completely separate disciplines. Metomancy was much more subtle than geomancy, as manipulating metal into the shape you wanted it to take was not as simple as summoning a rock pillar from the ground.

She thought about all of this while channeling metomancy through her body toward the shackles. She tried not to, as it distracted her greatly, but her nervousness and insecurity in her own magical abilities made her think about this stuff anyway.

Must remain calm, Durima thought, feeling the shackles on her arms and legs growing looser. *Calm, and focused. That's the only way to use magic effectively.*

Her concentration was snapped, however, when Huju looked out the window again and started.

'Started' was an understatement. He actually jumped a foot into the air, like he had seen a ghost, and when he landed, almost tripped over his own feet. He staggered backwards, clutching his chest as he did so.

As Namusa stood up from her chair, Valumor said, "Huju, what did you see? Was it—"

A loud *boom* exploded outside, cutting off Valumor before he could finish his sentence. This was followed by another *boom*, this one sounding like someone was punching the exterior of the house. The impact made the entire cabin shudder, though it thankfully did not collapse. It was a terrifying sound, one that made Durima wanted to get up and run, though the shackles around her arms and legs made that impossible.

"I saw ..." Huju took a deep breath. "I saw Uron. Oh my gods. I did not think I would actually get to see him in the flesh."

"He's here already?" said Valumor. His wolfish lips turned upward in a grin. "Excellent. Then that means—"

Another *boom* came from outside, and the eastern wall—the one with the window that Huju had looked out—fell inward. It landed with a crash against the floor, just barely missing Durima's toes, which she had curled to keep safe from being crushed. The rest of the building lurched slightly to the side, though it remained standing.

Standing where the wall had previously stood was Uron himself. He held his fist out, the fist wearing the God-killer, a fearsome scowl on his serpentine features as he looked at everyone. Behind him, Durima saw tropical trees and a waterfall, although she paid little attention to the outside now that Uron was here.

Huju grabbed at his hair, no longer looking quite as confident as he had before, while Namusa stood in front of her chair, though based on her expression, she clearly wanted to run.

The only one who didn't seem afraid of Uron was Valumor. He moved over to Durima and hauled her to her feet. He immediately placed his claw near her neck, where he could slit her throat if he wanted, thus ensuring that Durima would not try to escape.

"Uron," said Valumor, his breath hot in Durima's ear. "I am glad to see you finally decided to show your ugly face around here."

Uron lowered the God-killer. He didn't seem at all bothered by the way Valumor held Durima, though that was not very surprising, as Uron was so powerful that the Council members all probably seemed like nothing to him.

"How did you even find us?" said Huju. "We didn't leave you any clues."

"It wasn't hard," said Uron. He nodded at Durima. "Durima and I shared the same body for a brief time there. My connection to her is faint, much fainter than it originally was, but it was strong enough that I can track her down no matter where she is."

"It doesn't matter how you found us," said Valumor. He scratched one of his claws against Durima's neck; not enough to draw blood or cause any damage, but enough to make Durima tense. "What matters is that you are here, which is exactly where we needed you to be."

Uron tilted his head to the side. "Let me guess, your plan is to use Durima as a bargaining chip. If I give you the God-killer, you will spare her life."

"I won't ask how you guessed our plan so accurately like that," said Valumor. "I know how intelligent you are. You are cleverer than even the gods. But it doesn't matter how clever or intelligent you are, because we have you where we want you."

Uron folded his arms across his chest. "You assume I won't simply skip to the part where I kill you three in cold blood. I now understand why Durima hates you; none of you are very bright."

"We know how fast and strong you are," Valumor continued, "and how much you care about Durima. You and I both know you cannot move fast enough to save her from me."

"We win, Uron," said Huju, who had now moved to be behind Valumor. "There's no way you can get out of this deal. You know that we will kill Durima if you try to attack us. And we know that killing Durima would definitely put a dent in your clever little plans."

"You don't have to worry about us Council members deceiving you, either," said Namusa. "If you give us the God-killer, we really will spare Durima. Killing her would get us nothing if you agreed to our terms."

That was a big fat lie. Whether Uron acquiesced to their deal or not, that did not change the simple fact that Durima was a traitor to Martir. If the gods succeeded in defeating Uron, they would undoubtedly turn their wrath upon her. And unlike last time, when she and Gujak had been punished for a crime they hadn't even committed, this time they would be justified in punishing her.

So she looked at Uron with pleading eyes. She wanted his brilliant, clever mind to come up with a way to rescue her without having to give up the God-killer. Uron had thousands of years of experience and wisdom on his side;

surely he must have some kind of power that he could use to save her. Then she could help him kill the Council and resume their destruction of Martir.

Because there was no way Durima could save herself right now. She was chained and unable to open an ethereal portal. And she knew Valumor would not hesitate to kill her; he had been a General in the Katabans War, after all, and so had undoubtedly killed many people in the past.

Please, Uron, Durima thought, *do something. Anything. Just save me.*

Uron tapped his chin, looking thoughtful. He was irritatingly calm, like he did not understand the seriousness of the situation. Perhaps it was because it wasn't *his* life that was at risk here, but Durima found his nonchalance annoying.

The Council members appeared to watch Uron even more intently than she was. They were silent, so silent that Durima might have even forgotten they were there at all if she hadn't felt Valumor's horrible, hot breath at her ear or his claw still pressed against her throat.

Then Uron shrugged. "Kill her if you want. She is no longer useful to my plans."

Those words shocked Durima as much as if she had been electrocuted. Even the Council members seemed shocked by Uron's words, because she heard Huju and Namusa gasp and felt Valumor hesitate, perhaps thinking that this was all a trick on Uron's part; Durima wished it was, but she had heard how easily Uron had said those words. He hadn't been lying; he really didn't care if the Council members killed Durima or not.

A deep, powerful anger rose in Durima's heart. She wanted to scream at Uron, call him all of the worst names she could think of, but she was too angry to speak.

But her anger did not paralyze her. She wrenched herself out of Valumor's arms, causing him to cry out in surprise before she swung around and slammed her chains into his face with all of her might.

The blow knocked out Valumor like a light, sending him falling to the floor of the cabin with a crash. Namusa and Huju stepped back in fear, but Durima didn't pay them any attention. She just turned back to face Uron, who looked as calm and nonchalant as always.

Durima pointed one shaking finger at Uron. "You ... you betrayed me. I thought you cared about me. I thought you were my friend."

"Friend?" Uron said that in a flat voice. "I don't even find that amusing. But to be clear: We were never friends. I only used you because I needed your assistance; however, the final phase of my plan is about to begin, and you are not necessary in order for me to complete it."

Durima stepped forward, though it was a wobbly, uncertain step because her legs were still shackled together. "But you promised you would spare me, me and all of those katabans back on the King's Desert."

"I only said that to get you on my side," said Uron. He gestured at everything around them. "Everything on Martir is garbage that must be thrown out. It is a hideous caricature of Harnum, and that includes its inhabitants:

gods, humans, aquarians, katabans, whatever. All must be destroyed; none have a place in the old world I will restore."

Durima arms fell down. "So you just manipulated me. Just like how we manipulated Aorja."

"More or less," said Uron. He held up the God-killer. "I was hoping to make this revelation to you at a later point, but now that I have been forced to reveal this to you, I might as well end your life now, along with these Council idiots."

An ugly, purplish-black orb appeared in the palm of the God-killer. It grew larger and larger, its size expanding rapidly, until it was twice as large as Uron's head. A strange light flickered within, like lightning in a storm cloud; indeed, the orb even rumbled, an ominous sound that made Durima fear for her life.

"But what about the others?" Durima asked, trying to keep the panic out of her voice. "Garvan? The elder? And all of the other katabans who swore their allegiance to you? Will you spare their lives, at least?"

Uron smirked. "I will use them to help me destroy North Academy. If they ask what happened to you, I will simply tell them you were killed by the Council. And once North Academy is rubble, I will destroy them as well and then end Martir once and for all."

The sludge-like orb in his hand was so huge now that there was no way Durima or any of the Council members could possibly stop or dodge it. It even bubbled, like lava, which made Durima wonder just what the hell it was.

Not that it matters, I suppose, Durima thought. *Because*

it will kill us regardless of what it is.

"This is good bye, Durima," said Uron, without a hint of sadness in his voice. "You were a good and useful idiot while you lived."

Chapter Thirteen

G ujak?" said Darek. He looked more closely at the spirit before him. "You mean Gujak the katabans?"

The astral being who called himself Gujak looked at him with the blankest stare Darek had ever seen on the face of another being. "How do you know my name? And how did you know I used to be a katabans in my previous life?"

"Because I met you once," said Darek. "Granted, you were unconscious at the time because someone had ripped your arm off, but—"

Gujak grabbed his right arm, then tried to grab his left arm, too, because Darek hadn't specified which arm he meant, and ended up looking quite awkward as a result. "Who would rip off my arm? Did it hurt?"

Darek found Gujak's questions ridiculous before he remembered that Gujak, like most ghosts, had lost his memories of his old life.

So Darek patiently said, "Well, I didn't lose my arm, but I can imagine that it probably did. You went unconscious when it happened, though I think it was more from the shock than anything else."

Gujak looked like he wanted to ask more questions about his former life, but then Aorja snapped, "Gods, you're both so stupid. We don't have time to stand around talking about our lives back on Martir. We came here to see the Arbiter, didn't we?"

"Right on, beautiful," said Braim, giving her the thumbs up. "Though I gotta say, there's not much to see. The Arbiter is still out, right, Gujak?"

Gujak nodded as he continued to rub his hands together uncertainly. "Yes. He hasn't stirred at all."

"But why is Gujak still here?" said Darek, gesturing at the katabans. "I thought he would have moved on beyond the Gates by now."

"I got stuck here when the Arbiter fell unconscious," said Gujak. "I can't go anywhere until the Arbiter wakes up and decides my fate."

"Oh," said Darek. "That sucks. Sorry to hear that."

Gujak shrugged. "I guess it's not so bad. The biggest problem is the Dark Lady. If only the Arbiter was still awake, then I wouldn't have to worry about her anymore."

He looked at Darek more closely, scratching his chin, and then said, "I'm just surprised that I ran into anyone who knows me. I haven't run into any other ghosts who remember me since I got here."

"I didn't really know you while you were alive," Darek admitted. "I just saw you once."

"Oh," said Gujak. "Did I have any friends while I lived?"

Darek was about to say yes, but then Aorja punched him in the shoulder. The blow hadn't hurt—he was a ghost, after all—but it had been rude and annoying, so Darek glared at Aorja, who glared right back at him as if she wasn't intimidated by him at all.

"What did I say about wasting time talking about our lives back on Martir?" said Aorja. "Or am I going to have to drag you myself to wherever this Arbiter guy is?"

Darek sighed. "I hate to admit it, but you do have a point. Gujak, maybe we can talk more about your life on Martir later, after we see the Arbiter and figure out if there is anything we can do to help him."

Gujak frowned and looked down at his feet, still rubbing his hands together, but he didn't say anything. He looked very disappointed, though Darek tried not to feel bad about it because he knew they had far more pressing problems to address at the moment than a ghost's amnesia.

Now that they were no longer in a hurry, Darek looked around at their surroundings a bit more closely. It was a narrow, though elegantly-decorated, room, with two doors on either side leading off into other rooms that he could not see. It was very bright, even though there was no main light source that Darek could see—especially with the white walls and floor, the same shade as the road outside.

A tall spiral staircase, made out of the same gold as the Gates, wound all the way up to a solid platinum door at the very top. The spiral staircase's railings appeared to be made out of rubies, although considering this was the Spirit Lands, Darek figured that all of this was probably made out of some other kind of material that only looked like gold and platinum and rubies.

Along the walls ran painted-on chains. What they symbolized or meant, Darek had no idea, although he suspected that they might have just been on there for decoration. He supposed it didn't matter right now.

As for the smell, the watchtower, like the rest of the Spirit Lands, had no real scent to smell. The floor was firm under their feet, though it was made out of some sort of reflective material, because he saw his reflection and the reflections of the other ghosts in the floor.

"Why is this place so fancy?" said Darek, looking around at the watchtower's exterior. "Especially in comparison to the rest of the Spirit Lands, which are quite plain."

"I don't know," said Braim with a shrug. "The Arbiter said this tower has always existed and always will exist, if that helps."

"Where is the Arbiter?" said Aorja, putting her hands on her hips, her harsh eyes scanning the interior of the watchtower, as if she thought the Arbiter was hiding somewhere. She glanced at Braim. "Why don't you take us to him?"

"I was just about to suggest the same thing, beautiful," said Braim. He pointed at the golden staircase. "See that staircase? We climb it to the door at the top. Beyond that door is the Arbiter's room, which is where he's been sleeping ever since he fell unconscious."

Darek nodded, but then he looked at Gujak again and a new question came to mind. He did a quick look around the watchtower's interior to make sure he hadn't overlooked anyone, but when he only saw himself, Aorja, Braim, and Gujak, he decided that it would be okay to ask.

So he said, in a hopeful voice, "Braim—or Gujak, I don't care which one of you answers this question—has a wise-looking, bald-headed old man come through here recently?"

Braim and Gujak exchanged puzzled looks for a moment before Braim looked at Darek again and said, "Wise-looking, bald-headed old man ... hmm, sounds familiar."

"Yeah," said Gujak. He scratched his chin. "I seem to recall arriving at the Gates at roughly the same time as a ghost fitting your description. He was very kind and smart."

Darek felt his spirits rising. He knew they had to be talking about the old Magical Superior, Chen Wirm, who, if Darek recalled correctly, had died around the same time as Gujak. Because Gujak was here, Darek had theorized that the Magical Superior's ghost might also be here, which was why he had asked Braim and Gujak about it.

"Why do you ask?" said Braim, folding his arms across his chest.

"Because I was wondering if that guy's ghost hadn't been able to pass beyond the Gates yet," said Darek, gesturing at Gujak. "Like Gujak here."

Braim shook his head. "Nah. That guy was one of the last ghosts to be approved to go beyond the Gates by the Arbiter."

"Actually," said Gujak, holding up one finger. "He was *the* last ghost to go beyond the Gates. I should know, because when the Arbiter sent him beyond the Gates, the Arbiter immediately fell unconscious."

Darek's spirits crashed in his heart (metaphorically, of course, seeing as he lacked a heart as a ghost), but he tried not to show it. Still, he couldn't keep his shoulders from slumping, nor could he hide the disappointment in his voice as he said, "So he's gone for good, then?"

"Pretty much," said Braim. "Why? Did you know him?"

"He was a good friend of mine," said Darek. "Didn't either of you talk to him at all?"

"Actually, I did," said Braim. He shook his head again. "He was kind of weird. He insisted we used to know each other back when I was still alive, but I couldn't remember him at all. There was something familiar about him, though, I'll give you that."

That didn't really surprise Darek all that much, because Braim had already shown that he had forgotten many things. Still, thinking about how Braim no longer recognized his uncle and master seemed depressing to Darek. He hoped that he wouldn't forget who his mother was while he was here; in fact, he wasn't even sure if it was possible for him and Aorja to lose their memories as ghosts, seeing as they had technically not actually died.

Yet another reason not to delay, Darek thought. *The longer we stay here, the longer we risk losing our most precious memories.*

"Well, that guy is long gone now," said Braim. He walked past Darek and Aorja toward the stairs. "Come on, you guys. I think it's time you met the Arbiter, though I'm not sure what good that will do at this point."

Upon reaching the platinum door, Braim made a shimmery, ghostly key appear out of nowhere (at least that's how it looked to Darek, who did not see any pockets or anything that Braim could have taken it from), and then inserted it into the door's keyhole. It seemed like a rather ordinary way to open a ghostly door, but Darek was happy there wasn't some more elaborate way to accomplish that task, seeing as elaborate solutions were always more time-consuming than simple ones.

When Braim twisted the ghostly key, a soft *click* came from the door and he grabbed the doorknob and turned. Without looking back at the others, Braim entered the chamber first, followed by Gujak, who had been right behind him, and then Aorja. Darek hesitated for only a moment, mostly because he wasn't sure what to expect from the Arbiter, but then he, too, entered the room, prepared for whatever was waiting inside.

When Darek stepped into the room, he at first believed that he must have actually walked into some strange alternate universe—because there was no way that this massive, cave-like room, with stalactites hanging from the ceiling, could fit inside the watchtower. Even if physics worked differently in the Spirit Lands, Darek still didn't understand how any of this could possibly work.

A strange, red liquid dripped from the tips of the stalactites, a liquid which resembled blood. Skeletons— some clearly human, some aquarian, some completely unidentifiable to Darek, like the skeletons that resembled humanoid bird-like creatures—hung off the walls, without any clothes, though they, too, were covered in that disgusting red liquid as if a child had tried to paint them.

Stalagmites rose from the floor, crimson with that same liquid from before. One of the skeletons was even impaled on a stalagmite ... and unless Darek's eyes deceived him, it was actually looking at them, its bony mouth open in a silent scream.

Lying in the center of the cave-like room was a large, fat man. He wore robes that might have been a brilliant white at some point, but they were now stained with crimson blood. His hands were huge and a large hammer lay open in the palm of his right hand, a hammer that was a sickening black.

The sight of all of this redness—it was the red more than anything—would have probably made Darek throw up if he hadn't been a ghost. Even so, he put his hands on his stomach, as he did feel ill. Perhaps it was just his memories of his mortal life that made him act that way; whatever the case, he didn't want to be in here at all anymore. He would rather face Uron and the Void by himself than be in this room for even another minute.

"Oh my gods," said Aorja, putting her hands over her mouth. "What is all of this?"

Braim frowned. He looked up at the stalactites on the ceiling. "I forgot to tell you. The Arbiter's room is tied to the Arbiter's health. When he's doing all right, his room is all right; when he's not ... well, it looks like this."

"We didn't even know this would happen until the Arbiter fell ill," said Gujak. He stuttered every word, like he was just as frightened of the cave as they were. "The creepier it gets, the worse the Arbiter's health is."

"Does that mean the Arbiter is actually dying?" said Darek, shuddering at the thought. "Is that even possible?"

"We don't know," said Braim. He gestured at the unconscious giant in the center of the chamber. "I honestly don't think he can, since he doesn't have anywhere to go if he dies, but this has been so unexpected that I just don't know what will or won't happen."

Despite the unease in the pit of his stomach at the gruesome room they had just walked into, Darek had to admit he was happy to see Aorja looking so terrified. It meant that maybe there was still some of the old Aorja left in her, the one he had befriended a decade ago, the one that had actually been kind towards other people and who didn't harbor grudges against people she hated.

Then Aorja lowered her hands and smiled. "You know what? I actually like this place. The blood everywhere, the dead skeletons wherever you look, even the Arbiter himself adds to it. If I wasn't a ghost, I think I'd torture my enemies in here."

She said that while looking at Darek, as if she was thinking of torturing him when this was all over.

Maybe the Aorja I knew really is dead, Darek thought. *Or maybe I'm just a hopelessly naïve fool who doesn't understand that some people are just irredeemable no matter how much you try to help them.*

"Well, uh, beautiful, that's an interesting thought," said Braim, putting his hands on his hips as he very pointedly avoided looking at her. "Anyway, if you want to look at the Arbiter, you can. I doubt you'll get much of a reaction out of him; he's been so still, sometimes I think he's already dead."

"But you just said you don't think he can die," said

Darek.

Braim threw up his arms in exasperation. "There's a huge difference between thinking something—which is called having an opinion—and that thing actually being a reality. Maybe the Arbiter really can die; maybe he can't. Damn idiot's never been straight with me about anything, even after I've loyally served him for ... well, only he knows how long, I guess."

Though Braim called the Arbiter an idiot, Darek could tell that the Arbiter's current condition truly worried him. Braim was clearly frustrated at his lack of knowledge about what was harming the Arbiter, a feeling Darek understood, as he didn't like not knowing how to help his friends, either.

So Darek walked over to the Arbiter, Aorja following close behind. Neither Braim nor Gujak followed; no doubt the two, having already tried everything they could to heal or wake up the Arbiter, saw no further reason in looking at him any more than they already had.

Up close, Darek noticed more details about the Arbiter. His face was somewhat human-like in appearance, except he had two slits for nostrils, like a snake's. His eyes were closed, making it impossible to tell what color they were. If he had stood up to his full height, he would have easily towered over Darek and Aorja; even lying down, he was quite larger than either of them.

Darek folded his arms behind his back, frowning at the unconscious Arbiter. "I wish there was something we could do to help him. If he's going to stay like this, then how can we convince him to summon Uron's soul back to where it belongs?"

Aorja kicked the Arbiter in the side. The blow didn't so much as stir the Arbiter, like she hadn't kicked him at all.

"I don't know," said Aorja, shaking her head. "I'm not an expert on ... whatever illness is hurting him. Maybe our whole quest was in vain."

"No," said Darek, though he found he didn't believe that word much himself. "No. We didn't come this far just to give up and go home."

"You're right," said Aorja, though she clearly said that with great reluctance. "Who knows if we even *can* go home? The Ghostly God didn't say how we were supposed to return to our bodies once we completed this mission."

"We'll worry about that once we wake up the Arbiter," said Darek. "Right now, we need to think as hard as we can if we're going to save Martir. We need to pull all the stops. We need—"

A tiny, sinister laugh cut him off. Confused, Darek looked around for the source of the laugh. He thought that Aorja, for some unknown reason, might be behind the laughter, but then he noticed that she was also looking around. So were Braim and Gujak, which made Darek feel more than a bit uneasy.

The laughter continued to grow, becoming louder and louder until it was ringing in Darek's ears like a howling wind. And it wasn't just one laugh, either; it sounded like a multitude of beings laughing as one, each one as terrifying as a midnight storm.

The floor shook beneath Darek's feet—almost causing

him to stumble—before Aorja, much to his surprise, grabbed his arm and helped him regain his balance.

Still the laughter continued ... and then Darek saw it. Coming from the dark corners of the cave-like chamber were draggers; not just one, like before, but dozens of them, so many that even Braim and Gujak were forced to retreat to the center of the room, near the unconscious Arbiter. Braim raised his blade, but Darek doubted that Braim's weapon would be very effective against so many draggers at once.

"Where did these things come from?" Aorja asked. She glared at Braim. "Braim, you said that the draggers couldn't enter the Spirit Lands because of that barrier. You liar."

"Liar? I would never lie to someone as beautiful as you," Braim said as his blade glowed with the green energy. "I don't know how they got through. Maybe they found a hole in the barrier I didn't know about or maybe the Dark Lady —"

The laughter interrupted him when it turned into a loud cacophony, practically deafening in its volume. Darek slammed his hands over his ears, but he could still hear the laughter that seemed to permeate all of existence.

"Oh, you pathetic, silly little ghosts," said a feminine voice that Darek had never heard before, the voice of a bitter old woman who liked nothing more than to demean her enemies. "So dumb, so weak, so unable to comprehend what is really going on here. Of course you wouldn't, because the Arbiter never did tell you the truth, now did he?"

"The Dark Lady," said Braim, his voice equally part frightened and angry. "Nice of you to show yourself, you monster."

The Dark Lady still did not actually appear; she just laughed again. "Look at you, calling me such awful words. Did you learn that from the Arbiter? We can't have that in my realm, no we can't."

"I learned how to talk like this by listening to the greatest man I ever knew," said Braim. "Don't remember his name—or really anything about him—but I do remember he always taught me that it was unnecessary to speak nicely to women like you."

"Silly, silly, silly you," said the Dark Lady, her words dripping with cruel laughter. "But very well. If you won't be polite, then I will have my draggers here teach you the manners you obviously never learned. Though I cannot guarantee that their teaching style will be painless."

Chapter Fourteen

Uron hurled his massive dark orb at Durima. She raised her chained hands to protect her face, even though they probably couldn't do much to save her. It was an instinctive move; she knew that once the orb hit her, she and the Council would die.

But then—just as she was sure that they were doomed—the black orb exploded in midair. Chunks of weird, black, slimy grime flew everywhere, landing on the knocked down wall, on the ceiling, and even some on her feet, though none of it hit her or the Council members.

"What?" said Uron. He looked genuinely flabbergasted, as if someone had sucker-punched him. "How did that happen? Which of you katabans did that?"

Durima lowered her hands and looked at the icky blackness in confusion. It smelled awful, like unwashed snake skin, though she would rather have it all over the place than all over her body.

As for how that ball had exploded, she didn't know. She looked over her shoulder at the Council, but Valumor was still unconscious and Namusa and Huju looked just as shocked as she and Uron were at this sudden turn of events.

Uron shook his head and raised both of his hands. Two orbs, similar to the one he had made before, began growing from his palms as he said, "It doesn't matter. Perhaps I did not design that orb very well. These two will be better."

"You keep telling yourself that, brother," said a voice Durima had not heard in a while, but one she recognized due to the distinctive chattering of teeth that bordered the words. "And I will keep exploding them, until you give up."

Uron looked around wildly when he heard that voice. He hurled one of the orbs at a nearby tree outside of the cabin. The orb splattered all over the tree, covering it in more of that icky black gunk before it began eating away at the tree's surface. Then the tree fell with a crash, a sound that seemed unnaturally loud in the mostly quiet island. A few nearby birds flew away in fear, but the speaker of the voice did not show himself.

Then Durima heard the clickety, clackety sound of bone walking against wood. A moment later, a skeleton wearing auburn robes, a large ruby attached to his upper arm, and carrying a long wand made of crystal and gold walked past her. His sudden appearance made Durima stumble over her still-shackled feet, causing her to fall onto the floor on her side, but she barely paid attention to that.

Uron lowered his hands, an angry hiss escaping his lips as he said, "So the high and mighty Mysterious One finally decides to show himself."

The skeleton—known also as the Mysterious One, the God of Mystery and Magic—stopped a few feet from Durima. He didn't raise his wand; however, Durima could sense that the Mysterious One was more than willing to fight if necessary.

"You recognize me," said the Mysterious One. "I didn't think you would, seeing as it has been countless years since we last saw each other. Even I don't remember exactly how long ago it was."

"I don't remember you," said Uron. He pointed one of the God-killer's fingers at the Mysterious One. "We have never met, although I've been aware of your existence for some time now. It was thanks to you saving Durima and Gujak from the Void that I ended up inside the ethereal for that brief period of time. I should return the favor."

The Mysterious One sighed. "I see. You don't *really* remember me. I should have listened to our brother when he said you wouldn't remember."

"You are babbling sheer nonsense," said Uron. "Then again, I suppose that is why you are the God of Mystery and Magic, and not the God of Wisdom. Though I don't know how babbling like a fool counts as 'mysterious.'"

"I'm not babbling," said the Mysterious One. "Every word I have said makes perfect sense. You simply lack the memories necessary to understand them."

Uron let out another hiss, this one longer and more threatening than the last. "Your attempts to fool me are more than a bit transparent. I still have the God-killer. I will use it to kill you, just as I have done to many of your siblings."

"My siblings?" said the Mysterious One. He chuckled. "Oh, you mean the gods. I almost thought you were referring to yourself and our true siblings."

"More nonsense from the God of Nonsense," said Uron.

"You and I are not related. We are enemies. And we always will be."

The Mysterious One shook his head. "That is not an entirely inaccurate statement, though it misses several nuances; namely, that we were not always enemies."

Durima had no idea what anything the Mysterious One said meant. She wasn't even sure that he did. Was he just spouting all kinds of nonsense in the hopes that it would confuse Uron long enough for him to defeat him? Or did the Mysterious One have a completely different plan that just wasn't obvious to her?

She looked over her shoulder at Huju and Namusa. The two had dragged Valumor closer to the back of the cabin, but they clearly had nowhere to run. There were no doors or windows for them to jump through, and of course they couldn't leave through the ethereal. Durima was more than a bit pleased to see them cowering, unable to leave because of their own spell that was supposed to protect them.

Then Uron said, "Not always enemies? Pathetic deity, I have never even seen you until today."

"No, you have," the Mysterious One insisted. He gestured at himself with his wand. "You just don't remember. Though I am not surprised. Our other brother did say your memory was ruined after we banished you, though I thought it might have gotten better in the years since then."

Uron grabbed his head, like a severe headache had just come out of nowhere. "Shut up. Stop. Nothing you say makes sense."

The Mysterious One shrugged. "I suppose it doesn't have to. I decided to step in directly this time because you are coming far too close to destroying yet another world. And with our brother currently out of commission, I am one of the few things standing between you and the complete destruction of Martir."

"Destroying yet another world?" said Uron. His yellow eyes glowed angrily. "I did not destroy Harnum, if that is what you are implying. I tried to save it, but my people refused to believe me and my leaders demonized me. *Me*! A loyal scientist of Harnum, who had always used his talents and skills to better my world and my people—talents and skills I was always underappreciated for."

"No," said the Mysterious One. "You are a complex case, but in truth, you are no mere Harnumian scientist. Your name isn't even Uron. I wish you remembered your real name, but I can see that you don't."

"My real name?" said Uron. He pointed at himself. "It is Uron. It has *always* been Uron. You are trying to make me doubt myself, doubt my senses and my memory. I will not let you; I will not."

"If you don't truly remember who you are, why are you so interested in Castle Hollech?" asked the Mysterious One. "I have been watching you. You went to Castle Hollech and you found something you didn't like, something that has stirred some of your earliest memories, haven't you?"

"No, I haven't," Uron said, though Durima caught a hint of doubt in his voice, like he was trying to avoid acknowledging the truth. "I found nothing there, nothing but a bunch of piles of dirt in the top tower. I found—"

"You may fool the mortals, but you can't fool me, brother," said the Mysterious One. "I believe that your memories are already starting to return; it's why you were so interested in Castle Hollech, why you haven't simply destroyed Martir right away. You have been searching for answers to your questions about your true identity."

"What I have been searching for is none of your business," said Uron. "Nor will I tell you what I am looking for. Knowledge is power, and I do not share power with anyone."

The Mysterious One shrugged his bony shoulders. "I can see this discussion of ours isn't getting anywhere. I wish you would remember, but perhaps it's better if you don't; because if you did, you would be an even more dangerous threat than you are now."

Uron held up the God-killer again. "I'm done talking. I am going to destroy you, turn your bones into dust and scatter it across the foundations of my world, the world I am going to restore."

"You may try," said the Mysterious One. "But I doubt you'll succeed."

"And I will destroy Durima and the Council as well," said Uron. "Then I will march on North Academy and end the world there, exactly as planned, if not exactly on schedule."

The Mysterious One tapped his bony chin with a finger. "Now that is something I certainly cannot allow you to do. But I cannot beat you on my own right now, so why don't you play with this while I get these katabans to safety?"

Before Uron could even react, the Mysterious One waved his wand twice.

As soon as he did that, Durima felt a power spike in the world, much stronger than the kind of power spikes she usually associated with the gods. A moment later, the roar of a giant monster echoed through the still air, drowning out the sound of the waterfall.

Then something large, reptilian, and whitish-gray swooped out of the sky toward Uron. It moved too fast for Durima's eyes to follow; all she heard was Uron cry out in shock and a moment later the large creature was flying away, Uron clutched between its claws, although Uron was punching and kicking against its grasp viciously.

Then the Mysterious One whirled around and pointed his wand at Durima and the Council members. "You four. We must get out of here. That spirit dragon will not hold Uron forever; sooner or later he will break free, and once he does, he will try to kill us all."

"Go?" said Durima, glancing at the 'spirit dragon,' as the Mysterious One had called it, in the sky. "Where? Where on Martir could we run from Uron?"

"North Academy," said the Mysterious One. "The mages at North Academy have been working to take down Uron for a while now. We need as many allies as we can find."

"Will we be safe at North Academy?" asked Huju with a gulp. "Will Uron not be able to get us there?"

"He will," said the Mysterious One. "Once he deals with that spirit dragon, I have no doubt in my mind he will go there. Even if we don't go to North Academy, destroying that place is still a top priority for Uron. We must go there to tell the mages and help protect the school from his inevitable attack."

"Why not just destroy Uron here and now?" Durima demanded. She pointed at the Mysterious One. "If you're so powerful, can't you do that?"

"On my own? No," said the Mysterious One. "I wish to the sky that I could, but I can't. Uron and I may be equals, but let me tell you that Uron is not as alone as he thinks. Defeating Uron would not solve all of our problems, to put it plainly."

"What does that mean?" said Durima. "Isn't Uron the only threat to Martir?"

The Mysterious One glanced over his shoulder. "Oh, if only that were the case, Durima. All I will say is that the current situation has gotten so bad that I must tell everyone the truth about Uron quickly. I should have done so sooner, but reticence has always been a vice of mine, I suppose."

The Mysterious One raised his wand, perhaps to teleport them to North Academy, but then Durima said, "You can't take me to North Academy. Once the mages there see me, they'll kill me."

"I will protect you," said the Mysterious One simply. "I know exactly how you have supported Uron, but I also know that you no longer support him anymore. If anyone has a problem with your presence, they can bring it up with me."

Durima was about to say she found it very odd how the Mysterious One treated her that way, but then the Mysterious One flicked his wand. Her whole world melted away and the next moment—literally in one blink of her eyes—she found herself lying on the soft grass of the sports field of North Academy, along with the remaining Council members and the Mysterious One.

But they were not alone. A mortal man wearing black robes and a fox mask stood with about a dozen or so other mages, clearly in the process of teaching them something. Durima remembered that man as Junaz, one of the teachers at the school if she was not mistaken, who had also attacked her and Gujak when they had visited the school last year.

Junaz, the tip of his wand glowing like he was about to cast a spell, turned around in alarm to face Durima and the others. His students, also, looked at the newcomers, though unlike Junaz, their wands were unlit and at their sides.

"What in Skimif's name?" said Junaz. Then his eyes landed on Durima and he gasped. "Durima the Demon! What are you doing here?"

The Mysterious One held his wand in front of Durima. "She is under my protection, Junaz. I will explain more later."

Junaz's eyes darted to the Mysterious One. "And who are *you*? Why do you wear the robes of the Magical Superior?"

"I will tell you my identity later," said the Mysterious One. He nodded at the Arcanium towering above them in the distance. "Go and tell Jenur Takren about my arrival. I, the Mysterious One, God of Mystery and Magic, request an audience with her, Archmage Yorak, Auratus, the Ghostly God, Ranama, and any other major leaders here. It is of utmost importance that I speak with them right away, because it concerns the truth about Uron."

Junaz stared dumbly at the Mysterious One, his uncomprehending eyes not blinking through the eye holes in his fox mask. "Wait ... the Mysterious One? I heard about you. Didn't you help save North Academy from Jakuuth Grinfborn a few months back?"

"That I did," said the Mysterious One. "But please. Go tell Jenur. Time is of the essence."

Thankfully, Junaz did not ask anymore questions. He turned and ran up the sports field to the Arcanium. His students followed, none of them looking back, though whether it was due to their fear of Durima or their fear of the Magical Superior, Durima did not know.

She looked up at the Mysterious One, who was watching the retreating mages, and asked, "When you said Uron is your brother—"

The Mysterious One held up a hand to silence her. "Do not ask me any questions here. I will explain all in the Arcanium, once Jenur grants my request for an audience. And she will. Because if she doesn't, then Martir—and the Spirit Lands—will be doomed forever."

Chapter Fifteen

Darek counted four dozen draggers, but as more came from the shadows, he ceased counting entirely. All of the creatures left that same inky blackness wherever they came from, only for another dragger to crawl over it on their way toward the center of the chamber.

By now, Darek, Aorja, Braim, and Gujak had all gathered close to the unconscious Arbiter. There wasn't anywhere else to retreat to now. The draggers were so numerous that trying to climb over them was folly, and there was no other exit that Darek could see, aside from the door, which they were unable to reach thanks to the army of draggers pouring from the shadows. And considering how neither Braim nor Gujak had mentioned any secret exits, Darek was pretty sure that there were none.

"Braim, got any ideas?" said Darek, glancing at the man. "You've fought draggers before. You know how to deal with them."

Braim shot a blast of green energy at one of the closer draggers. This time, the blast actually caused the dragger to blow up into smoke, but it was replaced almost immediately by three of its brethren.

"Yeah, I know how to deal with them, but I've never

fought this many before at one time," said Braim, his tone frustrated. "And they just keep coming. No way I can beat them all, especially while protecting you guys."

"Then don't fight," said the voice of the Dark Lady, still as annoying as ever. "Allow my corruption to take hold. There is no reason for you to protect my brother; the idiot was never worth protecting in the first place."

"Your brother?" said Braim. He glanced at the Arbiter lying behind them. "The Arbiter is your brother?"

"Of course he is," said the Dark Lady. "Did he never tell you that? Of course he didn't. The Arbiter has never been a very honest arbiter, though I imagine the fool was too ashamed of our relation to tell you anything."

"But he told me you were just a mortal spirit who got a gigantic power boost," said Braim.

The Dark Lady laughed. "What a silly story. As I said, brother has never been very honest, especially with lesser spirits like yourself."

Braim looked too shocked by the revelation that the Arbiter and the Dark Lady were actually related to respond to that.

Darek, on the other hand, said, "It doesn't matter whether the Dark Lady even turns out to be your mother. We can't let anything she says get to us."

"Darek's right, for once," said Aorja. "So unless you want to get turned into a dragger yourself, why don't we spend less time getting shocked by big revelations and more time figuring out how we're going to get out of this alive?"

"There's no way we can," said Gujak, covering his face

with his hands. "We're going to get corrupted and there's nothing we can do about it."

Aorja punched Gujak in the shoulder. "Were you always this whiny or did you just become that way after you died?"

"I don't remember," said Gujak. "And that's what makes this whole situation even worse; once I become a dragger, I'll lose what little memories I didn't forget since I got here."

The draggers were now closer than ever. It would not be long before they were finally upon Darek and his friends, and once they were ... that was a thought Darek tried not to dwell on for long.

There's got to be something we can do to get out of here alive, Darek thought, his eyes darting around the place as he looked for some way to survive. *Anything. I mean, this is the Arbiter's room. Surely he should have something he could use to defeat the draggers, right?*

Darek took a step back and almost tripped. Looking down, he saw the massive, metallic hammer of the Arbiter lying at his feet. It still lay in the Arbiter's hand and looked too heavy for Darek to pick up, but at this point, he was desperate enough to try anything.

Not desperate enough to just pick it up, however. He looked at Braim and asked, "Braim, what does the Arbiter's hammer do?"

"Do?" said Braim, looking at Darek in disbelief. "It helps the Arbiter determine someone's judgment; at least, I think so, because that's all he's ever told me. Why are you even asking that question?"

Darek didn't answer. He just bent over and grasped the

handle of the hammer with both hands. He expected to have to exert his full strength in order to lift it up, but much to his surprise, he lifted up the hammer without much difficulty. He then returned to his full height and looked at the hammer with a little bit of wonder and curiosity.

But he had no time to examine it closely, because Braim shouted, "Darek, what the hell do you think you're doing? That's the Arbiter's hammer. Why did you pick it up?"

"Got any better ideas?" said Darek.

Before Braim could respond, Darek swung the hammer at the nearest dragger. The hammer connected, and when it did, the dragger shrieked in pain before exploding into a similar dark mist that the one Braim had killed had left behind after it exploded.

The sudden death of one of their companions caused the rest of the draggers to stop advancing on Darek and his friends. All of their soul-less, empty eyes focused on Darek; more specifically, they were drawn to the Arbiter's hammer, which glowed like a star in his hands.

"What's this?" said the Dark Lady. "A ghost thinks to use my brother's own weapon against me? Impossible. Only the Arbiter can use that hammer."

"Sure," said Aorja, rolling her eyes. "Because that's how Darek just managed to use it, right?"

"I've never seen a ghost use the Arbiter's hammer before," said Braim, his eyes locked onto the hammer. "I didn't even know it was possible for a ghost to use it."

Darek probably should have been as shocked as everyone else, but he knew it wouldn't be long before the

Dark Lady and her draggers recovered from their shock and resumed their attack.

Despite not knowing the full extent of the hammer's powers, Darek ran toward the draggers anyway, swinging the hammer as he did so. He hit two, instantly turning them into that same dark gas from before, and then smashed the hammer's head into the face of another dragger, killing it instantly.

He was amazed at how effortlessly he used the hammer. It felt as natural as if he had been born wielding it. Every movement was normal, so normal he almost forgot that he had never used the hammer before until just a few seconds ago.

It reminded him of how he had felt as a Limitless. That same confidence and belief in himself had returned in full measure now; he felt like he could destroy a hundred draggers if he had to.

Even the draggers seemed to understand his true power, because many of them were now retreating back into the shadows. Maybe the draggers thought Darek was actually the Arbiter or maybe they just didn't want to end up like their friends; either way, Darek liked it, though he decided to kill a few more just to scare them off for good.

He held up the hammer, but then stopped as the Dark Lady said, "Stop running, you cowardly draggers! The ghost is the other way. The *other* way! If you cannot match his might, then you can still overwhelm him and his friends with your sheer numbers! Show the bravery of those spirit dragons I influenced earlier to attack these pathetic weaklings!"

A few of the draggers hesitated upon hearing the voice of their lady, but that turned out to be the last mistake any of them would make because Darek slammed the hammer down on them, instantly turning them into dark gas. He then looked up at the ceiling; he had no idea where the Dark Lady actually was, so he decided to address the stalactites hanging above them.

"Why don't you come out and show yourself, Dark Lady?" said Darek, holding up and shaking the hammer. "Or are you afraid of a little ghost with a big hammer?"

"How dare you talk to me like that," the Dark Lady's voice rang out like the blast of a storm. "So disrespectful, so arrogant, so foolish. Do you even know what I am?"

"I know you're a monster that needs to be taken down for good," said Darek. "Now, are you going to appear in person or just speak to me from under whatever rock you're hiding under?"

"I would never stoop so low as to fight a common ghost, even if that common ghost was wielding my brother's hammer," said the Dark Lady. "I only fight my equals."

"Like the Arbiter?" said Darek. "If you wanted to fight him, then why did you poison him like that?"

"Because he has stood against me for too long," said the Dark Lady. "I tired of him preventing me from going beyond the Gates, to where all of those innocent souls rest. I wish to corrupt them all, to let them all know the horror and pain that I feel every day of my life."

The Dark Lady sounded hurt when she said that; in fact,

she sounded so hurt that Darek almost forgot that she was some sort of mad spirit hellbent on causing as much trouble as she could.

"Well, that's still not right, even if you actually are in pain," said Darek. "And anyway, your grand plan is falling apart all around you, in case you can't tell. Your draggers are running, while you yourself are so arrogant that you're unwilling to fight us just so you don't have to 'stoop' down to my level."

"My plan is not falling apart," said the Dark Lady. "It is coming along perfectly; indeed, its end is not far now. Only a little while longer—just a little while—and we will win this eternal battle once and for all."

"Right," said Darek. "But from *our* perspective, it looks like you are—"

A loud scream interrupted Darek, causing him to whirl around. Near the Arbiter's unconscious body, some of the draggers had cornered Braim and Gujak. Braim was waving his blade at them, shooting energy blasts at them, yet these draggers didn't seem as easily afraid as the others.

As for the scream, Aorja had somehow been separated from Braim and Gujak and was now surrounded on all sides by another dozen or so draggers. They didn't seem to have touched her yet; however, they were closing in and if Darek didn't do something quick, she'd end up looking just like them.

Darek ran as fast as he could to save her, even though he was also thinking that he shouldn't. If Aorja was corrupted, would it really be a great loss?

Whether it would or wouldn't, Darek had to at least try to save her. He raised his hammer over his head and brought it down on the nearest dragger, causing it to scream in pain before it exploded.

Half of its brethren turned to face Darek, while the other half continued to draw closer to Aorja. Aorja kicked at them, but she clearly didn't actually want to hit them (otherwise she'd be corrupted) and none of the draggers going after her seemed even slightly afraid of her hitting them.

Darek swung the hammer at the draggers in front of him. He smashed in the head of one, but the other ones actually ducked and avoided getting their heads crushed under the weight of his hammer. He swung again, but then the draggers melted into the floor, deep puddles of blackness that the hammer soared over without hitting anything.

The blow's trajectory almost sent him spinning off his feet, forcing him to regain his balance as the draggers' puddles mixed together. Soon they became one large puddle, still as black as ever, and then something rose from the puddle. The inky blackness fell off the thing in falls, revealing a larger dragger that almost towered over Darek.

Darek stopped when he saw it because he had not expected that to appear. The dragger crawled toward him, a strange hissing noise escaping its mouth as it came closer to him. He still heard Aorja yelling at the other draggers, but he had no way to get to her unless he killed this thing first.

So Darek swung his hammer at the large dragger's face. When the hammer stuck home, he expected it to die instantly just like its comrades, but much to his horror, the dragger didn't even flinch.

It raised one of its clawed hands and slashed at him, forcing Darek to jump back to avoid getting harmed. This put some distance between him and the giant dragger, but it wasn't a large gap by any means. Especially when the giant dragger resumed crawling toward him, its danging eyeballs flopping about wildly.

He was about to slam the dragger with the hammer again—he figured that he just needed to hit it again, only harder than before—when the dragger melted into the inky blackness once more. The puddle separated into multiple smaller puddles of blackness, which then surrounded Darek on all sides.

The puddles slowly began moving toward him, but Darek didn't just stand there and let them touch him. He jumped over the puddle in front of him, landing feet first on the stone floor, and then whirled around and brought the hammer down on that same puddle.

As soon as he did, however, the hammer got stuck in the puddle. He pulled as hard as he could, but the hammer wouldn't budge. It was like it had been glued to the floor, making it impossible for him to budge it even slightly.

Panicking, Darek looked over his shoulder at the others. Aorja was still being chased by the other draggers, while Braim and Gujak were doing everything they could to fight off the ones surrounding them. The only being who wasn't doing anything right now was the Arbiter, who was still unconscious.

Then Darek felt his hands burn and he jerked them back, letting go of the hammer's handle as he did so. The hammer was covered in what looked like black sludge now, like the dragger he had slammed it onto was devouring it. Looking down at his hands, Darek saw tiny burn marks on the tips of his fingers, which despite their size, burned as hotly as if he had stuck his fingers into a blazing fire.

But he had no time to stand around hurting. The other draggers were rising from their puddles, a few already crawling toward him again, and because he was unarmed he had to step back to avoid getting touched by them.

This is bad, Darek thought. A drop of blood fell on him from the stalactites above, though he barely paid attention to that. *Really,* really *bad.*

Without the hammer, that meant that only Braim could actually fight the draggers. But he was just one ghost, and the draggers just kept coming. Sooner or later, the draggers would get Braim ... and once he joined their cause, then everything would truly be lost.

There has to be something I can do, Darek thought, looking around wildly for anything that would give him even one hint of how to turn the tide. *Come on. This is the Arbiter's room. He should have something in here I could use to defeat the draggers, right? I mean, he must have thought something like this might happen at* some *point, shouldn't he?*

Unfortunately, Darek only saw the stalactites and stalagmites and the chaotic scene unfolding all around him. The situation was becoming so grim that he was starting to think that all hope was indeed lost.

I can't even ask the gods to help, Darek thought, glancing at the ceiling. *None of them have any power here, after all. Not even the Ghostly God does.*

"Feeling a little less confident now, ghost?" said the Dark Lady, who sounded as if she was speaking directly into his ear. "That pleases me greatly. Once my draggers have finished with you and your friends, do you know what I will do next?"

Darek kept walking backwards, because the draggers were still coming after him. Then he heard something dragging itself along the ground behind him and, looking over his shoulder, saw more draggers coming from behind, effectively caging him in.

"I will open the Gates and make all who dwell beyond it into my servants," said the Dark Lady. "And they will never have the sweet embrace of death to relieve them from my rule, because they cannot die and therefore have nowhere else to flee."

Despair gripped his heart, making Darek feel like giving up. He wished he still had magical power, because it would have been very useful right now. He just looked between the two groups of draggers drawing in on him, their eyeballs dangling, their movements erratic and unnatural.

"Nor is there any way for you to go, either," said the Dark Lady, "but that is fine, because I do not want you to go anywhere ever again."

There was too much truth to the Dark Lady's words for Darek to think of any comebacks. He looked this way and that, but it was mostly out of habit now, because his rational mind had completely given up on finding any sort of salvation.

The Arbiter, Darek thought, looking over the heads of the draggers coming from behind him, toward the unconscious Arbiter near the center of the room. *We* need *the Arbiter.*

But how was he supposed to wake the Arbiter? He did not have the time or knowledge to do that, especially with the draggers so close now that Darek only had seconds before they were upon him.

Yet Darek thought that if he could just get to the Arbiter, then maybe they would survive. It was probably his desperation making him think that way, as there was no logical reason for it, but he had to try it anyway. He had nothing to lose if it turned out to be a dead end, after all.

One of the draggers got to him before the others. It dragged itself toward him even faster than its brethren, but right before it could touch him with its corrupting fingers, Darek jumped right over its head.

He landed on the ground behind it and then took off toward the Arbiter, while remaining aware of the draggers now turning to follow him. Braim was still fighting off the draggers near the Arbiter, while Gujak and Aorja—who had somehow reunited with them, though Darek didn't know how—stood behind him, likely due to the fact that they were useless against the draggers.

Braim moved fast. With every slash of his blade, he took down at least three draggers and caused several more to stay back to avoid sharing the same fate as their brethren. Still, the draggers were definitely not going away, making Darek feel bad for luring the draggers chasing him in this direction, but he had no choice if he was going to get to the Arbiter.

When another blow from Braim left a gap in the draggers, Darek dashed through it as fast as he could. He skid to a stop past Braim, putting his hands on his knees as he panted—again mostly out of habit, because he didn't actually feel tired due to being a ghost—while Aorja and Gujak looked at him in surprise.

"There you are," said Aorja, slapping Darek on the back of the head like he had done something wrong. "Where did the Arbiter's hammer go?"

Darek gestured over his shoulder in the direction he had come. "Lost it."

"Lost it?" Aorja repeated. "Damn it, Darek, I know you're an idiot, but I didn't think you were *that* stupid."

"Without the Arbiter's hammer, how are we going to get out of this uncorrupted?" said Gujak, putting his hands on his face. "We're gonna die."

"No, we're not," said Darek, shaking his head. "While Braim holds off the draggers, we're going to figure out how to wake up the Arbiter. Waking him up is our best—and only—chance at survival."

He expected Aorja to call him an idiot for coming up with such a stupid plan and for Gujak to collapse into a fetal position at the mention of the word 'only.'

Much to his surprise, however, Aorja said, "All right. It's

the best idea you've come up with all day and I don't have anything better to counter it with."

"Same here," said Gujak. "But we gotta hurry. There are tons of draggers now, almost too many."

Darek looked over his shoulder again. While Braim was firing blasts of green energy as quickly as always, the draggers surrounding them were so numerous now that Darek couldn't even count how many there were.

Not that it mattered. Whether there were fifty or one hundred draggers, there were still far more than any of them could handle, even working together.

So Darek ran up to the Arbiter's prone body and pressed his fingers against the Arbiter's skin. It felt soft and even rubbery under his touch, which made no sense to Darek, though he didn't spend much time at all focusing on the sensations.

"How are we supposed to wake him up?" said Aorja. She, too, was touching the Arbiter, though with the same results as Darek so far. "Just hope he gets annoyed at us trying to interrupt his nap?"

Darek had no answer for that. He just kept touching and feeling, hoping that some answer would come to mind. *Any* answer, because at this point, he would have done anything if it would have offered even the slightest chance of their survival.

But aside from the soft rubbery-ness of the Arbiter's skin, Darek felt nothing. Well, he did feel a little foolish rubbing the Arbiter like this, but what else was he supposed to do?

Aorja shoved the Arbiter as hard as she could, while Gujak jumped from foot to foot, clearly too anxious to be of much help. His jumpiness made Darek even more nervous and irritable, which did not help him concentrate as well on their current situation as he should have.

That was when he felt something stir inside the Arbiter's body. It felt round and warm, and it was only for a minute, but he did feel it. It was not a product of his imagination, though what it could possibly be, he had no idea. Nor did he ask Braim or Gujak, who had already shown that their knowledge of the Arbiter was only slightly deeper than his own.

The screeching of a dozen draggers caused him to look over his shoulder. The draggers had forced Braim to back up closer to Darek and the others. He still fought them off, blasting the draggers with energy blasts, but they were well and truly trapped now, and it was only a matter of time before the draggers became too numerous for even Braim to fight off.

Without even thinking, Darek slammed his hands against the Arbiter's body. He didn't expect that to do anything, as he had done it mostly out of panic at their current situation, which was why he was shocked when his arms went straight through the Arbiter's skin and into the Arbiter's stomach.

He was so shocked that for a second he just stood there until Aorja snapped, "Darek, how the hell did you do that?"

He had no idea and would have said so had his hands not wrapped firmly around some kind of sphere at that moment. The sphere burned red hot, almost too hot, but Darek pulled it out anyway.

Upon pulling it out, Darek looked at what he had found. It was indeed a sphere, a fiery red one that reminded him of Aorja's old blood stone. Yet it was not a rock; it felt too soft to be one. He turned it over in his hands, unable to understand what he was looking at or why the Arbiter had had this weird sphere inside his body at all.

Nonetheless, something about the sphere washed away all of Darek's worries, as if this was exactly the thing he needed at the moment. He tightened his grip on it, feeling its heat course through him like a river. It wasn't as powerful as the feeling of absolute power he had experienced as a Limitless; however, it was better than what he had felt in a long time.

"Guys, you better come up with something quick," said Braim, causing Darek to turn and look at him. "Because I'm starting to get overwhelmed here!"

He was right. If the draggers had been innumerable before, they were almost infinite now. Some were even now reaching toward Darek and the others, even with Braim still firing energy blasts at them unceasingly.

There was no time to stand around examining the sphere, whatever it was. Darek sensed that it could do something great, so he decided to find out what it was.

He clasped both hands around the sphere and pressed it together between his palms. Energy flowed through his whole body; not just energy, but pain. The pain of betrayal, the pain of illness, the pain of anger ... all of it flowed through him and it took him a moment to realize that he was feeling the pain of the Arbiter.

But this pain, rather than weakening him, made him stronger. A buildup of power, unlike anything he had ever felt before in his life, surged through his body, causing him to shout, "Everyone down!"

Braim, Aorja, and Gujak didn't even ask him what he was about to do. They dropped to the floor, covering their heads. Because Braim was no longer fighting off the draggers, the corrupted spirits surged forward, clearly going in for the kill.

Then Darek held out both of his hands and shouted, "Take this!"

What 'this' was, was a mystery even to him until a wave of reddish energy—almost like fire, but not quite—shot out of the palms of his hands.

The wave struck the incoming waves of draggers, instantly incinerating every dragger it touched. The first wave of draggers didn't even make one sound as they turned into black gas, while the back waves shrieked in fear and surprise before they, too, were destroyed by the wave.

And not only did the wave go forward, but when Darek looked around, he saw it extending all over the room in every direction. The other draggers that had surrounded them on all sides were going down by the hundreds, their dark gas clouds forming together into a massive one before that, too, dissipated, as if by a powerful gust of wind that had come from nowhere.

And the Dark Lady was shouting, "No! Damn it! This

wasn't supposed to happen! My brother wasn't supposed to help you survive!"

Not that the Dark Lady's shouting and cursing did her any good. The draggers were still going down; a few of the smarter ones on the edges of the room tried to flee, but the wave was faster than they and consumed them as easily as a fire consumes a dry forest.

"Dark Lady!" Darek called out, pointing at the ceiling, even though he knew she wasn't actually there. "Why don't you come and show yourself now, you monster? Or are you too great to fight a mere ghost like myself?"

There was no answer from the Dark Lady now; in fact, Darek was under the distinct impression that the Dark Lady was gone. Where she might have gone to or whether—no, *when*—she would return, he didn't know, but right now he was glad she had left.

The wave of reddish energy Darek had unleashed had finally dissipated by now. And as far as Darek could tell, there was not a single dragger left in the Arbiter's room; not even the dark gas they turned into was present anymore. The room looked like how it had appeared when they first entered; still and deathly, with no one else besides himself, his friends, and the Arbiter, who had not moved one inch since the start of the fight. The Arbiter's hammer lay on the floor, no longer covered by the slimy blackness that had once been a dragger.

Braim rose to his feet, looking around as if to make sure that there weren't any draggers hiding somewhere ready to jump out and get him. There weren't, of course; there

245

weren't even any black puddles. Nonetheless, Darek understood Braim's carefulness, if only because the draggers had proved themselves to be rather hard-to-kill monsters.

Aorja also stood up. She stared at Darek in disbelief. "What was that?"

Darek looked down at his hands. He still grasped the red sphere he had taken from the Arbiter's body, but it wasn't as shiny or as red as before. It looked deceptively simple, like a child's toy ball, though he still sensed power inside it that was much greater than any mere toy.

"I don't know," said Darek. He held it out toward Braim. "You're the expert on the Arbiter. Do you have any idea what this might be?"

Braim leaned forward to peer at it more closely. Gujak, who still held his hands over his head even while standing up again, also looked at it; though based on the lack of comprehension in his eyes, he was probably just as ignorant of the sphere's nature as Darek was.

Braim, on the other hand, seemed to recognize it. He grasped Darek's wrist and brought the sphere closer to his eyes, as if he wanted to make certain that it was what he thought it was. He held Darek's wrist so tightly that it was starting to become uncomfortable to Darek, who tried and failed to pull his arm out of Braim's grasp.

"You look shocked," said Darek. "Have you seen something like this before?"

"Yes," said Braim, without looking up at Darek or letting go of Darek's wrist. "But I didn't think I'd get to see it again, not under these circumstances."

"Then what *is* it?" said Aorja, tapping her foot impatiently. "The Dark Lady might have run away, but it's not like we can just take our sweet time. Get to the point."

Braim then looked up at Darek. His eyes, once so happy and go-lucky, were now full of dread and sadness. It was a mesmerizing look, one Darek could not take his eyes off of, even though he wanted to.

Braim tapped the red sphere with the index finger of his other hand. "This sphere ... this sphere is the last remnant of the Arbiter's life."

Chapter Sixteen

Durima sat as close to the Mysterious One as she could while maintaining a respectful distance to allow him some space. She didn't sit next to him so closely because she particularly liked or respected him; she did it because she didn't want any of the other people in the room glaring at her to try to stab her while she wasn't paying attention.

'Glaring' was an understatement. Each of the beings present for this meeting in the study of the Magical Superior—Jenur Takren, Archmage Yorak, Durima's former master the Ghostly God, Ranama, and Auratus—stared at her with such bitter hatred that if looks could kill, Durima would not only have been dead, but also would have been annihilated from all of existence. Indeed, she figured the only reason they weren't tearing her to shreds right now was because the Mysterious One protected her and no one, not even the Ghostly God and Ranama, wanted to fight him.

The Council members were also present, sitting between the Ghostly God and Ranama, and they, too, glared at Durima. Valumor in particular glared at her with powerful hatred; his face was still bruised from where she had hit him with her chains, which explained his absolute and utter loathing of her right now.

Durima had expected these glares. Considering how she had been a loyal servant of Uron for the last couple of months and had even tried to kill a few of the people here, she knew she deserved far worse than a few angry looks. She tried not to look intimidated, though, because showing fear in the face of your enemies was always a mistake, whether in war or in argument.

Despite the glares, Durima did find herself watching Jenur, the only human in the room, closely. Durima had no idea what the death of the Human God might have done to humans; right now, Jenur looked normal, though her hair appeared to be graying. Either the full effects of the Human God's death had not yet fully happened, for whatever reason, or the Human God's demise had affected humans in less obvious ways that Durima could not detect through mere observation.

And neither the Ghostly God nor Ranama have said anything about his death, Durima thought. *Maybe they're more interested in listening to the Mysterious One than talking about the death of yet another god.*

The Mysterious One was the only person in the room who wasn't glaring at her. He sat crossed legged on the floor, his wand on the table before him, his hands resting on his knees. He seemed perfectly tranquil, despite the urgency he had shown earlier, though considering he was a skeleton, it was hard for Durima to know for sure just what he was feeling at the moment.

"I am pleased that you have all answered my summons," said the Mysterious One, looking at the assembled group of gods and mortals and katabans as if he met with them every week. "I was a little concerned at first that some of you might not, since none of you know me very well, but I can see that you all thought that a meeting with the Mysterious One of Martirian mythology was too good an opportunity to pass up."

"Why is *she* here?" was the first question that Jenur asked, her tone as sharp as an assassin's knife. She was pointing at Durima as she said that. "Do you even know what she's *done*?"

The Mysterious One patted Durima on the shoulder, though without looking down at her. "I am fully aware of how Durima aided Uron in escaping the ethereal. But don't worry; she isn't loyal to Uron anymore."

"How can we know that?" said Jenur. "How can we know Uron isn't somehow listening to us through her or that she's not trying to take us down from the inside?"

"Because I would know," said the Mysterious One simply. "Besides, Durima, you don't like Uron anymore after he tried to kill you, right?"

Durima nodded. She looked at Jenur from across the table, not even flinching under the woman's scornful gaze, and said, "Yes. I thought following Uron would lead to a better world for the katabans as a whole, but now I know better. I have no interest in taking down this group from the inside."

"And that is the last we will talk about that subject for now," said the Mysterious One, patting Durima on the shoulder again. "We have far more urgent things to talk about than Durima's loyalties."

"Ascertaining the loyalties of a known traitor seems very urgent to me," said the Ghostly God. He gestured at himself and Ranama. "But this is no surprise, coming from you, a very lazy, cowardly god who has been completely absent since Uron killed Skimif."

The Mysterious One shrugged. "I have always made a point of staying away from these sorts of conflicts. It has been a blessing and a curse ... and I am afraid to say that in this instance, it has indeed been a curse."

"The Mysterious One hasn't been entirely unhelpful," Durima said, even though she knew no one would listen to her. "It was because of his help that we managed to put Uron in the ethereal in the first place."

"And Darek said he helped save North Academy from Jakuuth's Army," Jenur added. Then she addressed the Mysterious One directly. "But I think the Ghostly God, as much as I hate to admit it, has a point. Why haven't you done more? Why haven't you been here helping us figure out how to defeat Uron?"

The Mysterious One raised one hand and rested his chin on it. "Because I have been distracted by many other things. There is far more going on than anyone here knows, except for myself, obviously. If we are going to defeat Uron, then I will need to tell all of you."

"Why didn't you just tell us right away?" said Yorak. She slammed her fist on the table, causing it to shake. "Why so mysterious?"

"I didn't think you needed to know, at least at first," said the Mysterious One. "I thought I could handle things from behind the scenes while you Martirians dealt with Uron here. It was a mistake on my part, however, a mistake all of us will dearly pay for unless we act quickly."

"So you *have* been working against Uron, then," said Yorak. "Just 'behind the scenes,' as you put it."

"Essentially, yes," said the Mysterious One. "Anyway, I am trying to figure out where to start. What I am about to explain to you all is complex and lengthy, so finding a good starting point is as difficult as shooting a target from a hundred miles away."

"Start with yourself, then," said Jenur. She pointed at the Mysterious One's wand and clothes. "What are you?"

"He's a god," said the Ghostly God, tossing a glare at Jenur, like he thought she was being stupid. "The God of Mystery and Magic, to be precise. Are you just going to ask more stupid questions like that?"

The Mysterious One chuckled. "Actually, that is a very good question to ask. Because you see, Ghostly God, though I hold the title of God of Mystery and Magic, in truth, I am not a god at all."

Durima expected him to say something like that (she had suspected for some time now he might not actually be a god), but to hear him just state it so bluntly and without reservation took even her by surprise.

She wasn't the only one surprised by this revelation, however, because the Ghostly God leaned forward and growled, "What? Impossible. Of course you're a god. You are a southern god, just like me."

The Mysterious One shook his head. "I have only pretended to be a god for all of these years in an effort to keep my true nature and identity a secret to everyone. I stayed in the southern seas because they are largely uninhabited, so I rarely had to worry about anyone stumbling upon me. I didn't even have to worry about you southern gods finding me; the aura of mystery I exude has proven to be more than enough to keep you gods away."

Ranama adjusted his glasses, frowning. "That does explain why you have always been impossible to detect. We gods can sense each other; sometimes with effort, true, if the god we're looking for is hiding, but it usually is possible. You, on the other hand, have always been hard to find, so hard that many of us didn't even believe you existed until just recently. Myself included."

"If you're not a god, then what are you?" said Yorak. "And why are you wearing Chen's robes?"

The Mysterious One glanced down at his clothes briefly, as if he had forgotten what he was wearing. "What I am ... oh, that's another complicated topic. To put it in a way you might understand, I and Uron are of the same kind. We're brothers, actually."

"Brothers?" said the Ghostly God with a snort. "You two look nothing alike. Uron resembles a snake man. You're a skeleton. Besides, Uron is from the Before World, so unless you also happen to be from there—"

"Wrong," said the Mysterious One, holding up a hand to silence the Ghostly God. "Uron only *believes* that he's from Harnum, which is the name of the world that existed before this one. He is confused, though I imagine his memory is returning. Once it does ... oh, he will be an even greater threat than he already is."

"Skimif told us that Uron said he was a scientist from the Before World," said Jenur. "I remember him telling us that."

"Skimif only knew what Uron told him," said the Mysterious One, "which isn't a slam against Skimif; simply a statement of fact. Ask yourselves this: How could Uron, a mere scientist, with no special powers or abilities of his own, survive for thousands of years beneath Martir and then rise again as strong as—if not stronger than—Skimif, the God of Martir himself?"

It was a good question, one that even Durima had not considered before. Based on the thinking expressions of the others, they, too, were considering that question.

"Now there was indeed a being named Uron who lived on Harnum before it's end," said the Mysterious One, nodding. "But he was not the noble figure that the Uron you know portrayed him as, fighting against a corrupt regime that tried to censor the truth of his discoveries."

The Mysterious One flicked his wand. A sphere appeared in the center of the table, a red world that Durima had never seen before and that didn't look anything like Martir.

"Nor did Harnum end thanks to a natural disaster," said the Mysterious One.

He flicked his wand again. The sphere hovering over the table cracked in half, but when it did, it left behind a tiny dark ball that was the same purplish-black as Uron.

"Harnum met its end at the hands of Uron," said the Mysterious One. "The real Uron was a bitter failure of a scientist, hated by all and mocked by his peers as a failure. He wanted revenge, so he turned to the old magic of Harnum to get it, the old magic that had been lost for eons and was practiced only by a select few in Harnum's distant corners."

"Hold on," said Durima, holding up a hand. "This isn't right. When Uron and I were going to the Old Ruins, he recounted many of his old memories to me. How could he remember them if he isn't the actual Uron?"

"Because of what the original Uron did," said the Mysterious One. The tiny black sphere shivered. "The original Uron used the old magic of Harnum to establish contact with the Almighty Ones, the mythical beings in Harnumian mythology said to exist in the afterlife."

"They must not be very mythical, then, if the original Uron managed to contact them," said the Ghostly God, folding his arms over his chest. "Who are these 'Almighty Ones,' anyway? Are they even still around?"

The Mysterious One chuckled. He tapped his forehead. "You're looking at one now. What did you think I meant when I said that I and Uron are brothers? We are both Almighty Ones."

The Ghostly God leaned over the table, his eyes locked on the Mysterious One. He looked as interested as if someone had offered him the secrets of the universe. "How many of you are there? Where are you? What is the full extent of your powers? What is the afterlife like?"

The Mysterious One held up his wand. "I will get to all of that in time, Ghostly God. Right now, I am in the middle of telling a story, and the more you interrupt, the longer it will take to finish."

With an impatient sigh, the Ghostly God sat back.

"All right," said the Mysterious One. "Where was I? Oh, yes. The original Uron contacted the Almighty Ones ... or perhaps I should say, only one of us: My brother, the one you know as Uron, whose real name is the Great Snake."

"The Great Snake?" said Jenur. She frowned. "I remember the Magical Superior mentioning that name a year ago, just after Uron first rose. He called Uron the 'Great Snake.' Did he know—"

"He got it from me," Ranama said, drawing all eyes toward him. "During that week before Uron's rise, the two of us worked together to translate the diary we found in the Old Ruins. We came across a passage talking about 'the Great Snake,' though it didn't make sense to us at the time. The Magical Superior told me later on that he thought the term 'Great Snake' was another name for Uron, though I did not believe him at the time."

"The Magical Superior was one of the smarter mortals to live," said the Mysterious One. "It doesn't surprise me in the slightest that he figured out there was a connection between Uron and the Great Snake, though it's obvious he never figured out the true relationship between the two."

"I still don't understand exactly what the Almighty Ones are, though," said Yorak, folding her arms over her chest. "Are they gods? Creations of the Powers, just like us?"

256

The Mysterious One shook his head. "We existed well before the Powers ever came here, even before Harnum's end. Due to our differences—the Powers are usually focused on the physical world, while we are usually focused on the next world—we rarely interact; indeed, I am the only Almighty One who chose to reveal himself to the Powers, though the Powers know of my siblings."

"Why?" said Ranama. He sat back in his wooden chair, though he didn't look very relaxed to Durima. "If you're not a god, why would you play the role of one and deceive us all for so many centuries?"

"I took on the title of God of Mystery and Magic in order to keep a careful eye on the Great Snake, naturally enough," said the Mysterious One. "His spirit lay dormant under Martir's foundations, so I came here to make sure he did not awaken or cause any trouble."

"Some good *you* were," said Yorak. She pointed an accusing finger at the Mysterious One. "Uron still rose again anyway. *And* he got the God-killer, too, if that wasn't bad enough."

The Mysterious One looked down, as if ashamed. "Well, yes, that was a failure of mine. The deal I worked out with the Powers was that I would protect the God-killer in Bleak Rock from being used by normal mortals and that I myself was supposed to use it in the event the gods became a threat to Martir. As you can tell, that did not work out the way it should have."

"Then why weren't you on Bleak Rock when Gujak and I ..." Durima had to catch herself, because her voice almost broke when she mentioned Gujak. "When Gujak and I went there in the first place? Why had the Spider Goddess made that her domain?"

"For once, Durima has a point," said the Ghostly God. "Leaving Bleak Rock under the care of my deceased sister was a foolish move on your part."

"True," said the Mysterious One. He placed his wand back onto the table. "This ties back to what I said originally, about working behind the scenes and trying to stop Uron without anyone noticing. I expected Uron himself to come for the God-killer, so when Durima and Gujak arrived instead, I thought that the Spider Goddess would be strong enough to take care of them. I did not expect them to actually use the God-killer and kill her themselves, albeit accidentally."

"Then why didn't you stop Uron after that?" said Jenur. "I wasn't there on that terrible night when Uron rose again, but I was told that dozens of gods answered Skimif's summons to battle him in the graveyard. Why didn't you answer as well?"

"Because I still foolishly and naively believed that I could stop him without having to tell any of you anything," the Mysterious One admitted. "Because even though I am so old that I don't even know how old I am, or if I even have an age, I still underestimate my brother."

He sounded truly broken as he said that, not even looking Durima in the eye. It made Durima feel a little less angry toward him, seeing the Mysterious One so broken over his mistakes, but she still didn't forgive him entirely.

She was also grateful that all of the anger in the room was now directed to the Mysterious One, rather than toward herself.

"Well, what's done is done and there's not much we can do about it now," said Ranama. He removed his glasses and wiped them on his shirt, revealing his empty eye sockets. "Now, Mysterious One, you still haven't fully explained the relationship between the original Uron and the current one who you called the Great Snake."

"I should finish that tale, shouldn't I?" said the Mysterious One, the sadness in his voice vanishing quickly. He looked up, though his skeletal face made it impossible to tell whether he was still as broken as he had appeared earlier. "As I said, Uron contacted the Great Snake. Uron explained that he wanted revenge on everyone who mocked and belittled him and his accomplishments. The Great Snake promised him that, and more, if he would only follow the Great Snake's orders."

"And then what happened?" asked Ranama. "What were the Great Snake's orders?"

"One, that the Great Snake possess Uron, in order that he may have a physical body to use to interact with the world," said the Mysterious One, holding up one finger. "And two, that Uron would obey every command the Great Snake gave him without question. Uron, being the sad, petty, vengeful man that he was, agreed to the terms of the deal. As a result, Uron and the Great Snake became one, a deal which was supposed to be temporary but which, like many temporary things, ended up becoming permanent."

"Why did the Great Snake want to destroy Harnum?" said Ranama. "And how are you and he related?"

"That is a bit tricky to explain using Martirian words, but I will try my best," said the Mysterious One. He flicked his wrist at the black sphere, which split into four spheres. "You see, there are four Almighty Ones total: Myself, the Great Snake, the Arbiter, and the Dark Lady."

As he said their names, he tapped each black sphere. The spheres changed shape into different forms; one resembled the Mysterious One in miniature, one resembled Uron (*No, the Great Snake,* Durima corrected herself), while the last two resembled a large man wielding a hammer and a scary-looking woman with long, sharp fingernails that looked like claws.

"We've existed in the Spirit Lands—the place all spirits go when they die, but before they are ready to rest in peace —for as long as any of us can remember," said the Mysterious One. "At one point, maybe we didn't exist, but now we do. We don't know if we were created by someone else or if we simply came into being one day. We call each other siblings, but only because we are equal in power and have worked together forever, not because of any actual blood relation like how you mortals are related."

"So you and the Great Snake are here," said Jenur, who sounded like she was trying her very hardest to understand all of this, but not having as much success as she'd like (a feeling Durima understood well). "Then where are the Arbiter and the Dark Lady?"

The Mysterious One pointed up with one bony finger.

"Both are still in the Spirit Lands."

"Why aren't they here helping you?" said the Ghostly God. "Surely, the three of you working together would be strong enough to defeat the Great Snake, wouldn't you?"

The Mysterious One actually laughed at that. It was a strange clacking sound, so abrupt that it almost made Durima jump. But she managed to catch herself before she did that and settled down as the Mysterious One's laughter faded.

"I forgot," said the Mysterious One, "just how little you Martirians understand about us Almighty Ones. While it would be wonderful if my other two siblings could work with me, there is a good reason I am the only one fighting the Great Snake right now."

"And why is that?" said Ranama.

"Because the Great Snake is not the only fallen one among us, sad to say," said the Mysterious One. "My sister, the Dark Lady, is as corrupt as the Great Snake. The two have been working together for eons to undermine everything we have worked to build, while I and the Arbiter have worked against them as best as we could."

"You don't sound quite so 'almighty' to me if you are fighting amongst each other," said Yorak. She rubbed her shoulder, like it hurt. "I am getting tired of sitting here talking. While we do this, Uron is—"

"Currently not anywhere near here," Jenur interrupted. "Yorak, I understand your restlessness, but listening to this story is the best thing we can do right now. Mysterious One, you may continue."

261

"Thank you," said the Mysterious One. "I do not like our in-fighting anymore than you do, Yorak, but it has been that way for centuries. You see, the Great Snake and the Dark Lady had always had ... how should I say it ... *darker* jobs than me or the Arbiter."

"Darker?" said Jenur. "What do you mean by that?"

"By 'darker,' I mean not as pleasant as what the Arbiter or I usually do," said the Mysterious One. "The Dark Lady, for example, was supposed to rule over the Unknown, a land where evil spirits are banished by the Arbiter for their wickedness. She was supposed to ensure that they stayed where they were ... unfortunately, my sister decided she would be better served by turning those souls into her servants to help her conquer all of the Spirit Lands."

"What did Uron—I mean, the Great Snake—do?" said Yorak.

"His job was to act as the guard between the Unknown and the rest of the Spirit Lands," said the Mysterious One. "If any wicked spirits escaped the Unknown, it was his job to catch them and return them to where they belonged."

"What about you and the Arbiter?" said Jenur. "What were your jobs?"

"The Arbiter's job was to determine the worthiness of a spirit," said the Mysterious One.

The four black spheres flew into each other and formed a miniature set of golden gates that looked impressive even from their tiny size. Where the golden coloring had come from, Durima did not know, as the black spheres had not had even one hint of gold in them.

"Good spirits went beyond the Gates to rest forever," said the Mysterious One. "Bad ones went to the Unknown, as I have already said."

"What about spirits that return to Martir?" said the Ghostly God. He jerked his thumb at his chest. "Over time, I have met many ghosts that came back here, usually without any memory of who they were or why they were here. Did the Arbiter send them back?"

"Sometimes, my brother the Arbiter would send ghosts back to Martir as a punishment for their crimes," said the Mysterious One. "Though of course, they never stay long, as you usually find them and send the back."

The Ghostly God stroked his chin. "While these are all very interesting answers, you still haven't explained what *you* do, Mysterious One, or what you are supposed to do, anyway."

"My job is simple," said the Mysterious One. He tapped the table with one bony finger. "I am supposed to be here in Martir, in the land of the living, to ensure that everything on this side is working the way it is supposed to. I occasionally return to the Spirit Lands to do work there—especially due to recent events—but most of the time I am here."

"Just where is the Arbiter?" said the Ghostly God, looking around the room as if he thought that the Arbiter might be hiding somewhere nearby. "Why isn't he here, helping us defeat the Great Snake? Is he unable to exist in the physical world or something?"

The Mysterious One sighed. "Before I explain that, I think I should continue with our story about Uron and the

Great Snake. You must first understand this before I can tell you more."

"All right," said Ranama, nodding. "Continue on, then. All of us are listening."

"Where did I leave off?" said the Mysterious One. "Ah, that's right. The Great Snake, controlling Uron's every move, had Uron manipulate Harnum's major political powers in order to bring about a worldwide war that would kill every man, woman, and child on the planet. To top it off, the Great Snake had Uron use his scientific knowledge to head down into the core of Harnum, where he would cool the core down to make Harnum uninhabitable."

"Hold on," said Jenur, holding up a hand to catch the Mysterious One's attention. "You still haven't explained why the Great Snake did that, or why the Great Snake and the Dark Lady are evil."

"They became that way gradually," said the Mysterious One. "The Great Snake had always been hungry for power. He aspired to be greater than any of us, even though there were no other height for us to attain. He believed that we Almighty Ones should rule both the spiritual and physical realms, as our power granted us that right. The Dark Lady agreed, though the Arbiter and I disagreed, as you know."

"So you've been fighting for untold years, then, about the proper role of the Almighty Ones in relation to the spiritual and physical realms?" said Jenur.

"Correct," said the Mysterious One. "And for many years, we were at a standstill because all of us Almighty Ones are equal in strength to one another. The Great Snake wanted to tip the balance of power in their favor by destroying Harnum, which would naturally supply the Spirit Lands with billions of new, easily corruptible souls that could be turned into a new army under their command."

"That's insane," said Jenur, shaking her head. "Completely insane."

"No, that was my brother," said the Mysterious One. "But yes, it was a mad plan, though a clever one I must admit. The Arbiter and I didn't even know about his plan until it was almost too late to stop it, because the Dark Lady distracted us."

"But you failed anyway," said the Ghostly God. "Harnum ended. Every life on that world perished ... save for Uron, of course."

"That is unfortunately correct," said the Mysterious One. "But it wasn't a total victory for my brother and sister. You see, the Great Snake's possession of the original Uron caused both of their souls to merge in a way that even I had not known possible. So when Harnum ended and Uron died, he and the Great Snake went to the Gates just like any normal spirit. The Arbiter didn't banish them to the Unknown; instead, he returned them to the ruins of Harnum, where, with no body to control, they hid deep beneath its ruined surface, awaiting the day they could return to the Spirit Lands and get their revenge."

"What about the citizens of Harnum?" said Ranama, leaning over the table slightly. "Did the plan to make them into an army of corrupt spirits work?"

"No," said the Mysterious One, "though the Dark Lady managed to corrupt a few, the Arbiter and I worked together to save the vast majority and send them beyond the Gates, aside from those too wicked to go there, of course. And since the Dark Lady was alone, that meant she could not fight us, so the Arbiter and I retained control of the Spirit Lands."

"Did it never occur to you to find the Great Snake and make sure he couldn't return or cause any more trouble for you?" said the Ghostly God.

"We thought he was going to remain asleep under Harnum forever," the Mysterious One admitted. "When the Powers came by and decided to build Martir on top of Harnum's ruins, that was when we became worried that they might accidentally reawaken the Great Snake. That is another reason I came here; I wanted to oversee the Powers' work and make sure that the Great Snake never awakened. It meant leaving behind my brother the Arbiter, but as he and my sister are equally matched, I was confident nothing would go wrong."

"Of course," said Yorak, in a sardonic voice, "things always choose to go wrong exactly when you decide that nothing can."

"Very true," the Mysterious One said, nodding. "Because despite my efforts, the Great Snake did awaken again, though he took thousands of years to rise again. And you all, of course, know the rest."

Durima rubbed her temples. Taking all of this information in was one of the most difficult mental things she had had to do in a long while. She hadn't expected to learn so much at once and she didn't understand all of it, though she understood enough to know that the situation was far more complicated than it had originally appeared.

"Sounds like we need the Arbiter, then," said Jenur. "He's still around, isn't he? If we have him helping, then we should be able to beat back the Dark Lady and Uron, right?"

The Mysterious One steepled his fingers together. "I wish I could say he was fine, but in truth, my brother is not. He was afflicted with a terrible curse, a disease really, that has rendered him unconscious. He hasn't been this way for long, but that leaves only me against the Dark Lady and the Great Snake ... and I am afraid to say that I cannot defeat both of my siblings together."

"Great," said the Ghostly God, rolling his eyes. "Wonderful. I can see now that we are well and truly doomed."

Durima agreed with the Ghostly God, though she tried to ignore the feelings of doom and gloom coming over her. There had to be some way they could win, some way they could survive, even if it wasn't very obvious right now.

Whatever it was, Durima still had a few more questions to ask the Mysterious One first, so she said, "Uron never told me anything about this when I worked for him. He acted like he didn't know you when you saved me and the Council from him."

"That is true," said the Mysterious One. He sighed again. "In truth, the being you call Uron and the one I know as the Great Snake is not really either. The fusion of the two souls has resulted in someone with memories and features from both. Because he was a ghost for so many years, Uron's memory began to fade, much like any ghost's, and he only remembered the name of Uron and Uron's own twisted view of himself as a rejected prophet of doom."

"So Uron has no memory whatsoever of the Great Snake or the Dark Lady?" Jenur asked, her voice hopeful.

"Initially, he did not," said the Mysterious One. "But I believe my brother's memories are beginning to resurface, which is why Uron seems so confused right now. Uron thinks he's still trying to bring back Harnum, but in truth, the Great Snake is trying to repeat on Martir what he attempted back on Harnum; namely, create a massive influx of ghosts that the Dark Lady can corrupt to create an army loyal to them. He doesn't know it yet, but he will soon."

"Is that why he went to Castle Hollech?" Durima asked, scratching the top of her head, which had started to itch. "Does it have something to do with his past?"

"Castle Hollech bears a striking resemblance to a certain place in the Spirit Lands that the Great Snake once knew," said the Mysterious One. "It was once a part of Harnum, but after Harnum's end, it was placed in the Void by the Powers as part of their effort to hide the remaining bits of Harnum that they did not use when they built Martir."

"Uron was also searching for something in the Temple of Xocion," Durima said. "Do you know what it was?"

"Probably his diary," said the Mysterious One, gesturing at the stone tablet that lay on the table in front of Ranama. "He probably thought it was in the Temple of Xocion because it had been kept there for a brief period. Right, Ranama?"

"That is correct," said Ranama, putting one hand on the diary. "I once lent it to the Monks for safekeeping, as the coldness of that place would preserve it against decay, though I can see that Uron apparently did not know we had moved it out quite some time ago."

"That is not surprising," said the Mysterious One. "My brother is still quite confused at the moment, so that is the most likely reason why he went there, even though the diary was no longer there."

"But you and the Arbiter can stop him, right?" Huju spoke up suddenly, sounding smaller than usual from his spot on the Ghostly God's right. "You did it before. Can't you do it again?"

The Mysterious One chuckled. "Weren't you listening? The Arbiter is out like a light and I can't wake or heal him. Uron will soon remember who he is, no doubt, and once he does, he will waste no time in contacting the Dark Lady. And that, my friends, would indeed be no good."

"Is that it, then?" said Jenur. "Do we have no hope of defeating them at all?"

"I wouldn't say that," said the Mysterious One. "Though I agree, our situation is extremely bleak, the bleakest I can remember in fact. And it will get bleaker, because I know what Uron's next move is going to be."

"What is it?" said Jenur. "Is there anything we can do about it?"

"Probably not," said the Mysterious One, "but it's

important for you to know anyway: Uron is coming for North Academy."

"We already suspected that," said the Ghostly God in annoyance. "Are you going to tell us anything that we don't already know or are you just going to tell us stuff we already know?"

"You clearly don't understand why this is important," said the Mysterious One. "I might as well state it bluntly: If Uron destroys North Academy, Martir *will* end. Guaranteed."

"But that doesn't make any sense," Jenur said. She looked around at her study, at the bookshelves along the walls and the statues of the gods standing on another table toward the study's entrance. "How? I know North Academy is an important school, true, but it's not that important, is it?"

"By itself, no," said the Mysterious One. "But what you fail to understand is that World's End has already fallen. World's End is the southernmost island in Martir, while North Academy is the northernmost. There is a reason both have traditionally been almost impossible for the average mortal to reach, and it has nothing to do with any sort of tests of worth or anything like that."

"Explain yourself," said the Ghostly God. "What makes World's End and North Academy so important?"

"Think of their relationship like the sun and the moon," said the Mysterious One, the golden gates on the table turning into miniature versions of the two orbiting satellites. "Both are necessary to allow life to exist on a world; similarly, North Academy and World's End have acted as the places that balance Martir's magic, which is ultimately what keeps Martir together at all."

"So what, exactly, will happen if Uron destroys North Academy, too?" said Ranama.

"There will be nothing to balance the magic that runs inherent through all of creation," said the Mysterious One, gesturing at the air around them. "Martir itself will unravel quickly, like the threads of a spool, and with it, every life on this world—god, human, aquarian, katabans, whatever—*will* die."

A shocked silence swept over the entire study, so stunning and depressing was the Mysterious One's revelation. Durima felt even more tense than before; it was as if she had been told she only had minutes to live and she didn't know how to live them.

"But how do you know this?" said Jenur. "Not that I don't believe you, but—"

"I know this because I helped establish those rules back when the Powers were first creating Martir all those years ago," said the Mysterious One. He sighed. "I might as well be blunt about it: I founded North Academy, specifically so it could act as one of Martir's 'magical anchors,' as I like to think of them as."

"*You* are the founder of North Academy?" said Jenur, the disbelief in her voice obvious. "I didn't know that."

"Few do," said the Mysterious One. "It is why I stepped in to defend the school from Jakuuth not long ago. And it was I who taught the first mages who came here to learn;

indeed, it was those first mages who went and spread rumors about me in the first place."

"This is all very interesting," said Yorak, causing everyone to look at her. "But irrelevant to our current predicament. Have we already forgotten about Darek and Aorja? They're still in these 'Spirit Lands,' as the Mysterious One called them, aren't they? Mysterious One, do you know what their current status is? We haven't heard from either of them since the Ghostly God sent their souls beyond this life."

"Darek and Aorja are still fine," said the Mysterious One. "But I doubt either of them will be of much help, because they are still ghosts and are just as incapable of waking my brother as I am. I wouldn't count on them to show up and save the day."

Jenur sighed in relief. "Oh, I'm glad to hear that Darek is all right."

"So my theory worked," said the Ghostly God, rubbing his hands together eagerly, apparently forgetting all about how grim their current situation looked. "I knew it. The secrets that lie beyond the grave are that much closer to being mine."

"Didn't you hear what the Mysterious One just said?" said Ranama, looking at the Ghostly God in disgust. "Darek and Aorja cannot help us. Maybe it would have even been better if we had not sent them to the Spirit Lands at all; at least if they were still here, they could have helped defend North Academy."

"Mysterious One, is there any way we can bring them

back?" said the Ghostly God, apparently ignoring Ranama's chiding. "Because I've been unable to determine if it is a one-way trip or not."

"I believe the Arbiter could send them back, if he wanted," said the Mysterious One, nodding. "But of course, he's unable to do anything right now. Though if the Great Snake and the Dark Lady succeed, it won't matter whether Darek and Aorja can or can't return, if you think about it."

"Do you have a plan for defeating Uron, then?" said Yorak. "Because we have been debating that exact problem for weeks now and would certainly welcome your input, if it will show us a new way of looking at the situation."

The Mysterious One tapped his chin in thought. "The best way to stop him would be to heal and awaken the Arbiter, which would allow us to counter him and our sister, but obviously we can't do that."

"Then reveal to us what your other plan is," said the Ghostly God. "Surely you must have one, given you are an Almighty One and know and understand the Great Snake better than any of us."

The Mysterious One looked at the Ghostly God in surprise. "What? Oh, no. I do not have any other plan to defeat the Great Snake. That is partly why I decided to tell you all about this; I thought one of you might be able to come up with an idea we could use if I told you everything I know."

Durima just looked at the Mysterious One in disbelief, while the Ghostly God gaped at the Mysterious One's answer. Ranama almost fell over in shock, while Auratus covered her mouth with her hand. Yorak looked like someone had smacked her in the face and the Council members began muttering among themselves, which, based on what little Durima could hear, consisted mostly of them wondering if they could sneak out of here without anyone noticing.

Jenur was the only one who had enough sense in her to say, "Oh, come *on*. Here I thought you were explaining all of this to us just so we would understand your plan better. I thought you were going to pull a plan from out of your robes that would solve all of our problems."

The Mysterious One shrugged sheepishly. "I may be an Almighty One, but that doesn't mean I know everything. If I had such a plan, I likely would have gone ahead and executed it, rather than sit here and tell you all about it."

"But this isn't *all* bad," said Valumor, rubbing his clawed hands together anxiously. "After all, Uron or the Great Snake, or whatever his name is, isn't even here yet. We still have time to digest everything the Mysterious One told us and then come up with an amazing plan that will no doubt be—"

Durima never got to learn exactly what that plan was going to be, because at that moment a gray ghost materialized in the air above the table. The sudden appearance of the gray ghost made everyone lean back, except for the Mysterious One, who simply regarded it as an interesting specimen.

The gray ghost resembled Junaz, the fox-masked mage from before. It floated down until it was in front of Jenur, who watched its progress with shocked eyes.

"Jenur," said Junaz's gray ghost. Its tone was urgent and fearful and it spoke quickly, almost too fast for Durima to understand. "I apologize for interrupting your audience with the Mysterious One, but an entire army of katabans have just appeared on the Walls, equipped with strange metal armor and weapons."

"What?" said Jenur, even though the gray ghost could not hear her. "Where did they come from?"

Her questions went unanswered, for Junaz's gray ghost was still speaking rapidly. "And they aren't alone. Some of the students have reported seeing a tall, snake-like humanoid who resembles descriptions of Uron exactly, which means that Uron himself is here and—"

The gray ghost stopped speaking. Then it exploded into gray smoke, forcing almost everyone to cover their faces with their hands instinctively. Only the Mysterious One allowed the smoke to pass over his face like it was nothing.

Durima lowered her hands from her face, still looking up at the spot where it had been floating previously. "Why ... why did it explode?"

Jenur stood up. "I don't know, but I do know that Uron has forced us to act now. Let's go. Maybe, if we move fast, we'll be able to save a few lives before Uron destroys us all."

Chapter Seventeen

The tiny orb in Darek's hand beat like a heart, though Darek hardly paid attention to it because he was too busy staring at Braim in shock.

"What do you mean, this sphere is the last remnants of the Arbiter's life?" said Darek. "I thought the Arbiter couldn't die. He's a spirit, isn't he?"

"Hey, I didn't say I understood it," said Braim with a shrug. "It's something the Arbiter showed me once a long time ago. He said it was his heart, what kept him going. He showed it to me because he said he trusted me, thought I needed to know what it was in case something happened to him in the future."

Darek stared at the orb again. Knowing that this thing had been inside the Arbiter made him feel a little unclean, but he didn't drop it. He held it tighter than ever, now that he knew just how important it really was.

"What was that power it gave me?" said Darek, turning the orb over in his hand. "Was that the power of the Arbiter flowing through me?"

"Probably," Braim said. "Though I don't know for sure, 'cause I've sure as hell never seen the Arbiter do anything like that before. Just don't drop it, all right?"

Darek of course would never drop it, but before he could

say so, Aorja grabbed it from him. Shocked, Darek said, "Aorja, give that back right this instant."

Aorja ignored Darek, however. Her focus was entirely on the orb she had stolen from him, as if it was the only thing in the world.

"Aorja?" said Darek. "Aorja, whatever you're thinking—"

"I'm thinking I—I mean, we, of course—could use this to become powerful enough to defeat Uron," said Aorja. She looked up at Darek, insanity in her violet eyes. "You saw what it did to those damn draggers. Who knows what it could do against Uron? We might stand a chance of killing the bastard."

Darek swiped the orb from Aorja's fingers again, causing Aorja to say, "Hey!"

Rolling it between his fingers, Darek said, "You're assuming we can even take this with us back to Martir. I doubt it, myself. It's probably stuck here, just like we are."

"Besides, I'd never let you two take that thing with you," Braim added. "It still technically belongs to the Arbiter. If you guys took it with you, I'd have no guarantee I'd ever see it again."

Aorja folded her arms across her chest and pouted. "All right. I just wonder how Darek got it."

"I don't know," said Darek. "I just stuck my hands through the Arbiter's stomach and grabbed it. I don't know why or how that happened. Braim? Gujak?"

Gujak—who had been almost hyperventilating, despite the fact that there were no more draggers in the area—shook his head wildly. "No idea. I don't know anything about the Arbiter, at least not any more than you guys do."

Braim scratched the back of his head, frowning. "It's a mystery to me, too. Only explanation I can come up with is that … well, that the Arbiter is so far gone that we can't ever wake him up. Maybe he used the last of his strength to pass that orb onto you."

Darek looked at the unconscious form of the Arbiter. The Arbiter's body was deathly still, even stiller than before. He did not sense any energy radiating from the Arbiter, though frankly his magical sense had not been working ever since he lost all of his power before, so he did not consider that reliable.

"Does that mean that the Arbiter is dead?" asked Gujak in a fearful voice.

"Not sure," Braim admitted. "We might be able to revive him, given time, but maybe we won't be able to. I wouldn't count on it, though, since I doubt he would have done this if he was going to be all right."

Gujak gulped. "But if the Arbiter is dead, then how can we possibly defeat the Dark Lady? She'll definitely corrupt us now!"

Gujak sounded so hopelessly afraid that even Darek began to feel a little doubtful. Still, he didn't think that the Arbiter was actually dead; at least, he figured there had to be a reason he had been given this thing.

"I don't know how we can beat her," said Braim, putting his hands on his hips as he looked up at the ceiling. "And she will be back. I've no doubt about that."

Darek clasped his fingers over the orb and looked up.

"Maybe, instead of her coming to us, we come to her."

Braim shook his head like Darek was crazy. "Did you even just hear what you said? The Dark Lady is on the same power level as the Arbiter. She lives deep within the Unknown; even I don't know where she is. We walk into there, she'll corrupt us, unless her draggers get us first."

"Do you suggest we just stand around here and do nothing?" said Darek. He gestured at the Arbiter's body behind him. "We can't rely on the Arbiter here. We're entirely on our own. That means we have to fight her ourselves."

"I don't know, Darek," said Aorja. "The whole reason we came here in the first place was to convince the Arbiter to take Uron back to the Spirit Lands. If the Arbiter can't do that, then why should we bother with this stupid Dark Lady?"

"Because we're all going to end up here someday anyway, even if we beat Uron," said Darek. "Do you really want to die and come here again, only to spend the rest of eternity under the Dark Lady's rule? And who knows, maybe by defeating her, we'll learn how to help the Arbiter."

"Good point," said Aorja. "Still doesn't change the fact that we can't actually do anything against her, though."

"Maybe with this, we can," said Darek, holding up his closed fist, which glowed slightly thanks to the orb within. "If it gave me that much power, what else do you think it could do?"

"Guess we'd better find out," said Braim. "We can go outside and test it out there."

"Where those dragons that attacked us from earlier are?" said Darek. "I don't think so. Instead, we're going to head straight for the Unknown and 'test' the orb on the Dark Lady herself."

Darek turned to leave, but then Braim stepped in his path. The older ghost was holding up his hands, like he was trying to calm Darek down, even though Darek wasn't angry right now.

"Whoa, there, Darek," said Braim. "Let's not get ahead of ourselves now. While I want to punch that Dark Lady in the face just as much as anybody, I don't think it would be wise of us to go out to her territory and fight her directly."

"Why not?" said Darek, sidestepping Braim and walking past him. "I'm tired of feeling useless and powerless. Going to the Unknown would be superior to 'testing' the power of the Arbiter's life remnants here."

A hand grasped Darek's shoulder, stopping him in his tracks instantly. He looked over his shoulder and saw it was Braim who had grabbed him, a hard look in his eyes.

"Listen, I understand wanting to do something, but this is way too dangerous for us," said Braim. "We got lucky this time; we go into the Dark Lady's territory, a place none of us know very well, and we'll be corrupted faster than you can blink."

Darek shrugged Braim's hand off his shoulder. "Didn't you just say she was going to come back? And when she does, do you think we'll be any better equipped to fight her than we are now? Way I see it, it's only a matter of time before the Dark Lady returns, and I for one am not going to sit around waiting for her to come here and wipe the floor with us."

"When did I say we should just sit around and wait for her?" said Braim in annoyance. "Testing the Arbiter's life orb is hardly what I'd call 'sitting around and waiting for her.' It's called taking action."

Darek turned around to face Braim again and looked him straight in the eyes. "So is entering her territory and taking her on directly."

"No, that's called suicide," said Braim. "Listen, I don't want to argue with you because I don't really like arguing with anyone, but if you're going to keep acting like an idiot, then I'll argue all day long and well into the night."

"An idiot? I'm not an idiot," said Darek. He held up the life orb and turned it in his fingers to show it in its entirety to Braim. "Clearly, the Arbiter must not think I'm an idiot, either, otherwise he wouldn't have let me get it."

"Who says he chose to give it to you?" said Braim, folding his arms. "Maybe he just wanted to give it to whoever could get it and you were just lucky enough to be nearby when he did it."

"He gave it to us because he knew it was what we needed to defeat the Dark Lady," said Darek. "And if we can do that, maybe that will help us defeat Uron, too. It's a win-win situation for all of us."

"Unless we just walk into the Unknown like dumb asses and let the Dark Lady corrupt us," said Braim. "Don't you remember how we were outnumbered by those draggers? And I bet that wasn't even half of her forces. There are probably even more in the Unknown and they're probably twice as dangerous in their home territory than here."

"If you want to stay here, you can," said Darek. "I know where the Unknown is. I'll just go there myself, by myself if I have to."

"I forget," said Braim, shaking his head, "when I was still alive, did we always argue like this or is this new?"

"I don't remember because I was five-years-old at the time," said Darek. "But I do remember not liking you very much. I never understood why, but if you were anything like how you are now, then it's not a mystery to me any longer."

"And I'd say that you're acting just like a reckless five-year-old," Braim said. "Listen, I know what it's like to want to act right away, but there's still way too much we don't know about the Arbiter's life orb to make that a realistic or reasonable thing to do."

"I think Braim is right," said Gujak, who Darek hadn't even noticed walk up to them. "Right now, we need to take this opportunity to plan and think. Rushing headlong into danger isn't wise."

Aorja walked past Braim and Gujak and then stopped by Darek's side. She didn't look at Darek; instead, she focused on Braim and Gujak, putting her hands on her hips as she did so.

"Darek is usually an idiot, but in this case he's right," said Aorja. "We should attack now, when the Dark Lady least expects it, rather than wait for her to attack us again."

"Both of you are being stupid," said Braim. "The Dark Lady isn't on the same power level as the rest of us. Even if you manage to defeat the draggers, she won't hesitate to corrupt you."

"Maybe she won't," said Darek. He shook the life orb in his hand. "Because we have this life orb, which contains the power of the Arbiter. That should put us on the same level as the Dark Lady, shouldn't it?"

"Maybe," said Braim, shrugging again. "Or maybe not. Like I said, I still don't know a whole lot about the nature of the Arbiter, but that doesn't justify recklessly running headlong into the most dangerous place in the Spirit Lands."

"This is getting nowhere," said Darek. "We're just repeating ourselves. You two can stay here and keep an eye on the Arbiter if you want, while Aorja and I go to the Unknown to confront the Dark Lady on our own."

"And just what the hell are we supposed to do if you two get corrupted?" said Braim. "'Cause there's a very good chance that we'll have to fight you if that happens, you know."

"You can figure it out on your own," Aorja said. "You're smart, aren't you? If we become draggers, then you just kill us or whatever it is that Darek did to those other draggers earlier."

"Draggers can't be killed," Braim said. "I said that already, remember? Those draggers that Darek 'killed' are going to reform sooner or later, probably sooner, which will replenish the Dark Lady's forces."

Darek turned around and resumed walking toward the door, without looking over his shoulder at the others. "I don't care. I don't know for sure how we're going to beat the Dark Lady, but as long as we keep moving forward and don't let our fear paralyze us, we should win."

"Ain't that simple, Darek," said Braim from behind him. "But go ahead. Get yourself corrupted. I wish you wouldn't, but I happen to believe in the importance of letting people make their own mistakes, even if those are stupid mistakes."

Then Darek heard someone coming up behind him and the next moment Aorja was walking beside him. He didn't so much as glance at her, however, because while he was glad she was coming with him (he needed all the help he could get), he still didn't like her very much.

He also heard Braim and Gujak muttering among themselves. They were talking too quietly and were too far away for him to hear what they were saying, but he could guess—and not care less—about what they were talking about. All he cared about was getting out of the tower and finding the Dark Lady, no matter what.

Then Darek heard more footsteps behind him and he looked over his shoulder. Both Braim and Gujak were walking after him and Aorja in order to catch up with them, making Darek wonder if they were still intent on convincing him and Aorja not to go.

If they're just going to keep arguing, then I might just have to knock them around a bit to make them realize how stupid they're being, Darek thought.

Darek stopped and turned to face Braim and Gujak as they approached. So did Aorja, folding her arms over her chest as the other two ghosts approached.

"What do you want?" said Darek. "Let me guess, you're going to try to convince us not to go, right?"

Braim shook his head. "Nah. I can tell neither of you are going to listen to a word I or Gujak say. Instead, we're going to go with you. Right, Gujak?"

Gujak nodded, though it was a trembling nod. "Y-Yes."

"Really?" said Darek. "Why? I thought you thought it was foolhardy."

"It is," said Braim. "But I figured if we all stick together, we have a much better chance at survival. Maybe we'll even figure out how the Dark Lady poisoned the Arbiter. Worth a shot, ain't it?"

Neither of them seemed to be lying, and Darek could think of no reason for them to deceive him and Aorja. He actually felt quite relieved; due to his distrust of Aorja, he had worried that he might not have been able to rely on her when they went to the Unknown, which was the last thing he needed right now.

"And anyway, while I've never been to the Unknown before, I do know a thing or two about it, based on what the Arbiter has told me," said Braim, gesturing over his shoulder at the Arbiter's unconscious body. "So it's not exactly like we're going in completely blind."

"Well, that's good," said Darek. "I just need to know that you two won't run when the going gets tough."

"We won't," Braim promised. "Right, Gujak?"

"Y-Yeah," said Gujak, rubbing his hands together worriedly. "I mean, we don't even have anywhere to run to, you know? If the Dark Lady wins, then that's it."

"We have no time to lose," said Darek. He turned around again. "We have to strike hard and fast before the Dark Lady's forces recover."

Before Darek could resume walking toward the exit, the life orb in his hand glowed a brilliant red. It happened so suddenly that Darek almost dropped it, but he redoubled his grip on the orb even as he was forced to look away to avoid getting blinded.

"By the gods," said Aorja. "What's going on? Darek, did you do that?"

"No," said Darek, now squinting his eyes to protect them from the ever-brightening light. "This light ... it's unlike anything I've seen before."

And then he felt it. Throbbing in his hand, the life orb sent a stream of white-hot energy through his body. It made Darek feel like he had been set on fire and he wanted to scream, but he couldn't even when he opened his mouth.

Then some kind of barrier exploded out of the orb. It covered all four of them, like rats in a cage, causing Gujak to shriek in terror, while Aorja swore and Braim said, "What the hell?"

Then Darek felt some kind of outside force pulling his stomach. He tried to fight against it, because he did not know what it was, but it was too powerful and all of his struggles against it felt as fruitless as struggling against the rising tide.

So Darek gave into it, and he was soon swept away, which was the best way to describe the sensations in his body. Looking around, he saw Aorja, Braim, and Gujak also swept along with him, in a dark void that reminded him far too much of the Void's darkness, making him worry for a moment that the Void had somehow gotten them.

Yet this swept away feeling, and the dark void in which they hurtled, lasted only a moment. The next second, Darek landed on his feet and staggered across the ground he had landed on. He heard more swearing from Aorja, but he paid little attention to her bad language.

Because he was distracted by the place in which they had landed. He saw nothing more than barren earth, dead trees, and mourning skeletons wherever he looked ... and the Dark Lady herself, sitting atop her throne, looking as surprised to see them as they were to see her.

Chapter Eighteen

Stepping out of the Arcanium's lobby and onto its steps, Durima almost believed that she had somehow traveled back in time to the Katabans War, because the battle playing out—with all of the screams and noises of war—before her reminded her far too much of that conflict.

It was Uron's katabans army, almost a thousand strong, against the students and faculty of North Academy and the Undersea Institute, as well as the Xocionian Monks who had escaped Durima earlier, a similar number to Uron's army. Half of the dorms were either destroyed or on fire; in fact, she saw several of the students using their magic to hurl chunks of the destroyed dorms at the katabans, sometimes crushing three or four katabans at a time with every blow.

Yet it wasn't just the sights that reminded her of the War, but the smells. Blood and death permeated the cool winter air, with smoke from the flames stinging her nostrils, even though none of the flames were close to the Arcanium just yet. It was hard to tell how many people on each side had died yet, but as the conflict had just started, it made sense that there were few casualties so far.

She also noticed the robotic Guardian—which resembled

a giant, mechanical lizard—fighting a group of about a dozen katabans near one of the ruined dormitories. Guardian had beheaded one unfortunate katabans and crushed another to death, but as Durima watched, the other ten katabans began pummeling it with flame and rock summoned from nowhere, each blow knocking chunks off of its armor. Still Guardian fought on, which surprised Durima, as she had never thought of automatons as being all that strong.

But aside from that particular conflict, it was impossible for Durima to make out more specific battles. Lightning flashed across the battlefield, while waves of fire and waves of water crashed into each other, creating massive steam clouds that were then blown away by tornado-like gusts that came out of nowhere. Even though the battle had just started, all of the fighters on both sides (she could not think of them as soldiers, because few if any of them had any actual military experience that she knew of) were so thoroughly mixed together that it was hard to tell for sure who was one of the mages and who was one of the katabans.

Even worse, she did not see Uron or the Great Snake or whatever his name actually was. She didn't even sense him, which alarmed her greatly, because Uron was not the kind of being you could easily ignore. He had to be somewhere in the fray, but it seemed like he wasn't here at all.

So she tried to run down the front steps in order to join the battle, but then the Mysterious One's skeletal hand grabbed her shoulder. Despite how thin his hand was, his grip was as strong as iron and stopped her cold as a result.

The Mysterious One didn't try to stop anyone else. The Ghostly God and Ranama both flew past, while Jenur, Yorak, and Auratus ran down there as fast as they could. Even the Council members dashed after everyone else, with Valumor leading the others like the general he had been.

"Why did you stop me?" said Durima, trying to shrug off his hand, but he still held her tight. "I was a soldier. I know how to take care of myself in a battlefield."

"I have no doubt that that is true," said the Mysterious One. "But the mages might mistake you for the enemy. Therefore, I think it would be wise of you to stay out of this battle in order to avoid getting hurt by friendly fire."

"But ..." Durima had to admit that the Mysterious One's warning made sense, even though she was still sure she would be fine if he just let her go. "Then what am I supposed to do? Just stand around and offer moral support?"

A particularly loud explosion practically broke Durima's ears; at least, that was how it felt. Her ears rang, causing her to cover them until the Mysterious One waved his hands. Her hearing returned full-force just then, allowing her to hear the screams of dying or wounded katabans and mages battling it out on the other side of the campus.

"You will help me find Uron," said the Mysterious One, who didn't even flinch when a loud *boom* of a thunderbolt happened nearby. "You don't see him either, correct?"

"Right," said Durima, nodding. "I can't even sense him. Do you have any idea where he might be?"

The Mysterious One looked over his shoulder at the

Arcanium for some reason. The tips of his bony fingers dug more deeply into Durima's shoulder, almost painfully so, though he seemed unaware of it, as if he was so focused by whatever he saw that he had become unaware of everything else around him.

Then he said one word: "There."

Before that word had even completely escaped the Mysterious One's mouth, everything around Durima faded into darkness and silence. It almost made Durima panic before she realized that they were teleporting, though to where, she did not know.

At least, she didn't know until the darkness vanished and Durima found herself standing amid many familiar-looking tombstones, tombstones that looked newer than they should have been. A waist-high wall formed the graveyard's perimeter, while to the south the Arcanium stood tall and red, reflecting the rays of the sun, the sounds of the battle between the mages and the katabans more distant. She could no longer see the battle, but she did not have to, because she now knew why the Mysterious One had teleported him and her here.

Standing beside the tombstone of Braim Kotogs, the God-killer shining as brightly as always, was Uron. His yellow eyes, as serpentine as ever, focused on Durima and the Mysterious One as if he had not expected either of them to come, though he didn't seem very surprised at their appearance here, either.

"Long time, no see, brother," said the Mysterious One in a sardonic voice, holding his wand before him like a sword.

"I see you must have gotten rid of that spirit dragon I set on you earlier."

"I killed it," was Uron's terse answer. "How did you know I was going to be here?"

The Mysterious One gestured at the graveyard. "Because this is where you first rose. You wanted to end it where this all began. This is exactly the sort of thing that the Great Snake would do; I should know, because we worked together for untold eons before you lost your way."

Uron grabbed the back of his head as if he had a bad headache. "The Great Snake ... that name is familiar—too familiar, as if I should know it, but I don't."

"You do," said the Mysterious One. "You do. But whether you do or not, I must stand in your way because I know what you are going to do."

"Shut up," said Uron. "What do you know about any of this? You know nothing about me. You only say those words to trick me, to make me doubt myself."

"I cannot make you do anything, brother," said the Mysterious One, shaking his head. "I am only pointing out the obvious flaws I see in you. I have not lied to you or tricked you in any way so far."

"Liar," said Uron, pointing at the Mysterious One with a shaking finger. "I can tell when someone is lying. And you are lying."

"Believe what you wish, but that doesn't change the facts in the slightest," said the Mysterious One. "Now, Uron, I would rather not fight you, so if you would like to talk, then we can."

"Talk? Talk about what?" said Uron. He gestured toward the Arcanium. "I did not come this far just to 'talk.' If you truly do not want to fight me, then run back to whatever hole you crawled out of, you pathetic excuse for a god, and allow me to do what I came here to do, what I was *meant* to do."

"Not unless we stop you first," said Durima. She didn't cower underneath Uron's glare, despite knowing just how powerful he was.

"Stop me? You two? I doubt it," said Uron. He held the God-killer up before him. "Durima, do you remember what I told you about the God-killer's other abilities? It was a while ago, but I hope you are smart enough to remember."

Durima furrowed her brow, thinking back to the time when Uron had told her about it. "Yes ... yes, I do recall you saying something about unlocking the God-killer's true power, but I didn't understand what you meant by that."

"The God-killer can do more than simply kill a god by touching them," said Uron. He closed his fingers, forming a fist. "That is the simplest way to use it, but also the least efficient. There is another power it has, one that would make all gods everywhere tremble in fear of its power if they knew of it."

"What else can it do?" said Durima, shivering slightly as a cold breeze blew through just then. She looked up at the Mysterious One. "Do you know?"

"Yes, I do," said the Mysterious One, though without looking down at Durima. "The God-killer used to be in my island, after all, so I probably know the extent of its powers better than Uron."

"Then you know that I need only to take the God-killer to the lowest levels of the Arcanium," said Uron, "and once I do, expose it to the power lying underneath the school. This will then send a shock wave of power throughout all of Martir that will kill every single god and goddess on this useless world."

Durima stepped back in horror. "How come you've never mentioned this before?"

"A clever being such as myself never reveals his full hand to anyone," said Uron, shaking his head. "And I wouldn't have revealed it now, either, if I had not run into you two. Not that it matters; the two of you could not defeat me even if you tried."

"You and I both know that that is not true," said the Mysterious One. "If anyone is the liar around here, it is you."

"If you could defeat me, you would have done so already," said Uron. "But I guess you have the right to try—and fail—to stop me. I ordinarily wouldn't waste my time with such obvious pieces of trash, but I can tell that I will have to do so if I am going to get anywhere."

Uron held his fists up in a fighting position while repositioning his legs, perhaps to give him better footing in the graveyard. The Mysterious One's wand began to glow brightly, while Durima just crouched lower, despite knowing full well that she could not possibly survive a fight against Uron, even with the Mysterious One by her side.

The only other alternative is to run away, though,

Durima thought. *And I will not run away. Not now, not this time, because there is nowhere to run to.*

When she blinked, Uron was gone, like he had vanished into thin air. His sudden disappearance would have taken her by surprise, but Durima, knowing what to expect, jumped forward just as Uron reappeared behind her and brought both of his fists down onto the ground.

The impact of his fists onto the ground actually created a brief tremor that sent Durima staggering. She caught herself, however, and turned around in time to see the Mysterious One jabbing his wand in Uron's face.

A huge stream of fire shot out of the Mysterious One's wand, flowing over Uron's face like a cloud. Uron hissed in anger and lashed out at the Mysterious One, but he merely jumped back out of his brother's reach, causing Uron's fist to miss.

But the Mysterious One kept up the stream of flame, which was so hot that even Durima could feel it, despite not being next to the fire. The stream soon grew wide enough to encompass all of Uron's body, completely obscuring his whole form from Durima's vision.

Then, without warning, the flames scattered everywhere. They rolled over the Mysterious One, who with a wave of his wand caused the flames to go around him without touching him, while Durima summoned a rock wall that protected her from the worst of it. Nonetheless, as the flames passed around the rock wall, a few sparks burnt her fur; not enough to harm her, but enough to make her doubt the safety of her wall.

Thankfully, the flames were gone in a minute, though the rock wall was now charred and smoking and smelled like burned stone. She looked around it to get a good look at Uron, who still stood where he had been standing when the Mysterious One had tried to burn him.

His skin wasn't even darkened, though it was hard to tell for sure due to his purplish-black skin. It was as though those flames hadn't touched him at all, which did nothing to raise Durima's courage.

Then Uron slammed the God-killer into his other hand and ran at the Mysterious One. He pulled his fist back and launched it at the Mysterious One, moving so fast that Durima's eyes could barely follow.

The Mysterious One, however, merely moved to the side, dodging Uron's fist. As he did so, the Mysterious One tapped Uron's back with his wand as the serpentine being's trajectory carried him past his brother.

Another flash of light, this time in the spot that the Mysterious One had tapped, and Uron went flying through the air uncontrollably. He flew through the air in an arc and landed flat on his back on the other side of the graveyard, between two tombstones made of some kind of black rock.

But Uron didn't stay down. He grabbed the two tombstones and used them to help him get back to his feet. He shook his head and then aimed the God-killer at the Mysterious One.

A loud *bang* issued from the God-killer, and a rope-like string of that slimy black stuff Uron could make flew from it. The string rapidly grew thicker and darker as it soared, until it resembled a thick snake, similar to how Uron had looked prior to gaining his current body, with giant yellow fangs that looked as sharp as swords.

The Mysterious One raised his wand and jerked it to the side. About midway between Uron and the Mysterious One, the strange snake-like creature exploded, but as it did so, Uron launched himself through the purplish mist left in its wake. He landed right in front of the Mysterious One and then delivered a devastating uppercut to his brother, with a loud cracking sound issuing from the Mysterious One's chin.

Durima gaped as Uron's uppercut launched the Mysterious One into the air. He went straight up, like a water spout, and seemed completely out of control of his trajectory.

At least, Durima assumed that, until the Mysterious One stopped in midair and floated there. His jaw hung beneath his mouth, like it was dislocated, but then he pushed it back into place with his free hand, creating another cracking sound that made Durima wince.

Then the Mysterious One tapped the magic stone on his arm as he pointed his wand at Uron. Some kind of strange, whitish-gray mist shot out of his wand, wrapping itself around Uron's body like a rope.

Uron struggled against the mist, but it must have been much stronger than it looked because it didn't budge. Then it began to encase his whole form, like a cocoon, but then the mist shattered as Uron broke through its smooth surface with his arms and legs.

Rolling his shoulders, Uron said, "Is that the best you've got, Mysterious One? Because so far I am unimpressed."

The Mysterious One said nothing in reply; instead, he disappeared and then reappeared behind Uron. Another wave of his wand and a dozen Mysterious Ones surrounded Uron on every side. They were all so lifelike that even Durima could not tell which one was the real one.

Uron whipped his head in every direction, like he was just as confused as she was. The Mysterious Ones all raised their wands and pointed them at Uron as their wands began to glow red. Durima did not know what kind of spell the Mysterious One was going to cast on Uron, but she doubted it was going to be good.

Uron must have had the same thought, because he lashed out at the nearest Mysterious One. His fist passed through its head, causing the illusion to vanish, while the one directly behind Uron fired a dark-red energy blast that burned through the air.

The energy blast struck Uron in the back, sending him staggering forward like he had actually been hurt. That surprised—and pleased—Durima, as she had not thought it was possible for anyone to actually harm Uron.

It wasn't the decisive blow, however, because Uron then turned around and fired a blast of dark energy in the direction of the real Mysterious One. The dark energy passed through the illusion, however, and then all of the fake Mysterious Ones vanished, although the real one was now nowhere to be seen.

Even Durima didn't know where the actual Mysterious

One had gone. No matter where she looked, she saw no sign of him anywhere, and she did not sense him, either. She doubted he had run away, but the more time that passed without even a hint of the Mysterious One's presence, the more she wondered if he actually had fled.

Then the Mysterious One abruptly appeared behind Uron. He rested a hand on Uron's shoulder, causing Uron to start.

That was the only reaction Uron could do, however, because in the next instant, both the Mysterious One and Uron disappeared. Durima looked around for them in surprise, but she didn't see either of them anywhere. All she saw was the empty graveyard, which now felt very lonely, despite the sounds of battle still raging from beyond the Arcanium in the distance.

Barely breathing—she wasn't sure why, probably because it was a tense situation—Durima stepped out from behind the charred, smoking rock wall she had summoned earlier. She expected Uron and the Mysterious One to show up any minute now, but as the seconds ticked by, she was starting to believe that both of them were gone for good.

That's a silly idea, Durima told herself. *They're not gone forever. Uron is probably trying to get back here as fast as he can. No way he will simply stay wherever the Mysterious One just took him.*

She heard something scraping against the stone path of the graveyard and, thinking it was Uron, looked to her right and raised her fist. A tiny insect—one with golden wings and a snow-white body, though she could not identify the species—crawled along the stone path, seemingly unaware of the chaotic fight that had been going on not more than one hundred yards away.

Sighing in relief, Durima lowered her fist. Maybe the Mysterious One had indeed succeeded in taking Uron away from North Academy; if so, then perhaps everything was going to be all right after all.

Then she heard the familiar *pop* of an ethereal portal opening and closing and whirled around to see who had arrived. Even before she turned around completely, she knew it had to be one of the katabans under Uron's control; who else would use the ethereal to sneak up on her, if they were not going to try to kill her?

And she was right. Standing about two dozen yards down the stone path of the graveyard was Garvan. He held a sharp-looking crystalline knife in his hand, but he did not look like he had been fighting with his fellow katabans against the mages of North Academy. In fact, he didn't look like he had been fighting anyone at all, based on the lack of injuries on his body, which made Durima wonder what he had been doing instead.

"Durima?" said Garvan in a fake surprised voice, though Durima wasn't fooled by his falseness. "I didn't expect to see you here. I thought you were back in that battle at the Arcanium."

"Cut the crap, Garvan," said Durima. She nodded at his knife. "I know why you're here: You came here to kill me."

Garvan's feigned surprised expression turned into a twisted smile. "I always intended to kill you, Durima. I planned to do it before the attack, but when Uron came by and told us that you had betrayed us, well, I was forced to put it off."

Durima pointed one of her claws at Garvan. "Let me guess: You're the spy that the Council hired to infiltrate Uron's army and kill me, right?"

This time, when Garvan gasped, his shock appeared entirely real. "How did you know? I thought I hid my tracks carefully."

"Because you were the very first to arrive and were too quick to become my biggest supporter," said Durima. "I have some experience dealing with traitors. Often, they'll try to become your best friend first, and once they succeed in that, then they drive the knife deep into your back when you least expect it. Though to your credit, I didn't even start to suspect you until the Council told me there was a spy in Uron's army."

Garvan shook his head and looked at her again. His confident smile had returned, even though Durima could still tell that he was more than a little shocked by Durima's seeing through his trickery.

"It doesn't matter how you figured out," said Garvan. "What matters is that I am going to kill you where you stand."

"Why?" said Durima, standing her ground even when Garvan took a step forward. "I no longer serve Uron. You should ask the Council; they can tell you all about my betrayal of him."

"You think I still care about what those old coots have to

say?" said Garvan. He laughed. "It is painfully obvious now that Uron is going to win. I used to be loyal to the gods and to the Council, true, but at heart, I am a pragmatist. Siding with Uron is the most pragmatic thing anyone can do right now; it is the only way to survive."

"Uron lied to you and to all of those other idiots who follow him," said Durima, nodding at the Arcanium in the distance as a loud *boom* echoed from beyond it. "He's not going to spare the lives of anyone on Martir, not even the lives of his allies. He's a monster through and through who sees everyone as either tools to be used or obstacles to be crushed."

"Just why should I believe a word you just said?" said Garvan. "Even if what you say is true, I am sure he will spare me, at least, after I cut off your head and deliver it to him on a silver platter. He was absolutely enraged when he told us about your betrayal; I almost think that your betrayal actually hurt him, somehow."

"I doubt it," said Durima. "Uron never actually cared about me. He's probably just angry that I don't support him anymore."

Garvan cast a cursory look around the graveyard. "Just where *is* Lord Uron, anyway? I thought he would be here."

"He's gone," said Durima. "You just missed him. And no, I don't know where he went. All I know is that he's nowhere in North Academy, maybe not even in the Great Berg anymore."

Garvan's face went even paler. No surprise there; while the katabans army following Uron was a formidable force, the mages had two gods on their side. Assuming Uron actually was gone for good, then that meant it was only a matter of time before Garvan's allies were defeated.

Not to mention Garvan himself was hardly a threatening force. He was quite thin and pale, and the awkward way in which he held his knife showed that he clearly had very little, if any at all, experience in battle. That could have been a ruse, perhaps, but Durima didn't think so.

Durima rolled her shoulders. "Well, Garvan, now that you've shown your true colors, I guess I don't have to hold back anymore. By the time I'm done with you, I doubt you'll be very recognizable as anything more than mush."

Chapter Nineteen

The Dark Lady resembled the carvings of her on the Arch back on the borders of the Spirit Lands, except far more real. Her hair was as stringy and gray as always, her eyes a terrifying red, and her yellowed fingernails as long as knife blades. She wore a long black dress with tattered edges and holes on the blouse. One of the holes was near her breasts, giving Darek a glimpse of her skin underneath, which was a sick-looking yellow that would have made him throw up if he had a stomach. It sharply contrasted with her face and hands, which were far paler than that.

The throne she sat upon was made out of bones. Mostly arm and leg bones, though the ends of the throne's arms were skulls with puncture marks in them. The Dark Lady's thin, long fingers gripped the skulls as she looked down on all four of them.

As for the rest of their environment, it was a wide-open plain with a depressing gray-and-red sky. Skeletons of all shapes and sizes knelt in a circle everywhere, their heads pointed toward the Dark Lady's throne, as if they were worshiping her. But Darek only heard mourning sounds from the skeletons, mutterings of regret and sadness, so bleak that even he began to feel depressed.

Twisted, dead trees dotted the landscape around them, trees with human-like eyes on their branches. There weren't many of the trees, but there were enough to make Darek feel unnerved, mostly by the dead, gray eyes on them.

About the only good thing about this place was the complete lack of draggers, which told Darek that he must have destroyed quite a few if he didn't see any around here. Of course, maybe the Dark Lady didn't like having her servants in the vicinity of her throne, but whatever the case, he was glad they weren't here.

Though considering we're standing right in front of the Dark Lady's throne, maybe I don't have as much to be glad about as I thought, Darek thought, looking up at the Dark Lady, who, sitting on her throne, was dozens of feet taller than all four of them combined.

The Dark Lady looked down at them with surprise. "What? How did you ghosts get here?"

The Arbiter's life orb burned in Darek's hand, as if the presence of the Dark Lady had set off some kind of alarm. He held the orb up to his chest and said, "We're just as confused as you are about how we got here, Dark Lady, but it's pretty obvious what we've got to do: Take you down."

The Dark Lady's surprise turned into amusement as she laughed. "You four tiny little ghosts, defeat me? Please. I am on an entirely different level from you four. I could crush you without even thinking about it."

"Then why don't you do it?" said Aorja, her voice steady as she stood beside Darek. "Come on. What are you waiting for? Are you afraid we'll bite?"

"Foolish girl," said the Dark Lady. She stretched out her hand toward them. "But very well. If corruption is what you seek, then corruption is what you will get."

Then the Dark Lady paused, like she had just remembered something important that she had forgotten earlier. Her red eyes focused on the orb in Darek's hand, which glowed softly beneath his fingers.

"Is that ..." the Dark Lady seemed hardly capable of finishing her sentence. "Is that ... my brother's life orb?"

"If by 'brother' you mean 'the Arbiter,' then yes, it is," said Darek. "I thought you'd remember it, given I used it to destroy your entire army of draggers just a few minutes ago."

"I remember it well," said the Dark Lady. "I can guess that my brother's life orb must have teleported you here so that you could confront me directly. My brother always did prefer direct confrontation to indirect confrontation, after all."

Then she raised one of her hands. "But I also know that it will not help you to survive my power."

She closed her hand, but just as she did that, Darek raised the life orb and fired a red energy beam at her. The beam shot through the air like an arrow, striking the Dark Lady directly in the forehead.

The Dark Lady lowered her outstretched hand as she yelled in pain, covering the spot Darek had hit with her other hand. Smoke rose from her forehead, like a fire had started on her face.

"Whoa, Darek," said Braim, sounding impressed. "How

did you know that would hurt her?"

Darek shook his head. "Just a lucky guess."

Sadly, the victory was short-lived, because when the Dark Lady lowered her hand, the hole was no longer there. Nor did it smoke anymore, although the Dark Lady still looked absolutely furious, as if she could not believe what had just happened.

"Lucky shot, you little bastard," said the Dark Lady. "You are the first ghost to ever land a direct blow on me. Not only that, but it hurt ... and I *hate* hurting."

The Dark Lady stood up from her throne. Darek held the life orb before him, while Braim held his blade in a battle stance, and Aorja stepped back in hesitation. Gujak, meanwhile, just cowered in fear behind them.

"I will make you feel pain worse than any you have ever felt in your life," said the Dark Lady, her voice deepening unnaturally. "And for you, it will never, ever end, because you cannot die."

Then the Dark Lady began to grow. She grew taller and taller; she had already been tall before, but now she was becoming gigantic. She became so big that she actually stepped on her throne, crunching it into pieces, and still she grew, seemingly without taking any notice of her now-destroyed throne.

And when she stopped growing, she was so tall that Darek couldn't have reached her face even if he jumped as high as he could. Her fingers had to be as tall as the Arcanium, while her feet were as wide as a flat-bottomed ship.

The skeletons bowing around her immediately got up and ran, though they made not a sound as they did so. They ran into holes in the ground or behind the hills that rose up all around. Darek almost wished he could join them, because he was not so sure now that they could defeat someone as huge as the Dark Lady herself.

"Feel the pain that you inflicted on me," said the Dark Lady, her voice bellowing like a cannon shot. "And feel it forever!"

She raised one bare, pale foot and brought it down on Darek and everyone else. The four of them scattered, even Gujak, who apparently wasn't as frozen by fear as he had appeared. The Dark Lady's foot crashed into the ground, creating a tremor that made Darek stagger before he regained his balance.

Looking up, Darek saw the Dark Lady's massive head turning this way and that, like she was trying to decide who to go after next. Darek knew that none of the others, not even Braim, stood much of a chance against the Dark Lady, so if she went after anyone except for himself, they would surely get corrupted by her power.

So Darek raised the life orb and fired another energy beam at her. The beam stuck her ankle, barely leaving so much as a scratch on her skin, but the Dark Lady must have noticed, because she turned her attention to Darek now, a deep growl emitting from her throat as she glared down on him.

"The others can wait," said the Dark Lady. She pointed a massive finger at him. "*You* will be the first to feel my pain."

A disgusting-looking brown wave flowed from the tip of her finger like a water fountain. The wave came toward Darek so fast that there was no time for him to dodge it.

But he didn't need to. He held up the life orb and squeezed it, causing a red barrier to form over his body just as the Dark Lady's wave of corruption hit him.

The red barrier flashed and cracked under the pressure of the Dark Lady's corruption wave, but it held and not even one bit of the wave got through. Unfortunately, the wave clung to the barrier like barnacles on the hull of a ship, but Darek just squeezed the orb again and the barrier erupted into flames, completely incinerating the corruption that had covered it.

As soon as the last of the corruption was gone, Darek dropped the barrier and looked up at the Dark Lady once more. He did not see her face because her foot was coming down toward him again, forcing Darek to jump back from underneath its shadow.

Thanks to the lighter than usual gravity in this place (assuming this place even had gravity at all), Darek's jump took him back far. But the Dark Lady must have known he was going to try something like that, because she immediately kicked forward, rather than bring her foot all the way down.

Having failed to predict that movement of hers, Darek was unable to dodge it. The tip of her foot's toes struck him dead on, hitting him with enough force to send him flying backwards even faster than before.

Darek crashed into the dirt, bouncing off it a few times

before coming to a halt. He couldn't get up because his body was paralyzed with pain from that blow, pain that felt just as bad as if he still had a physical body.

At least I still have the Arbiter's life orb, Darek thought through his pain-filled mind. *Right?*

That was when he realized that his hand was empty. He looked down at his hand, hoping that maybe he had just lost feeling in it or something, but no, the life orb was no longer between his fingers. He realized he must have lost it at some point when the Dark Lady kicked him, though that did little to help him figure out where it was now.

He looked around the bleak landscape, searching for any sign of the orb. Thankfully, he soon spotted it: It lay about a dozen yards from where he lay, which was within his reach if he would stretch a little.

Darek reached for it, but paused when the Dark Lady roared, "No, you don't, you little bastard!"

Alarmed, Darek looked back in the direction he had come flying from. The Dark Lady was walking toward him as fast as she could, each giant step of hers closing the ever-smaller gap between them. It would only be seconds before she was upon him again, which meant there was no time to waste.

He crawled across the ground, reaching out as far as he could with his hand, but the Dark Lady was getting closer and closer to him much faster than he was getting to the orb. He almost gave up, but when he remembered what the consequences of giving up would be, he kept crawling.

Then his fingers wrapped around the orb just as the

Dark Lady's foot appeared over him again. Without thinking, Darek raised the life orb and fired another beam of energy at the underside of the Dark Lady's foot.

The beam struck, causing her to shriek in pain, but her foot was still coming toward him even as he increased the output of the energy beam. No use. The foot came closer and closer and this time he was sure that he was a goner because even if he tried to run, he would not be fast enough to avoid getting stepped on.

But then the red barrier from earlier rematerialized over his body, although it looked stronger and thicker now than it had before. Just as it finished materializing over him, the Dark Lady's foot came down like a falling building.

Darek was certain that the barrier would collapse under the Dark Lady's weight, but much to his surprise, the barrier held. The underside of the Dark Lady's foot completely blacked out his environment, but thanks to the dim red glow of the barrier, he could see that the barrier wasn't even bending underneath the Dark Lady's weight.

As stunned as Darek was, he knew better than to just lie there and stare at the barrier with his mouth hanging open. He rose to his feet and squeezed the life orb in his hand again. He did not know if that would do anything, but he did not want to spend the rest of his days trapped underneath the Dark Lady's foot, so he had to try.

The red barrier brightened so much that Darek had to cover his eyes to protect his vision. At the same time, the Dark Lady's cries of pain told him that the red barrier must be hurting her somehow, unless someone else was causing that pain, though he doubted it.

Keep it up, Darek thought, tightening his grip around the orb. *Don't let that monster have even a moment to relax.*

He thrust his arm upwards. The barrier expanded sharply, raising the Dark Lady's foot up. That movement messed up the Dark Lady's balance, causing her to stagger backwards as she hopped on her left foot, her right foot burning from where she had stepped on the barrier.

Not only that, but she appeared to be rapidly shrinking down to a much more reasonable size. Darek wondered if this was because of the red barrier or if maybe she was doing this of her own free will; either way, size mattered little with her, because she still seemed as powerful as always.

Soon, the Dark Lady had returned to her original size. She was still quite tall, but no longer monstrously so. She gingerly put her right foot down on the ground, wincing as she did so, causing Darek to wonder how much he had hurt her.

"Decided that being a giant wasn't all its cracked up to be?" said Darek as the red barrier zapped back into the life orb. "Or did I hurt you that badly?"

The Dark Lady scowled, though she winced again due to the pain in her foot. "So arrogant. You think I need to be a giant in order to swat you like an insect." Her voice was still unnaturally deep.

"Hey, I didn't say you needed to be," said Darek with a shrug. "You just chose to do that of your own free will."

The Dark Lady pointed at one of the nearby dead trees. As soon as she did, the tree's limbs extended and twisted through the air toward Darek. They came at him fast as lightning, but somehow Darek could see their every movement, as if they were moving in slow motion instead. Perhaps the life orb was helping him see the tree limbs as they actually moved.

Whatever the reason, Darek lifted the life orb in front of him as it glowed red again. A solid wall of reddish energy appeared in front of him, which the tree's limbs slammed into so hard that they broke into twigs and fell to the ground with a clatter.

Lowering the shield, Darek said, "Is that your best shot?"

"Your puny ghostly mind cannot even comprehend my 'best shot,' as you put it," said the Dark Lady. She raised her skeletal, thin fingers again. "Besides, I see no reason to waste my best abilities and moves on such a pathetic creature."

"You're only saying that because you're angry you haven't corrupted me yet," said Darek, gesturing at himself. "Kind of throws your whole 'puny ghost' theory straight into the trash, doesn't it?"

The Dark Lady roared in anger, but before she could attack, the tip of a long green blade pierced through her chest. Shocked, the Dark Lady looked down at the blade, while Darek just stared, for a moment as ignorant as the Dark Lady was of whoever had stabbed her.

Then Braim's goateed face appeared over the Dark Lady's shoulder as he said, "Take this, you ugly monster!"

How Braim managed to sneak up on the Dark Lady and attack her like that, Darek didn't know. He just watched as Braim's blade glowed brighter and brighter, like it was charging with energy.

Then a massive *bang* erupted from Braim's blade and the Dark Lady exploded with green energy. Darek summoned a barrier with the life orb to avoid the worst of it, but the explosion was so enormous that for a moment Darek couldn't see anything but green wherever he looked. His hearing was drowned out by the roar of the explosion, so loud in his ears that it was like standing in the middle of a bomb going off.

Yet the explosion lasted only for perhaps a minute, and then it was gone just as abruptly as it came. The shield stood as strong as ever, having protected Dark from the explosion. Because the barrier was transparent, he could see Braim standing there, apparently unharmed from the explosion, holding his blade as if he was still stabbing it through the Dark Lady's chest.

The Dark Lady herself was nowhere to be seen. There was not even one trace of that horrible woman no matter where he looked. It was like she had been completely evaporated from existence, though Darek was skeptical that anyone, even someone like Braim, could actually kill her. That still did not explain exactly *what* had happened to her, though, or where she was now.

At that moment, Aorja and Gujak ran into Darek's line of sight. He didn't know where they had come from; perhaps they had been hiding behind one of the nearby trees, though he noticed that the one that the Dark Lady had used to attack him was now utterly demolished, likely a victim of that massive explosion.

Braim lowered his blade at his side, looking exhausted from the effort of that gesture alone. "Whew. That was tougher than I expected."

Darek tilted his head to the side. "Um, what did you do to her? Is the Dark Lady actually gone for good?"

"'Course she's not," said Braim, shaking his head. "I had no idea that I could even hurt her. I attacked her purely on a whim; if it had failed, I would have become the first male dragger. I gotta tell you, that probably would have been very horrifying and very awkward, all at the same time."

"Then what *did* you do to her?" said Aorja, looking around wildly, as if she expected the Dark Lady to return any moment. "Will she come back?"

"I blew her up," said Braim. "Duh. As for if she'll come back, yeah, probably. We ghosts aren't strong enough to kill beings like her or the Arbiter on our own, after all. I didn't even know I could touch her."

"What do we do now?" said Darek, scratching the back of his head. "I mean, if she's not a threat at the moment—"

Darek knew he shouldn't have said that, because as soon as he did, the ground rumbled beneath their feet. All four of them looked down at the ground, which continued to rumble and shake as if a volcano was erupting somewhere nearby.

Then the ground split open beneath them and they all fell down before they could even scream.

Chapter Twenty

Garvan raised his knife and ran at Durima, leaving a wide opening for her to attack once he was close enough. A rookie's mistake, which told Durima that this idiot clearly knew nothing about fighting.

So she dashed toward him, already thinking about how she would easily dodge his knife and then knock him out with a solid uppercut to the jaw. He looked so thin and fragile that she doubted she would even need to use her full strength to take him out.

Once Durima was within range, Garvan brought his knife down on her, but he was so clumsy that Durima simply moved a few inches to the right to avoid his attack.

But then Garvan's knife suddenly shifted in that direction as well and cut through Durima's shoulder. It wasn't a deep cut, mostly because Durima jumped back as soon as she felt the steel bite at her skin, but it hurt enough to throw her off balance. She staggered to the left, gripping her now-bleeding shoulder, while Garvan advanced on her with a wicked, crazy grin on his face.

"Thought I was some kind of amateur, did you?" said Garvan, his voice filled with hideous delight. "I fought in the Katabans War, too, you know. I was trained as a knifer by Ooka, the God of Shadows and Knives himself, and one of the things he taught me was how to take advantage of your larger enemies who think that just because you've got a knife, you're a weakling who can be easily beat."

There was no time for Durima to heal her shoulder wound, even though she wanted to. Garvan had gone from running clumsily to walking as smoothly as if he was skating across ice.

Durima staggered past one of the tombstones, which she slammed her fist on as she passed it. When her fist made contact with the tombstone, she activated her geomancy, taking control of the stone and making it her own.

Then she raised her fist and pointed at Garvan. The tombstone wrenched itself from the earth and went flying toward Garvan as though someone had thrown it, causing Garvan to gasp in surprise.

But his surprise must have been false, because he ducked, successfully avoiding the flying tombstone. The tombstone crashed behind him, knocking over another headstone as it did so, while Garvan stood back up to his full height and continued advancing on Durima.

"Throwing rocks at me won't do you any good, Demon," said Garvan, holding his knife before him threateningly. "All it does it make you look like a fool."

Durima kept walking backwards, trying to think of some move she could use to take him down. Unfortunately, Durima had never been good at fighting knifers, because they were often small and agile, much more agile than her large body could move. She remembered hearing stories about knifers during the Katabans War, how many of them gained reputations for efficient viciousness, and how she had sustained quite a few injuries from knifers on the enemy side, though she never had to fight any alone.

Now, however, Tinkar must have decided that she couldn't be that lucky anymore, if the fact that she had to confront Garvan by herself meant anything. She knew that Garvan just needed one good opening to strike like a snake and slit her throat like an envelope.

Can't focus on that, Durima thought. *Must focus on the fight.*

Garvan was much closer to her now, but still outside of her reach. There was murder in his eyes, plain and simple, a look Durima had seen in many of her fellow katabans during the War, and the only way to sate that lust for murder was for him to kill her in cold blood.

Then, without warning, Garvan lunged forward, his knife held out directly in front of him like a spear. He moved almost too fast for Durima's eyes to follow. She tried to jumped back out of his reach anyway, but the pain in her bleeding shoulder flared, temporarily distracting her and causing her to stagger and stumble.

She saw Garvan's knife coming for her face and she could not move fast enough to dodge it. The knife pierced her skull and for a moment all Durima saw, knew, or felt was pain.

And then a blissfulness unlike anything she had felt before came over her mind and she no longer thought or felt anything.

Chapter Twenty-One

The gray sky of the Unknown above quickly became a tiny circle as Darek and the others fell. Darek reached out toward it, despite knowing that it was well out of his reach, while Braim, Aorja, and especially Gujak screamed for their lives.

They fell and fell and fell for what felt like an eternity. As when they had flown on that spirit dragon before, there was no wind blowing through their hair or in their ears because there was no air in here. And though Darek looked over his shoulder, he did not see what might await them at the bottom, though he doubted it would be any good.

The pit into which they fell was pitch black, but Darek could hear skittering sounds across the walls all around them, like they had fallen into the hive of some kind of monstrous insect species. He couldn't see any of them, however, nor did he want to. Something told him that if he could, he would have gone entirely insane.

Then they hit the ground hard. The pain wasn't as bad as it would have been, perhaps, if they had had physical bodies; however, the impact was hardly comfortable and made Darek's head spin. He didn't drop the life orb, though, because even though he could not see anything in this darkness, he could see the orb, still shining as brightly and warmly as ever.

"Ow," said Aorja's voice from somewhere in the shadows around him. "Where are we?"

"Not sure," came Braim's voice from Darek's left. "Probably a trap set by the Dark Lady."

"I'm scared," said Gujak's whimpering voice. "So, so scared. I want to go home."

"Home?" came the familiar, aged voice of the Dark Lady from somewhere within the shadows. "Why, you *are* home, petty ghosts. This is the true home of all who are as wicked as you four have been."

Dull yellow lights flickered on all around them, though the lights were erratic, as if their power source was unstable. Even so, Darek was glad that there was at least some light by which to see, for the darkness down here was almost as black as the Void's, until he saw the Dark Lady.

She no longer looked like an unusually tall, evil woman. In fact, she didn't have a body at all. It was her face, enlarged to a hundred times its normal size, sticking out of the cracked stone wall opposite them. Her face looked like a skinless human face, with the muscles and blood and brain exposed, her teeth as blunted, yellow, and crooked as ever. Her eyes were like lamps in that they swept over the assembled ghosts, bathing them in her awful red light.

Gujak opened his mouth, probably to scream, but not a single solitary sound escaped his lips. He was stuck in a silent scream and Darek, for once, didn't think his cowardice was inappropriate for this moment. Because right now, he also wanted to scream at the thing that gazed down upon them like they were going to be its next meal.

"Did you honestly believe that blowing up that temporary form of mine would keep me away, even for a little while?" said the Dark Lady, her voice deeper than ever. "You silly ghosts. Only my brothers could even come close to scratching me, and right now they are nowhere to be seen."

"But I still have the life orb," said Darek, raising the orb above his head, trying not to show his fear. "It's the power of the Arbiter, who you keep calling your brother. Doesn't that put me on the same power level as you?"

The Dark Lady's laugh was harsh and cruel. "Funny, funny, funny. That little orb gave you a surprising edge, I will admit, but only we Almighty Ones can access the orb's true power. Besides, it is weakened, because its original owner is dying, so you are still only slightly stronger than you would be otherwise."

"Bitch," Aorja sneered. She stood up and gestured with one finger. "Why don't you get another body and actually fight us like a real woman? Or are you just all talk and no action?"

"I can fight you perfectly well in my current form," said the Dark Lady. "Indeed, I'd say this form is even better for corrupting you ghosts than my other form was."

A hand broke out of the floor nearby, causing Darek and the others to move to avoid it, but then they were forced to move again when another hand, identical to the last, burst out of the floor. The two hands were connected to arms, arms that were as skinless and veiny as the Dark Lady's face, with fingers as big as logs.

The hands reached toward Darek and the others. Darek raised the life orb, but before he could use it to protect them from the hands, the Dark Lady shrieked loud enough to startle him. Unfortunately, he also dropped the life orb, which rolled away out of his reach as soon as it touched the ground.

Braim aimed his blade at the incoming hands and fired off several energy blasts. The blasts struck the hands dead on, but the blasts barely fazed them, which kept coming as if they had not been hit at all.

"Suffer," said the Dark Lady, whose eyes now glowed even more malevolently than ever. "Suffer under my wrath, you pathetic worms. Feel my pain ... feel it!"

Darek and the others backed up away from the hands, but it wasn't like there was anywhere for them to run to. The pit had no escape routes, no doors or hallways for them to flee inside. They were trapped, it seemed, and they had no way to defend themselves, either.

His hands curling into fists, Darek could only watch as the massive hands drew closer and closer every second. He wondered what it would feel like to be corrupted before snapping out of it and telling himself to stop wondering about such useless things and to instead focus on finding a way to avoid getting corrupted by those hands.

But no ideas came to him. It felt like every good idea he had ever had rapidly drained from his mind like water into a sewer system. It was fear, he realized, fear of the Dark Lady paralyzing him like a poison. That fear must have always been there, but he had not noticed it until now, perhaps because of the Arbiter's life orb granting him his earlier confidence.

Right before the fingers of the hands touched them, they froze. Darek held his breath, despite technically not having any breath to hold, his eyes fixated on the now-frozen, meaty fingers hovering before them. He glanced at Aorja, Braim, and Gujak, who all appeared just as shocked as he was by this strange turn of events.

Before he or any of the others could ask what was going on, the Dark Lady's eyes widened. And she whispered, "Do you feel that?"

Darek was about to ask what 'that' was—although he wondered if he could even do that much, he was so paralyzed with fear—when two beings appeared in the shadows of the pit above them. It was like they had simply materialized out of nowhere, which was the only explanation that Darek could come up with to explain their sudden appearance, as he had not heard or sensed either of them arrive until the instant he laid eyes on them.

The dull yellow lights running along the walls barely showed much, but they did show that one of the beings was a skeleton wearing auburn robes, while the other was a naked, muscular humanoid with purplish-black skin. The two beings hovered in the air for a moment, maybe shocked at where they had ended up (though it was hard to tell for sure because Darek couldn't see their faces) before the one with purplish-black skin punched the skeleton wearing the robes.

The skeleton flew over the Dark Lady's frozen hands toward Darek and the others. He looked like he was going to crash into them, but then he vanished and reappeared standing next to them instead. His skull was cracked—likely from the punch from the being who had punched him—but aside from that, he didn't look as terrible as he could have.

Nonetheless, Darek could not help but stare at the newcomer, unable to believe what he was seeing. "The Mysterious One? What are *you* doing here?"

The Mysterious One rubbed the side of his face, the part where he had been punched, as he said, "To return Uron to where he belongs, of course."

"Wait," said Aorja, leaning forward to look around Darek at the Mysterious One. "*You're* the legendary Mysterious One I've heard so much about?"

"Of course," said the Mysterious One, nodding. He gestured at Darek and Gujak. "Just ask either of them. They know me."

Gujak—whose mouth had been open in a silent scream the entire time—closed his mouth, his eyes flickering in confusion. Then he said, "Wait ... I think I remember you. But my memory ... it's still bad."

"Don't worry," said the Mysterious One. He nodded at Uron, who was now floating down to the ground below. "You don't need to remember me. Just know that I am on your side and am ready to help you save Martir and the Spirit Lands."

Then the Mysterious One pointed his wand at the hands. A flash of light shot from the tip of his wand and struck the giant fingers, instantly evaporating them into nothingness. The Dark Lady growled in pain, but she did not say or do anything else because her eyes were currently focused on Uron, who now stood on the floor.

Uron kept looking in every direction, like he was trying to find out where he was and what was going on. The God-killer still covered his hand, which made Darek wonder how he had managed to take it with him from Martir. He supposed it didn't really matter, because Uron was a huge threat whether or not he had it.

"What?" said Uron. "Where am I? What is this place? How did I get here?"

"I took you here, brother," said the Mysterious One, gesturing at the pit's high, dark walls. "I took you home."

"Home?" said Darek, looking at the Mysterious One blankly. "What do you mean by that? And why did you call him 'brother'?"

"I mean exactly what I said, Darek," said the Mysterious One. "This place is where Uron—no, the Great Snake—used to live, but that is a long, detailed story we have no time to delve into right now. All you need to know is that this may be the only place where we can actually do Uron any real, lasting harm."

"Wait," said Aorja, glaring at the Mysterious One. "Could you have done this the whole freaking time? You know, just take Uron and teleport him here, where he can't escape?"

"It's not that simple, Aorja," said the Mysterious One, shaking his head. He lowered his voice, almost like he didn't want Uron or the Dark Lady to listen in. "Uron could escape from here if he wanted to or knew how; besides, I didn't want to take him here in the first place because that would mean reuniting him with the Dark Lady, which is a very bad thing. I only did this because I had no choice, considering what Uron would have done to Martir if I hadn't taken him here."

Darek was about to ask just how the hell they were going to defeat Uron and the Dark Lady, when the Dark Lady said, "Brother, is that you?"

Uron turned to face the Dark Lady, raising his head to look up at her. "Who are you, monster? Did you just call me 'brother'?"

"Yes," said the Dark Lady in a fervent tone. "I did. Because that is what you are, even if you don't remember. You are my brother, the Great Snake, and I am your sister, the Dark Lady. I know it has been countless centuries since we last spoke, but surely you must remember your beloved sister, shouldn't you?"

Uron put a hand on the side of his head. "I seem to remember ... seem to remember something. You do seem familiar, but I don't know where I might have seen or met you before."

"You know me," said the Dark Lady. Her face extended out from the wall a little bit further. "But even if you cannot remember everything about me, trust me when I say that you and I are working toward the same ends: The complete subjugation of all spirits under our collective leadership."

"Subjugation?" said Uron, lowering his hand, his voice harsh and skeptical. "I seem to recall that my goal is to

326

restore Harnum and its people to their original glory. When did conquering spirits—*any* spirits—become a part of this plan of mine?"

"You have forgotten," said the Dark Lady. She pursed her lips for a moment. "Of course you have. You were without a body for so long ... but it doesn't matter. Your memory is returning, isn't it?"

"I am not sure," said Uron, looking down at his hands. "So much of this feels familiar, like an early childhood memory, but I cannot help but feel revolted at the creature before me that claims to be my sister, of all things."

"Revolted?" said the Dark Lady. She didn't sound offended; just hurt. "Never mind. You will get over your feelings of unease once you remember. All you need to know, dear brother, is that I am on your side against our other two brothers."

"Other two brothers?" said Uron. "Do you mean the Mysterious One and someone else? Because I do not believe the Mysterious One is at all related to me."

"There is no time to explain everything," said the Dark Lady. "Just know, Great Snake, that by working together and combining our power, we can crush the Mysterious One and his cronies. The Arbiter has already fallen; once the Mysterious One is out of the way, there will be nothing to stop our plan."

The Mysterious One looked at Darek and the others in shock. "The Arbiter has fallen? What does—"

He stopped talking mid-sentence and turned his head, inclining it toward the floor. Darek followed the Mysterious

One's gaze and saw that the mystery god was looking at the life orb lying on the floor. Though the Mysterious One's skull face did not change its expression, somehow Darek could tell that even the Mysterious One had lost any hope he had brought with him when he initially arrived.

Nonetheless, the Mysterious One waved his wand at the orb, which flew into his free hand. He then held it out toward Darek, who took the orb and held it close to his chest, where it warmed his hand, though it no longer felt quite as warm as it once did.

"I see," said the Mysterious One, his tone flat. "So the worst has happened. I am now all alone in this world. What bitter, awful luck we have."

Darek was not sure what to say to that, but he did not have to say anything, because Uron said, "The Arbiter ... I seem to recall that name. Another memory."

"Indeed," said the Dark Lady. "But you don't need to worry about him, now that he's no longer a threat. Instead, face the Mysterious One and his followers who dare to stand against us."

Uron turned around. His yellow, serpentine eyes focused on Darek and the others. He did not seem to recognize them at first, but then recognition dawned on his features. He smiled.

"Darek and Aorja," said Uron in a mocking voice. "I wondered where you two were. How did you get here? Did you kill each other? I know how ... strained your relationship is, so if that's what happened, I am not surprised."

"It doesn't matter how we got here," said Darek. "What matters is that we're not going to let you and the Dark Lady succeed."

"Of course you aren't," said Uron, shaking his head. "You've fought against my plans every step of the way. Though as you have no doubt noticed, you have also failed to stop me every time. If even Skimif could not defeat me, what makes you think that *you* can defeat me?"

"So that's Uron, eh?" said Braim, holding his blade in front of him defensively. "The guy who stole my skeleton?"

"Yes," said Darek, nodding. "That's him, all right."

"And you are the famous Braim Kotogs?" said Uron. He gestured at his body. "I would thank you for allowing me to take your skeleton—which has proved quite useful in my plans to restore Harnum—but I never actually asked you for it, so thanking you would be useless and presumptuous."

"Good," said Braim. "I don't really know you, but if you're allied with the Dark Lady and even half as bad as what Darek and Aorja here have told me, then that's enough for me to conclude that you're no friend of mine."

"I don't need your friendship, or anyone's friendship for that matter," said Uron. He spread his arms. "All I need to do is destroy Martir and everyone and everything within it. I cannot do that from here; however, I can eliminate you idiots who have been in my way ever since I first got my new body, and then return to Martir afterward."

"With my help, of course," said the Dark Lady. "Right, brother?"

"We may work together for now," said Uron, without

looking over his shoulder at his sister. "We appear to have several common foes, so logically, forming a team between us would be the wisest course of action, at least until our enemies are demolished."

Darek looked at the Mysterious One. "What's the plan? Do you know what we can do to stop Uron and the Dark Lady?"

The Mysterious One tapped his chin, like he was thinking. "When I first took Uron back here, I did not have any plan, but now that we are all together here ... yes, I think I do have a plan, though I don't know for sure if it will work."

"A plan that might not work is better than no plan at all, in my opinion," said Darek. "What is it?"

The Mysterious One opened his mouth to speak, but then the Dark Lady shouted, "Do you honestly think we are just going to stand here and let you plan right in front of us? Think again, fools."

The ground trembled beneath their feet before another set of hands burst through the rock behind them. The hands extended into the air before bending down over Darek and the others, effectively cutting off all escape routes.

Then dark energy began swirling around Uron's hands as he walked forward slowly, but surely.

Darek and the others drew closer together, even though that did little to keep them safe from the hands, while the Mysterious One said, "Don't be afraid, my friends, because —"

One of the hands shot forward and grabbed the

Mysterious One. It lifted him above the others as he struggled against it, magical energy flashing from his wand, his magic stone shining brightly, but it was no use because the hand didn't budge even slightly.

"It looks like your end is very close now, pitiful mortals," said Uron, the energy swirling around his hands now crackling like lightning. "The only question I have now is, how much pain can the average ghost handle before he finally gives in to his fate?"

Chapter Twenty-Two

Durima awoke. She blinked rapidly and then felt her forehead. She expected to feel sticky blood, maybe even parts of her brains leaking out from the hole that Garvan's knife had undoubtedly made; instead, she felt nothing more than a smooth forehead that did not seem to have been pierced or wounded at all.

That thought should have encouraged her, but instead, it filled her with dread and worry. Even her shoulder no longer bled; it was like she had been completely healed, but that didn't make any sense because she could not remember anyone healing her. Her last memory was of Garvan stabbing her in the head, a blow she should not have survived at all.

She sat up and looked around at her surroundings. She was sitting on a white stone road, similar to the ethereal, but clearly different, as it felt harder than the ethereal. Some kind of whitish-gray mist or fog—it was hard to tell what it was for sure—hung all around her, making it impossible for her to tell where she was or if there was anything nearby.

One thing was for sure: This was not the North Academy graveyard. Or anywhere else in Martir, for that matter.

But if I'm not in Martir, then where am *I?* Durima

thought. *How did I get here? Shouldn't I be dead?*

Then again, maybe she actually *was* dead. She knew little about what lay beyond death—the Ghostly God had never thought to share any of his findings with her, even when she had worked for him, and she had always been skeptical of myths like the Heavenly Paradise—but it was the only thing that made sense in light of two facts: One, she *should* have been dead anyway; and two, her body was no longer that bear-like creature with red fur. Instead, she was white, slightly glowing, with proportions similar to humans, though her hands were still much larger than any normal human's were, as were her feet.

If I'm dead, then does that mean that I am in the afterlife after all? Durima thought, looking around the place. *Pretty empty afterlife, if I do say so myself.*

Because she was curious about her surroundings, Durima rose to her feet and began walking down the road. She had no idea what might lie in the mist around here, but she had not survived the Katabans War and everything that had occurred since Uron's rising by being afraid. The only way to get her answers was to move forward, even if danger lay ahead.

As she walked, Durima wondered what had happened to Uron and the Mysterious One. She wondered if they were still fighting, and if so, who was winning. She hoped it wasn't Uron, but her more cynical side made her doubt the Mysterious One's strength and abilities, even if he was as strong as Uron.

She also wondered how the North Academy mages were

doing against the invading katabans force. Considering how the mages had the Ghostly God and Ranama on their side, she could not see how Uron's army could possibly win unless Uron first defeated the Mysterious One and then returned to help his men. The God-killer would certainly make short work of those two gods. Of that Durima was certain.

The whitish gray mist was incredibly silent; even Durima's footsteps hardly made a sound when she walked upon the pavement below her. She kept her ears open for any sounds, but it seemed useless, because she did not hear anything.

Maybe this is what the afterlife is, Durima thought as she walked. *No paradise, where all of your wants and needs are met; no great court of justice, where the wicked are punished and the righteous are rewarded; and definitely not a big blue sea with plenty of room for everyone. No, the afterlife is the place where you walk and walk forever, all by yourself, with only your memories to offer you companionship.*

It was such a depressing thought, but so far it seemed quite true. Granted, the Mysterious One had basically said that there was far more to the afterlife than this, but if so, she didn't think she would see any more of it. She did not see the Arbiter or the Dark Lady or any other ghosts; at this point, she would have even been happy just to see Darek and Aorja again.

Then she heard it. Up ahead, through the thick mist, came the sounds of someone walking. It was an uneven walk, like the person had a limp or something. The footsteps were coming closer and closer and Durima did not know if that was a good thing or not because she still couldn't see who it was.

To be safe, Durima crouched, holding her fists before her, despite not knowing if it was even possible to fight in the afterlife or if she could hurt anyone here. Still, she was so used to taking on a defensive stance when faced with unknown enemies that she did it anyway; what could it hurt?

Then the being stepped out of the mist and into Durima's line of sight.

The being was white and thin, without any clothes on its body or genitalia anywhere to be seen over its form. It looked as though it hadn't eaten in years, especially with the way it limped. Its eyes were dull and gray, while its mouth was missing several teeth. It dragged along its left foot behind itself, making it look more like a walking corpse than anything.

Yet, despite its frightening appearance, the newcomer did not seem very threatening to Durima. Strange, yes, but hardly a threat. Then again, Garvan hadn't seemed much like a threat, either, so Durima decided not to let her guard down until she could figure out exactly what the hell this thing was and just what it was capable of doing.

The thing stopped. Its gray eyes landed on Durima. Its expression was impossible to read; maybe it was as threatened by her presence as she was by its, or maybe it was just curious and wanted to know who she was.

For the longest time—though it probably only lasted a few seconds at most—the two stared at each other, not uttering one word or making even the slightest sound. It was an awkward moment, one Durima wished would end, but she did not want to attack it first in case the figure turned out not to be an enemy.

Then the figure lifted up its right hand and pointed at her. Durima expected some kind of magical blast to come out of it, but when nothing did, she realized that the stranger was simply pointing at her, as if to confirm her existence.

"You ... are Durima?"

Durima blinked. That figure hadn't just talked, had it? It certainly didn't have such a steady, deep voice, one that was more befitting of a king than a being like itself. For that matter, it didn't make sense for this *thing*—which resembled nothing on Martir—to speak perfect Godly Divina, either.

Yet who else could have asked that question? Durima certainly hadn't; after all, she already knew who she was. The only question now was whether to answer that question. Seeing as she had no other choice if she was going to figure out just what the hell that thing was, she decided it was safe to answer. It was hardly like she was sharing the secrets of the universe with it, after all.

Still maintaining her fighting position, Durima said, "Yes. I am Durima. Who are you?"

The figure lowered its hand and made a deep wheezing sound that Durima soon realized was supposed to be laughter. "Oh, good. I was looking for you. The Arbiter told me you would come here eventually. I did not believe him at first, but I can see I was wrong to doubt his ability to predict the future."

"The Arbiter?" said Durima. "You mean the Mysterious One's brother? I thought he was unconscious due to being poisoned by the Dark Lady."

The figure nodded. "He is. He gave me this mission right before he fell, however, and forced me to swear an oath to complete it no matter what. Now I can complete this mission, and once I do, I can move on at long last."

He said that while looking up at the mist above them, like he was imagining himself sprouting wings and flying. (Durima only thought of the figure as 'male' because his voice was masculine, though there was no other sign that identified his gender aside from that.)

"I noticed you didn't give me your name," said Durima, keeping her tone civil, but warning, as she didn't want to get too friendly with whoever this being was.

The figure shrugged. "My name is lost to the mists of time. Even I don't remember it. The Arbiter always called me Helpful, so that is the name I have taken on."

"Helpful?" said Durima. "Are you sure he wasn't just describing how useful you were to him?"

"He probably was," said Helpful. "But a name is a valuable thing and I simply couldn't go without one forever. So I took Helpful as my own."

Durima still thought it was a stupid name, but she figured this was probably not the best time to argue the point. She lowered her fists, though still kept her guard up in case Helpful turned out to be trying to trick her.

"Let's move on to more important things," said Durima. "You mentioned that the Arbiter gave you a mission about me. What is it?"

Helpful pointed at himself. "He told me to send you to the Unknown. Do you know what that is?"

"I vaguely recall the Mysterious One mentioning some place called the 'Unknown,'" said Durima, nodding. "Isn't that a place where evil spirits go? Am I an evil spirit because I betrayed my people to Uron?"

"I do not know who Uron is," said Helpful. "But I do know that you are not supposed to be sent to the Unknown as punishment. Only the Arbiter can decide the fate of a ghost."

"Then why did he want you to send me there?" said Durima. "Is it some kind of weird practical joke?"

"The Arbiter said that he thought you would be of great help there," said Helpful. "Now he didn't say if you were going to be as helpful as me, but I imagine he must have thought you were. I don't even know what you're supposed to do there; thinking back, I probably should have asked the Arbiter these questions before he fell unconscious."

Durima stepped back. "What if I decide to run away? What if I don't want to go to the Unknown? You can't make me go anywhere."

Helpful looked to the left and then to the right before returning his attention to Durima. "Where would you go? There is nothing around here for miles in every direction. Of course, there might be a few draggers wandering around; I haven't seen any recently, but I do know that a horde of them just broke through the barrier separating the Unknown from the Spirit Lands. If you run into them, I doubt they'd simply ignore you."

Durima did not know what a dragger was, but she didn't like that name. She looked over her shoulder and saw nothing but mist, which made her think that Helpful was telling the truth when he said that there was nothing around for miles, although he could just as easily have been lying as well.

"Do you want to go?" said Helpful, holding out a hand toward her. "I know the Unknown is a terrible place, but I also know that the Arbiter wouldn't have wanted me to send you there without a reason."

Durima hesitated. No way in hell would she ever go to some place like that. Granted, she didn't know every little thing about it, but she knew enough to know that going to the Unknown voluntarily was suicide (or whatever the ghostly equivalent of that was).

On the other hand, the only other alternative she had was to wander aimlessly forever, dodging those 'draggers' that Helpful mentioned, while Uron continued to destroy Martir. She remembered how the Mysterious One had told her that Uron or the Great Snake or whatever his name was, had come from the Unknown.

Maybe going to the Unknown will help me figure out how to defeat Uron, Durima thought. *It's a stretch, to be sure, and even if I did find out a way to beat him, that doesn't mean much if I can't go back to Martir and use it. But it's still a risk worth taking.*

"Are you worried for your safety?" said Helpful. "That's understandable. Everyone wants to feel safe. Only problem is, of course, that safety is an illusion, which makes our desire for it somewhat problematic, to say the least."

Durima looked over her shoulder one last time before shaking her head and saying, "All right. I'll go. I don't have anything better to do, after all. Maybe something good will come out of this."

Helpful smiled. "Looks like I will be free from my oath after all. Now hold on."

Durima was about to ask what he meant by 'hold on' when she suddenly felt as if she had been blasted in the face by a cannon ball. The last she saw of Helpful was his body dissipating into the mist, like he wasn't real, his smile dissipating with it.

As Durima flew through the air, the whitish-gray mist quickly evaporated until she found herself flying through pitch-black darkness. The sudden change from the light mist to the dark blackness reminded her of the Void, but she knew she couldn't be inside the Void because the Void didn't exist in the afterlife (she hoped).

And then she landed on hard, rough stone floor, the trajectory of the crash sending her rolling across the ground. She came to a halt fairly fast, but the collision had still rattled her head.

But she had received worse blows in the past, and

survived, so she pushed herself up, shaking her head as she did so to clear it out. She had to recover quickly, because if Helpful had done his job, then she was currently inside the Unknown, a dangerous place from what the Mysterious One had told her.

Then Durima looked up. She blinked rapidly, unable to believe what she was looking at, but no matter how many times she blinked, the scene playing out before her remained exactly the same.

Over on the wall to her right, the face of a human woman —enlarged and skinless—sprouted, a hideous thing that made Durima want to run and hide. It did not seem to have noticed her yet, for which Durima was thankful, because she didn't want to be noticed by that monster at all.

Directly ahead of the strange face wall monster were four ghosts surrounded by four massive hands that had the same skinless appearance as the face. She did not recognize any of the ghosts, but she did recognize the Mysterious One, who was struggling against one of the hands. The ghosts themselves were covered in a red barrier, though how long that would last once the hands began attacking it, she did not know.

And then she saw Uron, walking toward them, black energy crackling in his hands. Now Durima knew there was definitely no way that any of those ghosts would survive against Uron, especially because he seemed to be working with that face wall monster.

Exactly what events had led up to this, Durima did not know. Nor did she know if this was what the Arbiter had sent her here for; that was also a mystery, though given the obvious seriousness of the current situation, she figured it had to be. That didn't explain how the Arbiter could have possibly known all of this would happen, but she had no time to worry about that.

She just started to think about how she could possibly help in this situation when the horrible red eyes of the face wall monster shifted in her direction. Durima froze, looking at the massive face, which seemed just as surprised to see her as she was to see it.

"Where did *you* come from?" said the face wall. "Did you stumble into here, little ghost?"

Durima could not actually answer that question, since she didn't really know how Helpful had teleported her here in the first place.

Uron stopped advancing on the four ghosts and looked over his shoulder, apparently wondering what the face wall had seen. His eyes widened when he saw Durima and he turned all the way around to face her. With his back now to the other ghosts, he began stomping toward her, black energy still crackling and even sparking in his hands.

"Durima," said Uron, the rage in his voice barely contained. "The traitor, the hero, and the Demon. I'm not even going to bother to ask how you got here; I am just going to teach you what happens to those who knowingly betray me."

Durima got to her feet and walked backwards, as she knew there was no way that she could take on Uron in a fight and hope to have even the slightest chance of winning.

Especially in this strange place, where she wasn't even sure she could *use* magic.

But then her foot slipped off a ledge behind her and she had to catch herself. Looking over her shoulder, Durima saw that this wasn't actually the bottom of the pit they were in; rather, it was a plateau. The actual pit ran deeper and deeper into the earth than it appeared, though how much deeper, she couldn't say, as it was too dark to tell.

Not that figuring out its exact depth was a pressing issue. Uron was still advancing on her, a low, angry hissing noise emitting from his mouth. And unless Durima thought fast, she would soon find out its exact depth for herself.

Meanwhile, the giant hands were now beating on the red barrier protecting the ghosts. The barrier held under the barrage of fists, keeping the ghosts safe, but how long that would last was anyone's guess. As for the Mysterious One, he was still struggling against the other hand that had grabbed him, though he unfortunately seemed to be having no luck in breaking free.

Can't worry about those people right now, Durima thought, turning her attention back to Uron. *Have to think of a way to stop Uron.*

"It's funny you talk about betrayal," said Durima, glancing over her shoulder at the pit below. "Because I am pretty sure that *you* were the one who betrayed *me* earlier. I guess betrayal is only good if you're the one doing the betraying, right?"

"Hypocrisy is an insignificant matter to think about when you are about to face pain worse than anything you've ever felt before in your life," said Uron, not slowing down his pace at all. "Though it's not surprising; you katabans tend to focus only on the tiny, insignificant things that mean nothing in the long run."

Durima's eyes darted to the left and to the right, searching for an escape route or anything she could use to escape Uron.

But then it hit her: There was nowhere to run to now. Uron would find her no matter where she went. And once he did, he would beat her so viciously that even her physical body would feel it.

So the next thing she did might have been foolish, something she would never advise anyone else to do in her situation. But when she thought about the sheer hopelessness of her current predicament, she realized that she had no choice.

Raising her fists, Durima ran at Uron as fast as she could. Uron actually seemed taken aback by this action, because he stopped and hesitated, like he thought this was some kind of trick.

But it wasn't. Durima reared back and punched Uron in the chin as hard as she possibly could. She put all of her strength into that blow, despite knowing that it would probably not do a thing to Uron because he was so far above her in terms of sheer power. Still, she did it anyway, because if she was going to be corrupted (whatever that meant), then she would at least go down fighting.

Just as she thought, Uron didn't even flinch. The look of surprise that had crossed his features quickly turned into annoyance. He grabbed Durima and hurled her over his shoulder like she was a piece of junk.

Durima tumbled through the air and crashed into the ground. Again, the impact did not hurt, but it was so sudden that it left her briefly stunned before her mind yelled at her to get back up on her feet lest she allow Uron to get her. The only problem was her shoulders, where Uron had grabbed her; they burned, likely from the touch of his dark energy, though she paid little attention to the pain because there was no time to dwell on it.

Without even thinking, Durima got back to her feet. Uron had turned around now and was walking toward her again, except he had increased his pace. Durima crouched low, like she always did when preparing for battle, but this time it was more out of habit than out of any belief she could actually beat Uron. That thought prompted her to start backing up, even though she knew she was only delaying the inevitable.

Durima, said a voice in her head, almost causing her to start before she recognized it as the Mysterious One's voice. *I need your help. I know how to end this situation and save everyone, but we can't do it as long as the Dark Lady is attacking the others with those fists.*

Durima didn't look at what the Mysterious One had mentioned, as she didn't want to take her eyes off Uron for even a moment. But she could hear those fists banging against the barrier like drums, so she replied, *What do you need me to do?*

Distract the Dark Lady, said the Mysterious One. *My*

sister is far pettier than Uron. If you attack and harm her, she will focus all of her energy on destroying you, even though you're not much of a threat to her, which will give the others the time they need to stop Uron.

Great, Durima thought, still backing away from Uron. *How do I hurt her?*

A jolt of power caused Durima to start, while the Mysterious One said, *I just gave you enough power to hurt my sister. It won't last forever—five minutes, perhaps less, as your form can't contain that much power for very long —but if you act now—*

Durima didn't even listen to the rest of his sentence. The power flowing through her body made her feel even stronger than the gods, but she did not allow it to go to her head.

Instead, she stood up and pointed a finger directly at the face wall monster, which she assumed was the Dark Lady. Without thinking about it, she unleashed a burst of white energy—shining brighter than the dull yellow lights above— at the Dark Lady's face.

Her attack flew straight and true. The blast hit the Dark Lady directly in the face, causing her to immediately roar in pain and agony. Uron stopped and looked at his sister in surprise, saying as he did so, "How in the world—"

"You hurt me!" the Dark Lady wailed, her voice so loud that the ground cracked underneath Durima's feet. "How *dare* you hurt me! I will make you feel my pain a thousand times over, you stupid ghost!"

The hands that had been beating against the ghosts'

barrier ceased pounding on it (though the fourth hand still held the Mysterious One). Then they went back into the earth, and a second later, burst out of the ground around Durima, surrounding her like a pack of hungry, wild baba raga.

All three of the hands formed into thick fists. Durima covered her head, despite knowing that that wouldn't protect her very well. She looked up at the fists, as big as boulders, and knew that her days had truly ended.

Then, without warning, one of the ghosts appeared in front of Uron, the two figures visible through the gap between the arms. She did not recognize the ghost, because his back was to her, but she noticed that he carried some kind of strange glowing green blade that she had never seen anything like in her whole life.

Uron stepped back, perhaps out of instinct, because he said, "What are you doing?"

"What I should have done when I first saw your ugly mug," said the ghost. He raised his blade. "Getting my body back, you bastard!"

The ghost drove the blade directly into Uron's chest. There was no reason that should have so much as tickled Uron; Durima had once seen a god stab Uron in the chest, only for him to respond by killing that god.

Yet rather than destroy the stupid ghost, Uron actually screamed in genuine pain. His whole body began glowing with purplish-black light, while the ghost stabbing him also glowed, though it was a white-and-gray glow, similar to the energy blast Durima had shot at the Dark Lady.

The giant fists above Durima froze, while the Dark Lady cried out, "Brother! What is happening to you?"

Durima wanted to know the answer to that question, too, but she was too stunned by this sudden turn of events to do anything more than watch as the spectacle unfolded before her.

The further the ghost drove his blade into Uron's chest, the more distorted Uron became. His whole form seemed to be evaporating; no, it was splitting. His scream of agony became two screams, one almost human-like, the other the hiss of a dying snake. Durima even thought she saw two beings standing in Uron's place; one a strange-looking man with purple skin wearing a white coat, the other a horrible snake that looked like the form Uron had worn during his time when he pretended to be a servant of the Ghostly God.

Then the ghost himself was sucked into Uron's chest. At the same time, a bright explosion—like the eruption of a volcano—erupted from Uron's form. It completely blinded Durima and filled her ears with the two screams she had heard before, the human one and the snake one, while the shouting of the Dark Lady also assaulted her hearing.

The explosion lasted so long that Durima was certain she had somehow died again, but then the bright lights and screams faded. Durima's eyes needed no adjustment back to the normal darkness of the pit, but she blinked several times anyway out of habit.

The ghost who had been stabbing Uron was gone. There was not even one hint of him anywhere. Uron was also gone, though unlike the ghost, there were two creatures floating in his place.

One was a long, deadly-looking purplish-black snake with awful yellow eyes, which Durima believed was the Great Snake himself. The other was a serpentine-skinned humanoid wearing a white coat, who was now looking around in alarm; the original Uron, the one who had made that terrible deal with the Great Snake so many eons ago.

But even as she watched, both the Great Snake and Uron rapidly faded out of existence. She thought her eyes were playing tricks on her at first, but when neither of them returned, she had to conclude that the two were indeed gone for good.

"What happened?" the Dark Lady roared, her sudden shout causing Durima to start. "Where did brother go? What happened to that foolish ghost that attacked him? I don't understand!"

"You never did understand the various mysteries and magic of ghosts, sister," said the familiar voice of the Mysterious One. "Or much else, for that matter, which I suppose is why you became the monster that you are today."

The Mysterious One walked into Durima's line of sight. The fists hovering above Durima immediately came down on her, but the Mysterious One flicked his wand in her direction and the fists turned into whitish-gray mist that evaporated quickly.

"Please don't crush innocent ghosts like Durima," said the Mysterious One, addressing the Dark Lady. "I know it is your job to punish evil spirits, but Durima is the farthest thing from that, despite her imperfections."

"Don't lecture me on my job, brother," said the Dark Lady. "Or use your stupid magic to interfere with my judgment. What happened to our brother?"

"Let me put it in the simplest words I can use," said the Mysterious One. He stopped and gestured at the spot where Uron and the ghost had been standing. "That ghost who assaulted Uron and the Great Snake was Braim Kotogs. I doubt you'd know that, sister, because you don't really pay much attention to individuals except when you can corrupt them for your own twisted ends."

"What does it matter who that ghost was?" the Dark Lady demanded. Her face extended from the wall even further. "I want to know what happened to my favorite brother!"

"It's important you know who that was so you can understand what happened," said the Mysterious One. "Anyway, I hope you know that our dear brother, the Great Snake, had borrowed the skeleton of Braim Kotogs in order to have a body that could interact with the physical realm, yes? And I also hope you know that he took that body here with him when I took him here?"

"I know that much, idiot," said the Dark Lady. "Get to the point already."

"Very well," said the Mysterious One. "You see, dearest sister, I had a theory that if Braim Kotogs's ghost came into contact with Uron's body, then Braim's skeleton would kick out both the Great Snake and Uron himself in order to make room for Braim's ghost, which is the rightful spirit of that body. I did not know if that would work, seeing as it has never, to my knowledge, been done before, but I was quite desperate and willing to try anything, which is why I had Durima here distract you long enough to let Braim attack the Great Snake."

"So Braim's alive again?" said Durima.

"Yes," said the Mysterious One, nodding. "He is probably back in Martir even as we speak."

"Then where is the Great Snake and Uron?" said the Dark Lady. "How come I cannot sense our brother?"

"That is also quite simple," said the Mysterious One. "You see, the Great Snake and Uron had essentially become one spirit after so many years of being together. Rather than make Uron stronger, however, this union gave the Great Snake's spirit the exact same weaknesses as Uron's. So when Braim's skeleton kicked out their spirit, it had the unusual effect of obliterating both of them from existence. Or nonexistence, as the case may be."

"What? That makes no sense at all," the Dark Lady cried. "Almighty Ones and ghosts cannot die. We are all eternal."

"I did not say they died," said the Mysterious One. "Granted, I did say they were obliterated, but what I mean by that is that they no longer exist as beings independent of the rest of the universe. I imagine that happened because their ghost had nowhere else to go and was already an unstable and unnatural thing to begin with; therefore, it had to cease to exist."

"Impossible," said the Dark Lady. "The Great Snake is simply missing. That's all. I will find him, find him and bring him back, and then we will crush you once and for all."

"Good luck with that, sister, but I'm afraid your threats don't mean much in the face of undeniable fact," said the Mysterious One, shaking his head. "Neither of us can sense him because he is gone for good. He will not be able to terrorize anyone ever again, nor will he be able to help you in your little schemes, either."

The Dark Lady looked so lost right now that Durima almost felt sorry for her. Almost.

"Then ... then I will still crush you all," said the Dark Lady. "I will corrupt every last one of you. I will find a way to get into Martir and kill everyone and everything that lives there. I will—"

"Do nothing except stew in your anger and think about what you did," the Mysterious One finished for her. "I am sorry, sister, but now that you and I are the only Almighty Ones left, it is my job to stop you if you try to harm anyone again. Because it is you and me, we are effectively equal, which is as the Almighty Ones should be."

The Dark Lady roared again, except this time it was a literal roar, like some terrible beast in the jungle. The ground began to shake, while the walls started to close in on them.

Durima thought for sure this was their end, but then the Mysterious One simply waved his wand.

The next moment, the Dark Lady's ugly, angry face had vanished, replaced instead by the interior of some kind of tower that reminded Durima vaguely of Castle Hollech. She looked around and saw the other three ghosts from before—

two of who were clearly Darek and Aorja, though she did not recognize the third one—standing nearby, looking as shocked as she felt about this sudden turn of events.

Nonetheless, even though the Dark Lady was nowhere to be seen, Durima thought she could still hear that evil spirit's roar of anguish and defeat. And she was quite glad that she was nowhere near the Dark Lady now.

Chapter Twenty-Three

Darek had no idea what just happened. Even though the Mysterious One had just spent the last twenty minutes explaining to him, Aorja, and Gujak the exact nature of Uron and the Almighty Ones, none of it made any sense to him. Indeed, Darek privately wondered if the Mysterious One had somehow gone insane, so wild was his story, but Durima nodded along at every point as if he spoke nothing but the truth.

The Mysterious One explained it all while the five of them stood in the Arbiter's tower. Darek paid full attention to the Mysterious One's story, but he still kept expecting more of those dragons from earlier to interrupt and attack. None ever did—perhaps because the Dark Lady didn't dare attack while the Mysterious One was around, but that did not make him feel any safer.

When the Mysterious One finished, Aorja said, "That has to be the most convoluted story I have ever heard. And that's after one of my fellow Rock Isle prisoners came up with the story of the teleporting, purple baba raga to explain what happened to my missing lunch."

"Every word of what I just said is true," said the Mysterious One. "I know it is all hard to believe, but trust me when I say that I am not lying."

"I don't think you are, Mysterious One," said Darek. "But it is a hard to believe story, that's for sure."

"The truth is always harder to believe than fiction, I'm afraid," said the Mysterious One with a sigh. "But now you know. And knowing really is half the battle."

"Right," said Darek. He looked at Durima, who aside from her occasional nods had not said a word during the whole explanation. "How *did* you get here, anyway?"

"I died," said Durima, her tone short. She gestured at her forehead. "One of the katabans attacking North Academy stabbed me in the head. I got to the Unknown because some being named Helpful sent me that way."

"Helpful?" said the Mysterious One, though he didn't sound surprised. "I thought he had deserted us after my brother was poisoned. I suppose I need to reevaluate my opinion of him, then."

Darek then looked at Gujak. Like Durima, he had been silent during the whole conversation. He wasn't even looking at Durima; instead, he was looking down at the Mysterious One, like he was still processing everything that the Almighty One had just said.

"Gujak, do you remember Durima?" said Darek, gesturing at Durima. "You two were friends when you were living, weren't you?"

Gujak looked at Durima, his eyes full of surprise. "Wait, you're the Durima that these two have told me about? The same one?"

"As far as I know, I am the only Durima there is," said Durima with a shrug, though she did not meet Gujak's eyes as she said that. "So I guess I am."

Darek expected Gujak to joyously hug Durima now that they were reunited; after all, the two of them had been good friends back when they were alive. That's what Darek would have done if he had been separated from a close friend for a long time, anyway.

But instead, Gujak rubbed his other arm, looking quite awkward as he said, "Well, uh ... thanks for helping. I wish I could remember more about you, but ..."

"It's fine," said Durima. Her voice choked slightly. "Not like I'm going anywhere. Now that we're both dead, I guess we have plenty of time to get to know each other again, you know?"

"I guess so," said Gujak. "But where do we start?"

"You two can start when you go beyond the Gates," said the Mysterious One, putting one hand on Gujak's shoulder. "Because I believe that that is what you both deserve, after all you have been through together."

"But how can we do that if the Arbiter is ... if he's no longer with us?" said Gujak, looking at the Mysterious One with frightened eyes. "He was the only one who could determine a ghost's fate, right?"

"Yes," said the Mysterious One, nodding. "But he did not leave us entirely. Darek, do you still have the life orb?"

Darek held up the red glowing orb between his fingers. "Yes. I do."

"Good," said the Mysterious One. "Then that means that *you* are the new Arbiter of the Spirit Lands. Congratulations."

Darek blinked several times. "Wait, what?"

"What?" said Aorja, louder than Darek had. "What do you mean, *he's* the new Arbiter of the Spirit Lands? Does that include the power of the Arbiter, too?"

"I mean that there is a very good reason that the Arbiter gave Darek his life orb," said the Mysterious One. "My brother would not have given you this power if he did not think you would use it wisely."

"But ..." Darek looked down at the life orb, which felt pleasantly warm in his hand. "I didn't sign up for this."

"I know," said the Mysterious One. "But Darek, after what I've seen of your character, I am confident you will make an excellent replacement for my brother. Your understanding of the difference between good and evil will help you in making the difficult, yet necessary, decisions that my brother faced every day when he was still with us."

"Really?" said Gujak, putting his hands together in hope. "Oh, that's wonderful. I was worried that I would be stuck here forever, since the Arbiter isn't around anymore. Maybe now I can finally rest."

Darek could not find it within him to celebrate with Gujak, though. He understood this was a good thing, of course, because the Arbiter's role was clearly vital to the maintenace of the Spirit Lands. Even so, he felt a resistance in the pit of his stomach that squashed any positive feelings he might have toward the situation.

"So Darek gets to become more powerful than a god, Durima and Gujak are back together and get to go onto the actual afterlife, and Martir is safe from Uron for real," said

Aorja. She folded her arms across her chest. "Does everyone get a happy ending around here *except* for me?"

"Don't worry, Aorja," said the Mysterious One. "I will send you back to your body back in Martir. Whether or not you'll get a happy ending ... well, that depends on how you live your life, of course."

Aorja scowled, like she thought she had gotten a raw deal, but then Darek held out the life orb toward the Mysterious One and said, "I am sorry, Mysterious One, but I don't want this."

The Mysterious One did not frown, because he had a skeletal face, though Darek could tell he was puzzled just the same. "Excuse me?"

"I said I don't want the title of Arbiter," said Darek. He shook his head. "Listen, I know it's a great honor and all that, but this isn't what I want to do. I don't want to spend the rest of eternity judging the souls of people who died. I want to return to Martir and help rebuild there."

"But you would make a great Arbiter," said the Mysterious One, his tone almost pleading. "My brother would not have given you his life orb if he did not think you were worthy of it."

Darek shrugged. "Maybe I would make a good Arbiter, but I still don't want anything to do with it, at least right now. Right now, returning to my home and to my friends and family is more important to me. Sorry."

It was hard to read the Mysterious One's facial expression, for he could not really make any due to his skeletal features. Yet even if he was disappointed by Darek's choice, Darek would not give in because he really, truly did not want to be the Arbiter.

But then the Mysterious One raised his hand and took the life orb from Darek. As soon as he did, Darek no longer felt as warm or powerful as he once did. He felt exactly like how he had when he first arrived here, though that did not trouble him much.

"Very well," said the Mysterious One, his tone flat. He deposited the life orb in one of his robe's pockets. "I suppose I will have to fill in the position of Arbiter for now. I will have to find a replacement later."

Aorja raised a hand, but the Mysterious One said, in a sharp tone, "Don't."

Looking frustrated, Aorja lowered her hand and muttered under her breath about how stupid the Mysterious One was. Darek rolled his eyes, but said nothing about her childish behavior because it needed no commentary.

"Maybe I'll take up the mantle of Arbiter later on," Darek said. "After I die, perhaps."

"I will keep that offer in mind, Darek Takren, when we meet again, whenever that might be," said the Mysterious One. Then he raised his wand. "I will also have to send both of you back now. Do you wish to return to Martir immediately?"

"Yes," said Darek. "I want to see if Uron's army has been defeated or not."

"I imagine it has been," said the Mysterious One. "It was an undisciplined mob, really, that wouldn't have even tried to attack if Uron hadn't gathered them all together like that.

I doubt they won, though of course I don't know for sure."

"I hope they lost," said Darek. "I also want to go see Braim. You said he was alive again, which means he's back in Martir, right?"

"Correct," said the Mysterious One. "Though I have no idea what he might be like, now that he's alive again. I imagine he'll remember this much, but as this has never happened before, I don't know for certain what his memory will be like."

"That's fine," said Darek. "We'll help him get back to normal. Much has changed since he died, so he'll need all the help he can get."

"Wait," said Aorja, looking at Darek sharply. "Who's this *we* you're speaking of? I don't remember volunteering to help an idiot like Braim readjust to the world."

"I suppose you don't have to if you don't want to," said Darek. "Just be aware that by refusing to do so, you will probably be returned to Rock Isle for your crimes. Which is technically what you deserve, you know, after everything you've done."

Aorja gulped. She looked away, as if she did not want to make eye contact with Darek, and said, "All right. Fine. I guess I can help, but that doesn't mean I have to enjoy it."

"I don't expect you to," said Darek. Then he addressed the Mysterious One again. "What about Skimif? Can you bring him back? The gods still need a leader, after all. His death left a huge power vacuum in the world, one that can't be easily filled by anyone else."

"Of that, I am unsure," said the Mysterious One. "Your

best bet would be to find some way to contact the Powers and see if they will give you a new God of Martir. Of course, Martir survived for eons without a God of Martir before, so maybe your world and the gods will adapt to this change."

"Maybe," said Darek. "How would we contact the Powers, anyway? Do you know how to speak with them?"

The Mysterious One shrugged. "The Powers haven't been anywhere near Martir for three decades, but I will see what I can do about contacting them. I will let you know what they have to say, assuming I have any luck in finding them."

That did not seem like a good answer to Darek, because he figured that Skimif's spot needed to be filled quickly if not immediately. Nonetheless, he knew they had little choice but to wait for now, so he simply nodded to show that he understood.

"And the Dark Lady?" said Aorja. "She said she's going to destroy Martir. Do you think she'll do that?"

"My sister is prone to hysterics and melodrama," said the Mysterious One. "But yes, she certainly does have the power to hurt you, if she wants. Don't worry about that, however, because I will keep an eye on her and make sure she stays where she's supposed to, though I doubt I'll need to do much, because I think the Great Snake's death traumatized her. She may well spend the rest of eternity searching for him, even though there is nothing to be found of his remains anywhere."

Aorja sighed. "That's a relief. I don't ever want to see that monster's face again, not after all this. Or any of her stupid draggers, for that matter."

"Now, I believe it is time for you to go home," said the Mysterious One. "Your mother and your friends were quite worried about you, Darek, last time I saw them. Best to let them know you are all right."

"I don't want to go just yet," said Darek. He looked at Durima. "I need to say something to you, Durima, something I've been meaning to tell you ever since Uron rose from Braim's grave last year."

Durima cringed, like she expected Darek to yell at her. Nonetheless, she said, "What is it?"

Darek took a deep breath and then said, "I wanted to thank you, Durima, for helping save the Magical Superior back then. You took him out of the graveyard so he wouldn't be hurt during that first battle between Uron and Skimif. Thanks."

Durima looked quite shocked by Darek's gratefulness, so shocked that she seemed to have temporarily lost the ability to speak.

Then she slowly nodded. "You're welcome, Darek Takren. It was ... my pleasure."

Darek smiled, though he did not comment on Durima's awkwardness. He just looked at the Mysterious One again and said, "All right, Mysterious One, you can send us home now. We're ready to go."

The Mysterious One nodded and flicked his wand.

The entirety of the tower melted around Darek and Aorja. The last thing he saw, as they left the Spirit Lands, was the Mysterious One speaking with Durima and Gujak, most likely to send them beyond the Gates, where they would rest for eternity, as they deserved.

Chapter Twenty-Four

The next thing Darek knew, he was sitting on the floor of the Chamber, Aorja beside him, his body so stiff that he thought he had somehow become a stone statue. There was no one else in the Chamber except for himself and Aorja, which made him feel a little alone, although he knew that that was because no one else knew about their return yet.

Aorja shook her head. She moaned, "Oh, I'm so stiff. I didn't think I'd wake up feeling like a wooden board."

Darek stretched his arms and legs. "Yeah, but I guess it's better than being corrupted and turned into a dragger, right?"

Aorja cracked her neck from side to side as she said, "Right, but this isn't exactly how I expected to feel. I will never do that again for as long as I live."

Darek rolled his eyes and began to stand up. The stiffness in his bones was rapidly leaving him, which he was glad for, although it seemed to him to be going away even faster than it normally should have.

As a matter of fact, as Darek stood up, he realized that he felt even better than he had before going to the Spirit Lands. His senses were alive; his robes were purer than ever, the dank scent of the Chamber was vivid and real, and he felt like he could run a sixty mile marathon in an hour.

But most importantly, he could feel the magic in the world again. He thought he was imagining things at first, but there was no way he could simply be imagining the flow of magic underneath, above, and all around him, like the water of the sea.

Doubt still lingered in his mind, however, so Darek raised his right hand and concentrated hard on summoning an ice cube.

Just as the thought entered his mind, a tiny ice cube— barely bigger than his small toe—appeared in his hand. It was cold to the touch, almost too cold, but rather than drop it, he held it tighter than ever.

"Huh?" said Aorja, who was also standing up now, stretching her limbs as she stared at the ice cube in Darek's hand. "How did you do that? I thought you couldn't use magic anymore."

Darek grinned. "Who knows? Maybe the Mysterious One gave me back my magical abilities, or maybe they just returned on their own. Either way, it's wonderful."

"Damn it," said Aorja, snapping her fingers. "I liked being more powerful than you. Now we're equals again."

"Yes, we are," said Darek.

Before he could say much else, however, he felt a familiar spike of magical energy enter the room. The next moment, the Ghostly God appeared in front of him and Aorja, his hands clasped together, a look of eagerness on his face.

"Welcome back to the land of the living, Darek, Aorja,"

said the Ghostly God, looking down on them both with glee. "I sensed your souls return to your bodies, so I came right away to see if you were really back. It looks like I was correct in that assumption; even better, I know that that ritual I used to send you two to the afterlife earlier worked. Now I just need to devise a way to bring back spirits I send and it will be perfect."

The Ghostly God drew out his notebook and summoned a pen from nowhere. He jotted down a quick note before discarding the pen, which turned into mist before it hit the floor, and stuffing the notebook back into his chest armor.

"Yeah," said Darek, nodding. "It's great to be back."

"Now," said the Ghostly God, leaning down toward them like he wanted to be sure he wouldn't miss a word they said. "Where is Uron? And the Mysterious One?"

"Uron's gone," said Darek. "For good. We don't have to worry about him or the Great Snake anymore. The Mysterious One is all right. I'll fill you in on the details later."

The Ghostly God sighed in relief. "Thank the Powers. For a while there I almost believed that Uron had indeed survived, but it looks like the gods of Martir shall continue to reign over this world for the time being."

"Right," said Darek. "Now, what's going on in North Academy? Did anyone die when the katabans attacked?"

"Some died, but not many," said the Ghostly God. "The katabans fought valiantly, but when Ranama and I spoke, they listened. They will all be judged by Grinf; right now, they are all in the sports field, where Zeeree and several of the Xocionian Monks are keeping an eye on them so they don't try to run away or do anything else—though I think it's useless, because right now not a single one of those katabans would dare go against anything Ranama or I ordered them to do."

"Zeeree?" said Aorja. "Oh, I'm so glad to hear he's doing all right. If I had lost him during that battle, I would have probably gone ahead and killed everyone here, mage or katabans alike."

That line even made the Ghostly God look at her like she was crazy, though Darek did not focus on it too much because he remembered something urgent. He did not know where it was, but he could guess.

"Ghostly God, can you take me and Aorja to the school's graveyard?" said Darek. "I know it's a strange request, but there might be something there that requires our attention."

"I am normally loathe to grant the requests of mortals, but because you two have saved Martir, I suppose I can," said the Ghostly God. He raised a warning finger. "But just this once. Don't get the wrong idea and think I enjoy serving you mortals or anything, all right?"

"I would never think such a thing about you," said Darek.

The Ghostly God snapped his fingers and then the Chamber was gone. They now stood outside in the graveyard, the sun shining down on them, a cold breeze blowing in from the southern Walls, but Darek barely paid attention to any of that.

He ran to the back of the graveyard, Aorja following

close behind, while the Ghostly God shouted, "What are you two looking for? There's nothing in this graveyard except tombstones."

Darek didn't respond. He just ran until he reached the back of the graveyard, where he found the tombstone he was looking for: The tombstone of Braim Kotogs, which looked quite new due to having been repaired after Uron and Skimif's initial battle here.

But the tombstone wasn't the only thing there. Lying in front of the tombstone, his red hair flecked with dirt, was Braim Kotogs himself.

Braim looked like he hadn't aged a day over thirty, even though he had been dead for that many years. His skin was smooth and young, his hair was a vivid red, and his muscles were clearly as strong as ever.

The only problem was that Braim was bare naked. Darek avoided looking at Braim's genitals, but he could tell that Aorja was staring. He would have told her to stop that, but he was so eager to see if Braim was okay that he wasted no breath in telling her off.

Falling to his knees at Braim's side, Darek cradled the man in his arms and said, "Braim, are you awake? Braim, can you hear me? Braim, wake up!"

Much to his relief, Braim's eyelids flickered open. His eyes were a brilliant green, like grass in spring, but for a moment they only showed a lack of understanding, as if he had no idea where he was.

Then Braim said, in a weak voice, "Hey, Darek. How are you doing?"

Darek could not help but smile. "I'm doing fine, Braim. How do you feel?"

"Like I fell from a three-story building," said Braim. He then looked down at his legs and grimaced. "Okay, who stole my pants?"

"No one did," said Darek, "but we'll get you a new pair anyway. How does that sound?"

"Better than lying naked in this cold dirt," said Braim. He shivered. "I forgot what cold felt like."

"You'll have plenty of time to remember that, and much more, once we get you back in shape," said Darek.

He looked at Aorja, whose eyes were still focused on Braim's lower half, and said, "Get Braim some clothes. The school should have some extra uniforms on hand, so grab one of those. And make sure it fits him."

Aorja started and looked up at Darek. He thought she was going to argue with him, but much to his surprise, she just turned and ran away. She passed the Ghostly God, who turned to watch her go, confusion spreading over his face before he turned back to look at Darek and Braim.

"I do not understand," said the Ghostly God. "I thought Braim Kotogs had been dead for thirty years. How is he back here?"

"Like I said, I will fill you in later," said Darek. "For now, could you tell Mom about this? I think she would like to know."

"Fine," said the Ghostly God. "The others need to know about your and Aorja's return, anyway."

The Ghostly God vanished in a burst of mist, though not

without first casting a curious glance at Braim. Darek had a feeling that the Ghostly God was not going to leave Braim alone later, if his curiosity meant anything, though he decided not to worry about that for now.

Then Braim said, "Why do you want your Mom to know about me? Is she a pervert like Aorja?"

Darek shook his head. "No. She was a close friend of yours before you died. I think she needs to know that you're back; she'll be ecstatic."

"If you say so," said Braim. He shivered again. "You know what? The cold actually feels kind of good, after not feeling it for a while. I kind of like being alive better than being dead, at least so far."

"That's good to know," said Darek. "Now once Aorja gets back here with your robes, we will show you to everyone else. Then we can start to work on rebuilding Martir. How does that sound?"

"Like a lot of work," said Braim. "But I don't have anything better to do, so why not?"

Darek did not respond to that. He was just thinking about how glad he was that this madness was finally over, even knowing that the days ahead were likely to be their toughest yet.

At least I'll have my friends at my side, if nothing else, Darek thought. *And a bit of magic, too.*

THE END OF MAGES OF MARTIR

Now available:

Tournament of the Gods Book #1:

Gathering of the Chosen

The mage known as Braim Kotogs is the first human to return from the dead, a fact which brings him more attention—and trouble—from mortals and gods alike than he wants. He doesn't remember who he is or much about his past, nor is he interested in winning the Tournament of the Gods. But when a mysterious assassin nearly takes his life, Braim must enter the Tournament in order to survive and learn the identity of his assailant.

As the princess of a powerful nation, Raya Mana believes that she is destined to win the Tournament and become the new ruler of the world. But when she is assigned to a bracket that she loathes, Raya must deal with shattered expectations, in addition to an anonymous letter writer who claims to know all her darkest secrets.

Carmaz Korva has known only poverty and hopelessness his whole life, having grown up on an island that the gods have abandoned. But when he is offered the chance to enter the Tournament of the Gods, he sees an opportunity to restore his people to their original glory while remaining ignorant of the tragedy that awaits him at the end.

And with a mysterious and malevolent force plotting their destruction in the background, winning the Tournament of the Gods may be the least of their troubles.

Buy *Gathering of the Chosen* wherever books are sold!

About the Author

Timothy L. Cerepaka writes fantasy and science-fiction stories as an indie author. He is the author of the Prince Malock World series of fantasy novels, the Mages of Martir series of fantasy novels, and the science-fantasy standalone *The Last Legend: Glitch Apocalypse*. He lives in Texas.

Read more and find links to his other books at his website www.timothylcerepaka.com.